A PRIVATE UNIVERSE

BY
ANDRÉ MAUROIS

TRANSLATED BY HAMISH MILES

*No man is by nature exclusively domiciled
in one universe. All lives . . . are passed under
at least two flags, and generally under many more.*
ALDOUS HUXLEY

NEW YORK
D. APPLETON AND COMPANY
MCMXXXII

A PRIVATE UNIVERSE

By ANDRÉ MAUROIS

A PRIVATE UNIVERSE

LYAUTEY

THE WEIGHER OF SOULS

THE SILENCE OF COLONEL
   BRAMBLE

BYRON

ATMOSPHERE OF LOVE

ASPECTS OF BIOGRAPHY

A VOYAGE TO THE ISLAND OF
   THE ARTICOLES

DISRAELI: A PICTURE OF THE
   VICTORIAN AGE

BERNARD QUESNAY

ARIEL: THE LIFE OF SHELLEY

CAPTAINS AND KINGS

MAPE: THE WORLD OF ILLUSION

CONTENTS

PART I

ENGLAND AND OTHER MATTERS

PART II

PRESENT AND FUTURES

CONTENTS

PART I

ENGLAND AND OTHER MATTERS

ADVICE TO A YOUNG FRENCHMAN LEAVING FOR ENGLAND

YOU are going to live in a far country. The distance is not in space (the journey is shorter than from Paris to Lyons), but in ideas and manners. You are going to live in a mysterious and difficult country. During your first days there you will murmur: "This is a hopeless business. I'll never get to know them; they'll never understand me. It is too wide a gulf to cross." But take heart. It can be crossed. Bear in mind that once they have taken you up, they will be your steadfast friends. Read Lawrence's book, "Revolt in the Desert," and you will see how that Englishman turned back alone into a perilous desert to look for an obscure Arab left behind by the caravan. The friendship of the best of them is like that. I myself put it to the test during the War. It well deserves the efforts needed to gain it. And remember too that, notwithstanding this seeming difficulty, it will suffice to observe a very few rules to avoid rubbing them up the wrong way.

Dress

Two principles, no more: dress as they do; dress simply. As they do, because they like conformity. If you play golf in riding breeches or dine in a regimental mess in "shorts," you will shock and grieve them. But you will shock them even more if you show such bad taste as to be "over-dressed." No too-perfect clothes, no too-new shoes. Jane Harrison, in her recollections, described her pleasure at seeing the Duke of Devonshire receiving an honorary degree at Cambridge and wearing shoes so worn-out that his socks showed through. Those socks, she said, convinced her that he was truly ducal. Don't imagine in London that you ought to dress like an Englishman on his travels. In London an Englishman is not on his travels; imitate him, and dress as you do in Paris.

Conversation

Until you have found your feet, don't talk much. Nobody will blame you for your silence. When you have held your tongue for three years, they will think: "He's a nice quiet fellow." Be modest. An Englishman will tell you about his "little place in the country," and when he invites you down there, you'll find that the little place is a mansion with three hundred rooms. If you are a lawn-tennis champion, just say: "Oh, I'm not too bad." If you have crossed the Atlantic single-handed, say: "Yes, I've done some sailing." If you have written books, say nothing. They will find out your qualities for themselves, in time; they'll tell you with a laugh: "I've been hearing something about you," and they will be pleased with you. If you are treated unfairly (that will happen—they are sometimes unfair) go straight and tell them just where you think they are mistaken. The odds are that they will admit it. They are always anxious to play the game. If France is attacked in your presence, counter-attack fiercely; they will take it in good part.

A golden rule: never ask questions. I have lived for six months in the same tent as an Englishman; we shared a bath; but he never asked me whether I was married, or what I did in peace-time, or what were the books I read. If you must offer confidences, they will be listened to with polite indifference. Beware of confidences about other people. Gossipy stories exist there as elsewhere, but they are at once more sparse and more serious. Between silence and scandal there is no golden mean. Choose silence.

Do not imagine that your intellectual worth gives you any prestige in their eyes (except amongst a very small set in London and at the Universities). Only one thing counts—your character. I doubt whether you could even imagine the contempt in which all literary culture is held by a certain type of Englishman. You are entering the only country where a man will unabashedly say to a writer: "Books? I've never read a single book. . . . When I try to, I can see I'm not getting hold of anything I read. . . . So what's the good?" But you are left at liberty to read, and you will be gently chaffed about it, rather as they might chaff someone who collected rhinoceros horns. A taste for rhinos would be more comprehensible.

Last night I tried to talk to a young Englishman who had been up at Cambridge for two years about the notable dons I know there. He did not know even their names. "How should I?" he said. "I took up rowing as soon as I went up, and when you row seriously you only live in a very small circle." And thereupon he began deploring the young generation who were spoilt by dancing and sports cars, "and refuse," he said, "to work for their college." The word "work" from his lips surprised me. I questioned him. He meant playing Rugby. I was reassured.

Alongside this "athletic" type, you must learn to know the "æsthete" type. For a long time you will feel a lesser being in the small "intellectual set" I spoke of. Cultivated Englishmen are few, but their culture is exquisite, their epigrams are swift and subtle, their taste exacting and perfect. They have a blend of relish and superciliousness which is dangerous to your self-respect. You will be anxious to please them and you will find it very hard to catch the right note. Try to find it in a blend of nonchalance and preciosity. Write one essay on cocktails and another on the Chinese poets. If you understand them properly, you may find Proust a strong bond in common. He is the one French writer who is close to them. They will guide you in your reading: I should advise E. M. Forster, Virginia Woolf, David Garnett, and the three Sitwells. Maurice Baring's novels will give you a true picture of the "Racine side" of English society.

When you seek to convince them avoid arguing too well. As a Frenchman you imagine the battle is won when you have proved that you are right. To them it is a matter of indifference whether logic puts them in the right or the wrong. On the contrary, they rather mistrust reasoning when it is too well put. When the French delegates at Geneva put forward the disarmament Protocol the English rejected it because it was so clear. "It won't work," they said. What they like is a policy tested and tried by time, ancient maxims, old usage. To induce them to do something new, show them that they have always been doing it. Give logic a rest whilst you stay over there.

Activity

Don't work too hard. Above all, don't be what they call "fussy." Wait until they ask you to do things. Don't rush ahead of tasks with excessive zeal. "Are they lazy?" you ask. Yes, a little; but the point is rather that they see a kind of pride in wanting to do too much. Look how they walk, with rather slow, too long strides. That is how they move through life. They don't like to jostle destiny. In the Army they used to tell me: "Never refuse a job; never ask for a job." Like all men, they have ambition; but they hide it pretty well.

Justice

Don't commit murder in England. You will be hanged. Before a French jury, given some imagination, a romantic mien, and a good counsel, you can fairly easily save your neck. But those twelve Englishmen will listen to your talk of sentimental sufferings with startled indignation, and will have you hanged by the neck until you are dead. True, they acquitted a Frenchwoman who committed murder a few years ago; but it was only an Egyptian that she killed. Be careful; steer clear of their law courts. Their judges are terrible, and will regard you as guilty

7

before you have said a word. The cross-examinations of their barristers are of such devilish ingenuity that you will confess to having stolen the Nelson Monument to get clear of that hail of questions. Remember that respect for the Law is greater there than elsewhere. "Keep off the Grass" in English does not mean "Walk on this Lawn."

Food

Before you go you will be told that you will feed badly in England. Well, cooks and chefs there are not so good as in France. But if you can time your hunger properly you can eat to perfection. The two excellent meals there are breakfast and tea; luncheon is middling; dinner, bad. Reserve your appetite for the first two. Learn to appreciate new delights—porridge, haddock, marmalade. At luncheon eat from the great joint of underdone beef, or some of the admirable pink ham. Pass over the dessert with a masculine air. Say firmly: "I don't care for sweets." In England every other shop is a sweet-shop, and yet the English are contemptuous of sweets. Leave them to the women and children.

Make the national drinks your own. They will tell you that whisky is "a clean drink." It is true; whisky leaves your mind clear, your tongue clean, your body warmed. Their beer is good, but beware of drinking it as you might drink French beer. During the War the Tommies used to tell me plaintively: "You can't get drunk on this French beer!" Which was perhaps true. But don't forget that a Frenchman can get drunk on English beer. Accept their champagne; they understand it thoroughly. Bring your-

8

self to drink a cocktail before dinner, port after dinner, and whisky at ten in the evening; you will make scant progress in their esteem if you remain a water-drinker. When Disraeli was in discussion with Bismarck, he forced himself to smoke although it made him ill. In such circumstances, he declared, the man who is not smoking appears to be keeping an eye on the other. Besides, you will get the taste for it, and their crusty port is excellent.

But above all, enjoy the general spectacle. You will like those landscapes that seem to have been drawn by Constable and Gainsborough. You will like the rather wild gardens, with their trim, close-shaven lawns. You will like London with its grey-gold fog and the red splashes of buses and the black splashes of policemen, like a vast Turner. You will like the theatres with their comfortable stalls, their attractive programme girls, their short intervals. You will like the enticing, multicoloured bookshops, like shops of exotic fruits. And more than anything you will like the books . . . (but don't say so).

FROM A HOLIDAY DIARY, 1928

JULY 31ST.—Finished "Climats" last night before leaving France. I have pangs of regret at having slain Philippe, and not having attempted a picture of happiness, in a third part. Difficult, no doubt. "Symphony in white major." And yet the curve of happiness has its variations no less than that of tragic lives. I shall try to do that later with different characters. Philippe had a taste for restlessness; he would soon have wearied of poise and tranquillity. Perhaps I ought to have made it clear that I see no inevitability in that surrender to one's self, that easy soft-heartedness of the characters in "Climats." This morning I brought along with me in the Paris-Calais train Alain's "Propos sur le bonheur." I agree with him that it is possible to *make* one's happiness, and that fatalism in sentiment is no less false than the fatalism of action. I feel more and more that the problem of Free Will is fallacious. Of course the universe is vast and complex, and of course we are small and weak. Nevertheless, we have a grip, rather as the touch of a child's finger-tip on a switch can set a huge factory into operation. Philippe and Odile and Isabelle are wrong in being what they are.

But that is how they were, and that's all about it. . . .

GUILDFORD. AUGUST 1ST.—It has been a troublesome journey. Five changes. The trains here seem to weave

10

unaccountable arabesques all over the country. One of them threads the seaside stations like a string of sea-pearls, then turns up in the direction of London, and drifts away again in the end to saunter through the countryside. Junctions everywhere. We are far from the Napoleonic Paris-Lyon-Méditerranée and from Laroche, the immutable and controlling factor amongst railway-stations, pacific and civil, dispenser of earthly possessions, fixed landmark of the travelling Frenchman. In England the trains go everywhere if you give them time, as thoughts do, or novels.

The house which the H.s have chosen for us is a small manor belonging to a retired colonel. Elizabethan, very plain, charming. It is surrounded by a green lawn which comes right up to the walls without a pathway, like a nailed-down carpet. Beyond a white fence lies a private golf-course, with flocks of sheep grazing amongst oak-trees à la Gainsborough. "Only nine holes," said the Colonel apologetically. I reassured him. In the park, a long avenue called the Monks' Walk, a small antique temple (three columns with pediment), a stream overhung by willows, and then a very straight hill, a curious ridge of chalk which cuts across the plain and is called the Hog's Back.

Here is the history of the house: from the date of its building until the War, that is, throughout four centuries, it belonged to the same family, land-owning gentry of the county. The dining-room walls are covered with their portraits—judges, soldiers, ambassadors. After the War these squires were forced by taxation and bad investments to sell. (They now occupy a small cottage quite near.) It was a time when the British Army, cutting down its millions of men to two hundred thousand, was forced to get rid of many officers of high rank. Our Colonel, having received quite a substantial gratuity, left the Army and bought this country-house. There he entertained his war-time colleagues, laid down tennis-courts, kept up the golf-course, and then, finding last year that he was ruined, decided to take "paying guests." And to-day, as a gentleman host, solicitous and masterful, he busies himself with his guests, rather as if they were his regimental horses.

I have just had a long talk with the Colonel. He is a cultivated man, in the English way: that is to say, he knows some history, the names of plants and birds, something about gardening, a smattering of architecture. A type of man I like; we shall get on well. Apart from him, we know nobody in the neighbourhood. "Yes, we do," the children told me after exploring the park; "we've got three friends already—a white horse, a brown cow, and a robin redbreast."

I was afraid I might be cut off from books, but there are good bookshops at Guildford. This analysing of sentimental difficulties has been too much on my mind for a year now, and I feel a strong craving for moral healthiness. I thought instantly of Kipling, and spent this first morning, now sitting on the lawn in the sun, now strolling in the Monks' Walk, re-reading "The Bridge Builders" and "The Man Who Would be King." Yes, that was the right antidote. From the dangerous machinery of passion, man's escape lies through action. *Primum vivere.* If I had not a family, an organized life, I think my true happiness would have been a post as an intelligence officer in Morocco or an administrator in Indo-China. Time was when I had a great fondness for being the head of an industrial concern; but there I suffered from the unresolvable discords of the workers. A collective activity, believed in by all its participants—that, I think, is one recipe for happiness.

In the afternoon I took another Kipling, "Puck of Pook's Hill," to read in this setting which has witnessed the passage, one after the other, of Saxons, Romans, Normans, the Canterbury pilgrims, and Kitchener's armies. In depicting the impact of the Roman world upon the British barbarians, he has obviously had in mind as model the impact of the English upon India. He is right. The passions of men are always more or less alike. . . . Kipling, it seems, lives not very far from here; I must see him. I liked him very much in London last year, when he talked to me so well about Cecil Rhodes. I emerged from this day of reading with all the admiration I felt for him in the days when I read him for the first time, at the age of thirteen.

AUGUST 3RD.—Some Boy Scouts have come to camp in our grounds; they are the sons of London working-class parents, in charge of an elderly scoutmaster with a white moustache. They have been working all day in clearing the river-bed of the black floating tree-trunks which were troublesome to boats. To-night they sat round a great fire of their own making, and sang. Our children went to listen to them. It is excellent, I think, this school of discipline with enthusiasm. We all sat down in the field, and our faces were lit up by the fire as in Rembrandt's "Night Watch." Long ago, in the same field, Chaucer's pilgrims halted to sing round just such a fire. The great art of the historian should be to extract the permanent from beneath the transitory, the "everlasting man," in Chesterton's phrase. No doubt, man's nature evolves; certain sentiments and desires vanish; but who shall say whether some tragic happening, suddenly shattering the social framework, would not revive within us the ancestors we thought were dead? "Our first movement is to murder those whom we hate." The characters in "Climats" are too civilized. My most dangerous weakness? Politeness.

AUGUST 5TH.—The past two days reading Trevelyan's "History of England." Greatly struck by the influence of armament on the political constitution of the country. Power follows actual force. When the Norman baron brought over his methods of mounted warfare and the idea of the fortified castle, feudalism triumphed. In the fourteenth century the bow became the national weapon; every village graveyard had the butts behind it, whence Crecy, Agincourt, and the Peasants' Revolt of 1381. A little later the invention of the cannon brought about the downfall of the feudal baron, by making possible the destruction of his stone walls from a distance. On the sea, the idea of placing cannon inside the vessel so as to fire through port-holes decided England's superiority over Spain. Drake saw a man-of-war as a mobile battery; the Duke of Medina-Sidonia saw it as a platform designed to carry his musketeers to the boarding of another vessel. It was the broadside that made the British Empire. If we really wish to give the League of Nations the means of imposing peace, it must be given *force* and the power of irresistible control.

More reading: Fauconnet's book on Spengler. At the moment I have neither the courage nor the time to make an attack on the text of the gigantic "Decline of the West." In any case, Fauconnet's analysis is made with much intelligence.

Essential idea: the relativity of all human ideas, even the mathematical. A system is never true; it is true for a given man at a given moment. One can grasp the possible thought of a Frenchman of 1795 or a German of 1917, but one does not grasp the possible thought of Man in general. "Hegel, German philosopher (1770-1831)"— that defines his doctrine.

Certainly, Spengler is partly right. Descartes and Spinoza were philosophers who came on the scene after a period of great development in mathematics, and, yielding to an intoxicating wave of geometry, they strove to demonstrate truth as theorems are demonstrated. Taine was born at a time of experimental triumphs, and yielded similarly to the materialist wave. His "Theory of Intelligence" could not have been written in 1720, nor in 1920. Russell, whom I was reading the other day, and to some extent Bergson, have been moulded by the new physics.

It will always be so, and no system in the world will be true for all men at all times. "If Nietzsche had gone to reveal the Superman to the Moslems, and Kant his categories to the Chinese, they would both have realized the historical and geographical relativity of their ideas."

But do we need a system? "Life," says Goethe, "finds its end in itself, and laughs at what is thought of it."

* * *

The children are working on the garden table at their holiday tasks; I have my own. I have promised to write a continuation to Sterne's "Sentimental Journey" for a series of "Sequels to Famous Books." That is to be my task for the month. Forced labour. I would far rather get back to my "Byron." I shall take on no more of these commissioned tasks. But promises already made must be kept. Let's try.

To start with, I shall have to put in a note somewhat on these lines:

"The reader will recall the last chapter of 'A Sentimental Journey.' Yorick has to spend the night in an Alpine inn alongside a young Piedmontese lady. Almost all the historians of literature are unaware of the fact that from that chapter a son was born. He was recognized by Yorick, and a family of Yoricks still survives in the little town of Sisteron, where travellers are astonished by this foreign name. The following narrative describes the first journey made by one of the French Yoricks to the land of his forbears."

A Sentimental Journey into England

by

Monsieur Yorick

Paris—Nord

—This much I like in starting upon a journey, said I, whilst the blue-smock'd porter was stowing my portmanteau in the rack, this much I like, that it delivers us from fancied woes.

What is an affront when he that offers it is distant a hundred leagues! What is love when the mistress is beyond reach! 'Tis only on our travels, I began again as I settled myself on the cushions, that we are truly ourselves. Here is Yorick—which is to say a body, a few desires, a few memories,—and no longer Yorick's house, Yorick's servants, the friends and foes of Yorick, Yorick's legend, Yorick's fortune. No more goods to have care of, unless it be the six shirts and twelve handkerchiefs and four-and-twenty volumes within that case. No more visitors to dread, no more bells a-jangling. And on that instant, as the train gathered speed and slid over the groaning rails of the *Gare du Nord,* I resolved to set down the account of my journey and to make an instant start with a *Preface in the Compartment*—

Preface in the Compartment

A traveller is a monk in motion. No convent of *Saint Bruno* has a rule of silence more strict than prevails in a carriage packed with strangers. How over-valued is

the courage of those who vow themselves to solitude!
They may dock themselves of small pleasures, but they
free themselves from great torments. Now my own
taste has been ever for the monastic and cloistered life.
I have viewed the Charterhouse of *Florence*—the cells
of the Fathers are charming—their windows look across
the Tuscan campagna, over roofs gleaming in the sunshine, and to the high mountains beset with cypress—
each Father has his garden, a dark mass of olive trees
lighten'd by the yellow of a lemon—and on the tables
you may see books sacred or profane.—'Tis very true,
said I to Stella, I have always thought it, and now I
know, that I was made for solitude.—You! answered
Stella laughing freely, you who crave for company at
all hours of the day or night!—How little you know
of me, Stella, said I sadly—for it is painful to be mis-
read by a woman who——

And I had reached that point in my preface when I
perceived a grave-featured young man who seemed to
be coming in my direction. Sir—says he—are not you
Yorick? Whereat I understood that I should not be
travelling alone, which afforded me great relief.

....

....

....

Enough for this morning. I am going down with the
children to see the robin's nest and the trout in the weir.

AUGUST 7TH.—Working all morning on that *pastiche*
of Sterne. It is difficult and I find it boring; there is

something false in that naivety of style. If the draft does not shape better to-morrow, I shall drop it and try writing a continuation to the "Pastiches et Mélanges" of Proust.

As consolation for these three stupidly wasted days, read a remarkable article by the Countess Vera Tolstoy on "the original of Natasha" (the Natasha of "War and Peace," of course). I knew already from the book by Tolstoy's son that Natasha was largely formed from Tolstoy's sister-in-law, Tanya Kuzminsky (or, before her marriage, Tanya Behrs), but here I have found exact details.

Tanya was a coquette. In 1863 Tolstoy wrote to her: "Tanya, my dear, you are young, pretty, gifted and kind. Take care of yourself and of your heart. Once given, a heart cannot be taken back, and a tortured heart keeps its scar."

Tolstoy was fond of living amongst the patriarchal family of his parents-in-law, and made it into the Rostovs' interior in "War and Peace." In 1862 Countess Tolstoy was writing to her sister Tanya: "I must tell you a great secret—Levoshka [Tolstoy's family name] intends to describe us when he is fifty." He only waited till he was thirty-six. A writer's scruples subsiding when once the work is ripe.

Tanya's first love, at the age of fourteen, was for her cousin Kuzminsky. When she talked over the situation with him she held out her large doll, Mimi, placing the doll's leather arms on her cousin's shoulder. That was the scene between Natasha and Boris in "War and Peace."

The whole Behrs family watched the publication of the novel with deep feeling and also with some anxiety.

When the first part appeared under the title of "The Year 1805," a friend, Polivanov, wrote to Tanya: "You will certainly have read 'The Year 1805' and found plenty of acquaintances in it, yourself included ... How much Natasha reminds one of you! In Boris there is something of me and ... Is not Natasha's kiss also something out of real life? You have probably told him how you kissed your teacher."

And Tanya replied: "You ask me about Levoshka's tale. It is true that Boris has a little of yourself in him. ... About Natasha he was quite frank with me: 'You think your life is pointless, do you?' he said to me. 'Not at all, I am noting every bit of you.' I am sorely afraid that he is also telling my adventure with Anatole. Papa is very angry, and says: 'Our friends will recognize Tanya, and that will do her harm.' For my own part, I like his novel very much. Almost all the readers whose opinions I have heard, either do not like or do not understand Peter Bezukhov. ... You think that Natasha's kiss comes from the time of our teacher? No, it was with Alexander Kuzminsky."

The story of Anatole in "War and Peace" is that of a real adventure of Tanya Behrs. Tolstoy did not even feel inclined to alter the name of the hero. Here is the actual story: When Tanya was sixteen a young man named Anatole S—— became attached to her, followed her everywhere, and spoke to her so freely that she came to believe that nobody understood her so well; above all, she felt pride in being regarded by him as a grown-up person. He was a brilliant youth, but unkind, yet Tanya loved him and believed herself happy. To her sister Sonia, Tolstoy's wife, she wrote: "This week at St. Petersburg has been a fairy-tale."

The Tolstoys invited Tanya and her brother Alexander to spend the summer with them, inviting also Alexander Kuzminsky and the said Anatole S——, who was known to Tolstoy. The young man's cynicism was distasteful to Tolstoy, who one day ordered the carriage and, without any explanation, sent a servant to tell Anatole that the horses were waiting to take him to Tula. For a long time Tanya remained sorrowing, but she consoled herself when Tolstoy's elder brother, Uncle Serge, was in love with her. He was living with a gypsy woman by whom he had had several children. Uncle Serge remarked to his brother: "Leo, Tanya is dangerously attractive. It would be as well if I didn't come here any more." In "War and Peace" the relations of Uncle Serge with Tanya became those of Prince Andrew with Natasha. Serge asked for her hand when she was seventeen; he himself was thirty-eight. The family asked them to wait for a year on account of Tanya's youth. "A whole year!" says Natasha in "War and Peace." "But why a year?" Then Uncle Serge's gypsy was informed; she wanted to kill herself, and seemed to be in such misery that Serge and Tanya felt it their duty to renounce their project of marriage. Tanya was very brave, but in despair. She spent whole days without saying a word. "Tanya," Tolstoy said to her, "where are all your pretty ways? Come, give us a moment of old times." Shaking her head, she smiled and answered: "I can't. All men now are to me just like our old nurse Trefonova." (In "War and Peace," Natasha had lost all desire to attract, and had not even the need to contain herself; she said and felt then that no man interested her any more than Natasia Ivanovna would have done.)

*   *   *

From first to last, Tolstoy drew that character from the life, and it is the most successful of all his creations. This is a lesson which the prentice novelist should ponder. Pride, and the need for confidence in his own magic, will easily induce a writer to favour above all else the characters and scenes of his own invention. Tolstoy's example shows that the transposition must be made with a set of real data. Little by little the fictitious character diverges from the model and begins to take on a life of his own; and at last the umbilical cord can be severed.

AUGUST 9TH.—I have dropped my Sterne, which was intolerable, and for the past couple of days have been working most enjoyably on Proust. I am not quite satisfied with the opening, but after three pages the substance of the phrasing, at once fluid and arborescent, becomes (I think) fairly Proustian.

Yesterday I took the children to Portsmouth and visited Nelson's flagship, *Victory*. They were delighted with the town, which was beflagged on account of a royal visit. The spot on the deck where Nelson was killed by a French bullet is marked by an engraved brass plate. The English removed their hats. My boys did likewise. "A pretty sight, sir," said the sailor accompanying us, "to see two little French boys taking off their caps to Lord Nelson." As we came away I asked them: "What was it you saw?"—"What did we see?" they said. "Well, we saw the place where Napoleon died."

This afternoon I climbed to the wood that is still called Chantry Wood because the Canterbury pilgrims used to sing as they went through it, and in the shade of St. Martha's chapel I read an American book, "The Arcturus Adventure," a very straightforward account of a naturalist's journey. I am fond of these observations of the habits of animals, mirrors of our human ways. Since learning that in the uttermost depths of the sea there are fish which can only exist so long as they are subjected to terrific pressures, and burst if they come up, I have wanted to write a story to be called "Fish of the Great Depths." I would show human individuals of extreme degradation who burst when they try to live in a purer atmosphere. I also find admirable the fact that certain blind fish carry in front of them a small light-producing organ which attracts their prey, and yet which they themselves will never see.

To live, every animal must perforce make an isolated niche for itself. As a species, an animal is calm and assured of survival as soon as it contrives to find happiness in something useless to other kinds. Sometimes the isolation is geographical (a species capable of living on the coldest or most desert islet lives in peace), but it can also be gastronomical, as in the case of vultures, whose sole rivals for carcasses are the jackals and certain insects. It

23

can be a question of the hour of feeding, as with bats, or an optical sanctuary, such as that of the insects whose resemblance to twigs makes them indistinguishable. The same law is true of mankind; the specialist lives because the other human specialists have no interest in preventing him from living. There are symbioses of specialists. In medicine, the general practitioner is linked to the ear-nose-and-throat specialist like the big bumble-bee to the orchid. The scholar who lives on corpses will respect the peace of the novelist, so long as the latter does not make attempts on his corpses, but will attack the biographer who comes a-hunting on his particular islet. In Parliament the administrative bats do not vex the meals of the eagles of foreign policy.

The law of compensation is another that is shared by animals and humans. The animal which has some admirable feature is often made ludicrous by several other features. The albatross, godlike in the air, walks the earth like Charlie Chaplin; the peacock, an aristocrat in its array, is a suburban in its voice; that great artist, the nightingale, dresses like a gipsy. The poet always pays in one way or another: Byron is lame, Keats consumptive; Balzac is poor and ambitious; Stendhal is ugly—the law of compensation.

The author of this book, William Beebe, describes the love-making of the albatross. When a pair of albatrosses make love, they stand up face to face about a foot apart. Suddenly one of them raises its neck and utters a grunt. His partner mimics him. The two birds bow profoundly to each other three times, and then, crossing their beaks and rapidly moving their heads, they go through a kind of fencing, with closed mandibles. At the moment of supreme ecstasy, one of the albatrosses opens its mandibles and the beak of the other is thrust in. Whilst Beebe was observing a pair of albatrosses engaging in this play, a third bird approached, bowed, and showed its desire to raise its neck and cry, but the others did not look at it and went on with their ritual. The naturalist thereupon took up a position facing the spurned lover and made him a profound bow. The albatross looked a little surprised, returned the greeting three times with great solemnity, and then put his beak up towards Beebe's face. Then, realizing the impossibility of a clash of beaks, he moved away with an air of solemn distress.

At Cambridge, last spring, Professor G. took me to see some astonishing dramas of sentiment in his garden. He had there two Argentine geese, superb black birds with white ruffs, Spanish grandees painted by Velasquez, and with a comically dignified gait. "When I brought them over," said the Professor, "I thought they were a pair, and I named them Don Carlos and Theolina. An odd mistake for a naturalist, for I soon realized that my birds were both males. The strange thing is that they appeared to share my mistaken belief. It may have been because they were the only specimens of their kind in Europe and found themselves condemned to a regrettable inversion, but the fact remains that Don Carlos paid shy court to Theolina.

"With springtime they became active and excited, and

collecting materials, they skilfully and lovingly built a nest just like that of all their kind. And then, their work finished, they awaited the eggs, which naturally did not appear. Their despair was comical, but profound. For whole days these two male birds remained pining beside their sterile nest. At last Don Carlos had an idea; going to the hen-run, he stole an egg, and along with Theolina he tried hatching it. A chicken came out. The foster-parents seemed to be taken aback, and then to be very angry, and they killed the chicken with their beaks. Then seeing that they again appeared to be depressed, I tried offering them a peahen's egg. Rather suspicious, but still intent on their great project, Don Carlos and Theolina again hatched the egg. For my own part, I felt anxious; I did not know how they would welcome the arrival of a little peacock. . . . But birds are like men; their pride overcomes all other passions. When they saw the gleam-ing plumage and the green and gold rings of the little bastard born to them, my two Spanish grandees were de-lighted. And for a whole summer I had the astonishing spectacle of a little peacock being taken out with solemn pride by a pair of Argentine ganders."

It was also Professor G. who introduced me to the White Pigeon Who Refused to Sit. "You know of course," he said, "that amongst pigeons it is usual for both the male and female to sit on their eggs, taking turns of duty. One of them rests and fetches food whilst the other remains motionless on the nest, and then, after a reasonable time, the rôles are exchanged. Well, amongst my white pigeons this year I soon noticed that one pair was behaving abnormally. For two days the male and female had sat in the proper way, but on the third day the female did not turn up at the right time to take the male's place. Exhausted and surprised, he summoned her in all sorts of ways, but she was quite indifferent, apparently not hearing, and was flirting with another male. The situation was so interesting that I did not leave my white pigeons; and really it was quite a moving sight, because the deserted husband seemed to be torn between two conflicting emotions—anger on the one hand, which seemed to make him wish to leave his nest and attack the adulterous couple, and pre-paternal love on the other, which forbade him to let the eggs grow cold. As it turned out, he did not move. . . . Before long the second couple likewise had eggs; the male seducer and the unfaithful lady began taking their turns of duty over this second clutch, in a nest placed only a few feet away from that in which the unhappy husband, had it not been for my aid, would have been dying of hunger. But what do you think this female bird did? After twenty-four hours she grew tired of sitting on the future children of her lover, as she had tired of those of her husband. Once again she refused to take her place and play her part. And look at them now. . . ."

And the Professor took me into a pigeon-house. Accompanied by a male bird, the female pigeon was strolling with an air of conceited, mischievous innocence, between two nests in which sat the two males, starving and exhausted, casting glances of impotent fury at each other.

from afar. The Professor gazed at her for a long time with scornful curiosity.

"A real lady of fashion!" he remarked.

AUGUST 12TH.—Kipling invited us to luncheon yesterday. There was no disappointment in store—the man *is* like his work. He lives in the lovely old house of a fifteenth-century iron-master; its wonderful garden is the one in which "Puck of Pook's Hill" is placed. He led me over the brook beside which Dan met the Dwarf. All the elements of the scene are there, in this actual countryside. Like Tolstoy, Kipling looks at Nature (peering through those keen eyes under their huge eyebrows); he accepts Nature as he finds her, imposing on her that slight distortion caused by the passage through a particular sensibility, and transforming her into a work of art.

"How true to life your Roman soldiers are!" I remarked. "One feels that things must have been exactly like that, along the great Wall of Hadrian, with those young tribunes, and that soldier spirit which has hardly changed ever since there have been men and they fought. . . . Did you get your inspiration from the outposts on the North-West Frontier?"

"Of course. . . . One always has to model the unknown with familiar material. . . . India is a good model."

"How I loved 'Kim'! I can't tell how often I've re-read it—twenty or even thirty times perhaps. . . ."

" 'Kim'? That was an easy job. . . . I had it all round me. But are there really young people in France who read my Indian stories?"

28

"Not only those, but 'Stalky and Co.,' and the 'Plain Tales,' and all the rest of them. . . ."

"In England the younger generation have rather moved away from me. They are looking for something different, and that's as it should be. If a young writer were unlucky enough to be over-fond of my books he would simply write Kiplingese, and would not find his own legs. . . . Yes, certainly, the young must be rather unfair to their elders."

"You know the lines—

> Young blood must have its course, lad,
> And every dog its day."

"Quite true. The years and the centuries must be left to discover what was solid and enduring in a literature."

"But in your case," I said, "the pendulum is already swinging back. I have been to Oxford and Cambridge this year, and the young æsthetcs are 'discovering' you again."

"Really?" he said. "No, it is too early. It would be a pity."

The tone of his remarks has a strong tinge of humour. What ingenious fun he would make of Philippe Marcenat in "Climats"! To him, the individual ought to be sacrificed to the collective and should find his happiness in the sacrifice. It is a bad hive where every bee is self-regarding and argues about the command of the species. Such hives ought to be burnt.

The dignity of his life commands respect for his ideas. He lives here, away in the country, far from the noise of his fame. "One must learn to choose," he says. A lesson for Philippe Marcenat. In love too one must learn to choose, and, having chosen, play out the game without regrets. One must make a marriage, or a country, or a work, to the best of one's powers, without seeking the why and wherefore. And the drive home passed thus, in a reverie screened in fancy by Kipling's brushwood eyebrows.

AUGUST 13TH.—Worked well this morning: result of my Kipling day. I am making an inventory of the maxims of life which I believe to be sound. There are two of Disraeli's: "Never explain, never complain"; and "Life is too short to be small." One should never regret what can't be changed, and always start from the present situation. Essentially it is what Descartes said: "I have made it my habit to alter my desires rather than the order of the world, and to consider that what has not come about is, so far as I was concerned, an absolute impossibility."

Choose.—Never sulk about your own actions.—Begin nothing without considered choice, and always finish what has been begun.—Never hate, but be able to fight nevertheless. (The maxim *"tout comprendre, c'est tout pardonner"* is true in the field of inner life, but false in the order of active life.)

Look for the best in everyone. I like those words of Cardinal Newman: "It is almost a definition of a gentleman to say that he is one who never inflicts pain. . . . He has no ears for slander or gossip, is scrupulous in imputing motives to those who interfere with him, and interprets everything for the best. He is never mean or little in his disputes, never mistakes personalities or sharp sayings for arguments, or insinuates evil which he dare not say out. Nowhere shall we find greater candour, consideration, indulgence; he throws himself into the minds of his opponents, he accounts for their mistakes."

As a writer one should learn to admire. "It is a sure sign of mediocrity always to be moderate in one's praise." I came across two fine remarks on that in Mark Rutherford this morning. One is from George Eliot, to the effect that denigration is an art within the reach of any donkey, and that what we need is to be taught to admire. The other is Goethe's: "If you have called a bad thing bad, you have done no great matter; but if you call a good thing good, you have accomplished much."

That autobiography of Mark Rutherford's is very remarkable. The story of a man who received a puritan education, who ceased to believe and yet retained respect for the mode of life instilled in him, and especially for chastity. Puritanism is false, but contains the essence of something true. It can produce two types of men: the Byron-Gide type, exasperated by the constraints they have undergone and avenging themselves by liberty of action while still remaining deeply imprinted with awareness of the Devil; and the Rutherford-Edmund Gosse type, men who pass judgment, but still admire, without active revolt. In this connection one should re-read "Father and Son" and "Si le grain ne meurt." Besides,

I shall have to re-read Gide in order to understand Byron properly. They have more than one point in common.

AUGUST 14TH.—Worked during the morning on my Proust, which I am enjoying. After luncheon, a walk with the children over the heather up on Hindhead. They were delighted with a vast round bowl in the land, several hundred feet deep and completely lined with heather. "We must stay," they said. "It's so beautiful." On returning I read an article by Bertrand Russell on the necessity of political scepticism. To ponder a piece of Russell's writing always gives me keen pleasure. I like that resolute thought, boring right through to the base of the problem, and unhesitatingly bringing up to the surface whatever it finds. His idea in the article I have just read is a bold one:

All party politics consist of setting up one section of the citizens against the rest of the country, and of trying to make that section a majority. It follows that an idea which would unite all the citizens against the rest of the country, is useless to the politician. *The politician requires myths, of such a kind as to be pleasing to as large a group of men as possible, and displeasing to the other group.* For example, the reduction of taxation on small fortunes, complemented by a crushing tax on large fortunes, is a wonderful line to follow in politics.

These propositions lose their validity only in the case of a foreign war, because it is then possible to unite the whole country against the common enemy, and hatred finds satisfaction. But in times of peace the politician's art consists of understanding, not what is useful to the country, but what passions are easy to kindle. *The most honest politician could not have a solely constructive programme, inasmuch as that programme will never assure him of power.* If measures must be applied of a kind to ensure the safety of the country, that cannot be done by a party government. How, then, can reasonable politics be combined with democracy?

Is it by a government of experts? No. Because (*a*) democracy won't choose them. Because (*b*) the expert makes the mistake of thinking that *his* science, and his alone, is important: if the country were entrusted to a laryngologist, he would cut out everybody's tonsils. Because (*c*) the expert has no understanding of vulgar passions. Because (*d*) he overlooks the impossibility of enforcing an unpopular law: a financial expert, for instance, might be conscientiously convinced that taxes on salaries were necessary; but he could not obtain their payment. And because (*e*), although the expert, not being in power, strikes us as more tolerable than the demagogue, if he were in power he would doubtless become a tyrant.

What, then, is to be done? It is certain that modern societies are feeling an urgent need to alter their mode of government. For over two hundred years politics has been based on sentiments (envy or hatred) which have had their uses in the struggle against classes that were too powerful and too sure of themselves, but are becoming dangerous in a great industrial society, for this society can live only by the co-operation of all the citizens. The life of a great capital like Paris, London or New York, is a miracle, sustained only by the very unstable equilibrium set up by the efforts of hundreds of varied organisms. Revolution would mean our starvation. But like the beavers, shut up in a library who, at the time of the floods, started to build dykes on the floor with books, we ourselves are following political methods which at the present time have become absurd, as they correspond with the standards of a pre-industrial age.

The War proved the possibility of abandoning those methods of inciting the proletariat against the ruling classes and the ruling classes against the proletariat— methods which, through fear and apathy, actually lead to war. During the War, confronted by a common foe, every country managed to attain, with no alloy of hatred, a marvellously effective national socialism. But in peace-time those same standards would be condemned, by proletarians as inadequate, and by the propertied classes as vexatious. So long as there is not a new generation trained to forswear hatred, the desire to hurt our enemies will be stronger than the desire to do good to ourselves.

The first aim of any great statesman, therefore, should be to see that children are brought up in an atmosphere of national co-operation, and meanwhile to concentrate hatred against the politicians and not against any single class within the nation. The peoples are ripe for such a form of hatred, and it would become a moral equivalent for war, from which, for a time, it would release us.

Government is only possible through myths. But neither the Marxian nor the conservative myth is the sole efficacious one. The myth of organized planning is quite capable of acquiring a quasi-religious influence for a hundred years, and this would be excellent. After that something else will have to be sought.

Such is the Russell theme. It is brilliant. I can anticipate, however, the democrat's reply: "That myth of government against the rich classes is far from having exhausted its useful consequences. There is still enough inequality to bear a century of battling against it." Possibly. For my own part, I believe that mankind's true enemy is neither the Rich Man nor the Politician, but the remnant of inhuman forces in the universe. Physical suffering, war, poverty—these are enemies formidable enough, one would think, for men to be grouped against them. The part for writers to play is to call to mind this cruelty of a harsh and indifferent world. That is why great pessimistic books leave behind them a sense of serenity.

AUGUST 16TH.—Began the "Life of Robert Louis Stevenson" by Sir Graham Balfour. At the beginning of the lives of great novelists there is nearly always a period of contacts with numerous and diversified classes of people. It was so with Balzac, Stendhal and Dickens, and it was so with Stevenson in Edinburgh. During his early years he sought the company of "seamen, chimney-sweeps and thieves." Amongst these people he was known as "Velvet Coat," and amongst them he found the types which

35

enabled him to write "Treasure Island." The curious thing in him was that the will to write was anterior to the gift of writing. "I kept always two books in my pocket, one to read, one to write in. As I walked, my mind was busy fitting what I saw with appropriate words; when I sat by the roadside, I would either read, or a pencil and a penny version-book would be in my hand, to note down the features of the scene or commemorate some halting stanzas. Thus I lived with words. And what I thus wrote was for no ulterior use; it was written consciously for practice. It was not so much that I wished to be an author (though I wished that too), as that I had vowed that I would learn to write. That was a proficiency that tempted me; and I practised to acquire it, as men learn to whittle, in a wager with myself. Description was the principal field of my exercise; for to anyone with senses there is always something worth describing, and town and country are but one continuous subject. But I worked in other ways also; often accompanying my walks with dramatic dialogues, in which I played many parts; and often exercised myself in writing down conversations from memory.

"Whenever I read a book or a passage that particularly pleased me, in which a thing was said or an effect rendered with propriety, in which there were either some conspicuous force or some happy distinction in the style, I must sit down at once and set myself to ape that quality. I was unsuccessful, and I knew it; and tried again and was again unsuccessful, and always unsuccessful; but at least in these vain bouts I got some practice in rhythm, in harmony, in construction and the co-ordination of parts.

"I have thus played the sedulous ape to Hazlitt, to Lamb, to Wordsworth, to Sir Thomas Browne, to Defoe, to Hawthorne, to Montaigne, to Baudelaire and to Obermann."

He frequently re-wrote one story in the style of several different authors. "That, like it or not, is the way to learn to write. It was so Keats learned, and there was never a finer temperament for writing than Keats."

Another sound idea expressed by Stevenson is that a writer ought to work every day and not wait for inspiration. He says that the lives of Goethe and Balzac taught him much from that point of view. I think this is true. A writer thinks only on paper. Reverie is good, but it should be a material already sketched in the rough. Reverie entirely lacking in object is totally unproductive. A writer can extract a good novel from a detestable tale. But out of nothing, nothing can come. This *pastiche* of Proust, undertaken against the grain, gives me several ideas for possible novels.

Another book begun last night: Jung on "The Unconscious." I find Jung more remarkable than Freud, as being less inclined to harp on one string. To both of them the clash with one's self is the sign of the civilized man. An inevitable clash. The social man is an animal; he has retained animal instincts and desires, and suffers from being obliged to repress them. But at the same time the human animal is social, and morality has become one of his instincts. Morality is not extraneous to man; it is not something given one day on Sinai to a creature who had never thought about these problems. Morality has taken shape slowly; like all human instincts, it is a product of evolution. The immoral man is always a neurotic subject. His attempts at self-liberation by satisfying his animal desires at the expense of his social obligations are futile. If he does so, he suffers from a "repression of morality" no less painful than the repression of sexuality. That is the whole story of Byron.

AUGUST 18TH.—To-day we had a pleasant visit from Thornton Wilder, the American writer, unknown until his recent fame as the author of "The Bridge of San Luis Rey." An ingenious theme: the old osier bridge of San Luis Rey, near Lima, breaks one day (about the end of the eighteenth century), just when five people were crossing it. Hurled into the ravine, they perish. An old monk who saw the accident wonders why God sanctioned these deaths, and for the strengthening of his faith he proposes to seek out the causes in the lives of these five people. . . . The sobriety of style reminded one of certain French classics, particularly of Mérimée.

A charming man, quite young. "I'm thirty," he told me, "like all writers of twenty-six." He holds a university post.

"My weakness is that I am too bookish," he said. "I know little of life. I made the characters of 'The Bridge' out of the heroes of books. My Marquesa is the Marquise de Sévigné. In my first novel, 'The Cabala,' the hero was

Keats. The method has served me well, but I don't want to use it again. I shall not write again before I have actually observed men better."

"And on what subject?"

"It hardly matters. Don't you think that in the whole of the world's literature there are only seven or eight great subjects? By the time of Euripides they had all been dealt with already, and all one can do is to pick them up again. He took them from history, or from foreign tales. Have you ever studied the sources of Shakespeare? I believe that the only character he created himself was Ariel in 'The Tempest.'" (I've never understood why certain critics should stand amazed at Shakespeare's erudition or find it extraordinary in an actor. After all, Shakespeare was not a "humble player"; he lived at court. All his erudition is to be found in the little books which were to his age what bookstall volumes are to ours.) "The Romans took their subjects from the Greeks, Molière from the Romans, Corneille from the Spaniards, Racine from Corneille and the Bible. . . . Ibsen seems to me the only dramatist who has really invented themes, and isn't that just his real greatness? No, there is nothing new that a writer can hope to bring except a certain way of looking at life. . . . In my own case, for instance, what I seek everywhere is the mask under which human beings conceal their unhappiness."

"So you think that all human beings are unhappy?"

"In social life, yes, all of them—in varying degrees. . . . They are solitary, they are consumed with desires

39

which they dare not satisfy; and they wouldn't be happy if they did satisfy them, because they are too civilized. No, a modern man cannot be happy; he is a conflict, whether he likes it or not."

"Even those tanned, ruddy Englishmen with their boyish eyes?"

"Just like the rest. And the proof is that they have humour. Humour is a mask to hide unhappiness, and especially to hide the deep cynicism which life calls forth in all men. We're trying to bluff God. It is called polish. . . . Our young people in America, it seems to me, express that cynicism more honestly than most Europeans do. Freud has helped them a lot."

"But also spoilt them a lot. . . . In Freud there is a sexual obsession which simply is not true of the majority of men. . . ."

"Possibly. . . . There, again, I answer 'possibly' just to please you. Sexual life is so important."

The whole afternoon passed in pleasant conversation. He talked very well about music, especially about Bach. Then of the theatre.

"I saw 'Le Misanthrope' in Paris the other day," he said, "but I was disappointed in the acting. They made Célimène into a most unattractive coquette. . . . No. . . . The terrible thing about Célimène is that she was very nice."

"I once thought of writing Célimène's dairy," I told him. "It would have shown that her 'betrayals' were often, in her own eyes, merely attempts to placate Alceste and make him happy."

About five o'clock he rose. Unfortunately we shan't see him again. He is going for a walking-tour with Gene Tunney, the boxer.

"A strange companion."

"Don't think that. I'm very fond of him."

AUGUST 22ND.—We discovered yesterday that Box Hill, the little country-house where Meredith lived so long, is quite near us here. So of course we went over. I know few pleasures more acute than a literary pilgrimage, made to a spot consecrated by the presence of a great man. A deep affection for letters produces the same effect as love. The sight of a certain bush, or a certain stone bench, kindles strong emotions in the visitor, because Marcel Proust plucked a sprig of hawthorn from that bush, or because Madame de Récamier sat on that bench beside Chateaubriand. You bring with you the books appropriate to recall or to read again; a page that hitherto has been cold and obscure becomes clear and human; if the actual landscape does not come up to that described by the artist, you enjoy the realization of that beautiful distortion to which genius submits Nature, and if you have been able to choose worthy companions for your pilgrimage, conversation is stimulated, as if the *genius loci,* evoked by genuine piety, returned to mingle for one evening with these kindly reveries in earthly scenes.

Here we were escorted by a niece of Meredith (a most attractive French face, a Vulliamy of Monancourt. She showed us the log summer-house, a sort of Swiss chalet,

41

which was Meredith's study, and described him to us, his vigour, his eloquence, his habit of teasing. Last night I was re-reading the opening of "Richard Feverel." Ramon Fernandez is right in his belief that the philosophy of Meredith is the one we have most need of in this time of over-acute sensibilities. Observation, not feeling. . . . Man's rôle in Nature should be active. . . . Once again the teaching of Alain, and of Kipling. The difficulty is to find the strength to apply it. Meredith himself was torn between a romantic sensibiliy and a will to create. But, as he says, we must not grant an exaggerated value to the conventions or to worldly respect; we must not allow our selfish emotions to outweigh the great realities of a noble, active, passionate life. A gust of fresh air to sweep away spurious grievances. I should like my next novel to have more air moving in it than "Climats" had. I like the life we lead in this countryside. I see only children, animals, streams and trees. I haven't heard a bitter or mischievous remark for a month past. I have walked, run and rowed. When I found a good book I was able to read it right through and with relish. In a word, I have been alive. And yet such retreats are healthy only if they are not too long. Meredith wrote his best books before Box Hill.

First sentence of Meredith in the letter announcing his marriage: "I shall work better than ever." There speaks the true writer as lover!

AUGUST 28TH.—Visit to our friends the S.s, near Richmond. In the evening they opened a small box containing family relics. Amongst them I found a letter written by one of their ancestors to his wife in 1746, on the eve of the Battle of Culloden, in which the writer of the letter was to die. It is so fine that I want to transcribe it. Coming after that conversation with Thornton Wilder, it made a striking impression on me, reminding me of the happiness that man can find in a certain purity. It is perfectly true that a cynical brute lies asleep deep within us, but the Princess de Clèves exists, and Dominique.—

My dear, I am just now come to my Quarters, it is about Eleven at Night. There is nothing in my mind, but God, and you. I cannot go to Bed until I tell you, that I never think myself entire but when I am with you. I would be very happy if I could now Lye Down in your Arms. I shall Lye down with regret: With no more Comfort, than my Conscience can afford. I Bless God for the peace of mind I have. And for the gracious assistance he has given me, by you. Our engagements are such, that we must be Happy, or not, in Excess; I do think that Indifferency, if ever we allow it to Enter our Minds, would soon turn to Hate. You do give me, and can continue to me, all the pleasure that a Wife I Love can give; you afford me all the Happiness that a Virtuous Companion can produce in a mind already full of you. It is in your power, to make me more miserable than I can tell you, it is beyond Expression, it is more than possibly you can Imagine. I am satisfied of the Truth and Strength of our Affection and hope it shall end only with Life itself. In the strictest Truth of my Heart, I assure you, I am wholly yours.

Now I am just going to Bed. I know not if ever I shall Sleep; or if I do Sleep, I know not if I shall ever Awake, it may be the Sleep of Death. I thank God for his past Mercies. I beg a Continuance of them. I cannot breath, once, without them. This is a Serious Subject, but it is what one will reflect upon, if we die as we would wish, not a sudden Death. From which Good Lord deliver us.

God Bless you and our Dear Boy. I am

Your affectionate and faithful Husband,

THOˢ WEDDERBURN.

To-morrow we start on a Byronic pilgrimage of several days. We are going to Harrow, and then to Newstead Abbey.

AUGUST 29TH.—Harrow-on-the-Hill. The red brick School buildings are very plain. I liked the graveyard and that stone where Byron used to go and sit. The very wide view was veiled with haze. The name on the tomb is PEACHEY. Who was this Peachey over whom Byron meditated so often? In the class-room with its oak woodwork he has carved his name thrice. One can recognize his Napoleonic "B" and the peculiar formation of his "y." The Library contains a portrait of Byron as a child; he was already handsome, whatever the majority of his biographers may say. The features are perfect in their regularity, the hair a light reddish colour, the

44

eyes wonderful. I can see him limping along the cobbled path of the graveyard, Clare on one side, the Duke of Dorset on the other.

A long journey north. Old, flowery villages. Posting inns with handsome red-and-black signs. At last, Nottingham. A glance at that gloomy street near the castle, where the quack Lavender kneaded poor Byron's legs. In the village of Hucknall Torkard we found the church where he is buried. As he requested, the stone bears the single word, BYRON. The sexton tells us that for five centuries all the Byrons were buried in that vault. "Wherever you walk," he said, pacing the choir, "here, and there, it's full of Byrons." He is very proud of this litter of Byrons. The eating-house opposite the church is called the Byron Fish and Oyster Bar.

We set off for the Abbey. It comes into view at a turn of the road. Of the church, a ruin, nothing remains but a tall ogival façade through which the trees are visible. The main body of the building is intact. It is a place that one loves at first sight with a curious fondness. We cannot tear ourselves away. I now understand Byron's attachment to his domain. "Newstead and I stand or fall together." The pleasure of finding all the expected relics. Here are the miniature forts built by the Wicked Lord, and the avenue of yew trees where the monks paced, reading their breviaries, the fine tomb of the dog Boatswain, Byron's oak (a trunk cut to a man's height on which he liked to write), and the tree on which he and Augusta carved their initials. In Byron's room, portraits of the old servant Murray, and of Jackson, the boxer.

45

Beside it, the haunted room. We spoke to some English friends of renting Newstead for a summer. "Don't do that. It's full of ghosts!"—"But I should like to meet Byron's ghost."—"Yes, but think of your poor children!"

Between Newstead and Annesley (Mary Chaworth's home), we follow the long line of trees that joins them. Here is the Diadem Hill, crowned with trees, from the top of which Mary scanned the fields for Jack Musters, her betrothed, whilst Byron, poor Byron, watched Mary's eyes. The house is still occupied by a descendant of the Chaworth-Musters'. Mrs. Musters showed us the door at which Byron fired his pistol: the wood is riddled with bullets.

"Have you a portrait of Mary Chaworth?"

The "Morning Star of Annesley" had a kind, tender look. How valuable it is to place real pictures beneath the accounts of history! Everything seems to take on consistency and strength. Evening was falling. We went to take a last look at the walls of Newstead in the twilight. Byron loved that hour when the bats flit under the bare vaulted roof of the church. To-day it is roofless. Coming out we looked at the great oak which the neighbours saved from the Wicked Lord. It was here that Mrs. Byron halted one day in 1798. The nurse, May Gray, had the boy Byron on her knee, and the child was deeply moved to know that in a few minutes he would at last be seeing a castle of which he was the lord. . . . The very spot, the same tree. George Gordon Byron, a boy with russet hair, rested his eyes on that bush. And that stout woman, her arms laden with brace-

lets, rolling her r's. . . . It all seemed suddenly so real
to me that for a moment I forgot that these things were
happening a hundred and thirty years ago. Yes, there
are ghosts at Newstead.

OCTOBER 2ND.—On deck. A clear sky, very pale blue on
the horizon, bright overhead. From Dover the French
coast could be seen. I feel that I am returning transformed and soothed. For some weeks past all my reading
has brought me back to one central idea—*you can make
your own life*. "God leaves us to ourselves." My companion during those recent months, Byron, with his belief in Fate, almost the unique source of his unhappiness,
has joined in teaching me. I began yesterday an admirable book of Eddington's, "The Nature of the Physical World." We are far from the mechanistic universe
of Adrien Sixte or Taine. To the modern scientist a
man's destiny is no more determined than are the movements of a molecule; the laws of history, like those of
physics, can only be statistical, and this leaves the individual free. An insurance company can accurately fore-
cast how many men of a particular generation will be
living in fifteen years' time, but of what will happen
to a particular man it knows nothing. Exact though
mortality tables may be, it is useful to teach children
that they will be run over if they walk in front of cars,
and this teaching will modify the life-duration of those
who learn it. Human will is restored to its place in the
world. The universe is hard to penetrate and heavy to
move, but it is indifferent. Every man can fashion his

own niche therein. "It is because destiny is immutable that our fate is in our own hands."

And what is to be made of this liberty, a real thing, but in the last resort a matter of thought? "Life is too short to be small." Not one moment should be lost in hating those who hate us. Not one thought should be given to our enemies which could be given to our friends. We must not be made the slaves of ambitions and needs which we do not feel, and which common men seek to suggest to us in order to hold us. During these weeks in London I was happy in a life stripped of all trappings. I rented a small room near the British Museum. Every day, from nine to one, I worked in that vast room, the circular form of which is so favourable to work, because, wherever you look, your eye finds nothing to catch hold of and is thrown back on to your desk. I lunched in clean and humble restaurants, sitting at small tables with clerks and typists. A novel on my knee, a cup of tea, a slice of ham, two pennyworth of jam. An hour's stroll round the chessboard squares of Bloomsbury, in the midst of that foreign crowd as heedless of my activities as the waves are of a swimmer's. Then work again, from two to six. The wonderful solitude of a great city.

The air on deck here smells of damp wood, brine, and pitch. Two lines are running one after the other round my mind: one is Mallarmés

Le tendre, le vivace et le bel aujourd'hui . . .

and the other is Madame de Noailles', I think—

L'étendue alentour est enfantine et nette . . .

The pale sea shows hardly a wave, a smooth surface ruffled by faint tremors like those on the close-trimmed coat of a slightly winded horse. What does one need for happiness? A patch of blue sky overhead, mildness in the air, and peace of mind.

Calais. A great wave, washing up as we enter, runs leaping alongside us between the jetties, a dog scampering at the vessel's side.

CHELSEA WAY: PROUST IN ENGLAND *

IT was during a dinner at the Pré Catelan that I learned from M. de Norpois how the government of the Republic had decided to recall him to the active list, and send him to London at the head of the French delegation to the Conference on Air Armaments. In congratulating the ex-Ambassador, I made a point of mentioning that I had long been anxious to see London, and that his presence in England might well induce me at last to undertake the journey. He replied, I think, that the work of the Conference would unfortunately leave him scanty leisure, but I was hardly listening, as my attention had for a moment been engaged in observing the solo violinist, who, boldly cutting loose from the orchestra and wandering out among the tables like some venturesome and resonant outpost, still with amazing precision, remained in unison with the rhythm and movement of his colleagues, all as if some invisible headquarters-staff, by veiled and exact instructions, had maintained liaison between this mobile patrol and the main body of the melodious forces. With the closing bars of each piece, the violinist bowed in the direction of the blonde American ladies whose brightly coloured gowns enframed the

---

* Marcel Proust himself, in his *pastiches* of Flaubert, Saint-Simon and others, showed that these exercises can help a writer to understand a style different from his own—and one that he admires.—A.M.

50

glazed wooden platform, lowering his bow as if saluting with a sword, and then turned back to his comrades, who were waiting with calm curiosity for him to bring back a report about the enemy whose pink camp-fires they could discern beneath the far-off bushes, and so enable them to launch a new offensive of harmony. With his head thrown back and eyes dim with happiness, he turned the caresses of his responsive bow on to the great air from "Pagliacci" or from "Samson," and one felt that under cover of these long, sustained, insistent notes, he was inwardly and securely violating the hearts of those haughty damsels, like some Julien Sorel, schooled in the Conservatoire, reading a doubtful love-tale to the proud Mathilde de la Môle. But as ten o'clock drew near, there loomed up behind the musicians several large negroes in dinner-jackets, whom the fiddler watched with a look of anguish so affecting that, when one white-eyed giant of these blacks placed a saxophone beside the violoncello and a drum beside the viola, it seemed to me as if a really despairing and quite beautiful grief were lending its nobility to the waltz he played, which was a very antiquated pre-War favourite; for there is no music that is absolutely bad; through even the flimsiest, an impassioned player can say all that there is to say, and we ourselves are that player when, deeply stirred by some grave personal misfortune, we transfer our own distress, and thereby a genuine and affecting beauty, to the jingle of a hurdy-gurdy or the raw symphony of a wayside fair.

Precisely on the first stroke of ten o'clock, one of the negroes, who, erect and resplendent, had been dominating this picture like the black slave standing in the foreground of Lorenzo the Magnificent's procession in the fresco of Benozzo Gozzoli, laid hold of the drumsticks, bent forward, and proclaimed with a loud, long-drawn rattle of the drum that the days of easy languid life and artlessly voluptuous phrases were over, that the fierce, streaked, mechanical hour of swift rhythms, of skyscrapers and streamline cars, had struck at last. Across the tables that throbbing rolled as the drums of mobilization had rolled over France fourteen years earlier; even in the most secluded bushy corners, its sustained, muffled energy tightened the muscles of bodies limp in the softening languors of peace, and made warrior Amazons of those pale madonnas of the luminous gloom.

"I do not disguise from myself," said M. de Norpois, "how complex are the duties of a French emissary in England. Nevertheless, he can, I think, steer his barque safely through somewhat menacing reefs provided he keep two guiding principles in sight—the first, that he is representing France, the second, that he is representing her in England, which amounts to remembering, on the one hand, that he is charged with the acceptance of our government's views by a friendly but dissimilar nation, on the other, that he must interpret to the former the frequently peculiar (and to a Frenchman, most surprising) ideas of the Foreign Office. And pray note that I say, in speaking of France, 'our government,' and in speaking of England, 'the Foreign Office,' and not 'the Cabinet' —no, nor even '10 Downing Street'; and I draw this distinction of set purpose, for the permanent officials of the Foreign Office have their own policy, one which is often successfully opposed to that of the Cabinet."

But I was no longer listening to the Ambassador, my whole attention being absorbed by the fascinating and manifold spectacle which the orchestra was by now presenting to me. As soon as that prolonged kettle-drumming rattled out, as if to give warning of the Last Judgment or the perils of the triple somersault, the solo violinist was apparently seized by some mortal, animal fear, rather as the flies which a cruel, heartless keeper thrusts into the metal cage to be devoured by the chameleon, and which, at sight of the monster, cling vainly to the farthest corners of the walls. Thus my violinist (who was not unlike Morel, but could not be Morel, who would not have been playing in a restaurant), ever since observing the entrance of the negroes, had borne his languishing melodies away amongst the farthest tables, even away beneath the firs of the Bois, as if hoping that in colonies so remote from the metropolis, barely even linked to it by far-travelling *maïtres d'hôtel,* he could perhaps maintain a tenderly Pucciniesque régime for yet awhile after the wild tambourining revolution of the Pré Catelan. But the negroid rattling had drowned his phrases as Santerre's drums did the voice of the dying King Louis, and the extremity of his alarm reminded me suddenly of all the heroes of story and legend tortured by the dawn of some tremendous day of reckoning, of Faust or of Peter Schlemihl at the hour when their souls are claimed by an infernal and ruthless creditor, or of Cinderella on the night of the ball when the twelve strokes of midnight ring out.

He stopped short and hastened over to the band, and I imagined, seeing him lean over to the Benozzo Gozzoli negro, that he had managed to extract a promise from his black conquerors to let him triumph just once again, as he came forward, blissful and triumphant, and began with an all-too-tender stroke of his bow on "Plaisir d'amour ne dure qu'un moment. . . ." But his pleasure was briefer even than that of love, which is not so very short (being not, as is supposed, the pleasure of making love, but that of experiencing it), because suddenly a little fury-faced monster with a napkin in his hand, conjured up by the first tearful notes, sprang upon the musician and held out his watch with a gesture of domineering brutality. Pursued by this monster, who was the manager, the fiddler and "Plaisir d'amour" backed away towards a yawning doorway (that of Hell, no doubt) which engulfed the musician, whilst the infernal gnome, with an imperious flick of his napkin, unleashed the negroes, who were joined, as I noticed with feelings of scorn, by a traitor to white music in the person of the violoncellist, who now became the diminutive prop of a gigantic silver instrument from which he drew certain discordant sounds.

"The mission with which I have been honoured," said M. de Norpois, "will be made a trifle easier for me by the fact that France and England no longer possess either divergent interests or common and disputed zones of influence. No French statesman nowadays has any serious thought of reviving our claims to Egypt, still less to Canada. As for an attack on India, that is for the moment placed in the sphere, if not of impossibilities, at least of improbabilities, both by reason of the inadequate radius of flight possessed by the machines in actual use, and by the temporary impracticability of maintaining subsequent supplies. . . ."

But the voice of the jazz-band swamped that of the Ambassador in my ears, just as for the fair Americans it had swamped that last plaint of the violinist, and powerless to hear anything else, I observed the strange exactness with which it evoked the rhythm and movements of love. Admittedly, this was no fresh observation, and I recall how, being at a concert one evening with Saint-Loup, I had analysed a Beethoven symphony and discovered how it moved forward through phases of repose, resumption, and torment, towards the crowning deliverance of perfect accord, as a pair of lovers towards that brief shock which will mark the simultaneous term of their pleasure and their pain, but comparing the songs of my doomed violinist with the syncopated twitchings of the negroes, these two musics seemed to correspond with two conceptions of love, the one romantic and factitious, seeking to believe in a perfection of understanding between bodies and souls, in the unbroken classic progression of sentiments, a conception expressed in the melodic simplicity of Puccini, of Gounod, and even of Schubert, the other cynical and realistic, accepting fitfulness as a law of love which it seeks amid the wailing dissonance of a unique and elsewhere undiscoverable rhythm, a doctrine transposed with stern clarity into a language of sound by the short, panting, spiteful confession of saxophone and drum.

Meanwhile, there began to roam among the tables certain dark and restless animals, their eyes seeking a prey in the darkness. They emerged thus every evening, at the hour of the violinist's withdrawal, just as the darting of bats succeeds that of the swallows, or as the tiger goes questing at nightfall. These prowling, famished beasts were the professional dancers. And I noticed that, like all carnivora they preferred their prey plump. They did not go over to those delicious, parti-coloured nests of pink and green and blue girls twittering round the lake-side tables, but kept peering into the gloom of the jungle to find some quadragenarian bovine, tethered to the base of a striped parasol by a halter of large pearls. Our table was on the boundary-line between the hunting-grounds of two of their number, and when they passed close to each other I could observe a strange glance of hatred and complicity. For a long time I wondered why both their bodies seemed to incline in one direction, as if in fear of reprisal from some harsh and invisible master, a master whose hiding-place seemed to be hinted at by their deflected glances, just as the warped apple-trees on the plateau of Méséglise, all leaning towards the same quarter, serve, even in calm weather, to point the direction of the prevalent winds, or again, just as street-walkers, hurrying alongside the passers-by in the yellow shadows of nocturnal streets, will reveal, by the unconscious orientation of their anxiety, the lurking-place of the pimp who is keeping his eye on them. And at last, by gauging the exact angle of fear of these dancers, whom every check made thinner and more avid, I espied, half-hidden behind a tree, the diabolic little manager, his flapping napkin giving them reminders of the pains of Hell and the wretchedness of their lot, like those cruel winged spirits who mingle sometimes on the canvases of Breughel with the throng of the living.

So deeply interested had I been by this spectacle that I did not notice that M. de Norpois, contrary to his general habit, had for some time been sitting silent, apparently in expectation of a reply from me. Not knowing what he had said to me, I asked whether he would be seeing Desmond Farnham, the novelist, in London, and whether he had read his books, of which I myself was fonder than of any author's then living.

"I know Farnham's name very well," he said. "He is a brother of Lord Shalford, and I have heard mention of him in Rome, Vienna, Tokio, and Paris as well, for he belonged at one time to the service and has been stationed in all these capitals. He is, I believe, a gifted fellow, but I have not read his novels myself, although excellent judges assure me that they are remarkable. For my own part, I must admit, I remain loyal to Walter Scott and Dickens, and especially to Thackeray, who to my mind represents the essence of the English spirit (but no doubt I ought to say 'British' for the author of 'Waverley' was a Scotsman, and you know the strong attachment of the two races to nationalist distinctions, which nevertheless are no bar to close understanding, for the United Kingdom could not be described as a house divided against itself, although up in Scotland in the days when I had the honour of being invited to Balmoral by King Edward the Seventh, I have frequently heard natives of the Northern Kingdom, when they were going to England speak of 'going out of the country.' . . ."

But seeing that the Ambassador was again well under way, and in no danger of stopping for a considerable time, I passed the remainder of the evening in watching my violinist, whom I had descried sitting gloomily behind the jazz-leaders, like a captive king fettered in the train of a conquering barbarian's triumph.

Although M. de Norpois had scored a great diplomatic success in contriving to bring that evening at the Pré Catelan to a close without having invited me to pay him a visit in London, I nevertheless made the crossing a few days later. The name of a train on the lips of Bloch (a frequent visitor to London, where his plays were performed with much success) had abruptly decided me to undertake a journey both distant and formidable in my eyes. This train was called the "Golden Arrow," a name which evoked that symbolic and delicious arrow of gold to which Sainte-Beuve longed to fasten his equivocal friendships, and that Zeno, "cruel Zeno, Zeno of Elea," whose swift, motionless arrow I could fancy linking with its quivering, gilded streak the sandy dunes of Calais and the white cliffs of Dover. Unable, alas, to bring Albertine, I had persuaded Andrée to vouchsafe me her company, and we started together from the Gare du Nord by that splendid midday train, which, by the central, culminating

and majestic hour of its departure, set there in the middle
of the day like a royal box in the middle of the sweep
of a balcony, acquires a glamour over and above that
of the winged emblems on its long blue coaches.

There could be no doubt that this crowd on the platform was already an English crowd, and for a long time
Andrée and I kept wondering what gave it this undeniable British character, for men nowadays are dressed
exactly alike in every country in the world, and English-
women wear clothes bought in the Rue de la Paix or the
Champs-Elysées, and yet, now in the train as later on
the deck of the boat, as we sat beside our suit-cases in
the midst of a huge encampment where squatting families
watched over the tribal baggage, whilst our tongues could
feel the salt tang of the sea on our lips, our minds, little
by little absorbing these unknown faces, were quite unmistakably tasting the flavour of England, a flavour which
came partly from the types around us, for the males of
the Continent can never show those bright pink com-
plexions on which the white moustache stands out pure
and snowy, as the brittle, lunar peak of a lofty mountain
will stand sometimes against a rosy sunset sky, and partly
too from the clothes, for although a "foreigner" can at-
tire himself in tweedy clothing, yet, on him, its very in-
formality has a touch of affectation and deliberateness,
whilst it is only on the English that this carelessness is
really unstudied, and therefore elegant. Near us on the
deck was an old lady, wearing a grey dust-coat and
crowned with an incredible hat of green tulle, who looked
so lamentable a figure that Andrée, convinced that she

must be on the first-class deck by mistake, was commiseratingly awaiting the arrival of the boat's ticket-inspector and his doubtless gruff expulsion of the poor old beggar-woman to the steerage. I reassured Andrée, and advised her to go over and read the name painted in white letters on the old lady's luggage surrounding her where she sat. A moment later Andrée returned, slightly confused, and told me that the bags belonged to the Duchess of Surrey, who was, of course, a cousin of the King's, and that the old lady must be a maid. But I told her that I thought that this was the Duchess in person, and actually it will be seen that I proved to be right when I met her during a week-end at Lord Shalford's.

Behind us the French coast became paler and more faint, in the same degree as the English coast ahead of us grew sharper and more distinct, so that I seemed to be watching some mysterious transfusion of strength, such as one can see taking place in some of those cruel and fantastic films in which the scientist, with his long alchemist's beard and surgeon's overall, makes use of a living woman to animate a statue, and one sees the beautiful body outstretched on the table becoming limp and collapsed whilst the artificial creature opens its eyes, comes to life, and smiles all round. Thus it seemed as if that romantic castle, rising clearer every instant in the white Dover cliffs, were fashioned of the flesh and blood of the Calais watch-tower and the lighthouse of Cape Gris-Nez.

This crowd on the boat differed also from a Continental crowd in two rather subtler characteristics, one being its relative good-humour, not marked by any positive action, yet apparently permeating all the social relationships of this mobile gathering. A smile came into spontaneous being on every face one met. The Pullman official, for instance, moving to and fro along the deck in his blue frock-coat, entering up the seat-reservations for the English train, did not show that combination of obsequiousness and officiousness which a like functionary on the Continent would doubtless have assumed, but was self-respecting, kindly, and yet inexorable, in his efforts to satisfy our wishes without going beyond his rights, and accepted a half-crown tip with the startled dignity of an admiral and the pleased gratitude of a poor man, and with an air which made it clear that the service in question had been rendered before any question of the half-crown had arisen, and consequently that it would have been rendered even if you had not been a gentleman and had forgotten the tip.

Thanks to him, Andrée and I were able to find ourselves in opposite seats in the train from Dover to London, with tea laid before us in blue-and-white china on which Chinese dragons were battling with Dutch windmills. And whilst we were enjoying all those details in the carriage, the clothing of the attendants, and the manner of serving tea, which struck us as different from France (for in travelling we find something acceptable in anything out of the ordinary, because, in our fundamental awareness of the vanity of these transplantations and the trifling sum of real pleasure which they bring us, we act like those shady men of business who inflate a balance-sheet by crediting worn stock and worthless plant

61

at full value, and we place to the credit side of our journey the most minute variations of manners, be they quite insignificant in themselves—the actual debit side being so burdened with the weight of our headaches, our fatigue, our ravaged stomachs, our uprooted intestines, and with the sense of having lost a whole day, that every single item must be entered to make a balance), the train was sweeping us through stations to which we felt grateful for their being English, and for having the outward appearance thereof, for being called "Folkestone Junction" and not "Embranchement de Louviers," and for proclaiming "Mazawattee Tea" rather than "Quinquina Dubonnet." We were passing through small towns made up of strings of identical glazed-brick cottages, each protruding its two bow-windows which bulged into infinite distance like the lines of beautiful, athletic, and full-breasted maidens on the friezes of the Panathenæa. It was pleasing to observe that the sheep in the fields did not look like the Norman sheep, but were smaller and woollier than ours, their legs being hardly visible, which made them look like the ill-carved toys of a Swiss wood-worker, and that the trees, though of the same stuff and substance as the trees of Tansonville or Méséglise, were nevertheless planted in an English style, not in the straight lines that we know, but isolated in the midst of wide grassy fields, and were also lower and more bushy (this coming no doubt, as Andrée pointed out to me, from the nature of the soil, which does not allow the roots to plunge deep and forces the tree to expand in girth rather than height), which makes an oak, even when standing alone, look like

a landscape of Gainsborough or Constable, whereas it
could not possibly be an oak of Corot or Daubigny, and
further, that the grass appeared to be of a closer texture
than French grass, which in point of fact is quite true,
as I found later when I lay on English lawns and discovered how closely this green tissue is fitted to the
ground, veiling the tiniest patch of its original soil with
its clipped, curving blades, rather as the vigorous, close-
trimmed hair of a young soldier spreads its dark, air-tight
coating over the pinkness of his scalp.

Andrée, who was an even greater enthusiast in this
game of differences than myself, pointed out to me the
beauty of English graveyards, sullied by no fearful erections of iron and glass, but ranging their lines of flowery
graves on a carpet of mossy grass only broken, here and
there, by the decorative triangular shape of an arbor vitæ
or a cypress, or by the drooping tresses of a weeping-
willow, a beauty which is one of the countless and touching products of that English craving to veil the seamier
side of life, which is a key to the melancholy humour of
Dickens and Charles Lamb, to the cheerfulness of English soldiers during the War, to the graciousness of their
hospitals, and which results in there being no more instant evocation of the happiness of being alive than a
nursery of lovely fair-haired children, reared on porridge
and rhymes, in some great house in Belgrave Square, or
than the flowery, smiling serenity of the cemetery at
Folkestone.

At last it grew dark. On the outskirts of the small
towns through which the train was passing, the white

tennis-players grew pale like those phantasms of which Madame de Sévigné speaks in the "moonlight" letter, and beside me my English travelling companions, with dignified and disdainful deliberation, were beginning to bestir themselves. Hats coming down from racks, venerable and initialled leather suit-cases emerging from the depths of the carriage, and the bustling of the admiral of the Pullman—all told me that we were entering London. When I stepped out of the train, I saw that alongside us, on the other side of the platform, a long rank of taxis was waiting, and the fact of these vehicles, attributes of the city, being actually *inside* a station, left me as much surprised as I might have been by the entry of a motor-omnibus into a cathedral. The mixture of two elements took me aback; I felt that the French method of penning up railway-trains in the stations behind closed barriers allowed these monsters to preserve a glamour essential to our enjoyment, and retained in travel that element of mystery and the nether world which is doubtless its sole charm, and then, linking this trait with others in the British character, I discovered a fascinating symmetry in the intellectual edifice which I was raising, for railway-trains, amongst this maritime race, came in like ships alongside a quay, and it was quite natural that access to *terra firma* should be unrestrained; those bare-headed young men in dinner-jackets, accompanied by those girls with their fair-skinned pallor who were drawing the mauve feathery collars of evening-cloaks closer to their throats, coming to meet the ruddy-faced old general, must surely have emerged from some neighbouring casino, and

in my eyes Victoria Station came alive with the faintly
swinging masts and all the kindly twinkling of a harbour. But when once our wits have found an explanation
that strikes us as ingenious, we derive so keen a pleasure
from it that we seek to carry it always a stage further,
and as I crossed the narrow platform alongside which
the coaches were moored, and was gliding still on the
rails of the taxi, I reflected that this people is one loving
in all things imperceptible transitions and open barriers.
Just as the tides of the railroads pour freely into the heart
of the city through those great docks that are called Victoria, Charing Cross, or Paddington, so the English aris-
tocracy likes to plunge sometimes into the commonalty,
not only mingling with the latter in its games, but also
returning to it through its sons (for a great-grandson of
the King himself might be plain "Mr. Windsor"), and
welcoming the better plebeians without any water-tight
barrier surveyed by a functionary in a peaked cap, or so,
again, in English history, the monarchy assumed the form
of democracy not by a bloody revolution, but without its
being possible to point to any single year as that of the
change, with the result that Lord So-and-So, an all-
powerful nobleman, holding rights of territorial jurisdic-
tion, having the gift of seats in the Commons in his hand,
and being proprietor of four towns, is at the present day
bereft of all real power, may see his own son a defeated
candidate for those same seats, and yet is not left humili-
ated or with any feeling that a change has taken place,
so, seated beside Andrée in a taxi of old-fashioned build,
I found myself wafted all unawares from the peaceful

shelter of the Pullman into the lurid turmoil of Bucking-ham Palace Road.

On arrival at the hotel, I enquired for the room I had engaged, and the porter, a small mischievous-faced fellow who looked like that old man with his nose blossoming in a huge pimple who is teaching a child his letters in one of the rooms of the Louvre, answered me with a particu-larly agreeable smile, but in French, which at once pleased and vexed me, for although knowing that I spoke English with a foreign accent, I was incapable of detecting that accent. Listening to Andrée, I was instantly struck by the odd turn of her English phrases, by the over-stressing and over-sibilance of her "the's," but I myself, speaking worse than she, kept thinking with every new phrase I uttered that I would suddenly, by some phonetic miracle, catch the exact sound, for we match the sounds we pro-duce, not at all with the real sounds which an Englishman would give to the words (and which we can no longer remember), but with a sound preserved by our memory, one that is already inexact, for if it were exact, we should know English like an Englishman, which is not the case.

Next morning, after a deft and silent chamber-maid had pulled up the black paper blinds which had cut me off from the light, and brought me that sleepy morning cup of tea with which the English wash the night's burden of digestion from their tongues and cleanse their brains of the last lingering images of dream, I lost no time in call-ing Andrée and hurrying to the window. How delight-ful! From our rooms on the sixth floor we overlooked Hyde Park. As far as I could see stretched the green billows of trees, their greenery becoming more and more blue as they receded into the distance. Of London itself one saw only the misty outlines of houses on the farther bank of the Park, like those vague white towns in pictures by Turner (whom I then knew only through Ruskin, but to whom I was soon to be indebted for enjoyment as keen as those to which Swann had quickened me before Vermeer or Mantegna), which shelter the loves of Dido or Armida. When we came out into the street after breakfast we tried for a long time to find just what it was that gave this dreamlike aspect to a city which we had imagined to be entirely mercantile and maritime. Was it those red motor-buses revolving in long files round the Marble Arch, seemingly in ant-like obedience to some obscure law which bade them for ever follow as close as possible on each other's heels, or was it those dark policemen who seemed at one moment like Fates, their diligent fingers spinning the thread of British destinies on some invisible distaff, and at another like Spanish dancers, the outstretched left arm holding a transparent, impalpable guitar and the right twanging its single string whilst the traffic speeded before them? But no, it was neither the omnibuses nor the policemen; on the contrary, these all shared an equal appearance of solidity, metallic or carnal. Faced by this impression, I felt now, as formerly I had felt before the three trees at Tansonville, the duty of explaining it. And at last, as I came up Whitehall, I was struck by the fact that I was walking, not through a town, but through the drawing of a town, or more precisely a washdrawing, or perhaps one of those frenzied romantic draw-ings in which Victor Hugo loved to heap up black and white cathedrals, in a sort of mediæval Babel, high above walls and battlements. And this idea of a pen-and-ink drawing suddenly threw light into a whole dark tract of my consciousness. As London is a city whose air is laden with dust and fog and coal-smoke, each one of the grey houses along the street we followed was streaked with strange shadows, with gleaming white shapes which, being quite unrelated to those of the building, distorted the latter and deprived it of the aspect of a construction planned by human hands, so that these blacks and whites seemed to have been placed there by those unwitting artists of genius, chance and smoke, who had given the city this air of fantastic yet moving unreality which is only possessed by the comedies of Musset, certain dialogues of Shakespeare, and the hall of the Gare Saint-Lazare.

Towards noon I went downstairs to the apartments which the French delegation occupied in the same hotel, and had my name sent in to M. de Norpois. He received me almost immediately. "I am all the more pleased to see you," he said, "because circumstances enable me to do you a service (I say 'circumstances' and not 'my intention,' for I discovered, long before being summoned to represent France in the country where the phrase has been made proverbial, that honesty is the best policy). For I must tell you that last night I happened (a curious coincidence, on the eve of your arrival) to be dining at Lord Shalford's, and there made the acquaintance of his brother, the Desmond Farnham of whom you spoke to me and whom you are anxious to meet. I told him of your admiration for his works, and if you wish it, I can easily give you a line of introduction to him. As a matter of fact," went on M. de Norpois, "I cannot say that I care much for his novels; I have made an attempt to read them, as well as those of the other English writers you mentioned during that pleasant dinner, but I shall remain faithful, if you don't mind, to my old friends of the Victorian age, whose humour, and whose narrow, but praiseworthy, conception of life conformed in my opinion much more closely to the authentic British temperament than these new works which have been subjected to the dangerous morality (or, as I ought to say, immorality) of the Russian novelists. Since being here, I have discovered the existence of a young England which would cause me much alarm on our friends' behalf, did I not feel it to be numerically weak, and powerless against the compact and vigorous bulk of traditional England. But this does not alter the fact that your friend Farnham, or, as everybody calls him here, 'Desmond,' is a delightful and courteous person."

M. de Norpois wrote a few words on a card and rose, to let me understand that he had more weighty functions to fulfil than his reception of myself; an English man-servant, who looked like that admiral with a purplish complexion portrayed by Reynolds in the National Gallery, showed me out with a slightly more pronounced degree of politeness, as appropriate to someone whom the head of the delegation had received without causing him to wait. I rejoined Andrée, and found her with a lady's maid whom she had engaged by telephone during the morning, a dark little person dressed entirely in black, about forty years old, who reminded one of an engraving intended to represent in human form the ant of the fable in some illustrated volume of the Romantic period, and who doggedly answered Andrée's enquiries as to her name with the words: "Tuttle, ma'am."

"Tuttle?" said Andrée.

"Yes, ma'am—Tuttle," repeated the maid.

"Tuttle?" said Andrée.

"Tuttle," said the maid.

"I am glad to see you back again," Andrée said to me. "You know, I thought my English was fairly correct—at least my governesses kept telling me so, and you remember how when I was translating George Eliot with you I was only very seldom obliged to look up a word in the dictionary, but this woman doesn't seem to understand what I say, and answers me with a word I simply don't know."

I then explained to Andrée that in England a master and mistress invariably address a lady's maid (and likewise a butler) by her surname, a usage which strikes me as more reasonable than the French one, the relation of master to servant being of a social order, like that of captain to soldier, or judge to prisoner, and in no way of a sentimental order, as that of husband to wife or lover to mistress. And so Andrée's English maid was perfectly right in answering "Tuttle" to my friend's questioning, Tuttle being her surname.

I must say a word about this Tuttle, who was with us throughout our visit to England. During the first half-hour of life in common, Andrée and I thought her stupid, because she answered any orders given with "Yes, ma'am," replying with such extraordinary rapidity, even, as it seemed, before she could have had time to transpose the sounds of our voices into thought, but we were not long in discovering that we were mistaken, and were convinced within a few days that Tuttle was a person of admirable intelligence, gifted with a sense of organization bordering on the marvellous; for if Andrée had said to her at six in the morning, "We are leaving at noon for Constantinople, Bagdad and Calcutta. Pack the bags, take tickets, and see to the passports"—Tuttle would have answered, "Yes, ma'am," Andrée and I could have gone to sit in the lounge and read *Punch* (the subtlety and intelligence of whose comedy, for all its simplicity, delighted us both), and about half-past eleven we should have seen Tuttle appear, and Andrée would quite casually have asked her, "Is everything ready, Tuttle?" and she would have answered, "Yes, ma'am," which would be quite true, and if I had added, "Will you please order a taxi, Tuttle," she would have given me a slightly surprised and much offended look and said, turning not towards myself but to Andrée, "The taxi is at the door, ma'am," thus making it perfectly clear not only that one general order sufficed and that detailed arrangements ought to be left to her own initiative (like a good chief-of-staff, pained if the new general wants to meddle with transport lines, and giving him respectfully to understand that he knows his job), but also that she was in Andrée's service, that she was a lady's maid, and that if the gentleman saw fit to travel without a valet, he did not thereby acquire any right to turn a lady's maid into a courier. On these two points, during the whole time of her being with us, Tuttle remained as obdurate as the Duc de Saint-Simon on the question of his wife's stool, or as the Duchesse de Guermantes in her resolve not to receive Madame de Cambremer. She did not refuse to perform services for me, and was admirable in the art of running the iron down a pair of trousers or in folding waistcoats in a suitcase, but she declined to take the order to carry out these functions, although in themselves they were a pleasure to her, from myself. If I did ask her for such favours, she went to see Andrée in the adjoining room, consulted her, and then, having received confirmation of an order which, as it was signed by a personage without due authority, she had been unable to take at its face value, she made ready to execute it.

I sent M. de Norpois's card to Desmond Farnham, adding quite a long letter to it, and whilst awaiting a reply, Andrée and I began our visits to the museums of London. At the Tate Gallery we spent long hours in front of the Turners. Spiralling in long whorls, the trails of white, golden and vaporous cloud floated across skies far different from those, with their rotund cloud-shapes, of Constable or Gainsborough. Strange cities, where Grecian temples mingled anachronistically with feudal keeps, seemed to soar upward into a pale mist from green unfathomed ocean-beds. Placed within the field of this wavy and distorting vision, every landscape suffered an engulfing sea-change, every city became an Atlantis peopled with swirling phantoms. Following the life of the painter along the walls by means of the dates of his pictures, I could trace his growing obsession with images of the sea and the idea of dissolution. As a young man he observed sunken boats and shipwrecked vessels, and loved to fondle the deep, green, white-flecked hollows of towering waves. Then the whole universe became for him one billowy ocean. The saffron and the pale-rose hollows of the valley of Orvieto softly unfurled themselves, the walls and trees took on that strange rich air of the deep-sea forests of Shakespeare, and his palace of Calypso seemed to be awaiting the bleached bones of the drowned mariners of "The Tempest." Standing with Andrée near the entrance of that long room, I pointed out to her that, viewed from a distance, each picture seemed like a breaking wave of colour, on the crest of which floated an ocean pine, one fragment of uprooted flotsam, toppling upon floods of red coral and amber. We went over to "Childe Harold's Pilgrimage"; the trees of the Italian landscape drooped on to the rocks like seaweed; a sandy beige, gripped in Rembrandtesque fashion by a yellowish light, formed a neutral background for the enamel tints, and then, in Turner's old age, the sea itself was dissolved, and the "Morning after the Deluge" became, in the eye of a floating God, no more than a whirlpool of light drawing down to itself the pale bodies of sirens.

I tried to show Andrée that landscape painters could be grouped under two heads, which, in a quite personal and in no way pedantic classification, I called the "glossy" and the "distorters," the former being the men of objective habit, whose main care is for accuracy, who concentrate on rendering the wonderful simplicity of all natural transitions, and are in painting what the Tolstoy of "War and Peace" is in literature; the "distorters," on the other hand, being the subjective minds, more concerned with a manner of seeing than with the thing seen, and like a Renoir or a Monticelli, transmuting the visible world as a Giraudoux or a Virginia Woolf does the world of sentiment.

"Look at the Corots of the Roman Campagna," I said to Andrée, "those in the Moreau Collection at the Louvre, or, if you like, at that little view of Avignon here in London, or amongst the English school, at that man I am so fond of, Richard Parkes Bonington. These are pure 'glossy' painters. Now come and see these Gainsborough landscapes, with trees like ostrich plumes; there you can just catch a beginning of the 'distorting' genius."

"Of which Turner would be the climax," said Andrée.

"You are most intelligent, Andrée dear. Yes, Turner, and also of course some of our own Impressionists. Rembrandt bequeathed them his light, as I showed you in Turner, and as I could also show you in certain Constables. But Constable is particularly interesting because he was skilled in both schools of painting. You remember the other day how we admired that small landscape in which he depicted so well the 'painted wood' aspect, the 'quilted sofa' aspect, of certain grassy downs in the limestone districts of England—just like the Italian Corots. Now, on the other hand, look at this farmyard; it has all the strange gleam, all the 'sheet silver,' of Turner. And that twofold aptitude makes me prefer Constable to

Turner, just as I prefer Boudin to Monet. We must go and see the Boudins at the Tate; they are excellent, and they'll show you that Boudin, like Constable, does not harp on one string. He is 'glossy' in the manner of his painting, in the exactness of the vivid colours, so few and so well detached on the sandy uniformity of the backgrounds, but in his drawing, with its sparse, black, enchanting lines, he is a 'distorter.'"

Passing without stopping (for Andrée did not like them, but I knew I should have found some pleasure, perhaps artificial, in them) through the Pre-Raphaelite rooms ("And yet, Andrée," I said, "you declare that Millais is very bad, and I certainly grant you that almost always he *is* bad, but look at that tiny picture in which a woman in a pale yellow gown is seated under a blue umbrella beside some tiny red flowers which look like Signorelli's—how good that is! Now come, you are often unjust in your judgments, and even you and I, who believe we are open-minded, will be victims of a fashionable opinion."), we went over to the portrait-painters, amongst whom I was especially glad to find Reynolds again, and his Robinetta, so triangular, voluptuous, cruel, and frank.

Three days after my arrival, the hotel porter (who, although I was a guest of no importance, was very friendly towards me, because he spoke French with a very pure accent, so that I gave him an opportunity of displaying a talent, and this is a much more potent cause of good feeling than a tip) handed me a letter, the typewritten address of which presented the most astonishing appearance, its lines heaving up and down like a stormy sea, some characters being blue and others red, quite meaninglessly, and yet this untidiness and incoherence, far from offending the eye succeeded, on the contrary, by an astonishing victory of man over keyboard, in giving that cold mechanical writing the air of intimate and privy courtesy in a handwritten address. When I opened the letter, I was stirred when I found it signed "Desmond Farnham," and read that he was inviting me to lunch that same day, at half-past one o'clock.

I did not note, when I was recounting my conversation with M. de Norpois, how greatly surprised I had been to learn that my favourite novelist was the brother of Lord Shalford. Certainly I had never cherished that prejudice, foolish enough, but widely spread amongst intelligent men, which consists in regarding talent or genius as reservations of the commoner classes, and refusing to recognize them if they appear in a man of high birth, or even in one who merely mixes in the best society (which, in the seventeenth century, would have meant denying genius to the author of the "Maximes," and in the eighteenth, to Saint-Simon), but Farnham's name, and the nature of his novels, had always led me to imagine a gentle, shrinking, solitary man, traits of character which I could not readily associate with the name of the Shalfords, famed and gallant Cavaliers in Stuart days, who for three centuries have been giving England a numerous band of ministers, generals, admirals and viceroys. Andrée, who made "Debrett" her favourite companion in the hotel reading-room, informed me that after the name of Lord Shalford, G.C.B., G.C.M.G., G.C.V.O., 9th Viscount and 15th

Baron, there occurred this entry: "Brother living: Honble. Desmond Farnham . . . educated at Winchester . . . secretary of Embassy . . . Colonel . . .War, 1914-1918 . . . D.S.O." So not only was the frail and delicate author of "Tiziano Sorelli" the son of a lord temporal, but he was also a diplomat and a colonel; and yet (although Debrett, with strange shamefacedness, did not add that he was one of the great writers of our time) there could be no doubt about his identity, a revelation which forced me to a total refashioning of the image I had formed of him, just as I had to do, even more curiously, a few days later in the House of Commons, where I had asked to be taken, when a Labour member rose to question Sir Austen Chamberlain on certain points of foreign policy, and I pleasantly pictured to myself this man of the people patiently training himself in the moments he snatched from his manual toil, and poring over the map of Europe and its history when he came up from the mine or out of the workshop. I asked my guide the name of this socialist, and he told me without further comment that it was Arthur Ponsonby, which I accepted as quite satisfactory. Well, it happened a few days later that M. de Norpois was speaking of King Edward VII in my presence, and saying, "It was not easy for him to forgive Arthur Ponsonby his opposition, for after all, as he said, Ponsonby was born in the purple." I asked what this phrase might mean, and M. de Norpois, looking at me with some surprise, replied, "What could it mean, except that Arthur Ponsonby was born in Windsor Castle?"—which gave me yet one more proof that we do not perceive reality, but perceive what we believe to be reality, for I had in all good faith been admiring the hereditary features of a great aristocrat as the toil-worn face of a worker. And when I became more familiar with them, I took great pleasure in those complicated names of English families, and just as Françoise at home loved repeating to herself that the son of the Duc de Guermantes was the Prince de Laumes, and the sons of the Duc de la Rochefoucauld were the Duc de Liancourt and the Prince de Marsillac, so I was delighted to discover that the charming Eric Phipps, who was at the British Embassy in Paris, was descended from the Marquesses of Normanby, that the eldest son of the Marquis of Headfort is that Earl of Bective whose pleasure it is to do electrician's jobs (so that in many London houses the maid will come in and announce, "Lord Bective, ma'am, has come about the bells"), his second son being called Lord William Taylour, and even such blended historical and topographical information as that the Duke of Westminster's family name is Grosvenor, and the Duke of Bedford's, Russell.

It had been my hope to lunch alone with Desmond Farnham, but when the butler who opened the door of the small Chelsea house to me, with tortoiseshell spectacles planted on his very youthful features, and having at once the air of a student of an eminent family and that of an overgrown child (an aspect which all British butlers have in my eyes, on account of their striped trousers, which, in conjunction with their silk-lined coats, brings back to my mind that costume known as "Eton," so much so that even to-day, after encountering him a score of times, I cannot set eyes on the venerable and almost centenarian butler of the Duchess of Surrey without thinking of a senior schoolboy), took my overcoat, I saw that other coats were already lying on the seat where he placed mine, and I gathered from his haste that I was the last arrival. For I had not yet learned that in punctuality the English are the second people in the world, the first being the Swedes, who, if they are invited for seven o'clock, arrive in a body two seconds before seven and only press the button of the door-bell at the precise moment when the hour strikes so as to enter then in a steady stream while the seven strokes are sounding, like those figures in the Strasbourg cathedral clock who emerge at noon from their gilded abode, while the English, with more indulgence, grant, if absolutely necessary, a respite of two minutes (but yet some of them do not grant that, for Lady Oxford said to me one day: "I don't wait for anybody, except the King"). I had barely time to observe as I entered the drawing-room that the decoration was French, and Second Empire, for Farnham came up to me at once with a very kindly smile, whilst I murmured a few words, to which, however, he did not listen, for he was engaged in presenting me to Lady Shalford, his sister-in-law, to Lady Patricia Crawley, to Lord Shalford, his brother, who was like Sargent's portrait of Lord Ribblesdale, and to Osbert Sitwell, who looked like Sacha Guitry in his youth, a brief formality after which the conversation was resumed as if I did not exist, a conversation which it was difficult for me to follow, primarily because it was in English and extremely fast, but more especially because its theme was the life of certain mysterious beings whom I did not know, and who in any case, being mentioned only by their Christian names and even, frequently, by their nicknames, were impossible for a foreigner to identify. Lady Patricia, who had just returned from Italy, brought news from Florence:

"Aldous and his wife are flourishing; Aldous is working on a long novel. Sybil is with the Berensons. Diana is at the Lido, Tiny at Danieli's. Your father was away, Osbert. Gladys is at Siena with Mr. Wilkins, who's getting more and more like Queen Victoria; I went to their place and Mr. Wilkins met me at the station himself in his Packard."

It was plain that the very names of Mr. Wilkins and Gladys contained an inherent comicality, invisible, as it seemed to me, but no doubt luminous to the initiate, for whenever they appeared in any sentence, everybody laughed except myself, who literally did not know what to say. I had rehearsed a few amiable remarks, quite genuine though certainly awkward, on Farnham's books and the influence they had had on my life, but I now felt that it would be not only ludicrous, but shocking and inept, to utter them, and so I could only try to ask in a whisper who Gladys might be, at which he laughed without replying, and asked Lady Patricia to explain Gladys to me.

"It's a long saga," said Lady Patricia (and I set myself the problem of deciding whether the word had been restored to fashion by Galsworthy and his Forsytes, or whether, the other way round, Galsworthy had used it because it had remained current). "How is one to begin, Desmond? Ten years ago Gladys was Gladys Weston. In those days she was a young American who, shortly before the War, took London by storm in a single night because she turned up at quite a serious party dressed in a man's jacket and with white satin trousers. Her husband was Douglas Weston, who had a good voice."

"And for whom, you remember," interrupted Lady Shalford, "she extracted some lessons from old Van Dyck, who no longer gave any to anybody, by just going and sitting on his doorstep until he agreed to receive her."

"Do you remember the little studio, Desmond?" said Lady Patricia to Farnham. "Gladys and her husband" (she went on, addressing myself) "had rented a small studio down here in Chelsea where the greatest musicians in the world used to come. You heard Cortot, Pablo Casals, Arthur Rubenstein, Chaliapin. About four in the morning the music stopped, and everyone went to bed, just anyhow, on the divans covered with cushions which went right round the studio. Most of the musicians were going back by the morning boat-train, and they used to leave there straight for the station. Sometimes one would go with them. It was charming. And then the War came, and the studio was closed, and that was the end of Gladys Weston in London."

At that moment we went in to lunch, and while the young Etonian with his tortoiseshell glasses passed round the caviare with such a perfect air of it being a matter of course that I really took him for a butler, Lady Patricia went on:

"In New York, apparently, the Westons went on having an amusing time. Gladys went quite mad, but really charmingly so. She used to steal the firemen's axes in Broadway theatres, and leave them in taxi-cabs, and then she would put an advertisement in the *New York Times* saying: 'Left in a taxi, fireman's axe stolen from Theatre Guild. Please return to Mrs. Gladys Weston. Reward.' A fortnight afterwards she had a letter from the taximan: 'Madam—I beg pardon for not having returned the axe sooner, but I have had cramp in the stomach. If you still need it, it is at your disposal.'"

And so the saga of Gladys Weston was unfolded throughout luncheon, Lady Patricia alternating with Lady Shalford like the two parts of a Greek chorus. I was told how Weston was dead, and how Gladys had married a very rich banker, who was mentioned only by his Christian name, Edward, and how, when travelling with Edward in New Mexico, she had caught sight, through the door of the railway carriage, of an Indian who looked just like Queen Victoria, and had said to Edward, "I'm sorry, darling, but I love that Indian and I'll have to leave you." (A phrase which enabled me to suppose, though it was not said, that the Indian was Mr. Wilkins.) These stories were told in a very agreeable vein of humour, and I should have found them most amusing had I not arrived at Farnham's with the absurd but persistent idea that it was my duty there to make exposition of my soul, and likewise to garner exact and fresh ideas regarding the younger English writers, with the result that I was gradually overcome by despair when I saw that an hour which I had so much looked forward to was being frittered away in chatter which, though possibly charming, was certainly pointless. For a moment the presence of Lord Shalford, who was a member of the Cabinet, led me to hope that my taste for the serious might be satisfied, and that we should at least have some talk of English politics, but he gave a long description of the state of health of two of his friends, Stanley and Austen, so that I ceased listening until, surprised at the interest Farnham showed in these medical remarks, I asked him who these two gentlemen were, and received the reply, "Stanley Baldwin and Austen Chamberlain, the Prime Minister and Foreign Secretary."

But now, as I was on the very point of yielding to my despair, it turned out to be just this conversation on Sir Austen Chamberlain's illness that saved me, for Lady Shalford said:

"At last, I'm glad to say, they've managed to convince him that he must take some rest, and he's going to take a sea-voyage. I went to Hatchard's this morning to find some books for him."

"I hope, Alice," said Farnham, "that you remembered my Americans?"

"Of course," she said. "I sent him the 'Bridge,' the Willa Cather, and 'The Great American Band Wagon'."

In this way books were introduced, and for a quarter of an hour they remained on the stage, which at last enabled me, as I so eagerly wished, to hear Desmond Farnham talking of literary matters. In point of fact, he and his friends talked of them in a way quite different from that in which a French gathering of the same intellectual standing would have done. Here again, authors were referred to only by their Christian names, so that it took me some time to realize that Arnold was Arnold Bennett; Virginia, Virginia Woolf; Harold, Harold Nicolson; and Maurice, Maurice Baring; moreover, pedantry was so scrupulously avoided that one sometimes had the impression of an affectation of nonchalance and frivolity in passing judgment. Lord Shalford, in particular, a most cultivated man, tried to make one believe that he read nothing but detective stories and only went to see "mystery" plays, and when his brother recommended Gerhardi's "Futility" to him—"It will amuse you, Howard: you know such a lot about Russia"—he asked with feigned apprehensiveness, "But isn't it rather Virginia Woolfish?" Whereupon his wife said to him, "Really, you're intolerable, Howard. . . . You pretend you don't understand 'Mrs. Dalloway' and you simply can't put the book down."

"Not at all, Alice! The truth is that I *try* to understand because I'm jealous of your high-brow friends. . . . It's perfectly true, Patricia. Alice is terribly high-brow, you know. . . . She is quite ashamed of me in front of you, Sitwell, or in front of M. Jean Cocteau when he comes to see us at Antibes."

"Oh, Howard. . . . How *can* you say I'm high-brow? Why, I'm simply terrified when I do happen to find myself amongst a Bloomsbury set!"

During my stay in England I was very often to hear the two expressions which had just taken me by surprise (I mean "high-brow" and "Bloomsbury"), and although their meanings were outwardly very different, the former

84

indicating a physiognomical trait and the latter a district in London, yet in point of fact they were both applied to one particular group whose æsthetic and literary judgments were regarded as important, consummate, not to say extreme, by the very people who spoke of them ironically, for, like those saints whose virtues touched the hidden hearts of the agnostic patricians who sent them to the torture, the aloof and subtle critics of Bloomsbury perturbed these English spirits who were the most hostile to their tastes, leading them to voice their glorying incomprehension with a vigour the very excess of which was an immediate pointer to its weakness. The timidity of the all-powerful Lord Shalford, a Secretary of State, in the face of this group was not feigned, for a few weeks later I saw him reduced to speechless uneasiness when confronted by an old lady living in a thatched cottage near Cambridge, who had written a book on John Donne which had been praised by Bloomsbury, so that really it is a great mistake to say, as people will, that the intellectuals in England have not the same status as they have in France. True, they have not, and would not wish for, the same position in society, but by the very fact of this detachment they maintain the unimpaired lustre and the consecrated character which are the only fitting attributes of intellectuals.

Greatly pleased by Lord Shalford's ingenuousness, whether feigned or actual, I manœuvred myself into closer proximity to him, and asked him whether, as he was the Air Minister, he had had occasion to meet M. de Norpois in the course of the recent negotiations.

"Yes," he replied. "And I feel a certain admiration for M. de Norpois as one who, unlike so many European statesmen, is no slave to formulas. It is to America, and in a more general way, to the popular Press, that we owe the dangerous habit of the 'slogan,' the telling phrase, on which a minister imagines he can construct both a programme and a platform, and of which he merely becomes the servant. Your friend Norpois certainly has a taste for formulas, but he likes them multiple and contradictory, and this leaves them for the most part innocuous. If he is not altogether my diplomatic ideal, that is only because he is too perfect a diplomat, a quality which inspires a certain distrust in one who has to deal with him. I have always felt that the best negotiators are men like Mr. Balfour, who will pursue a conversation with unwavering precision, but will always keep an air of being lost in some erudite reverie or making a mental translation of a Greek poet, or else, in a different but equally effective style, men like Lord Derby, whose joviality and, as you call it in France, '*l'air bon enfant*,' preclude any lurking Machiavellism."

Now, obviously, nothing could have been more likely to interest me than these observations of Lord Shalford's, and I should have enjoyed them keenly had I not received the impression whilst we were talking, that he was inexorably eyeing the light-coloured uppers of my boots, uppers for which I was not really responsible, as my bootmaker had persuaded me before I left that these kid uppers were fashionable in England, and I now noticed, not only that I was alone in advertising my lower extremities with this startling conspicuousness, but even that everybody else's were extremely old, and Lord Shalford's indeed almost in holes. Now this indifference to elegance, this loyalty to things old, struck me as admirable virtues, contrasted with which the insolent newness of my almost white uppers struck me as ostentatious and damnable. I was conscious that nothing accorded less with my character than a desire to attract attention by such means that, on the contrary, I had ordered these hateful boots through a craving for conformity and simply because of my boot-maker's remarks, but of this Farnham and his friends knew nothing, and, thinking that they would doubtless judge me by this detail and by a few awkward words which had not (my English being only middling) exactly conveyed my thoughts, I felt desperate. But just when I was painfully and clumsily taking leave, convinced that I must have left a very bad impression on these Englishmen and that they would not invite me again, Farnham suddenly asked me, with a great deal of kindly concern, what I proposed to do in England. I told him it was my intention to remain for a few weeks so as to see the English country-side.

"A good idea," said Lord Shalford. "You ought to come and stay somewhere near me, in Surrey. . . . Look, there is a beautiful house that has just been turned into an hotel by an old friend of mine, Major Low. . . . You know Ashby Hall, Desmond?"

"A capital idea," said Farnham. "That's it—he must go to Ashby Hall, and as we're all going to Bosworth, my

brother's place, next week, we can be neighbours"—turning towards myself with these last words.

And with the sudden discovery of this extreme kindness, this determination to be pleasant to me, amongst
people whom I thought I had shocked, not to say dis-
gusted, I felt such a surge of inward happiness that I now
saw them as the most interesting and charming group of
people I had ever before known, and when I returned to
the hotel I sang their praises to Andrée with fondness and
vehemence.

"You know," I said to her, "I think they're right. We
ought to go and stay near them. I should greatly like to
see one of these great English houses, and it will be very
pleasant to have the Shalfords as neighbours. I shall try to
get an invitation for you too, and in any case we shall be
able to take lots of walks together, for Ashby Hall is in
splendid country. What we must do is to hire a car for
the time of our stay, and we can send Tuttle by rail with
the trunks. . . ."

Andrée called Tuttle, who was of course in the next
room, for she never moved far away and when not working for Andrée remained reading "Home Chat." Tuttle
gave us a look of authority, self-effacement, and dignity,
and awaited Andrée's orders.

"Tuttle," I said (and for an instant she turned a surprised head in my direction, then fixed it again toward
Andrée, judging, I suppose, that although she could not,
alas, suppress me, still the sounds emanating from me
would then, by refraction from Andrée, reach her from a
proper direction). "Tuttle, we are going to stay at Ashby

88

Hall. It is a country hotel lying between Guildford and Dorking. I don't know which station is the nearer. . . . You are to go there with the luggage. We shall go by car, but we shall have to find a chauffeur. I know that this is all rather complicated. . . . If you fetch me a time-table, I shall tell you the time of your train. As for the car . . ."

Here Tuttle stopped me, gently and firmly.

"If you will just tell me, ma'am," she said in a tone of polite reproach, "what time you wish the car to be at the hotel, and what time I ought to meet you with the luggage at Ashby Hall . . . ?"

And sure enough, at the appointed time, in front of the door of the Hyde Park Hotel, we found a car driven by a French chauffeur whom Tuttle had somehow or other discovered in London within an hour or two, and when we arrived at Guildford that evening, we likewise found Tuttle, there in Andrée's room, having already unpacked our trunks, and seemingly having spent all her life in this house, and yet being ready to leave it without any regrets at five minutes' notice.

The hotel Lord Shalford had told us about was an old red-brick manor-house, which Farnham had told me was beautiful and not unlike Ham House, where Lord Dysart lived, but for the first few days I could not succeed in grasping this beauty, which, for all I could see, was no more than that of any other brick house; for our æsthetic pleasures are built up of unconscious comparisons with examples we have already encountered and recorded, and just as during the first days of a sojourn amongst Negroes or Eskimos, all the women seem to our eyes ugly until the moment when a certain picture of the norm of the Negress or the female Eskimo enriches us with that seemingly eternal idea, in the light of which alone we are able to view objects, so for several days Andrée and I were always surprised to read in the guide-book, "Note at *Dunsfold* the Clock Hotel, one of the finest Georgian houses in England," and then to see a quite ordinary house, its porch, with a triangular pediment, resting on twin white pillars, while its red façade was relieved at the top by a narrow band of stone with only a trace of carving. Well, a week later we were both in love with this supremely simple architecture, delighting to draw each other's attention to the exactness of the proportions, to the perfect grace of this or that sash-window, to the fanlight surmounting a doorway, or to the colour of a brick here and there, its half-vitrified red recalling the glowing warmth of some Egyptian jewel.

Round Ashby Hall spread a broad, mown lawn, its tightly-stretched carpet seeming to be nailed down right against the walls of the house, and ornamented by four immemorial yews clipped in the form of gigantic bowls, the insides of which seemed as if they might have formed as it were a darkened rest-room, had not the eye distinguished the monstrous network of their thick twisting stems, the foul framework on which that luxurious, almost insubstantial, shell of bosky green was stretched. Beyond a white rail lay wide meadows with a stream flowing through them, and these, being as free and untamed as the lawn was trim and clipped, made a pleasing contrast with the latter. This wide stretch of land was doubtless marshy, for the grass covering it had the shaggy, wavelike, and almost aqueous appearance of water-plants, a sea of rushes and tall swordlike stems whose tide, when the wind stirred its yielding surface, beat against the strong, solid breakwater of the lawn. A few miles from Ashby Hall rose the high hills of Hindhead, covered with yellow furze and with heather, the dead colours of which I liked, the crackling rosy purple and dull green, that aspect of being at once dead wood and flowered beds which invested these heaths (as those in Scotland) with a subtle and mysterious charm. Farther on, the road ran through a small town, old and flowery; a black clock-face with gilt numerals jutted out, slightly askew, over the High Street; the white inn with its black beams still bore the same name as in the days when the Portsmouth coach came cantering in beneath its archway with the post boy cracking his whip. The little, grey stone houses, with their twin bulging windows, had kept their lattice-panes cross-hatched with lead. Andrée was surprised to notice how the old house-fronts blended decorously with those standardized shop-fronts which seem in England like the *leitmotiven* of urban life, the red pediment, flat yet noisy, of Woolworth's, the rounded, multiple and very unpharmaceutic window of Boots', and the glazed tile strip of W. H. Smith & Sons, Booksellers, but I tried to show her that the peculiar genius of England lies in her incorporation of a quite modern life within an antique setting, and that a small town like Guildford is a very close image of the mind of a young Englishman as shaped by Oxford and Cambridge, for that mind, like the charming houses of this steeply-pitched High Street, will be found to contain a timbered building of the sixteenth or seventeenth century occupied by an intellectual Boot's or Woolworth, (say Freud, or Einstein, Ltd.), a character which makes the English High Street very different from the American Main Street, because in the latter neither the intellectual nor commercial branch-shops have found a pre-existing and picturesque framework waiting for them to step into, and are left to provide their own background, modern, still and monotonous.

To Andrée and myself, who had both been devoted to English history and English literature, nothing was more moving than to be here, suddenly, in the very places where that history had been enacted, those books and poems written. At first I thought we should be disappointed, for I have noted elsewhere that names, and especially place-names, are fraught by ourselves before any actual contact with certain images of great beauty which represent their essential content, and that reality is often powerless to surpass or even to match these. But we quickly realized that this is not so with England, the beauty of whose poetry, humanity, and woodland, remains tangled enough to shelter the dreams of her poets. Looking at the map, I saw myself ringed in by names which I wreathed with wondrous, if perhaps deceptive, visions. Eton, which I pictured as girt by those fields on which Waterloo had been won and Shelley's boyhood lost; Winchester, which I would have sterner and still more aristocratic; Marlborough, which I mistakenly associated with the Duke and Queen Anne; Bath, whose Roman and Georgian renown evoked the fair Miss Linley, and the graver beauty of Mrs. Siddons, but what was true of the names of towns was still more true of proper names, for when, thanks to Lord Shalford (a telephone message on the day after my arrival at Ashby Hall invited me to take tea over at Bosworth), I was able to meet under his roof some of the bearers of those names so dear to me, I could not help painting in behind each of those faces a background which recalled the history of its family. The soft, dazzling beauty of Lady Diana Cooper, when I learned that she was the granddaughter of John Manners, stood out to my eyes against the glowing mirage of Belvoir Castle; in the fine features of Lord Lytton I pleased myself with the fancy that I was beholding the very author of "Pelham"; and in the face of Lord Shalford himself, the charming, tender, poetic traits of the friend of Charles I.

Because of a certain smoothness, amounting almost to softness, which infused their ease of manner, their courtesy, the surface calm of their faces, a smoothness that inevitably reminded me of their springy, well-trimmed turf, I had been tempted at first to regard these Englishmen as blissful and insensitive. But little by little, as I came to know them better, as much by my personal observations as by the stories of Desmond Farnham, with whom I had reached terms of intimacy, I discovered that the tranquil tone of their voices was capable of masking the same passions and sufferings that stir other men; thus, Lord Shalford really did feel shy before his wife's high-brow friends, and Desmond, telling me of the veiled loves of a friend of his, described how this man's jealousy reached such a pitch that when a clumsy hostess, at a river-party on the Thames, did not allot him a place in the same boat as the woman he was fond of, he jumped into the water in evening-dress to rejoin this lady (which confirmed Stendhal's theory, for no Frenchman, from sheer pride, would have done such a thing), the difference between the English and my Continental friends residing in the fact that these dramas, for all their violence, left no trace on their pink cheeks or in their blue eyes, but were enacted on a different plane, far removed from the observer and yet coinciding with the perfectly tranquil presence of the hero himself, rather like those secondary pictures which a cinematographer will sometimes throw upon the screen simultaneously with the principal picture, to evoke a memory or suggest a comparison.

One evening (we had been staying at Ashby Hall for about a fortnight) I was struck on my way back there by a curious and quite powerful sensation which I recognized as that of wonted habitude. For the first time since being in England I seemed to be "coming home," and on analysing this impression I found that it arose from my memory having gradually recorded, exactly and infallibly, the pictures which made up the Ashby road and the park surrounding our house. I now knew, when I saw a certain white rail beside which stood a cottage of grey stone with its windows framed with lead strips, that a hundred yards farther would bring me to the beginning of a long alley of lime trees, and sure enough, one minute later, the real alley of limes actually arrived and set itself with scrupulous accuracy over the one already outlined in my mind, this evoking in its turn a clump of three oaks, a dark curtain of yews, a rose-garden, and once again the three oaks, the sombre yews and the vivid roses of nature came and played themselves in the concave matrix which, graven within me by an artist of marvellous accuracy, was awaiting them. Now the sentiment of "home" is nothing else than this coinciding of our expectancy with reality (an impression that is agreeable because in all of us, as a legacy from the long centuries of terror when the universe, a monster with unknowable reactions, made men afraid, there survives a taste for whatever is fixed and familiar), and it had needed only a fortnight for this impression to become as powerful to me in this foreign land as it might have been at Combray, or later at the Hotel at Balbec. And so, reflecting that what was true of places was true no less of persons, that now Desmond Farnham as once Bergotte, now Lord Shalford as once the Duc de Guermantes, were becoming in my eyes straightforward characters, whose reactions, whose ideas, nay, whose very answers I could foresee, discovering also that, if I let myself go, Lady Patricia would soon inspire in me those sentiments which I had formerly owed (different though they were) to Gilberte, then to Albertine or the Duchesse de Guermantes, I realized yet once more that our sentiments are independent of the objects that give them birth, and that we carry with us to new places and even into new countries, certain possibilities of emotion which all, sooner or later, find in our environment their means of satisfac-

95

tion, a reflection which might well have led me also to question the worth of national sentiments if, after seeking in my new life the sentimental equivalents of all the elements in my past life, and after finding, as I said just now, Ashby Hall for Combray, Farnham for Bergotte, and Shalford Abbey for the Guermantes mansion, I had not noted that after the experiment, at the very bottom of the retort, there remained a sort of indescribable residue, slight but irreducible, and such that not all my efforts could produce an English substance with which it had any affinity, a residue that seemed to me unsatisfied, almost plaintive, powerless to achieve a stable compound with anything in my present environment, and which, by its microscopic presence (just as some slight aberration in the orbit of a planet, constant, vexatious, and inexplicable by any mathematical error, is proof to the astronomer of the existence of some invisible heavenly body) made me continually aware of the presence, the distant, veiled, silent, and yet unmistakable presence, of France.

PART II

PRESENT AND FUTURES

RELATIVITY

I

A TOUCH OF INFINITY

"BEAUTIFUL," she said, "are the architectures of God." Around us the gleaming crests of snow ringed the valley with a diamond circlet. Snow covered one side of the hollow, a mantle of pines the other half. In its depths the grass was of an almost liquid green; bare, pale trees seemed to be mirrored in a verdurous lake with white banks.

"Look down at the road beneath our feet," said I. "Do you see those deep parallel ruts made by the cart-wheels? Just imagine that down in the hollow of that bend, in between those two curves of upturned snow, there are living certain creatures of infinite smallness, invisible to our eyes. 'Let us admire,' they are saying, 'these snowy crests and the architectures of God. . . .'"

"And are they wrong?" she said. "Was it not an intelligence which made this road, and fashioned the curve of the track and this twofold harmony of the bend?"

"Human intelligence," I answered. "It is the will of a poor being, ignorant of the aims of the Universe and seeking only the maintenance of his fleeting and frail existence. . . . Our friends in the rut are at this moment

worshipping the work of the farmer's cart, not the work
of a divine architect. Who knows whether the astounding order which you and I think we can discern in the
world, may not be in its turn, the manifestation of the
activities of some vast animal which, on some incon-
ceivably gigantic planet, is seeking its love and nourishment?"

"Perhaps," she said. "But that animal, with its love
and its food, still forms a part of God's plan, just as the
farmer's cart does, and just as you yourself, with your
doubts, do. . . . Do you remember the day when we went
to the observatory to see the sun-spots?"

We were on the bridge of an inter-stellar liner. The
aged, silver-haired astronomer called out the longitudes
to the celestial steersman. The cupola swung round
towards a dart of light. Projected on to a white card, the
spots looked like some leprous disease of the sun, the livid
purple bruise from some blow. Solar storms, said the
astronomer. Nobody knew much about it, said the
astronomer. (The evening before, another scientist had
shown me cups of cells under the microscope in his
laboratory. In a circular world grey plains were sprinkled
with lakes of darker tinge. Little was known about the
morphology of cells, said the biologist. Nobody knew
much about it, said the biologist.) The sun-spots looked
very like the cells. Shapeless landscapes. Inhuman landscapes. Probably the surface of the Earth would look
thus to a dweller upon Sirius. "Spots," the Sirian would
say, "shapeless spots,"—and it would be Paris, and this

garden, and ourselves. Under his eyes he would have our sufferings, our hopes, a day of revolution, a day of festival. Under his eyes he would have the Paris of July 14, 1789, or the Paris of November 11, 1918. "One degree to the left," he would say to the man under his cupola, "shapeless granular formations." In the cells also, and in those black chromosomes, living beings were reviving at the fires of the microscope their infinitely brief existence. "It has been calculated," they were saying, "that the Great Light has been flooding the Universe for one hundred billion chromosome years."

The cupola turned, the rollers swivelled round, the telescope swung up. "Venus," said the astronomer as if announcing the next station. "In the realm of the stars," said the astronomer, "deaths are more frequent than births. This universe has begun; this universe will end. It has begun its ending. . . . Stick a stamp on a penny" (said the astronomer) "and put the coin on the Obelisk. If the height of the whole is taken as representing the time that has elapsed since the world came into being, the penny on that scale represents the time since mankind has walked the earth, and the thickness of the stamp, the time since parts of mankind have been civilized. . . . Add one stamp for each five-thousand-year period of civilization, and carry on until your obelisk is as high as Mont Blanc. You will still be far from the probable duration of man's future. This image, which I borrow from my colleague Sir James Jeans, is more or less accurate. And it is consoling . . . But the day will come when not only man, but also the Earth, and the Universe too, will return into Nothingness. . . . Perhaps it was but a fleeting thought that crossed the mind of God."

The helmsman announced Venus. It was a pale pink globe. . . . I thought of a postage-stamp . . . of a mountain of postage-stamps. And Homer's three thousand years of veneration. . . . Fame—half a postage-stamp, I reflected. "I wonder who the devil created this world," said Byron, "and the fellows of colleges, and women of a certain age, and myself more particularly?"

"The Universe," said the astronomer, "is finite in space as in Time. It is curved, and after millions of years light comes back upon itself. It is almost empty. Imagine that the Grand-Palais contained nothing but three or four particles of dust, and you will have an idea of the distances separating the stars of the Milky Way from each other. Beyond that, you would have to go thousands of miles before you found another grain of dust. . . ."

To bring us back to the metal staircase of the terrestrial landing-stage, the cupola creaked, turned, and sank. I wonder, thought I, who the devil created this world? Who the devil created this curving and almost empty world? What mind was it—a mind impossible even to imagine—that said to itself: "I am going to throw a few specks of luminous dust into a corner of the Void. Upon one of these specks, dark, chilled, and just like thousands of others, lost in an infinitely small globule of the Infinitely Great, which in itself is but a globule of the Void, I shall bring into being some living and sentient matter. I shall allow it to imagine that the whole world, the stars in their courses and the abysses of the heavens, are only a stage upon which purely human dramas are enacted. And then, to a few, I shall grant the power to measure the vastness of the abysses, the vanity of their own existence, and the obscurity of my designs . . ."—what mind said these things?

The spiral staircase touched land. A door opened. The heavenly bodies restored us to the light.

"Put on your hat," said the astronomer. "It's easy to catch a sunstroke."

Beware of a touch of the sun. Beware of a touch of the infinite, I thought. On that terrace at Meudon shone the human sun, nearer than that of the scientists. That ball of fire, unable to consolidate itself, was familiar and obvious. Galileo was wrong. The astronomer was wrong. A little girl in a green dress was kicking a rubber ball with stars painted on it. A train was crossing the viaduct. White smoke rose above the roofs. Seated on the benches of the Grand-Dauphin the Meudon mothers and their children were warming themselves in the real sun. The world was vast and beautiful. Something on our own scale.

II

PRIVATE UNIVERSES

I LIKE the abrupt dive into an unknown life which one gets from a remark caught on the wing. This morning, on the pavement in front of the Lycée Pasteur in Neuilly (the dry leaves, brown and crackling, were sliding along the asphalt round me like skaters), I overtook an elderly couple. The wife was stooping, thin and yellow; the husband very upright, with a white beard. "You criticize everything," he was saying sadly, "you criticize everything, you don't like anybody, and it's all because you're old and plain." What a subject for a Flaubert novel, I reflected, or perhaps for a digression of Proust! The ageing woman's view of the world, a view altering not because people and things have changed, but because the face becomes lined, because the body shrivels like those dead leaves.

"To argue against Carlyle's 'fire-eyed' despair is futile," I thought as I passed on beyond the old people, "because it is to argue against Carlyle's digestion." Where had I read that the evening before? Oh yes! In an essay on Pascal by Aldous Huxley. He spoke there of those individual views of the world, impenetrable each to others, which men take as truths and yet are merely projections of their own states. Speak for yourself, Huxley was telling Pascal. Valéry once told him: "The eternal silence of these infinite spaces does *not* terrify me. But the intermittent chatter of our small finite societies gives me reassurance. . . ." A sick man's philosophy, said Huxley. The fevered ascetic could not comprehend both sensuality and happiness. Making a virtue of necessity, he decked out his weakness with pious epithets. Pascal's "intolerable headache, griping of the bowels, and sundry other ills," made it extremely difficult, if not impossible, for him to be a pagan. His sick body, as Huxley says, was *naturaliter christianum*. And (Huxley continues) not only did he accept sickness for himself, but he tried to impose it on others. He wanted mankind to accept a metaphysic and a psychology which presupposed dyspepsia, insomnia, griping of the bowels, and headaches. "Those of us, however, who are blessedly free from these diseases will refuse to accept Pascal's neuralgia-metaphysic, just as we refuse to accept the asthma-philosophy of a more recent invalid of genius, Marcel Proust."

Huxley is not far wrong, I reflected. (The children were emerging from the Lycée; each mother picked out her own. The wind was gathering strength. The leaves no longer slid, but rose spinning together like flights of crows.) Huxley is not far wrong, but it is clear enough what a modern Pascal would retort; it is clear enough what Charles Du Bos would retort. "Speak for yourself," Du Bos would say in his turn to Huxley (and from his window one would see the basins of Versailles and the bronze deities, and on the wall that lovely portrait of Keats), "speak for yourself. I find nothing less satisfying than that philosophy of the healthy and sensuous humanist, that universe of the hedonist physicist, the scientific dionysian. And nothing could be more spurious, for man can soar above his own body, and the sick mathematician calculates as well as, or better than, the athlete . . ."—"But I am talking for myself," answers Huxley, "for myself and for those like me. That is my whole theme. I am a relativist in morality, as I am in metaphysics and in physics." And rather sorrowfully Charles Du Bos would light his pipe.

Yes, I reflected, it would be an interesting discussion, but, like all discussions, a vain one, for the cosmos of Huxley and that of Du Bos are impenetrable. Leibniz was right. Each one of us is a monad, eternally sealed. Stay, what was that phrase which had once struck me so much?—"And the brain of the person we love best. . . ." I was taking a course on the early Greek philosophers. The benches were hard and narrow. I was a student. Beside me on the tiers was a fair-haired girl who filled my universe. "We are alone," the lecturer was saying. "We are alone, eternally alone; we know nothing; we shall never know anything; and the brain of the person we love best remains irremediably closed to us." I looked at my neighbour, imagining beneath her hair that bony wall, hard and brittle, and irremediably closed.

"Private universes," said Huxley. (Black twigs were falling from the trees, and stood tremulously upright in the roadway.) Private universes, with no link of communication between them. The relations between Tolstoy and Turgeniev for instance. Tolstoy blames, Tolstoy is a man who passes judgment. On the evening at Isnaïa Poliana when Turgeniev, to amuse the children, showed them how the *cancan* was danced in Paris, Tolstoy solemnly noted in his diary: "Turgeniev, *cancan,* depressing." But to me, as a spectator, Turgeniev is neither less great nor less profound than Tolstoy. He is a weak man. He himself would show his thumbs and ask: "What can a man do with thumbs like these?" How could his universe be anything but different from that of Tolstoy, a strong, brutal, passionate man? Or from Dostoievski's? Or from Zola's?

In nearly all cases the formation of the individual cosmos can be reconstructed. There is education. I read that Ramakrishna beheld the goddess Kali in his trances. That is a world which I know I cannot enter. Whatever befall me, even if I become mad I know that I shall not see the goddess Kali. But set my birth in a different country and cram my childish brain with other images, and who can say what my view of the world might have become? Byron discerned in the Universe tokens of the wilful activity of a cruel fate hostile to mankind. I myself see a powerful and pitiless universe, indifferent to the individual. Who is right? Byron was reared amongst the Calvinists. An infirmity, a sequence of unfortunate accidents, and travel in the East had moulded his fatalism. The optimist philosophy of Meredith is that of a good walker. Amiel's sentimentalism is physiological. The equilibrium of George Sand . . .

It was beginning to rain. A group walked past me, three girls, working girls no doubt, laundresses I dare say. One of them was carrying a big white basket, and was speaking with an obvious passion that gave her eloquence. "Well," she said, "if you force me to it, very well, I'll tell you the whole truth . . . I wanted to have a velvet dress. . . ." A dive into another private universe. "The eternal silence of these infinite spaces terrifies me," said the sickly ascetic. "I'll tell you the whole truth—I wanted to have a velvet dress . . ." says the laundry-girl. When she is old and plain she will find the world hateful, and an old man will tell her that she doesn't like anybody. Not only is the cosmos individual, but it alters with age. Who ever thought like Marcus Aurelius at twenty? When the passions settle down with the wearing out of the body, one's philosophy takes on more serenity. The man who is ill or dying rejects the philosophy that serves him in health. In one single day the normal man changes his philosophy ten times over. The atheist has his moments of mysticism. "The most religious of men," I remarked to S., who is a devout Catholic, "doubts at least once a day."—"Once!" he answered. "A hundred times a day! For my own part, I think that the man who believes fully in his religion for five minutes a day is a great believer." But most men do not admit these things. They have a spiritual patriotism, and exercise a mental censorship over themselves. They are, as Huxley says, chauvinists of mysticism, chauvinists of agnosticism. And yet, I wondered, is there not a common universe which would embrace all these universes, a country of the monads, a truth that is communicable? For, I reflected as I reached my own door, if I can understand Pascal's universe and Huxley's universe, I am approaching a synthetic universe which seems to be of a different sort. That truth is relative, is an absolute truth.

But just then my key slipped into the lock, and my universe was transformed.

III

THE MYTH OF MYTHS; OR, THE
RENUNCIATION OF THE ABSOLUTE

I

IN his preface to the "Lettres Persanes," Valéry has shown that the era of order is the empire of fictions. Human societies are made possible by the acceptance of serviceable myths. It is untrue that incest is forbidden by the Gods. It is untrue that Justice always overtakes the guilty. It is untrue that Jupiter protects those who sacrifice victims to him. But if a large number of men lend the support of credence to such "houses of enchantment," that will suffice to enable these structures to provide a shelter for these men.

The pagan images are succeeded by the Christian and the civil images, but civilizations are always supported by abstract fictions. The Law is strong, not because of the omniscience of the police (nothing remains easier than the unpunished crime), but because the myth of the Law has its temple in our spirit. Kings, Ministers and Parliaments hold sway, not because they represent a real power (their armies are only composed of their own subjects), but because a convention admitted by all sees in their persons an incarnation of the fictitious forces.

And then, "in order, heads become bolder." The myths

and conventions are scrutinized disrespectfully; their true nature and their transparent weakness are exposed; men resent the obedience they have given them. The individual, whose desires have been so long dammed by this imaginary wall, reproaches himself for his scruples and cowardice. The day of the emancipated and the "enlightened" mind is dawning. Sincerity and revolution become myths in their turn. The convention of the unconventional, the most tyrannical of all, succeeds the other. "Disorder and the status of *de facto,* of physical violence, revive at the expense of order." Before long there must come a renewed "desire for police or for death."

2

Such, for the ten or twelve thousand years since men have existed and lived under governments, have been the ebb and flow of human societies. The Roman Empire did not outlive the myths which it had deified; the ensuing disorder made the fortune of the Asiatic theologies. The eighteenth-century philosophers, believing that they recognized the myth underlying royal power, cut off a King's head in order to convince themselves that he was a mere man, and then placed a crown on the head of a man in order to worship the myth of an Emperor.

Are men, then, fated to this alternation of order and disorder? Must civilizations necessarily crumble one after another? Are the sufferings of anarchy the only thing that can recall us to a respect for those conventions without which no society can live? It seems as if some wiser race would break free from this Wheel. But the conventions accepted by other days are not necessarily the best. They sometimes require transformation. How would they be so transformed if not by those who deny them?

3

The reality of History would seem to be something more complex than this cycle of Order—Disorder—Desire for Order, Conventions—Upsetting of Conventions—new Conventions. The myth begins by being a myth, that is to say, an affirmation, *verbum,* a word, and is then made flesh. The myth is graven upon the human body. After ten thousand years of life in society, the thinking and sentient man is not the same as the wild man of the primæval forest. The appetites of the individual remain strong. He still suffers from the repressions and constrictions imposed on him by the Laws. But upon the individual instincts there has been superimposed a social instinct.

The complete individualist who rejects the Conventions to attain self-mastery (Gide's "Prodigal Son" and Byron's "Corsair"), finds neither equilibrium nor happiness. The herd is there within him, despite himself. It is not by "society" that he stands condemned: society is a myth from which man can free himself. But the image of society that exists within each one of us is not a myth, but an indestructible reality. The herd instinct is as powerful as hunger or thirst or lust. The man lost in the desert and certain of never again setting eyes on men, who yet killed a child or violated a girl, would have no further peace with himself. The Law Court is a "house of enchantment," but "the moral law within our hearts" is not. A sin against society, or against God, can be imaginary, but not so the sin against man. The social man was a fiction, but from that fiction he was born.

4

So a distinction must be drawn between those new, and also quite formal, conventions, which remain for us as images or words, and those others which, assimilated by hundreds of generations, have become things of instinct and substance. The former may become objects of criticism or revolt; but revolt against the latter is rebellion against oneself, of which the individual will perish. "The sense of modesty is neither Victorian nor Christian, but human." Marriage laws will change; marriage itself will perhaps vanish to give place to new forms of union; but a certain sexual discipline, like courage, will retain a value of its own.

Private experience shows us that the myth thus transformed into instinct is more potent than any social or divine convention. I do not believe that I shall be struck by Jove's thunderbolt if I break my oath, nor do I believe that I shall be damned if I fail in a solemn promise; but I do know that I shall despise myself if I do not keep a promise made to a child. Justice has been a myth, but men have ended by creating the Gods.

5

Even when the social myths have become instincts, can they withstand the analysis that betrays their hidden nature? The end of the Roman Empire saw philosophers who, for reasons of political prudence, would have liked to prop up the images of the Gods on their plinths. But Jupiter failed as a serviceable convention from the day that he was recognized as a convention. Suppose that the Prodigal Son, having observed in his mind and flesh these strong resistances of social nature, is able to label them and recall their origins: will he not then have exorcised them?

It seems to me that the human spirit can escape this form of destruction, and even that *the whole mental drift of our time is towards a respect for certain fictions accepted as fictions.*

Science is renouncing the knowledge of the absolute, and no longer claims to build up a true system of the world. It puts forward hypotheses which enable us to explain known facts, and seem also to enable the forecasting of facts unknown. It is ready to alter these hypotheses should they cease to accord with the phenomena. The scientist is quite aware that the electron is a fiction, but in so far as our means of observation enable us to judge, everything happens as if this fiction were a reality. One day, the electron will doubtless be condemned. But this acceptance of relativity does not make science an impossibility. It ensures the solidity and the future of science. Jupiter dies when he is recognized as a fiction, because his priests had pointed to him as absolute. But the hypothesis does not die, it is transformed.

It is desirable that politics, following the example of

science, should renounce a knowledge of the absolute, and consent to respect conventions (known to be such) so long as they remain useful. Anger against political myths is no less insane than would be a rebellion against the ether or a rising against the Hertzian waves. The King of England is a myth, but a convenient, and therefore a venerable, myth. The right of property is a fiction. It is permissible to regard that fiction as out-of-date, as likewise to consider it indefeasible, but to hate it is comical, and to worship it is puerile. Science cannot live without hypotheses, nor human societies without those images. A people destroys one system of conventions only to bow down before another.

<h2 style="text-align:center">6</h2>

Myths are condemned by relativity inasmuch as they are dogmas, but *qua* myths they are upheld by it. The human mind is simultaneously aware of its impotence and its strength. Impotence, in its straining after an absolute; strength, in its readiness to limit the search to purely human ends. Many political and moral conflicts in the past have sprung from the refusal to admit that conventions were no more than conventions, or from the refusal to understand that, notwithstanding their conventional nature, they were necessary. It would seem that our time is at last ready to accept images *qua* images. We know Justice to be a myth, but we also know that no society, no human life worthy of being lived, can survive without it—"Does this generation, then, believe in nothing?"—Say rather, that it desires freedom to treat fictions as fictions. But what does that matter if it believes in the necessity of the fictions? What does it matter if it believes in the myth of myths—in the necessity of maintaining human society through respect for contracts? "The era of order is the empire of fictions."

IV

CREATION OF THE GENEVA MYTH

I

OVER a great part of this planet men are protected against all violence by the transparent and fictitious sword of Justice. "You can go unarmed from London to Paris," says Ramsay MacDonald.—"Because of the policemen," answers Paul-Boncour. But the policeman himself is a fiction. The instincts of several thousands of passers-by are not restrained by that single man in uniform in the middle of the Place de l'Opéra or Piccadilly Circus, but by the majority of civilized men, of whom the policeman is the symbol and who would rally, if need be, to the defence of the law. In practice the police only rarely appeal to this unwritten contract. The State asks nothing of us because we have promised it everything. So great is the strength of societies that in them the image takes the place of action. In the oldest periods of history this image has to be something real; a sword is borne before the early kings and rods before the consuls. Then the image itself becomes superfluous, and the myth holds sway by force of a habit of trust and of unspoken consent.

2

And yet these hidden forces, ensuring so silently and easily the tranquillity of individuals, seem to be impotent when whole peoples are concerned. Of their own accord men give up wearing coats of mail and walking abroad armed, and, in order to protect what they hold most dear (their persons, their families, their goods), they place their trust in words and images; but they are afraid of each other as soon as they view each other in the form of nations. They set up courts of international justice, but have no faith in the power of these tribunals. And their lack of faith is enough to nullify that power in actual fact. The myth can exist only in the minds of the faithful.

3

What would the Geneva myth have to be, in order to ensure peace in the world? It would have to be to the relations of the peoples what the Justice myth is to those of individuals. If all the denizens of the civilized world could be brought to believe, (a) that any conflict between them would be judged with as much impartiality as can be expected from a human tribunal; (b) that the decisions of this tribunal cannot be infringed without facing a clash with invincible powers; and (c) that every nation in the world is ready to join a League of Nations, so that any possible aggressor may be treated as a bandit—then the notion of a revolt against the sentence would be manifestly absurd. Such a revolt would only occur as it were accidentally, like a crime in a well-policed country. The peoples, like individuals in the past, would have accepted the rule of law. The myth of the international tribunal would be born. Like all myths, it would operate through its fictitious presence, and at Geneva the aeroplanes of the League of Nations would correspond to the policemen on duty at the doors of the Law Courts.

4

To certain Frenchmen it seems that the Geneva myth could have been brought to birth by the Protocol of 1924. But that Protocol was rejected by Great Britain, as the League of Nations itself was rejected by the United States. To Frenchmen that attitude resembles that of a vigorous individual who says: "Nobody has greater belief than myself in tribunals and in the necessity of justice, but don't ever count upon me in putting a decision into execution." The instant result of such a resolve, if adopted by all the citizens of a country, would be a return to the state of nature and individual self-defence. The myth of public security would be destroyed. It would no longer be possible to walk abroad unarmed. All potential thieves and murderers would become such in fact. The man refusing his signature to the social pact would find himself forced to endless combat whereas, under "the empire of fictions," he is never called upon for his promised support.

In international life things might well be likewise. If one country, tempted to attack another, were sure of mustering against itself the whole economic, financial and military power of the world, the act of aggression would not take place. The participants would have nothing to give because they would have promised everything, whereas between 1914 and 1918 they were brought to give everything because they had promised nothing.

5

The tragic character of this epoch lies in the fact that peace could have been assured in it, not for always (men do not build for eternity), but for a long time, if the peoples so desirous agreed upon the method of its maintenance. But whereas a Frenchman desires to bind himself and bind others by a contract similar to the social contract, the English and Americans view such a contract with misgivings, and decline in their own words, to become "policemen for the world." But the policing of the world would be a pacific undertaking. There would not be much to do. The policeman keeps the peace by his presence, not with his fists. It needs nothing more than the image of a blockade, the phantoms of great fleets ready to starve the peacebreakers, to impel the wavering statesman towards a lawful solution. In New York the traffic policeman is replaced at night by a red lamp, but the driver pulls up when confronted by that symbol.

6

Respect for such a myth does not imply that men have suddenly become good, generous and reasonable, nor even that they have forsworn the use of the institution of Geneva for the safeguarding of their particular interests. The attitude of the nations towards the League ought to be that of two individuals laying their cause before a civil tribunal. Each is anxious to win his case, but at the same time the disputants are citizens subject to the laws. They pay their taxes, and therefore their judges, and they never question the actual idea of the court. There are many who think it chimerical to imagine that a similar state of mind could one day become that of the European governments. Perhaps our great-grandchildren will have even more difficulty in understanding how it was that men, for several thousand years, were able to believe in the myth of war. But it is also possible that weaknesses, misunderstandings and waverings may render the acceptance of the rule of law impossible. In that event, as the advances of destructive science are swifter than those of the minds who conceive it and ought to stem its current, we should behold all too soon the end of a European civilization.

V

THE ABSOLUTE IN THE RELATIVE

ORDER and disorder are co-existent in the universe. Order, because man observes fixed laws therein; disorder, because the desires of living beings do not coincide therein with actuality. The aim of every civilization is to profit by natural order to induce a human order. Experience has shown that this is possible.

The natural order allows of the forecasting of events, but does not allow of this in every case. In particular the happenings that affect us most, those depending on the passions, are unforeseeable to the scientist. The human order allows of forecasting in more frequent instances because it is abstract. Societies built by human minds, and based upon a few simple principles, are more readily intelligible than the complexity of the natural universe.

Order is a good in itself. The possibility of foresight is the most precious good. Nothing is more distressing to man than doubt and anxiety. That is why ceremonies have from primitive times been pleasing to the peoples: by controlling words and actions they suppress for a moment the anxiety of expectation. Ceremonies are to be found in every civilization. The Soviet Government has its own as the Catholic Church has; the pygmies of Central Africa have theirs, and the citizens of Washington theirs. It suffices to witness "Parsival" to realize that if the theatre resumed its ceremonial character it would recover its ancient prestige. Europe will begin to exist when there are European ceremonies.

Order is a good in itself, and therefore every organization, even if it be bad, is something better than anarchy. There, no doubt, lies the sense of Goethe's saying that he preferred an injustice to a confusion. I prefer an injustice to a confusion, because confusion is itself injustice. But the lovers of order must as far as possible make ready the paths of justice. Unjust laws open the way for disorder.

Laws are "the necessary connections arising from the nature of things." They are the relations between two orders—the order of institutions, and the order of facts. Where a constant connection exists, the variation of one term is matched by that of the other. Whenever facts change, institutions must alter. Neither the Roman Empire, nor the Holy Roman Empire, the absolute monarchies, the plutocracies which to-day are styled democracies, nor the rule of the Soviets, are external forms. The data of a problem being what they are, only certain solutions are possible; but if the data are modified, the first solutions cease to be true. Peoples, like individuals, are always on a tight-rope: none can stand there motionless.

But does not human nature contain certain fixed elements to which there correspond certain fixed elements in laws? If one term of the connection (*facts*) contains constant alongside of variable data, must not the other term (*institutions*) be composed in the same manner?

123

One primary fixed element appears to be the survival in all human beings of an animal nature alongside of a social nature. The "Original Sin" of the Bible and the "repressed unconscious" of the psychiatrist, are but names for that violent, lusting beast which has to be chained and placated. Laws, both religious and civil, have to resolve this twofold problem. They are well framed when they maintain an even balance between protection and liberty, badly framed when they go beyond the point of balance between the two tendencies. Puritanism is an example of bad laws in the direction of excessive protection; and others no less dangerous in the direction of excessive freedom can be imagined.

The bonds of the family are a second fixed element. An institution like marriage has been altered to allow for economic and spiritual changes. But the principle holds good. Women have not found happiness in complete emancipation. The psychological data in the problem of the child are no longer entirely the same as they were a century ago, but a large number of these data have not altered. It is prudent to be slow in adjusting codes to ephemeral standards of morality. One function of law is to keep the verbal expression from outstripping the instincts.

Supreme amongst the constant data is the need for order itself, and the concomitant necessity of a hierarchy. Human order is an abstract order which is valid only through clarity. Where everybody is a ruler, that abstract order will find itself supplanted anew by the anarchy of the world of passions.

The social order can be stable only if the relation $\dfrac{\text{institutions}}{\text{facts}}$ is constant. Every variation in that connection is matched by an injustice, and every injustice by a disorder. The unwavering care of the true friend of order is to adjust institutions to facts. Disraeli made the Conservative Party a popular party. That was no paradox. An intelligent conservative is always a reformer.

VI

POLITICAL STABILITY IN FRANCE AND ENGLAND

LOOKING at the history of France and England during the past few years, one is struck by the frequency of political oscillations in France. To many Englishmen it was particularly surprising to see the French Chamber upsetting a ministry in the course of such weighty deliberations as the Naval Conference, as also to observe the downfall, on the first day of its life, of the Cabinet which had replaced it. "Such a thing," says the Englishman, "is inconceivable in our country. In England, if the voting in the House of Commons showed that a stable majority was impossible, the Prime Minister would take steps to dissolve Parliament, and a general election would show just where the real majority in the country lay. Why isn't it so in France? Why don't the French modify a constitution that makes continuity of policy so difficult?"

I

It is misleading to lay the blame for political instability in France on the Constitution of 1875. That Constitution does not forbid the formation of great parties taking their turn in power, as the Whigs and Tories, Liberals and Conservatives did so long in England, or as the Democrats and Republicans have done in the United States. It allows for, and admits of, dissolution.

In point of fact, no President of the Republic has exercised this right since 1877. Marshal MacMahon then dissolved the Chamber, but he did so very clumsily and at the wrong moment, and the electors retorted with a slap in the face by returning the same majority. Ever since that abortive move, the idea of dissolution, which ought to appear both lawful and natural, has become associated in Frenchmen's minds with the idea of the *coup d'état,* an image which has haunted the Republicans since the 18th of Brumaire and the 2nd of December. After more than forty years the memory of MacMahon remains an historic cause of instability by jamming a useful gear-wheel in the parliamentary machine.

Now, contrast the feelings of a French deputy with those of an English Member of Parliament, towards the ministry in power, assuming both men to be more or less equally endowed with ambition and patriotism. If the English politician should vote against his party and help to upset a Cabinet, what can he hope for? Nothing advantageous. He will put himself outside his party, and that will make his re-election difficult, if not impossible. He will have no chance of replacing any of the ministers, as the Cabinet will almost certainly have recourse to a dissolution. What is more, this dissolution will oblige him to face fresh election expenses before the normal time. Even if, through some single vacancy, he joins the ministry without there being a dissolution, a commendable custom obliges him to seek re-election in his own constituency. If he turns against a party, he can do so only by carrying his constituency with him. That is not easy. The personal interest of the English politician, therefore, weighs down the balance in favour of stability. In England no prizes are held out to the breakers of Cabinets.

In France such prizes exist, and the deputy's personal interest weights the scales in favour of instability. What need he fear if he helps to turn out the ministry? Will he be forced to run the gauntlet of an election once more? Certainly not, for we have seen that custom has hardened against dissolutions. Will he be turned out of his own party? Possibly; but there are so many parties in the Chamber that he will immediately find another. Will he, on the other hand, succeed to the place of the defeated minister? Admittedly, he has a chance. The head of a government, in forming his ministry, often takes account of the support given him by this deputy or that in some skilful manœuvre against the previous Cabinet. Whence, to even the most honest of French politicians, comes a temptation. Custom has held out rewards to the upsetters of ministries.

2

The temptation would be less strong if power were disputed by large organized parties. Such parties would themselves maintain their own internal discipline. In opposition they would have their "Shadow Cabinets" prepared to take up the real portfolios after a favourable election. Nobody in England at the time of the 1929 Election was in any doubt as to whom the King would summon if the Labour Party carried the day; everyone knew it would be Mr. Ramsay MacDonald, just as they knew it would be Mr. Baldwin in the event of a Conservative victory. There may be a struggle within the party for the position of leader (and such struggles are frequent), but in Parliament itself a certain loyalty is traditionally looked for.

In France, great parties do not exist. In the Chamber will be found Communists, United Socialists, Republican Socialists, Radical Socialists, a Radical Left, a Social and Radical Left, Republicans of the Left, National Republicans, a Republican Democratic Union, Independents of the Left, Independents, deputies so independent that they decline to form part of the group of Independents, non-party members, and a deputy who is not a member of the non-party party. Why this granulation of parties?

Every people has its qualities and its faults. Each must be governed with due regard for both sets of characteristics. In governing the English, their pride must not be overlooked. In governing the French, it must never be forgotten that they are individualists. France has shown her capacity for discipline in time of war and in time of financial crisis. In calm weather the French love to criticize their captains. Since the two Napoleonic experiments in particular a large number of Frenchmen have harboured an almost instinctive horror of any man who climbs above his fellows too high and too quickly. For a politician, popularity in the country at large is almost a source of weakness before the Chambers.

This deep sense of the equality of men, this stubborn individualism, hinders any blind loyalty to the leaders of a great party. In any parliamentary group, apart from a few mute, ingenuous and submissive figures, every deputy with a shred of talent thinks that he ought to be at least an Under-Secretary of State, and that he will be. If he disagrees with the senior members of his group, or even if, without disagreeing on doctrine, he observes that he is outweighed by too many brilliant and exacting personalities, he is tempted to form a new group. Thus, from time to time, a little swarm of youthful malcontents is to be seen, and round them will be buzzing men who have broken away from neighbouring groups.

The political game favours secessions of this kind. As no great party is numerous enough to assume power alone, every ministry leans upon a coalition of factions. To obtain their support it must open its doors to their representative men. Thus, a man who, in the rank-and-file of the Radical Party, would never have been a minister, will become one because he is the president of some social and anti-clerical group which he founded himself with a score of friends and is needed by the ministry to round off its majority.

The method of recruiting parliamentary commissions, their inflated importance, and the hierarchical promotion from a *rapport* to a portfolio, all tend towards the same confusion. Minor posts are covered with the same intensity as major ones, because the former lead to the latter. The proportional representation of the several groups in every commission produces the same measuring-glass operations that go to the compounding of a new ministry, and lead likewise to the further splitting-up of factions. An ambitious man obtains "his finance commission by joining in with fifteen others who want something else. Finally, as successful work within a commission is the image of, and the prelude to, success in the Assembly itself, men strive less there to collaborate with the ministry than to hamper it and prepare its downfall. A Premier is so fully occupied with self-protection against his successors that he has no time left to rule, and the supplanters will complain in their turn, when they have won power, of the bad faith of their opponents.

But these ambitions should not be singled out for condemnation. They exist in every country. Spinoza has shown that men's passions are always more or less the same, and that the good institutions are those which take advantage of human failings to lead a nation to a wise conduct of affairs, just as animal-trainers make use of greed and fear to obtain harmony of movements. The English politician as a man is very like the French politician. Like the latter he is mean, generous, ambitious, jealous, admirable and detestable. But as the rules of the game are different, the Englishman is led to shape his political career within a team, the Frenchman to blow up the party. (Examples of schism exist in the political history of both England and the United States—Disraeli and Roosevelt—but they are fewer, and their pretexts lie in rather deep ideological differentiations.)

3

Individualism, as a trait of national character, is not the sole reason that has prevented the existence in France of great parties holding power alternately. Great parties correspond to simple divisions in the country. In the United States, beneath the cleavage of Democrats and Republicans lies the opposition of North against South. In England the cleavage of Whigs and Tories divided the rebellious nobles from the partisans of the King and the Established Church. When that line disappeared, it was replaced by the line dividing Conservatives from Liberals, which marked off two philosophies. To-day, although the situation is slightly more fogged, the cleavage of Conservatives and Labour remains fairly clear. In France the lines of severance are more numerous.

Before the Revolution, France had more internal fissures than other countries. Privileged seigneurs, exempt from taxation and hardly ever in local residence, were more remote from the peasant than was the English squire, himself often close akin to the country folk and subject to the same taxation as his farmers. The Church annoyed an otherwise devout people by its privileges and its alliance with the nobility. Men spoke of "Church and Château," and had no liking for one or the other. The Revolution came to widen this fissure between two nations. To the long-standing hatred on one side there was opposed, in the other group, a just resentment. It should not be forgotten that there exists in Paris a small graveyard where the oldest French families are buried beside their guillotined ancestors whose bodies were flung into the common trench. That cleavage of Revolution and Counter-Revolution tends slowly to become obliterated, but it has been, and still remains, an important feature of the French political landscape. Only lately the president of the Radical Party was speaking in the Chamber of "Whites against Blues."

Now, it should be noted that the division of Revolution against Counter-Revolution does not follow the same lines as that of Riches against Poverty. In many provinces a rich peasant will not be in the same party as his landlord of the château. The Riches-Poverty cleavage might possibly be the dividing-line between two great parties—a socialist and a conservative party. Between the two (and without so much as taking into account of the innumerable shades), France can show a very large radical party grouping together both wage-earners and middle-class people. There we discern a new line of fissure, Clericalism and Anticlericalism, which does not imply for or against religion (nearly all Frenchmen are Catholics *de facto*), but for or against the political influence of the Church. Thus, some modest bourgeois, thrifty, quiet-living, and a hundred times more conservative than many English Conservatives, will vote for the radical candidate because of an invincible suspicion of "the curés." The sentiment is astonishing when one knows the poverty and inoffensive virtue of the majority of French parish priests, but it is linked up with ancestral memories. These memories turn proposals affecting schools and education, which elsewhere would not be really party questions, into grave political issues.

To these main features of the relief map must also be added innumerable secondary folds in the land. Reflect that France has clefts of North and South, of industrial regions and agricultural regions, farmers and wine-growers, that even amongst the socialists there are nationalists and internationalists, amongst the radicals, purists and opportunists. Reckon in also questions of personalities, of the small groups gathered round a leader because he is useful to them, and it can be understood why it was almost impossible in France to form the two large blocs whose alternation in power would ensure a more stable political life.

It must be added that, in France, the crystallization of such blocs is undesirable, for the violence of political passion would tend quickly to give it a revolutionary character.

4

"Well and good," the Englishman will say. "But when once the powder of your groups has coalesced into a bloc numerous enough to take over power and uphold a ministry, why doesn't it remain solid through at least one legislature? When a Chamber has been elected on a certain programme, how does it contrive to put the opposition into power? For that is what we've seen happen twice during the past year or two. The Chamber elected in 1924, the Chamber of the *cartel* of the Left ends off its four years under the authority of a man whom it began by setting aside—Poincaré. The Chamber of 1928, the Chamber of the National Republicans, the Centre, evolves so far as to make possible the appearance, if only for a day, of a Radical ministry. Why is this? And through what machinery?"

It is not very hard to grasp. As parties in France are rather ill-defined, the discipline of the groups is not strict. It is much more so in opposition than in power. It has been a little more so in the life of the present leigislature. Certain groups have expelled deputies who did not respect the collective decisions. But the outlaw can always tack himself on to the neighbouring group. In the centre sections of the Chamber are to be found "hinged" groups, half of whose members vote for, half against, the ministry. These groups exert great powers of attraction, because their medial position enables them always to have some of their members in the ministry, whether it be a government representing the Right or the Left in the Assembly, and because their numerical balancing power in a majority entitles them to a representation proportionally greater than their effectives. If need be, the errant deputy will find refuge amongst the independents. And so an opposition, like a government, can always try to crumble away the hostile bloc.

To that end, there are various paths. The ministry has posts, decorations, cordiality at its disposal. The opposition can make use of promises and play upon disappointed ambitions. Above all it has on its side, first, that sense of weariness produced by any lengthy reign ('I am tired of hearing him called 'the Just'"), and also, the inherent difficulties of all action. A man in power makes mistakes. Leave him rope enough and he will hang himself, as Disraeli used to urge. That is what nearly always happens. When the opposition feels the ministry to be shaky it can raise some issue which alarms the electorate, and so put the deputies of the majority in such a position that they must choose between their loyalty and their re-election. It is not loyalty that wins the day.

So unstable is the equilibrium of a Chamber that frequently the movement of one sitting will alter the whole political situation. A famous politician has said that a speech might sometimes have modified his opinions, but never his vote. Witty, but inaccurate. Fifty votes can be shifted over by a deft speech, or an awkward one. A French Chamber is susceptible to eloquence. Unlike the British Parliament, it is not formed of watertight parties on which nobody can hope to produce a reaction. It contains hesitating *individuals* who are swayed by the passions born of eloquence. I have seen Briand win over a hostile Chamber. I have seen Briand and Franklin-Bouillon, within ten minutes of each other, win the unanimous applause of the Chamber for speeches urging totally opposed arguments. To an able tactician, no battle on such a field is utterly hopeless.

5

It is sometimes urged that there are advantages in this instability, and that it is perhaps even preferable to the two-party system. Does it not enable the currents of public feeling to be more accurately reflected? Does it not keep the deputies free from too rigid a loyalty towards a party chief when he is seen to be incapable of holding power?

Nothing, as a matter of fact, proves the English or American methods to be superior to the French. The American Constitution, it is true, ensures the stability of the Cabinet, but if its members are in conflict with either of the houses of Congress, that stability is useless, because no measures can be passed into law. In England, for some years, political life was falsified by the existence of three parties, and by the fact of power being held by a minority government. In any case, no political institutions are good at all times and in all places for a quite abstract man. Answering the Athenian who asked what was the best form of rule, Solon wisely asked: "For what people, and at what time?" Laws are the machinery intended to use the individual passions for collective ends, just as the sail may serve the mariner to use the force of contrary winds to drive his vessel forward. The proper rigging depends on the seas he is sailing, the strength of the wind, the weather, and the vessel. The American Constitution or the British Constitution would not provide the right canvas for the good ship France.

But a machine can always be improved, and the French one does not seem at present to be working to full capacity. That is no reason for scrapping it, but rather for overhauling it. Between the two-party system and the present anarchy of ambitions there should be room for a better ordering of political life. Do there exist simple remedies, adapted to the historical formation of the country, which would abolish the weak points in the motor? The question should be put to the technical experts; here one can only try to indicate a few of the vulnerable points.

(a) We have shown how the constant splitting-up of parties makes loyalty difficult and makes treason the path to power. Cannot this disruptive tendency be checked? The Socialist Party, and more recently the Radicals, have succeeded in imposing discipline on their members. Would it not be possible to form five or six large parties to cover the whole of the Chamber? And would not this regrouping be facilitated by a slight alteration of the control levers of procedure? For instance, the method of electing commissions could be changed, and any commission entrusted with the examination of an important project, such as the Young Plan, should be appointed by the government departments. This would mean the abolition of prize held out to the party of fifteen members. It may seem a small reform; but the surgeon knows that it is often by touching an apparently secondary organ in a diseased body that the disquieting symptoms disappear.

(b) The first advantage of a re-grouping of parties in more compact masses would be greater ease in distinguishing the opposition leaders, and in allowing them to collaborate in certain questions with the government itself. This usage exists both in England and America; established in France it would be indispensable. Political liberty would not be lessened; the struggle would go on with equal energy on the points where it would be thought necessary, but the ruin of the country for questions of personalities would be avoided. To give a recent example, I have never yet met a deputy, of the Right or the Left, who did not admit, speaking as man to man, that the budget voted in March, 1930, was demagogic and dangerous. All the good work of four years was sacrificed in a few hours. The financial consequences of these votes will cramp the grip of all statesmen, whatever their opinions, who come into power during the existence of the next legislature. But no party could take responsibility for compromising the re-election of its members by making them take up a hostile attitude to measures that seemed to have a popular appeal. An understanding between the head of the government and the opposition leaders would nullify such responsibilities by sharing them out.

Agreement between opposition and government, when a matter of national interest was involved, would have to become a rule, and the existing camaraderie would have to be replaced by definite collaboration. The opposition would thereby lose the advantage of certain skirmishes, but would gain a greater measure of tranquillity for itself when its own turn for power came. It is striking to note how all men taking office in recent years have been smitten, one after the other, by a "persecution complex." Herriot, Briand and Tardieu have all complained of the unfairness of the Chambers, and all with reason. The evil arises from the tendency of the opposition (whether of the Right or the Left) to forget too quickly that it is not, as in England, "His Majesty's Opposition," but the opposition of the French Nation.

(*c*) It would be wise to widen the powers of the Presi-

dent of the Chamber and allow him sometimes to recall
the Assembly to its true rôle. Control is like certain toxins:
in proper doses it is necessary, and stimulates the execu-
tive system; in excessive quantities it is fatal. For some
years, in France, the organism of control has tended to
become a permanent government. M. Poincaré recently
showed how the war period transformed the great parliamentary commissions into irresponsible ministries. A
vote of confidence is now put forward almost daily, and
often several times on the same subject. Clearly, the
Government cannot be given the right to refuse a debate.
But could not the President of the Assembly be given
the right to prevent the multiplication of debates which
are identical with one another?

6

The experts, when they venture to speak out, mention
these remedies and some others which would be easy to
apply. The rôle of the "man in the street" is only to draw
attention to the fact that the national organism is not at
the moment entirely sound. Not that instability is so
great as people outside France suppose. In certain countries the surface looks solid and the rift is deep. In France
the surface shows fissures and the depths are homogeneous. Precisely because the lines of cleavage are innumerable, there is little real opposition between the
programmes of the different heads of the government.
Certain men are labelled "Left," others "Right." If one
did not know their political pasts, it would be hard to
understand why. In any case, the President of the Re-

public ensures a relative continuity by the choice of the men he calls upon. The President appears to be devoid of powers. Actually he is more powerful than the King of England, and can do much to correct, quite silently, the instability of parliamentary institutions.

But notwithstanding these counterweights, it is certain that governing with care for the general interest has been becoming too rare in France. If a few very simple adjustments to parliamentary formulas can (as politicians of all parties believe) induce personal interest to coincide with national interest, it is desirable that they should be carried out. Nothing can purge men of personal passions, but the rôle of the legislator is so to transform institutions that those very passions keep men moving along the paths of peace and loyalty.

VII

THE PAST AND FUTURE OF LOVE

AS the physical appearance of human beings, both men and women, has changed little for quite five thousand years, the observer is tempted to suppose that their sentiments and instincts have likewise remained the same. Hunger, thirst, sleep and love remain the essential needs of the human body.

But is it true that love is to-day what it was to an Egyptian lady of the time of Sesostris, to a Greek woman in Homer's day, to a thirteenth-century Frenchwoman? I don't think so. The social rules, conventional to begin with, have been transformed by time into instincts which have themselves transformed older instincts. Love, like the Gods, evolves, and we can distinguish certain laws of variation in the sentiment.

(a) *In a society where woman is a slave, passionate love does not exist.*

When Achilles is robbed of his captive woman, his fury rises from wounded pride; he is not "in love" in the modern sense of the term. His thoughts are not of Briseis, but of the men who have stolen her from him. The captive herself knows that she is the prize of strength, and resigns herself. Things remain thus so long as physi-

142

cal strength plays a large part in human societies. The woman cannot struggle; she accepts her conqueror.

Helen admits the defeat of Paris and the triumph of Menelaus. She has known the meaning of desire.

Yielding to it, she is content to regard herself as the "shameless woman." But when she has seen the Greeks attacking the walls of Troy, she resigns herself. She recounts the episode to Telemachus with no embarrassment: "Whilst the women of Troy were wailing their despair, my heart rejoiced, for my mind was changed and already I was in hopes of returning to my home; I bewailed the fatal mistake into which Aphrodite had cast me on the day she led me thither, far from my beloved country, parting me from my daughter, from my marriage-bed, and from my lord and husband, unsurpassed in wisdom and in beauty." And Menelaus answers: "Yes, all that you say, woman, is in conformity with truth."

Under the reign of force, one does not seek to vanquish a mind, or to make oneself pleasing; one takes hold of the object of desire, and feelings follow facts as best they can.

(b) *Passionate love is born in a society wherein the strength of social conventions overrules physical strength.*

The social conventions do not shackle men so securely as physical strength. They are open to argument; their validity can be questioned. As soon as instinct raises its voice a little, man is tempted to think that this validity is non-existent. That is the moment of conflict between duty (that is, the social being) and desire (that is, the individual being). Type of such conflicts—the story of Tristram and Yseult. Both respect the husband, King Mark. But they have drunk the magic philtre, and thereafter nothing could quench their mutual desire. The philtre is to them what Aphrodite was to Helen, but whereas Helen, a woman in a primitive society, treated her adventure with an almost lighthearted common sense, Yseult can find refuge only in death.

When once a total communion is desired, when once the wish is to possess not only a body but a soul, then one is drawn fatally towards the desire for death, for it is only in death that possession can be enduring. This, the true romance form of love, is always the source of tragedies, because the lovers who have enjoyed for a moment the sense of possessing something perfect and superhuman, long to make that moment eternal. But it is the nature of all things human to be fleeting. Only death can hold them fixed, or give the illusion of so doing.

(c) *In a society where men and women are nearly always kept apart by work and the mode of life of the two sexes, the birth of chivalrous love is possible.*

I offer two examples: mediæval society, and the America of pioneer days.

Chivalrous love is a deification of woman. It cannot survive if men and women are constantly with each other. No woman, even the most lovable in the world, is a goddess. The man who lives with her learns her moments of weakness, her days of plainness as well as her virtues.

Constant proximity wears down sentiment. The face that once seemed so beautiful, he no longer sees. He tires of those childhood memories, those stories which once seemed so delightful, and wants to hear no more of them.

On the other hand, when the woman is not seen, she daily approaches nearer and nearer to perfection. Don Quixote may be a caricature of the heroes in the romances of chivalry, but he is a caricature with very little distortion. He achieves great deeds for his Dulcinea del Toboso, a vulgar and ugly farm-wench. This is not ridiculous, but natural. As he never sees her, she is as good as any other woman. The knight-errant is, by definition, errant; he does not wear away his love in a common life.

To a certain extent the age of chivalry is recalled by the America of the pioneers, and even (apart from the younger generation) by present-day America. There, too, woman is deified. To achieve high exploits for her sake is the aim of the majority of men. Nowadays it is a question not of giving battle to windmills or cleaving three giants in single combat, but of creating great factories and vanquishing rival bankers. But the goal is the same. The dollars thus won will be laid by the business man at the feet of his lady, just as were the trophies of vanquished knights.

And the deeper reason is identical. It is simply that men and women see little of each other. The knight-errant of Wall Street does not scour the highways of Europe for wrongs to redress, but he leaves home in the morning, lunches at the club, and comes home late. His wife goes off for a trip to Europe; and thus distant, she becomes the "lady of his dreams."

Chivalrous love is perhaps an artificial sentiment, but it is one that enhances a man by giving him a liking for sacrifice.

The common point shared by love as it was imagined by the chivalrous society of the Middle Ages, and love as conceived by Anglo-Saxon societies, is a horror of reality. Just as the knight-errant refused to know what his lady really was, the English or American novel for a long time strove to convert woman into an immaterial being, almost disembodied, except perhaps for lovely eyes and rosy lips. The realistic nature of love in women, the strength of their instincts, their failings, were all wilfully ignored, and women themselves encouraged a literature which made their own game so easy to play. Byron had already noted that women detested his "Don Juan" because it was truthful. Bernard Shaw, in "Man and Superman," demonstrated the material advantage that women have in self-protection through a romantic convention that shackles the man whilst leaving the woman herself ample freedom, just because he turns a blind eye on her real nature.

But here again, the love described in the chivalrous romance or the English novels of 1880, is possible only in societies where men and women see little of each other.

We should note that chivalrous love contains an element of pride which does not exist in the passionate love of, say, Tristram or Fabrice del Dongo.

(d) *In a leisured society, and where men and women live in company, a flirtatious love and a laxity of morals arise to stifle chivalrous love.*

This transformation takes place in two stages. First comes leisure, which gives men and women time to reflect on their feelings and so teaches them to recognize the nuances, with their ever-increasing subtlety and complexity. Then arise the moralist writers, like those of France in the seventeenth century. A whole people caught the taste for these analyses, and has kept it to our own times.

But a society like that of the French seventeenth century, although it mingled the two sexes, still imposed strong bonds of restraint upon them. It was a religious society, with a powerful pressure of public opinion, and chivalrous love remained the ideal of its actual heroes (Louis XIV) no less than of its fictitious ones (Princesse de Clèves).

In the eighteenth century, with the weakening of religious beliefs, and with absolutism and security, morals became freer. One cause of lax morality is boredom, and boredom waxes with prosperity. The noble sentiments of chivalrous love then give place to the petty guiles of physical love. These are the same in all ages and all lands. Examine the "Ars Amatoria" of Ovid: it holds true for London in 1750, for Paris in 1840, for New York in 1930. The modern novel of America shows that there, too, the chivalrous period is being succeeded by one of libertinism. Ernest Hemingway's "The Sun Also Rises" is a book with the same remorseless sincerity of the novels of Marcel Proust in France, of Aldous Huxley in England. The pioneer's respect for an imaginary woman has vanished. Its place is taken by an intelligent, but depressing, clearsightedness.

(*e*) *Freedom in morals leads back to simpler forms of love which bear some resemblances to the primitive forms.*

The youths and girls of the present day, going about together, bathing together, are much nearer to the ancient Greeks than to their own parents. If we compare the women's dress of 1929 with that of the preceding epochs, we find that it has a closer resemblance to that of the eighth century B.C. than to that of 1840. Osbert Sitwell has remarked that the women of Crete wore short and simple dresses which would not be out of place on Fifth Avenue. Pure physical desire, with no alloy of intellectual feeling, tends to assume a great place in life as it does in literature, and this attitude will doubtless cause the temporary disappearance of chivalrous morals. For some years past it has been the young girl who is becoming romantic. It was so in the day of Theocritus. But the day of Lancelot was to follow.

* * *

What will be the future of love? Any prophecy is difficult. The social value of physical strength is lessening. The most powerful machines can now be handled by a woman or child. In all things, bodily strength will be replaced by mechanical strength. Nowadays women drive their own cars, and if we ever again see a war and an army, they will fire the heaviest guns and open the cylinder-taps to free the poison-gases. They can die as men die; they can fight as men fight, for a woman with a revolver is stronger than the strongest of boxers. They pursue the same studies as men, and earn their living in the same occupations.

How do the consequences affect love? The human couple was first founded upon brute conquest and upon the slavery of woman. True, certain societies had a matriarchal form and had respect for woman, but even then she was dependent on man, the hunter and warrior, for her protection and nourishment. In order to dominate, she slowly, in the course of centuries, forged a weapon— coquetry, the art of pleasing; and gradually, with the help of poets and artists, she succeeded in establishing the fiction of chivalrous love, the humble devotion of man to woman. For a long time she used these weapons to conquer the strong man who could ensure her safety; in times nearer our own, she has used them to enthral the rich man who ensures her economic liberty.

Economically, the modern woman will be less and less dependent on man. Her need for devotion will therefore be less. Capable of securing her own sustenance and her own safety, she will tend in love to seek greater equality and greater freedom of choice. She will no longer accept the masculine axiom which, in Europe at least, maintained that a woman's infidelity is serious whereas a man's is trifling.

With this companion, more closely resembling a man, it is possible that sentiments become less acute; sensuous friendships will arise between men and women, to which they will attach less importance than formerly. This is what is happening in Russia, where the words *love* and *fondness* are under a ban as such emotions are held to sap the strength of political passions. Many of the intelligent youth are anxious for the death of romantic love.

They are wrong, I think. Humanity would gain some time thereby; it would recover certain spiritual forces, and be able to save certain luxury charges for which a great section of men now toil. But in this it would lose incalculable forces which have been generated by romantic love. Directly or indirectly, it has inspired our finest works of art, our greatest works of action. Nearly the whole of our Western civilization is born of a social system based upon respect for woman and upon the value of love.

I do not say that other systems could not have produced good results. Acceptable philosophies have been engendered from different values in the Far East. But for the moment we ourselves have no values to set up in replacement. It can already be observed in many young people that the lapsing of sentimental love is balanced by gloom, bitterness, and a cynical distaste for life.

In young Russia the stage and novels display, especially amongst women, a regret for the romantic convention. It is impossible to find a motive force in life to replace this wonderful blend of physical desire and intellectual unity. "Physical desire," said Proust, "has the wonderful power of giving intelligence its due and of giving a solid basis to moral life." The problem of the generation following ours will be to refashion (notwithstanding the great sensual freedom which has by now coloured our morals and will be slow to disappear) amorous friendships of a kind not unworthy of romantic love.

VIII

HYPOTHETICAL FUTURES

I HAVE been reading a few books written by physicists, chemists and biologists, on the future of their several sciences. Anticipations of this kind have always given me great pleasure; I enjoy pondering the probable image they offer of a mode of life which will perhaps be ours. The modern prophets are modest, and for half a century now discoveries have been outpacing their predictions. In 1902 Wells shyly announced that heaver-than-air flying machines would perhaps begin to be useful for warlike purposes about 1950. To-day, scientific paradox is to-morrow's commonplace.

For some years it has looked as if wireless television, the transmission of a moving image from a broadcasting station, will become readily practicable. Before long all telephone subscribers will certainly be able to see and hear others at a distance, with the aid of an apparatus which will work by wireless, to be called perhaps the tele-photophone. Pocket models will enable one to continue a conversation with a friend during a walk or a journey. Lovers will make their rendezvous at 4h. 20m. 16s., wave-length 452. An ether police will keep certain wave-lengths for the secret communication of the Government. Terms of subscription will enable one to reserve a fixed wave-length for five, ten, or fifteen minutes, and in a certain direction. There will be wave-lengths for ladies only, others for educational institutions.

Life will be quite transformed by this continuous two-fold presence in image and sound. Absence and separation will drop several degrees in the scale of sentimental value. Lying will become more difficult. For some time we shall still retain control of the power to give or withhold visual communication at will, but later, thanks to a selenium-plated lens, we shall certainly be able to transmit whatever is visible from an aeroplane passing over a garden or a countryside. Besides, now that the long-distance control of aeroplanes by wireless is conceivable, we may imagine small appliances which any of us could control from bed, guiding them over a map while a screen would display the shifting images of the towns, streets and people over which the distant machines were flying.

One professor of physics threatens us with a more formidable invention for the coming century. It is certain, he argues, that human thought, being composed of words and images, must correspond to the emission of certain light and sound waves. These waves it will some day be possible to capture; the problem is only one of amplifiers. And thereafter, in any conversation, thanks to a sort of radioscope which everyone will have in his pocket, it will be possible to read the thoughts of one's friend whilst they are taking shape, and to ponder, simultaneously with him, the images that he is evoking. Conversation will then bear a close resemblance to what is now a solitary and silent meditation. A will look at B thinking for a moment or two; then he will think his answer and B will watch him thinking. This will mean the necessity of naturalness and the death of hypocrisy.

When communication over long distances becomes easy, speed of transport will be less important, but obviously can only increase. In theory, says one of my authors, speed is limited only by the speed of light. A more serious matter will be the total transformation of our methods of producing energy. Coal and oil will be superseded, on the one hand, by maritime power-stations making use of the differences of temperature between superimposed currents, and on the other, by the wind, the force of which will be collected by perfected accumulators. These inventions will completely transform the distribution of industrial regions. The factories at present grouped round coal centres will slowly migrate towards districts where winds are constant. Certain desert territories, hitherto regarded as of no account, will become the most populous areas in the world. Wars will be fought to have and hold them. At the same time, when chemistry has refashioned most foodstuffs by synthetic methods, on a basis of atmospheric nitrogen, agriculture will almost certainly vanish. The appearance of the earth will change. Forests and garden will take the place of fields.

The sources of light which we now use are extremely primitive. Professor Haldane has said that 95 per cent. of the radiations of these heated bodies are invisible. The lighting of a lamp as a source of light, he declares to be a waste of energy almost equivalent to the burning of one's house in order to toast a slice of bread; and it may safely be prophesied that in fifty years' time light will cost one-fiftieth of its present cost, and darkness will be completely abolished in all towns.

That is alarming, but certain biologists are still more disturbing. They believe that the explanation of our emotional and sentimental life can be found in the abundance or shortage of the secretions of certain endocrine glands. "Injections of the products of these glands would make people violent or timid, sensual or otherwise, just as desired. Assuming the existence of an oligarchic state, powerfully organized, it would be possible to inject a masterful temperament into the children of the ruling class, and a submissive frame of mind into the children of the proletariat. Against the injections of the official doctors, the best opposition orators would be powerless. The only difficulty will lie in combining submissiveness at home with the ferocity that is required against the outside enemy. But official science would doubtless solve that problem."

A paradox? Certainly. Nevertheless, the following experiment was lately described to me by a French scientist.

Some virgin female mice are selected, and some new-born mice placed beside them. The grown mice go on eating and playing and running about without paying any heed to the little ones, and even let the latter die beside them without intervening. The same mice are injected with the products of certain glands. Instantly these amazons are changed into admirable mothers; they are seen to give up their play and concern themselves only with these children, who are not even their own; they even die in their defence. In this case we are dealing only with a simple and powerful elementary instinct. But reflecting on these experiments, we can foresee a day when skilful blends of glandular secretions will enable us to obtain shades of sentiment of increasing subtlety. There will be joint laboratories for psychologists and biologists, where novelists and scientists will collaborate in the production of ampoules of Fond Friendship (guaranteed free of all sensual elements); and just as certain excessively stimulating products are counteracted by others, intended to sustain the action of the heart where the stimulation affects it, so tablets will be compounded, which will combine verbal romanticism and inward indifference.

These are strange thoughts. Need we regard them as depressing? I do not think so. If our present-day life could have been very precisely described to the men of 1880, they would doubtless have thought it terrifying. But many of these men are still alive, and have imperceptibly adapted themselves to a mode of life which would then have struck them as distressing and extravagant. And it will always be so. We do not know what life will be like for those of us who survive to 1957. But these survivors will no doubt find it normal and monotonous, and will turn inquisitive thoughts upon a future which we cannot so much as conceive.

IX

FRAGMENT FROM A UNIVERSAL HISTORY PUBLISHED IN 1992 BY THE UNIVERSITY OF ***

Morals—Puritanism and Repressions—Freudism and its Influence—Aberrations and Excesses of Freudism (1930-1940)—Symptoms of Reaction (1940-1950)—Schmidtism—Triumph of Schmidtism—Reversal of Values

Sexual Morality in the Early Twentieth Century

BEFORE the World War of 1914, especially in the Anglo-Saxon countries, official morality had remained very much the same as during the preceding century. True, even in England there were writers like Wells, Arnold Bennett, George Moore and Galsworthy, who had ventured to treat sexual questions rather more boldly than the novelists of the Victorian epoch. Actually, and in the capital cities especially, morals were distinctly lax, but this laxity did not extend to the middle classes, and even in aristocratic or artistic circles was not openly admitted. In America as in England, puritanism was still powerful enough for a sentimental scandal to ruin the career of a statesman. Vices existed, as they always have existed in every human society, but to be tolerated they had perforce to borrow the mask of hypocrisy and the language of virtue. . . .

157

Freudism and Its Influence: 1910–1930

The human animal, thus constricted by a rigid society, took strange and perilous revenges. "Repressed desires" (as they were later to be termed) took refuge in the unconscious, where they provoked grave discontents. An old seer of the eighteenth century, William Blake, had already proclaimed that *"he who desires but acts not, breeds pestilence."* This pestilence took the form of nervous afflictions and mental disturbance, and above all roused a general sense of ennui, pessimism and anxiety, which was possibly one of the hidden causes of the War of 1914.

This is not the place to set forth the doctrine of Freud; but we know how this great Austrian doctor and psychologist showed that such repressions lay at the root of most nervous afflictions. This teaching met with no great success in the Latin countries, which, having always enjoyed a measure of sexual liberty, were unfamiliar with the malady and had no need for the remedy, but in the Teutonic, and particularly the Anglo-Saxon countries, it was a genuine emancipation. Under cover of a scientific vocabulary, it became possible, permissible, and even easy, at last to speak freely of subjects which for centuries had been banned. Psychoanalysis, becoming widespread, confronted a large number of puritans with their real minds, and made them more tolerant of the desires of others. A certain freedom and boldness in morals was encouraged by the doctors, who deemed it their duty to free their patients from repression that might bring them to insanity. From about 1928 writers like Joyce and D. H. Lawrence displayed a boldness which was to seem half-hearted to the readers of 1940, but which in its day was something new. Physical shame disappeared at the same time as intellectual and verbal shame. Women shed more and more of their clothing. About 1935 men and women in complete nudity could be seen on numerous American and European beaches. In Germany and the Scandinavian countries the "nudist" sects multiplied. Tolerance of sexual liberties and even sexual abnormalities, became general. . . .

Excesses and Aberrations

Human morals swing like a pendulum, continually passing the middle position. In the beginning the Freudian influence was beneficial. It seemed to be true that excessive austerity was contrary to the moral and bodily health of such human beings as were neither saints nor impotent. It is a fact that from 1930 onwards the number of cases of insanity diminished, both in America and Europe.

But before long, on the ground of respecting the desires of everyone, a point was reached when all social contracts were broken. The ancient institution of marriage was completely destroyed by the coming of divorce by simple declaration, by companionate alliances, and by the refusal to bear children. Strictness of morals, under the rule of the older morality, had lent value and charm to harmless delights. In the nineteenth century, historians show, young men and girls had enjoyed being together for purposes of innocent games, sports, or studies. From 1935 oward, most gatherings assumed the character of a debauch. Public feeling had changed so completely that in England, formerly so strict a country, anti-puritanism became a positive virtue. It was not imposed by law, but custom was sovereign and the social sanctions were merciless. In 1954 the Prime Minister, Mr. Shallow, found himself forced into retirement by public opinion and the Press, because he was suspected of conjugal fidelity. It was he who had formerly passed the Act for Compulsory Psychoanalysis in Nursery Schools. He was accused of hypocrisy. More than one Continental newspaper opened a campaign to show that sexual liberty in England was a pretence, and that in actual fact, underneath all the extreme freedom of speech and literature, it cloaked a large number of chaste lives. It was an unfair accusation; but the fanaticism of the "emancipated" became ferocious. . . .

Symptoms of Reaction: 1940–1950

About 1940 the graph of cases of insanity rose quite rapidly. To the unprejudiced observer it would have been obvious that this was symptomatic of a check to the new morality. But the "emancipated," in their blind intolerance, nevertheless made a bid for new audacities. Signs of reaction, however, began to show themselves. So far they were slight, but they were unmistakable. In 1942 there appeared anonymously that curious book, "Confessions of a Child of the New Century," in which the inward confusion of the younger generation, and their craving for sentimental feelings, were set out with a naïve shamefacedness. Its success was enormous, even to the pitch of several writers, emboldened or jealous, trying to exploit the same vein, notwithstanding the danger of legal proceedings being taken against them. In 1943 Miss Brushwood's famous novel, "Conjugal Happiness," was published, in which, with an audacity that then seemed incredible, she depicted the pleasures of fidelity, normal love, and indissoluble marriage.

The book was banned by the English censorship, but was immediately reprinted in France, and thousands of copies were surreptitiously imported. An international group of writers protested against the Home Office decision and claimed the right to freedom of virtue. The body of the "emancipated" were furious, in the name of morality. The campaign roused lively curiosity, and the circulation of the book, which was translated into every language of the world, reached immense figures. More than 1,300,000 copies were sold in the United States, 800,000 in Germany, 300,000 of the clandestine edition in England, 70,000 in France, and 20,000 in Holland. The young people of both sexes seemed to find a pleasure which the classic moralists styled "unhealthy" in reading these descriptions of forgotten sentiments and modes of living.

The influence of "Conjugal Happiness" and the new "chastitist" school soon became obvious. Small groups, still rather timidly but in increasing numbers, tried to live their lives according to the principles of Miss Brushwood. Aged Americans can still remember the New York and Boston fashion during the winter of 1943-1944 for giving "conjugal parties," secret of course, to which were invited only married couples who passed the whole evening together without separating. These "goings-on" caused scandal, but Europe followed suit. In Hyde Park the police were forced to prosecute married couples who came in broad daylight and sat reading verses together on the grass. In Paris the Prefect of Police had to establish a special body of police on motor-bicycles to cleanse the Bois de Boulogne of women wearing the so-called "virtue" dresses, which, buttoned up to the neck, were shocking respectable passers-by. In one ancient European university a professor of philosophy was expelled for impenitent asceticism. It was becoming manifest that the morality of freedom, though still clung to by the masses, was no longer being respected by the elect. . . .

Schmidtism

In 1954 Dr. Schmidt, the Lausanne physician whose name was to become so famous, published his book on the repressions of modesty. Nowadays his doctrines strike us as self-evident, but at that time they came to innumerable readers as a revelation. Dr. Schmidt maintained:

(*a*) That as man had been a member of organized groups for more than fifteen thousand years, social morality and the constraints imposed thereby had become an instinct in him, no less powerful than the sexual instinct or that of self-preservation. (It was the old theory of Trotter.)

(*b*) That in thwarting this instinct by an artificial reversion to a completely animal life, repressions of modesty were caused in men, just as painful and dangerous as those of desire had been.

(c) That a great many nervous maladies could be cured by making the sufferer aware of this secret modesty and by sanctioning his obedience to it.

In support of this theory, Dr. Schmidt produced numerous psychoanalytic cases which disclosed the existence of repressed social elements.

His doctrine became known as Schmidtism and enjoyed widespread success, especially in the Anglo-Saxon countries, where its scientific vocabulary made permissible the confession of sentiments and scruples which had long been taboo. From 1959 onwards there was an excellent course in Schmidtism at Columbia University. In the following year the Institute of Schmidtian Psychology was inaugurated at Baltimore, and became the nucleus of a body of Schmidtian doctors. In 1960 Dr. Schmidt came in person to America, and was enthusiastically received by students and patients.

The happy effects of Schmidtism were soon manifest. Persons with conjugal, virtuous or normal inclinations no longer felt themselves regarded with hostility, and lost the uncouth manners and haggard appearance which had for some years become familiar to them. Their writings became less violent. The curve showing cases of sexual insanity, which once again had risen in a very alarming manner, began to drop. This period, to which Professor Gilrobin has given the name of "period of reversal of values," lasted approximately from 1960 to 1975.

At the moment of writing (1992), it is undeniable that

the Schmidtian reaction has in its turn been excessive. A new puritanism, more aggressive than the old, threatens to dominate our activities and our thoughts. What Freud or Schmidt, as yet unknown, will rise to free us from this evil spirit?

X

CHILDHOOD AND WISDOM

THERE are moments in life when everything seems to point one way towards one knot of ideas. Talking the other day with a friend about Cocteau's novel "Les Enfants Terribles," he remarked: "Yes, Cocteau is right: childhood is often a time of tragedy. . . . I have a son of my own, sixteen years old, in whom I can watch the passage from childhood to adolescence. . . . My dear fellow, it is a far cry from what the optimistic novelists describe to us! To certain beings youth means years of sadness and despair, sometimes a dreadful longing for death. . . . It is maturity that brings happiness. . . ." And that evening, reading Walter Lippmann's book, "A Preface to Morals," I found in its pages a theory of adolescence and maturity which seemed at once to confirm and explain the remark that had struck me in the morning.

Earliest childhood is a time of magical power. Alain, in his "Les Idées et les Ages," has shown how the child knows nothing of real obstacles. The sole denizens of the Enchanted Isle in which his helplessness makes him live are godlike forces, a mother or a nurse. If these are favourable to him, all things are possible, and he can make them favourable to him, first by cries and signs (period of omnipotence by magic signs [1]), and later by

[1] Dr. S. Ferenczi.

words and phrases (period of magic incantations). Experience does not teach the small child that things can be conquered by acting or working upon them. During the first fifteen months he is carried towards objects, or else objects are brought to him. His image of the universe holds no resistances other than wills. Through this period we all pass, and to it, no doubt, corresponds the incurable fondness that we harbour for the marvellous. Every mother is a fairy to her child, every father a magician. "Cook and gardener, door-keeper and neighbour, are sorcerers and witches whose attributes are duly ordered and who are the object of a special cult." When these divinities have been propitiated by the magic of cries and words, the child reigns over the apparent world.

But once able to move alone, the child is forced to recognize that he is surrounded by unheeding objects and hostile beings of whose existence he has hitherto been ignorant. Cats scratch, dogs bite, fire burns; cries and magic words don't work against these sources of pain. Through them the child leaves the enchanted world and enters into contact with the actual world. But it is only very slowly, through twelve or fifteen years, that he sheds his sense of omnipotence. If he is spoiled, brought up nearly alone in a fond family, he remains for a long time shielded from natural laws. Whence comes the necessity for contact with other children, and the formation of character through school. And during the whole progress of the painful apprenticeship to reality, through the fighting and bullying and ragging of schooldays, the sense of magical omnipotence is fighting for its own survival.

Cocteau's heroes keep fetishes and amulets in a drawer. All children with lively imaginations set up alongside the religions taught to them a personal mythology and barbarous observances. Most parents know nothing of the primitive cults counting their secret and discreet devotees under their own roofs. George Sand worshipped the goddess Corambé. I myself know a little boy who, before any decision, goes to consult "Mr. Lucky" in a corner, always the same corner, of an empty room. "Maturity begins when the adult abandons magical practices and accepts the conditions imposed upon his desires by reality."

That definition shows how few men actually achieve complete maturity. In most of us the enchanted universe and the real universe remain two countries with shifting frontiers. The story of the slow advance of that frontier is the novelistic theme *par excellence*. A man accepts (or refuses to accept) the existence of an outer world swayed by physical and psychological laws: that is the subject of Stendhal's "La Chartreuse de Parme," of Balzac's "Le Lys dans la Vallée," of Goethe's "Wilhelm Meister," and of every great biography.

In adolescence the period of first love brings a recrudescence of magic. During several years real human beings are once more replaced by divine creatures who can work our weal or woe by a single word. Certain men never mature; that is, they never accept the lessons of experience and continue to believe that the world consists only of their desires. Great wealth, power, or success won without a struggle, all tend to make a man into a child who never grows up.

The symptoms of "adult childishness" are familiar: the idea that there is a hidden conspiracy of men and things to thwart one's will, a sense that life is one's debtor, that the duty of the universe should be to care for one, the quest for an optimistic philosophy promising a disappearance of evil, just as a mother comforts a hurt child with kisses and assurances that the naughty table will be punished. Even in those of us who have at last admitted the heedlessness of nature and the defensive selfishness of other men, there often survives a childish sadness and a melancholy regret for the illusions of early years. We know that the world in which we live is imperfect, but we imagine it as another, wherein we shall be able to find once more the golden age of our childhood. True maturity, true wisdom, are attained only by those who can wholeheartedly say with Marcus Aurelius, "All that accords with thee, O world, accords with myself," or with Descartes, "I have made it my habit to vanquish my desires rather than the order of the world, and to think that what has not happened is, with regard to myself, something totally impossible."

It will be noticed that here the Wise Man joins hands with the Child. His desires having fallen into harmony with the nature of things, the Wise Man also is living in a universe that conforms with his desires. He can unleash his passions, not like a child because others will see to their consequences, but because he is master of the pack and can call them to heel at will. Very few men attain this childhood of wisdom, and the passage from the Enchanted Isle to the "strange carnival" of actual existence remains the great drama of human life. The most secret tragedies, and perhaps the most poignant, are played out in those school playgrounds where, everyday, some ten-year-old Hamlet discovers injustice, envy, malice, outruns them, accepts them, and becomes a man.

FROM A JOURNAL, 1930

JULY 19TH.—Rented for this summer the house of our friends the S.s, near the entrance to Richmond Park. Before leaving Paris, luncheon with Paul Valéry. He had a bad cold, coughing and shivering, but was in good form, weaving his clean-cut aëry patterns.

"I admit only two moral rules," said Valéry. "The first is, not to cause suffering (so far as that is possible, which is not always so); the second is, to try to be a little superior to other animals, and to respect in oneself a fairly lofty idea of mankind. . . . But that too isn't always possible."

"I like your moral system," I remarked. . . . "For my own part, I feel that man's great drama lies in his being at once an inferior animal, with the violent instincts of the brute, and a social being in whom the desire for approval and affection has become an instinct no less compelling. Whence the conflicts of which our novels are born."

"I don't think it is quite fair," said Valéry, "to set up the animal and the social being in opposition. The true conflict does not lie there, for there are social animals, like the ant, which have achieved their balance by a sacrifice of the individual. No, man's misfortune (and his originality as well) is that he has declined to make the choice. He began by evolving in the same direction as the ant, and then he stopped and said to himself: 'This is all very well, but I want to be a great beast of prey as well.' Now, it is hard to be both. In modern man, who has wanted to develop at the same time social organization (the ant) and individual liberty (the beast of prey), there is bound to be a conflict. It is impossible to stand upright on two legs that are always straddling further apart. So what's to be done? That is the problem of all morality."

"I don't know," I said. . . . "Learn to walk, I suppose. . . . You know Aldous Huxley's metaphor? Man is an acrobat on a tight-rope, moving painfully forward, holding a balancing-pole with the brute instincts at one end of it and the social instincts at the other. . . . There is no rule for making a good tight-rope-walker except to put one foot in front of the other and learn to use the pole."

"Yes," said Valéry. . . . "And that amounts to saying that the best type of man is the virtuoso. I have always thought so, in art as in morality."

JULY 25TH.—The Paris-Calais-Dover journey, in tearing weather. The rain lashed the carriage windows, but I had an excellent book, Malinowski's "Sexual Life of Savages." It is a very intelligent study of the natives of the Triobrand Islands in the Malay Archipelago. Came back upon some familiar ideas.

(a) The primitive races, more than any others, respect the conventions and ceremonies. This confirms what Valéry was maintaining the other day. Man began like the ant. The Triobranders are social animals. They observe the utmost decency in language. For excrement and for the acts of love-making they have both a polite word and a crude word, and it is always the polite word that they use in public. Their taboo subjects of conversation are more numerous than those in England. It is an insult to talk to a husband of his wife's beauty. This code of the proprieties is of course different from ours, but it gives the same results, that is to say, it upholds order and makes life possible. The convention is valuable *qua* convention, not by its absolute value. (That is what I tried to show in "The Myth of Myths.") For instance, unmarried girls in the Triobrand Islands can have lovers, and in this case they cease to sleep in their parents' houses, although continuing to have their meals there. Every village has its *bukumatula,* a collective house for the unmarried, where the unwed couples sleep together. The missionaries are shocked by this promiscuity. As a matter of fact, it is made "decent" by a general code of strict rules. No couple ever allows itself to watch the love-play of another pair; the liaisons are lasting and affectionate. In short, the *bukumatula* is a club for bachelors, the regulations of which are strict, but to which members can bring their betrothed. In some villages the missionaries have managed to suppress it; the results have been bad. The old convention is of greater value than any new convention, which long remains verbal.

(*b*) The family régime of the Triobranders is matriarchal. It rests upon a simple idea which seems to us extraordinary: these savages do not believe that the father plays any part in the procreation of a child. Their theory is that a spirit comes during the night and strikes on the woman's head. Her blood is thus driven inwards and so forms the child. The missionaries make great efforts to teach the natives our ideas about generation, as it is hard to bring the Christian religion to tribes to whom the notion of the Father and Son is unintelligible and the idea of a Virgin Mother perfectly ordinary. The missionaries have failed. Malinowski himself, who speaks the language of these islands, has seen the savages burst out laughing when he tried to explain the phenomena of conception according to our view. Their arguments are curious, because they show how the process of reasoning can serve to prove the most absurd thesis with apparent completeness. "How could the child come from lying together?" they say. . . . "Look at Tilapo'i there, the ugliest woman in the tribe. No man would want to be her lover. But she has children. Look at the albino women, who are repellent and impure; but they have children. On the other hand, our young girls make love in the *bukumatula* and never have children."

The consequences of such ideas are remarkable. As the father does not procreate, he is only the friend of his children; and they themselves are the relatives of their mother and the maternal clan. Incest between brother and sister is much more grave than between father and daughter. A girl may act or talk with full freedom before her father, but not before her brother. Also, when there are festivities or canoe expeditions, care is taken not to invite a brother and sister at the same time, for they are embarrassed at being together. If a child dies, the mother and the maternal clan, having lost a piece of their own flesh, affect a stoical indifference, but the father and his clan, for politeness' sake, heap ashes on their heads and wail dismally.

It would be amusing to write a "Sexual Life of the Natives of the British Isles," supposedly written by a native of the Malay Archipelago. The author would describe all the amorous customs of the Tea-Drinkers. He would regard them as crazy, would not understand why London possesses no *bukumatula,* nor why men accuse their wives of infidelity if a child is born in their absence, nor why Europeans like children to resemble their fathers. But he would come to the conclusion, if he were sensible, that these conventions, for all their absurdity, produce good results, and that forms of decency are found amongst the Tea-Drinkers which are almost comparable to those of the Pacific civilizations.

AUGUST 1ST.—Richmond Park. Squalls shot through with bursts of sunshine. "Further outlook: unsettled," says *The Times.* . . . The crazy English climate. . . . It is impossible to foretell one hour ahead whether we're to have storm or heat-wave. Whence (as Taine would rather ingenuously have said) the Englishman's horror of engagements long in advance. But no matter, we like our house here. To reach it, you come across Richmond Park. Herds of does and stags browse freely over the wide grassy expanses, broken here and there with solitary oaks. The does stop in a friendly way, one foot upraised a few steps from the car. In front of our windows is Ham Common, a lingering relic of collective ownership, a waste of furze and blackberries and bracken, a piece of wildness preserved, the refinement of an æsthetic race, a contrast which serves deftly to enhance the civilized charm of the Park itself.

AUGUST 2ND–6TH.—Rain. Reading. Annotating with great interest a difficult book, Gerald Heard's "The Ascent of Humanity." It is a history of civilization. If I arranged my library, as Charles Du Bos does, by spiritual affinities, I should place Heard between Auguste Comte and Spengler. Let me try to analyse this book, interpolating the reflections he has aroused.

A mind strongly obsessed with an idea tends to identify it everywhere. Here I once more find the Beast of Prey-*cum*-Ant idea. Heard sees man starting off with an attempt at an ant-heap. The primitive tribe, the herd, is a group in which collective life is the essential, where the individual as such hardly exists.

It is quite likely that in the beginning the individual units in the human pack are interchangeable. Every man can be the leader for a time, rather as in flocks of wild geese or herds of sheep, amongst which any one bird or animal leads the way and is then replaced by another. Primitive men instinctively react as the group does. A decision is taken, not after a debate of the parliamentary type, but because all the members of the group feel that it is demanded by the collective mind. (The "antennæ" of a politician like Briand, a primitive man in his kind, might be a survival of this collective sense. He thinks *with,* not against, the Chamber.)

The first conscious individuals to emerge from the

group are the magic-men. The classic type of the priest-king. Then comes the hero. The hero is the priest-king, who decides to do something original, something that will go beyond the group conventions. Every civilization passes through an heroic age, a time of glorious deeds performed by individual men. It is then that, in art, the recital of heroic exploits (epics and tragedies) supplants the collective magic of the ritual dance. Note that epic poems are always composed by singers *on* the hero. Later on, in the periods of introspective individualism that follow the heroic age, comes the day of autobiography, the self-written epic of inglorious life. *For the descendants of the hero are quick to discover the vanity of the life of action.* The conqueror scores the earth with furrows that are instantly obliterated by time. The heroic age is succeeded by the contemplative age. And that is when religion (no longer the magical religion of the tribe, but the individual religion of the man seeking his own salvation) comes to the forefront of human thought. Every stable period in human societies is marked at its close by the fondness of the masses for democracy and by mysticism amongst the elect.

The priest (the guardian of magical rites) is not a danger to society; indeed, he preserves it by imposing upon it collective ceremonial. The danger comes when someone other than the priest, the *paganus,* the pagan, becomes religious. Then Reformation and Revolution are drawing near. The individual, unable to find happiness in its heroic form of action, begins to seek it under some imaginary or supernatural guise. In seventh-cen-

tury Greece, the Dionysian or Orphic mysteries are orgies
working for the appeasement of the individual in a way
comparable to the action of a stupefying drug. A future
life is an opiate. Belief in the immortality of the soul,
Heard argues, is spiritual egotism.

Concern for salvation in another world is always a sign
of individualism. Inasmuch as man identifies himself
with society, he is interested in its duration, and his own
death strikes him as a matter of no importance. He shows
hardly any anxiety about survival. The religious revolution is marked by the concern for personal salvation, as
also by the conflict (in Semitic societies a violent one)
between prophet and priest. The priest is social, the
prophet revolutionary. Aware of a clash between himself and society, the individual fails to understand that
his uneasiness springs from an inner change. He believes
that some day soon everything will be transformed,
whether by the advent of a Messiah or by a political
upheaval, and that man will once more find his primitive
Eden. The Jew did not yield too readily to the notion
of a future life; his Sheol remains rather vague. But not
having built his paradise in the heavens, he could not
resist the craving to destroy his hell on earth, and from
this sprang the Apocalypse, the earliest form of the revolutionary ideal.

The Roman Empire tried to save the State by the tolerance of all religions. The same thing will be done later
by the British Empire and the French Republic in their
colonies: individuals may freely concern themselves with
their own salvation, provided that they leave temporal

policy entirely to the central government. After the fall
of the Cæsars, Catholicism brought forward a remedy of
the same class, a blend of the Jewish and the Roman solutions—the monastery. In Catholicism the average man
can find his metaphysical anguish healthily soothed by
the intangibility of dogma. The individual who is excessively conscious of his self, and might thus be dangerous
to Church and State, must withdraw into a monastic
house. A monastery is a place where a certain number
of men escape from social life and concern themselves
with their personal salvation; it is a collective egotism
which, by being collective, becomes constructive again.

The Renaissance, on the other hand, is the triumph of
the individual over the collective body. It is the time of
monstrosities—Cæsar Borgia, Henry VIII, Elizabeth, the
Emperor Frederick II. Cæsar Borgia is amoral, that is to
say anti-social; he is the beast of prey. The morality of
the human beast of prey has been defined in Machiavelli's
"Prince." But there is an ingenuous element in Machiavelli's cynicism, for he makes no allowance for man's in-
heritance as a herd animal. A Borgia society cannot last.
The beast of prey is very quickly devoured by the race of
ants. What is more, he devours himself. The greatness
of Shakespeare lies in the fact that, in the full tide of the
Renaissance, he expressed that anguish of the individual
unable to find happiness in self-centred action. Whence
Hamlet, and Macbeth. Romanticism is always the remorse of the beast of prey (Byron).

Reaction was bound to come. After a period of classical

stabilization in forms (the seventeenth century), there was the renaissance of sensibility (the eighteenth century). The day of monstrosities was over. Torture, which had seemed so natural, was suppressed. These changes were not ordained by reason, so dear to the sons of the eighteenth century. Hume remarked that it was not contrary to reason for a man to prefer the destruction of the world to the scratching of his own finger. It is the primitive instinct of social sympathy which has been wounded and is reviving. "The age of humanism becomes the age of humanitarianism."

About 1789 man cherished hopes of salvation through political revolution, just as a few centuries earlier he hoped to save himself by religious revolution. The nineteenth century was essentially revolutionary. The age of heroes had succeeded that of the herd when a few men became fully aware of their individual desires. The second revolutionary age began when a large number of men had the same feeling. But the political revolution (1789-1830) did not succeed in establishing a balance. The individual was unable to find salvation through politics, and seeks it in an economic Apocalypse. After the abortive sketch-plan of 1848 came the Russian Revolution, the most recent episode in the history of civilization. It will fail, in Heard's view, as the revolutions preceding it have failed, if it overlooks the chief factor in the problem. It will succeed if it contrives to rebuild for a time a consciousness of the *homogeneous* group, and not a class-consciousness, which leaves a large number of individuals unsatisfied.

Modern societies, composed of men who are too much egotists, are threatened with death because they are loose individual particles. But the enormous economic systems which support them demand a man's devotion to society. If our civilization is to endure, the individual must be outstripped. Is that possible? Are we to fear that human history must for ever sway between the neurasthenic beast of prey and the hardly conscious ant? Heard does not think so. He hopes that an objective and scientific generation will be able to bring forth, after the pre-individual (that of the primitive tribes) and the individual (of the Renaissance), the super-individual—the man who will realize that an intense individual life is only possible inside a perfectly organized society.

This super-individual would be the conscious ant; he will be freed from anti-social individual desires because he has gauged their emptiness, and although he respects the herd conventions, he will be freed from these also because he will respect them *qua* conventions. Is this too optimistic a conclusion? That supreme revolution could only be effected within man's own nature. Is it really possible? Perhaps. (After all, Valéry, Bertrand Russell, Aldous Huxley, Walter Lippmann, are drafts of the super-individual.) But even if it did succeed, it would only produce a state of unstable equilibrium. A great classical epoch would begin, to last for fifty or a hundred years. Then humanity would once again start off on its clumsy see-saw advance. A good thing. Equilibrium would mean death.

AUGUST 7TH.—*Richmond Park.*

Jardin royal où paressent les biches,
Où les amants cherchent la fausse mort;
Arbres profonds, creux sanctuaires, niches
Où sont cachés les dieux d'un peuple fort . . .

This morning *The Times* expert is still talking of cyclones coming from the Atlantic, low pressure ridges over Ireland, and rain. But there is a cloudless blue sky.

Signs of a fine day in the Park here. A faint haze lies over the stretches of grass and the trees, already bathed in sunlight; it is like a young girl's brooding, the expectancy of love. Then, through the luminous mist, come into sight the ponds, the bracken and, higher up, the moist crowns of the beech-trees. Birds are singing, the sky gleams almost white on the horizon, bright blue over-head, and the deer lie hidden in the grass, its burnt hue merging with the colour of their skins. Only their heads, the antlers of the stags, stand out above the waving blades of grass. In the bracken there—two moist eyes, or two dewdrops?

AUGUST 8TH.—Amongst the books in the library here there is one which is becoming popular with us. Its title is "Children's Questions":

"Daddy, what is the universe?"

And Daddy, according to the book, should answer: "The universe is everything."

"Daddy, what is sugar made of?"—*Answer:* "Put a lump of sugar in the fire and watch it. It melts, gives off gases, and is transformed into a little ash. That ash is carbon."

"Daddy, what is carbon?"—*Answer:* "Carbon is carbon."

And now, every morning, the children come down to breakfast and ask me: "Daddy, what is carbon?" And I answer: "Carbon is carbon." In twenty years, I dare say, a new edition will have to be prepared, in which the father will answer: "Carbon is a particular combination of the elements of the atom of hydrogen."

"Daddy," the children of 1950 will say, "what is hydrogen?"

"Hydrogen is hydrogen."

Per sæcula sæculorum.

AUGUST 9TH.—Work.

I have promised to write an introduction to "The Portrait of Zélide," by Geoffrey Scott, which Philippe Neel is translating. To help me, Mrs. Leplat-Scott has sent me her brother's other book, "The Architecture of Humanism" (Scott was an architect as well as a writer). I am very fond of these books by technical experts. This is a brilliant defence of Renaissance architecture, and of the Baroque in particular.

Scott is eminently a classicist, but he deals well with romanticism. He views it as a development of the sensibility in the direction of whatever is far-off. Far-off in past time (the taste for the Middle Ages), far-off in space (the eighteenth-century taste for *chinoiseries,* or for the exotic, as with Chateaubriand or Bernardin de Saint-

Pierre). Why does romanticism make for the far distances? Because it expresses the discontent of the individual, and the discontented always seek to thrust their unsatisfied desires into an imaginary past or into unknown lands. Being a projection of desire, romanticism is vague, and it likewise fails in philosophy, in the sciences, and more particularly in architecture. It is not plastic; it is poetical and, if need be, musical. In poetry and music it produces great works. The reason is obvious enough: it is upheld therein by form. A great romantic poet like Byron imposes the most highly rhythmic and ordered forms upon his thoughts. The wildness of the ideas is saved, as in Victor Hugo, by the classicism of the work itself. In architecture, on the other hand, there are *only* forms. Architectural romanticism confuses them, and nothing is left.

Second idea: the romantic is attracted by nature, always because he is discontented with society. Nature is another form of remoteness. It is viewed as a refuge. The age of sentimentalism and Rousseau's "natural man" is likewise that which attacks the French style in gardens. The garden was half-way between architecture and nature. They wanted to make something "purely natural" of it, which was impossible: only the virgin forest is "natural." Geoffrey Scott quotes the recipe for a garden in the so-called English style, given by a French nobleman of the eighteenth century: "Make the gardener drunk, and then follow in his footsteps." These so-called natural gardens, in fact, were so only in a symbolic manner. The park of the Petit Trianon and that of Bagatelle were well fur-

nished with grottoes, woods and waterfalls, but these orna-
ments were grouped in the most conventional arrange-
ment. No handiwork of man can be nature. In architecture, the efforts of the romantics to be natural produced
the fake ruin, or the house swathed in ivy or Virginia
creeper concealing its lines. Scott speaks with indignation
of Trinity Chapel at Cambridge, shown to visitors as an
object of admiration *because* of the plants covering it, the
fact being overlooked that underneath these creepers is
one of the most graceful monuments of any age.

"There is a beauty of art and a beauty of Nature. Construction, when it relaxes the principles of design, does not
become Nature; it becomes, more probably, slovenly art.
Nature, for a living art, is full of suggestion; but it is none
the less a resisting force—something to be conquered,
modified, adored. It is only when the force of art is
spent, when its attempt is rounded and complete, that
Nature, freed from the conflict, stands apart, a separate
ideal. It is thus the last sign of an artificial civilization
when Nature takes the place of art."

Against that may be set the fact that order, unaccom-
panied, is entirely powerless to create beauty. Some of the
most dreadful wall-papers, some of the dullest academic
buildings, have order in perfection. Order brings intel-
ligibility and helps our thinking. But easy comprehension
of an ugliness does not make that ugliness any pleasanter.
True classicism is not order in nature, but nature ruled
by mind . . . *Homo additus naturæ.*

One last, and essential, point: in Scott's opinion, with
which I think we must agree, romanticism is an enduring

force, and necessary to the spirit. It is a protest of the individual against devitalized conventions, and its strength will later help the same individual to refashion live conventions. The history of the arts has its eternal rhythm: classicism—fake classicism—romanticism—fake romanticism—classicism . . . *per sæcula sæculorum.*

AUGUST 11TH.—The Assembly of Bishops of the Church of England at Lambeth. Several features strike me:

(*a*) The extent of the territories represented. This assembly is an œcumenical council presided over by the Archbishop of Canterbury. The English, Welsh, Scottish and Irish Bishops are joined by the American Bishops (who have picturesque titles—the Bishop of Eua-Claire, the Bishop of Fond du Lac, the Bishop of the Panama Canal Zone), and also by Canadian, Australian, New Zealand, Indian, Japanese and Chinese Bishops, and by a few isolated ones like the Bishop of Corea, the Bishop of the Upper Nile, and the Bishop of Zanzibar. Proposals of union have even been made to Churches with slightly differing creeds. The Orthodox Churches have sent a representative, the Patriarch of Alexandria, to the Conference; the Archbishop of Utrecht heads a delegation of Old Catholics. An attempt to create another Universal Church alongside of Rome. But Rome has the advantage of single dogma.

(*b*) The Imperial tendency. Just as the British Empire tends to form, alongside of Europe, a federation of free states with the person of the King as its sole and fragile link, so the Church of England seems to be trying to set up, beside the Catholic Church, a federation of autonomous national churches. It would gladly grant them, as it were, "dominion status," provided that by attending such Conferences under the presidency of the Archbishop of Canterbury, they recognize both the unity of the Church and (though this would never be avowed) that of an Anglo-Saxon Empire. To maintain the Empire, His Majesty's Government does not hesitate to grant the Dominions wider and wider measures of freedom, even to the right of secession. The Church of England, on its side, is prepared to grant the local Churches the most astonishing rights of modification. At Lambeth, for instance, the Churches of Southern India have been authorized to set up a single Christian Church, uniting with non-episcopal bodies like the Presbyterians and Wesleyans. In religion as in politics, Britannic flexibility contrasts with Roman intransigence.

(c) The Bishops assembled at Lambeth have devoted a great part of their debates to sexual questions. This may be surprising, but I think that they are right: the maintenance of sexual discipline is one of the most important tasks of any Church. Without such discipline humanity moves speedily through orgy to self-destruction. "Among the tasks that confront the Church to-day," say the English Bishops, "none is more noble or more urgent than that of rescuing the whole subject of sex from degradation in thought and conversation. . . . We believe that the way to do this can be summed up in one word: education. . . . If the children have learnt from the first to connect sex instincts with the beauty and goodness of

186

God, they will not only themselves be proof against some of the worst evils of our age, but also become diffusers of that moral atmosphere where purity lives. . . ."

A curious point is the sternness shown by these Anglican Bishops towards divorce. This is surprising when one recalls that the break with Rome was caused by Henry VIII's desire for a divorce and the refusal of the Holy See. The Conference does not wish the marriage of an adherent whose first spouse is still alive to be celebrated in church, save in exceptional cases to be decided upon by the local Bishop.

On the other hand, it speaks with veiled indulgence of the practice of contraception. This Protestant encyclical certainly declares that the institution of marriage exists primarily for the foundation of a family, but, "where there is a clearly felt moral obligation to limit or avoid parenthood, the method must be decided on Christian principles. The primary and obvious method is complete abstinence from intercourse (as far as may be necessary) in a life of discipline and self-control lived in the power of the Holy Spirit." Each couple has to decide for itself, regarding itself as under the very eye of God, after careful and conscientious reflection, and if in doubt, after taking competent advice, both medical and spiritual. The question which every married couple has to face in this connection is: "Are there reasons which, in our case, would make it blameworthy to produce a new life?" If they reach the conclusion that it would be unmistakably a fault, and if the couple has good reasons for not being able to resort to abstinence, then the Bishops say that they cannot condemn the use of scientific methods of preventing conception. It is plain that a Protestant doctrine of personal judgment is set up against the rigid Catholic teaching, more rigid than ever since the Papal Encyclical of January, 1931. (This resolution was carried by 193 votes to 67.)

The following resolution was added: "Sexual intercourse between persons who are not legally married is a grievous sin. The use of contraceptives does not remove the sin." Obviously.

(*d*) The Conference was much concerned with new scientific teachings and their defensive value to religion. "There is much in the scientific and philosophical thinking of our time which provides a climate more favourable to faith in God than has existed for generations. New interpretations of the cosmic process are now before us which are congruous with Christian Theism. The great scientific movement of the nineteenth century had the appearance, at least, of hostility to religion. But now, from within that movement and under its impulse, views of the universal process are being formed which point to a spiritual interpretation. We are now able, by the help of the various departmental sciences, to trace in outline a continuous process of creative development in which at every stage we can find the Divine presence and power."

The Bishops here purpose to make use of scientists like Eddington or Whitehead for a new system of apologetics. I find this a surprising attitude. If the Churches really hold the truth of the prophets and apostles, of Moses and St. Paul, why should they need Eddington? The truth is that the modern scientist, unlike certain of his nineteenth-century predecessors, does not claim to explain the world, and freely admits that he will never explain it. It is also true that he recognizes that the spiritual cannot be reduced to terms of physico-chemical mechanism. (Mr. Haldane was quite clear about that at Oxford the other day. But other scientists might perhaps be of a different opinion . . . Langevin, Painlevé?). But it is inaccurate to say that confirmation of the Biblical stories is found in modern science. The word "God" is used to-day in different senses. As Walter Lippmann observes, the God of the deist physicists is not the God of the Bible; he plays a useful part in the vocabulary of the agnostic but cannot satisfy the passions of a believer. He does not rule the world like a King, nor watch over his children like a Father. He is no longer a *person* concerned with the affairs of this world. From the religious point of view he is no longer God at all.

It is permissible to ask whether a well-constructed language would employ one single word to designate ideas so different. Certainly many modernist and religious minds no longer believe, as Lippmann remarks, in the God of Genesis who walked in the cool of the evening in the Garden of Eden, and called Adam and his wife, nor in the God of Exodus who appeared unto Moses and Aaron and to seventy of the Elders of Israel. To say that modern science allows one to believe in the literal truth of the Bible because the relativity of Einstein justifies both Galileo and the Inquisition, is not perhaps a very honest way of thinking.

To which Lippmann doubtless replies that, all the same, it is better to retain the word "God," although it may mean one thing to the mass of the faithful and something else to a minority of scientists and philosophers, because the semblance of a certain community of sentiments is thus preserved. For, as he remarks, it is not merely expedient, it may also be wise to wish that men should not be too deeply divided by intellectual distinctions. This thesis can be upheld in good faith. Most words in our vocabulary represent a zone of "suggestion" rather than a clearly defined object.

To-morrow we are to have a visit from an English scientist, Professor N., one of the best pupils of Rutherford and J. J. Thompson, and the author of a fine book on the mechanism of the universe. I shall talk to him about the Assembly of Bishops.

AUGUST 16TH.—"The image I form of the world after reading you," I said to the Professor, "is of a vast concert of vibrations. They are there in all sizes, from the minutest waves of *gamma* rays, to cosmic rays, to the huge waves of wireless. Quite a simple mechanism and not without beauty. But what the devil is the use of it all? Why should a world of vibration have been created?"

"Possibly," he said, "because it was easier than creating a motionless world. Oscillation is the mark of souls and bodies that have not found their equilibrium."

"You remind me," I remarked, "of Madame de Charrière explaining to Benjamin Constant that God did exist, but that he died during the creation of the world. 'And so the universe which you behold,' she said, 'is only the scaffolding of a universe that will never be built.'"

Whereupon he spoke about the Englishman's religion, and quoted this definition: "One-quarter, lofty spirituality; one-quarter, base materialism; one-half, a sentiment like nothing else and defying all analysis."

"In any case," I said, "it is a very powerful sentiment amongst you, for hardly any English scientist can write a technical book without rounding it off with theology."

"True," he said, "but I confess that from a religious point of view that strikes me as weak. Why should one want religion to be scientifically true? There are several kinds of truth. When a mystic tells me that he has had the experience of meeting with God, what can I reply? He is right, just as much as the biologist who has seen a spermatozoon and an ovule under his microscope."

"I don't think it is quite the same thing. . . . The biologist can repeat his experiment, and it can also be repeated elsewhere by myself. The mystic's experience is unique. . . . The system of nature, as framed by science, is singular in its solidarity. I feel that the best argument for religion should be precisely the fixity of laws in nature, for the loyalty of the universe is something really surprising. . . . It is really the greatest miracle of all. Admit the disloyalty of the universe to its own laws and science becomes a sheer impossibility. Suddenly the sun's rays would reach us zigzag, and when I take away my hand the plate would soar gently into the air."

"Do you really believe in the loyalty of the universe?"

said the Professor. "Scientific laws exist because men make them. Mankind has abstractly isolated certain systems in the confusion of nature and found an order in them. Whence he has long concluded that a universal order exists. But the most important facts escape the grasp of science. Are there any laws of love, or even of rain and fine weather?"

"There are not," I said. "But a determinist like Berthelot or Bertrand Russell would reply that we are still imperfectly acquainted with the details of the mechanism, and that everything goes to show that by a perfect mind these laws could be discovered."

"I don't think so," he said. "Nothing seems to me to prove that a scientific psychology, or even a scientific meteorology, could ever be pieced together. . . . No: for my own part, I believe that the universe is crazy—with pockets of sanity."

Same evening.—"We all succumb," says Alain, "to that passion for conjecture instead of exact observation. But what are the odds in favour of our petty reasoning coinciding constantly with that great dice which the universe is flinging against us? Politicians never cease their prophesying; and one of the most powerful passions hidden in every one of us makes us admire and enjoy the realization of a prophecy. An eclipse can be foretold to within a second or two; but that need not turn our heads when we cannot foretell two hours ahead whether or not there will be clouds. And in politics and finance the prophets are still more ludicrous. . . . Our status as men does not admit of any such security, even in the field of misfortune;

events are more like the waves of the sea, and the able pilot steers as the wave comes."

True, very true. But the able pilot keeps himself informed by wireless regarding the movements of cyclones, and shifts his course to avoid them. Fog is hard to foresee, but we shall soon have instruments which will make collisions almost impossible. The advance of economic cyclones can be noted, as ocean storms can. Some day a bankers' weather bureau will have to be set up. The pilot knows that he cannot alter the wave and he steers accordingly, but he also knows that he is sailing to Havre and is certain of reaching there.

"But some vessels sink."

"I know. But is that any reason for not steering?"

AUGUST 21ST.—To-day attended a session of the K. Police Court. A tribunal of this kind differs from the French equivalent in that the judges are not paid officials, but local notabilities appointed by the Lord Chancellor on the recommendation of the Lord Lieutenant of the county. Formerly, magistrates were nearly all of the squire class. On the Bench to-day were an elderly General, a Colonel, the local Labour M.P., and four other magistrates about whom I know nothing.

A bare room. At one side the raised bench of the magistrates, and beneath them the clerk of the court, his shorthand writers, and numerous policemen. In the centre a table round which were seated the lawyers. On the other side a fair sprinkling of the public on benches. It is odd to see for the first time policemen without their helmets. Hitherto they had held in my eyes the unreal, abstract character of mediæval knights or the wax figures at Madame Tussaud's. Here one feels them to be at home; the armour softens; they are smiling men, with white or fair hair. It is like suddenly being present at a session of the tribunal of Saint Louis. He too was certainly surrounded by men of flesh and blood, like other men. To the traveller no less than to the historian the problem is one of detecting humanity beneath the legendary.

The clerk of the court calls the first case. The paper in front of me defines it in these terms:

Metropolitan Police v. *Waddell*

Charge: Driving a motor-car in a manner dangerous to public safety.
Maximum Fine: £20.

Waddell is standing on the small wooden platform reserved for accused persons. A common fellow; collar with rounded points; grey flannel shirt; jacket too square at the shoulders.

The prosecution, represented by a young man in black, stands at the lawyers' table and gives an account of the case. Last Sunday, on a certain wide and excellent road in the neighbourhood, three cars were following each other. In the first was Mr. D., an officer of the Coldstream Guards (his name was that of one of the great English political families); in the second was a friend of his, Mr. P., an engineer; in the third was the accused. Lieutenant D., and P., in their more powerful cars, had just overtaken the accused, and were slowing up on account of a bunch of cyclists who were taking up the right-hand side of the road. At that moment the accused took advantage of their slowing up to pass them himself, thus pulling out the third abreast on the road—the cyclists, one car, and the accused.

As a car was approaching in the other direction, Waddell had abruptly to fall back into line, forcing D. and P. to brake hard in order to avoid a collision. Lieutenant D. was furious and gave chase to the accused, caught him up and signalled to him to stop. The accused did not stop. The chase continued at seventy miles an hour. At last, in a favourable place, D. put himself across the roadway, forced Waddell to get out of his car, and asked for his name. "Give me yours!" he replied. D. refused, and summoned a policeman who happened to be near, reporting the accused for dangerous driving.

During this statement I watched the magistrates' Bench and tried to divine their thoughts. Most of them were gentlemen, two of them retired officers. Class solidarity ought to have tempted them to uphold a Guards officer. On the other hand the question of road courtesy is one that is frequently discussed in England, and therein as elsewhere, the English like the rules of the game to be observed. All of which seemed to me to tell against Waddell. Moreover the man seemed violent and irritable; one could easily imagine him driving brutally.

A stout pink-faced policeman opened the door of the witnesses' room and called: "Mr. Joseph D." Enter a fair handsome young man of the true Eton-Oxford type (though it would probably be Sandhurst), with a grey flannel suit and a red tie. He stepped on to the stand matching that of the accused, and took the oath, Bible in hand: "I swear by Almighty God . . ." The prosecuting lawyer then questioned him with obvious kindness and made him repeat the story as above. D. spoke in a very low, measured voice, adding a few supplementary details: "The accused," he said, "was driving an American car." A stir amongst the magistrates and public showed that this was an aggravating circumstance. The accused had had a lady with him, and when at last confronted by D. he had said: "If it weren't for the lady here, I'd smash your face in!" The young black-coated lawyer put one last question to the lieutenant: "And you took all this trouble, didn't you, Mr. D., in a purely disinterested way, to help in maintaining good order on the road?"—"Yes" —the word came in that same flat, toneless voice.—"Thank you," said the lawyer sitting down.

At this moment a small man in a blue coat, with a hard intelligent face, rises at the central table. This is Waddell's defender: a typical provincial lawyer, possibly a friend of the accused, having come from a distance to help him. The trenchant tone of his first words alters the atmosphere of the proceedings, and something revolutionary is infused into the commonplace business. It is no longer man against man, but class against class. To the little man in the blue suit this absurd case has arisen only from the resentment of two "gentlemen" (the word is frowned upon by English writers, but survives in popular usage) at seeing themselves overtaken by a mere tradesman. "But the road is everybody's, isn't it?" A common-place line, but this man has a fluent and cutting tongue.

"Lieutenant D.," he asked, "was it in the spirit of a Crusader that you set off on your drive last Sunday?"

"I don't understand the question."

"But it is perfectly clear. Do you regard yourself as bound to redress the wrongs of the Infidels of the high-way?"

"No."

"Don't you know that there are road police who do their duty properly and don't need any help from you?"

"No policeman saw this particular incident."

"Lieutenant D., what speed were you going at the moment of this particular incident?"

"About forty miles an hour."

"Don't you regard that as a dangerous speed?"

"No."

Here the chairman of the Bench intervened, obviously annoyed: "What does it matter what speed the witness was going at? Your client was going still faster, because he overtook him."

"I beg your pardon. Lieutenant D. is driving about the roads in a crusading spirit, eager to preach the Gospel amongst car-drivers. Am I not entitled to prove that this paladin is himself a dangerous driver? Lieutenant D., have you ever been convicted of driving at excessive speeds?"

"Yes."

Obvious surprise of the magistrates.

"Recently?" asks the little lawyer sharply.

"No."

"You say 'No,' Lieutenant D.? Were you convicted of driving at an excessive speed last year?"

"Yes."

"And you don't call that recently? Do they teach you evasions in the Coldstream Guards?"

A murmur of annoyance on the Bench. To attack an old and honoured regiment in defence of a common driver seems to these old gentlemen in the worst possible taste. A very clumsy lawyer. He will get his client convicted. But he persists:

"Lieutenant D., your car is a very fast sports coupé, isn't it?"

"It is a very fast coupé, but not a sports coupé."

Clearly the lawyer wishes by the word "sports" to suggest an idea of speed and elegance, in contrast to his client's decent, slow, ordinary, family car. The latter stands absolutely impassive in the box.

"What gave you most pleasure in this man-hunt, Lieutenant D.? The hunt itself or the denunciation?"

"It wasn't a hunt."

"Chasing a man at seventy miles an hour—is not that a hunt?"

"No."

"The truth is this—is it not, Lieutenant D.?—that you were annoyed at finding yourself, you, an officer of the Guards, and a sportsman (I beg your pardon! I forgot you had objections to the word 'sport' . . .) outstripped by a modest British citizen, and that you wanted to have your own back? When you spoke to him, you were excited and arrogant, were you not?"

"No."

"If the defendant refused to give you his name, did not you equally refuse to give him yours?"

"I should have given him mine if he'd given his. It was for him to start."

"Really? And why so, Lieutenant D.? Do you think that traffic should be held up because an officer of the Coldstream Guards wonders whether he should give his name first or second?"

I admire D.'s calm under this rain of ironic questions. The little man in the blue suit is standing with one foot on his chair, elbow on knee, chin in hand. He would have been a remarkable member of the Revolutionary Convention, but I still feel that he is doing his client harm. At last D.'s ordeal is over, and with a smile he crosses to a seat on the public benches. The policeman calls: "Mr. P.!" This is the Lieutenant's motoring friend: the same Public School type. The barrister will be able to continue his sarcasm. But P., a very adroit witness, does not let himself be pulled to pieces. "Yes. . . . No. . . . I don't share that view. . . ." The magistrates follow the match with evident favour towards the witness, although letting no trace of their feelings become visible.

"Your friend had a very fast car, Mr. P.?"

"No . . . a fast car."

"A sports coupé?"

"No . . . a coupé."

"Why won't you admit it is a sports coupé?"

"Because it was not a sports coupé."

"You say, Mr. P., that my client had an American car?"

"Yes."

"Mr. D. told us the same thing."

"I don't know."

"You don't know? Have you never discussed this affair with Lieutenant D.?"

"Oh, yes, often. The last time was five minutes ago."

"So these two gentlemen came to the Court together and have decided that my client's car was an American car. . . . What would you say, Mr. P., if I informed you that it is French car? Would you take that from me as a fact?"

"Yes."

I observe that the fact of having driven a French car, and not an American one, strikes the magistrates, witnesses and defendant as an extenuating circumstance. The blue advocate, seeing that nothing can be got out of P., thereupon lets him go.

One more witness: the policeman who brought the summons at D.'s request. An elderly man, twirling his helmet in his hands and rather embarrassed. He too will have a taste of the defending lawyer's irony.

"Tell me, officer, when Lieutenant D. came up to you, did he tell you that he had just been chasing this man at seventy miles an hour?"

"He did, sir."

"And you did not summons him for exceeding the speed limit? Really, officer, you lost a fine chance there!"

With this the hearing of witnesses was closed. "That is

my case," ended the black advocate. "That is my case,"
replied the blue; and the defendant crossed the room and
entered the witness-box. Bible in hand, he repeated the
formula of the oath, and then his counsel began examining him.

One cannot help being struck by the self-control shown
by this man of the people. It is his turn now to attract
sympathy. The lawyer gives leading questions:

"Did you do anything at all to rouse the anger of this
young Guards officer?"

"Nothing at all."

"How did he look when he caught you up?"

"He was white with rage."

"Was your car an American one?"

(Certainly this would appear to be the kernel of the
case.)

"No, French."

"How long have you been driving cars?"

"Twenty years."

"Have you ever had an accident?"

"Never."

The prosecution then take their turn with the witness.
Counsel tries to make him admit that by pulling out beyond both the cyclists and one other car, he must have
gone over the middle of the roadway, which is forbidden.
But he resists.

"I had all the room I needed. Four feet for the cyclists,
four feet for Mr. D.'s car, and four for my own. I didn't
go over the crown of the road."

I listened to this cross-examination wondering with

some embarrassment what I would do if I were on the Bench. The evidence is contradictory. There are no solid proofs. I should be for acquittal. But I thought that Waddell would be found guilty because the magistrates had been irritated by his counsel.

The Court retired. Both of the lawyers, and the policemen, engaged in friendly conversation, and after five minutes' deliberation the Court returned. Waddell is acquitted! The blue counsel is triumphant. In spite of my feeling of sympathy towards D., I am satisfied, because, given the evidence, this was the just solution.

Later, in conversation with the magistrates, I was interested to learn the grounds for their judgment. It had been a curious deliberation. The two retired officers, annoyed by the little lawyer, had insisted on *acquittal* because they mistrusted their own passions and were afraid of being prejudiced. The Labour M.P., on the other hand, had shown himself in favour of a small penalty, for the same reason. Complex reactions: but they showed me two things—firstly, why parliamentary government has so long been practicable in England; and secondly, how easy it would be to deceive through excess of honesty.

Second case. . . . But the second case was of the kind which in France are tried *in camera*. It was extremely curious. . . .

AUGUST 23RD.—Finished re-reading Eckermann in the new translation. I should like to try to define more exactly the causes of that resistance which I often feel in men whom I esteem, when they are faced by the wisdom of Goethe.

(*a*) Goethe displeases the faithful because he is at heart an agnostic. I know that he speaks of God with respect, much as he speaks of the Grand Duke of Saxe-Weimar and the King of Bavaria, though with less affection. But he has a strong dislike of all metaphysics. "Man is not born to solve the problem of the universe, but to seek whither that problem leads, and then to take his stand within the limits of the intelligible. . . ." And again: "I should not like to be deprived of the joy of believing in a future life, but some things are too remote from us to be an object of speculation that troubles thought. . . . To concern oneself with ideas of immortality is all very well for fashionable persons, especially for fair ladies who have nothing to do. But a superior man, who is already aware of being something here below, and must consequently work, battle, act, leaves the next world in peace and is content with being active and useful in this one." His morality is bold and straightforward: "Always hold fast to the present hour. Every state of duration, every second, is of infinite value. . . . I have staked on the present as one stakes a large sum on one card, and I have sought without exaggerating to make it as high as possible." It should not be forgotten that at the end of the second "Faust" he makes Faust an engineer. Provided that activity is possible, world systems seem to him useless.

Scorn for all doctrines that are still such. Contrast with that Péguy's remark: "Not to be concerned any longer with great questions is like smoking a pipe, a habit which you take to when age is gaining on you, whereby you believe you are becoming a man although the truth is merely that you have grown old. Happy the man who keeps his youthful appetite for metaphysics."

(*b*) Goethe is distasteful to all rebels. That is natural, because he accepts life. Revolutions seem to him inevitable, not desirable. "If one could make humanity perfect, a state of perfection would then be conceivable. Until then everything will go in a so-so way. One party will have to suffer whilst the other will enjoy well-being. . . . The wisest thing is that everyone should do the job for which he was born and which he has learned, and should not prevent others from doing theirs. . . ! In art as in politics, Goethe has a horror of criticism: destruction, he thinks, is vain; beauty lies in building. To which it would be simple (and fair) to reply that acceptance of the world is too easy when one is Goethe and a minister of State. But to scorn the world is no less easy when one is Jean-Jacques or Julien Sorel. The true triumph of the spirit would be to outsoar all these egocentric philosophers. The rebel can be a hero only when his rebellion is pure. If I detect in it traces of wounded self-love, then I am a rebel in my turn.

(*c*) This morning I heard J. de M. reproach Goethe for his success at the Court of Weimar: "People don't do that," she said, "unless they have a certain weakness of character. On the contrary, the essence of genius lies in its inability to accept and acclimatize itself." The problem, I think, is really more complex. Because a man is maladjusted, unhappy, touched with genius, he imposes a respect for his originality on a great number of others (Goethe, Byron, Proust). From the moment when he makes good and becomes to them a great man, he has *succeeded,* whether he likes it or not. . . . He may remain troubled in spirit. What human being is not? But he is no longer so as he was in the days of "Werther" or the "Nourritures Terrestres." . . . Has he thereby ceased to be a great writer? I cannot see that he has. But it was fear of success that made Wilde crave for catastrophe, and say that, without Saint Helena, Napoleon would have been less great. "Nothing fails like success," said (I think) Blake. In any case, are there any unalloyed successes? Suffering is the most fairly distributed thing in the world. Look at Goethe's despair after Marienbad, in the conversations with the Chancellor Müller. Goethe was not *born* in success: he conquered his liberty.

(*d*) Goethe annoys not only romantics (for he was in his way a classic writer, and René Berthelot is right in saying that his wisdom has affinities with that of Voltaire), but also the self-analysts that we all are to-day, for in his eyes a great work of art is objective. The notion of seeking to know oneself is to him absurd. "With all his senses and all his aspirations man strives outwards, towards the world surrounding him, and he has quite enough to do to become familiar with it, and observe it in so far as it is necessary to his ends. He is conscious of himself only in experiencing pain or pleasure. Man is an obscure being; he is ignorant of whence he comes and whither he is going. He knows little of the world, and even less of himself. I do not know myself, and God preserves me from knowing myself." In this respect he is at one with Flaubert, and at odds with our own generation; but that he is wrong remains unproven. Thibaudet has shown how the only really truthful confessions are those made with a semblance of objectivity under the mask of a character (Madame Bovary, Mlle. de Vinteuil).

We must not forget that a man's mode of life in practice helps us to judge his theoretic code of morality. Eckermann's description of the aged Goethe is a very beautiful one: "He was seated in a wooden armchair before his writing-desk; I found him amazing gentle, like a man suffused with heavenly peace, remembering an unspeakable happiness that he had once enjoyed, and which was returning once more to float over his spirit." But once again, it is easier to inspire love if one is a Nietzsche or a Shelley than if one is a Goethe or a Meredith. This does not prove the inferiority of Goethe or Meredith. It merely proves that those men who seek a compensation in literature ("reading, that unpunished vice . . . ") are for the most part unhappy men who can recognize themselves best in another unhappy man. The men of action, who ought to like Goethe, do not read or read but little. In art there is a premium on madness. "If I wanted to pursue fame . . . " says Valéry. But one must remain true. . . .

AUGUST 25TH.—In France, I think, we are ignorant of the place still held in England by love as a passion. The novels of Maurice Baring (such as "Daphne Adeane" or

"Cat's Cradle") may have helped some Frenchmen to realize the "Princesse de Clèves" element which exists in present-day England alongside the cynicism of Huxley's characters. The English keep their passions well hidden because of their strong sense of modesty in matters of sentiment, but when these passions break through the surface impassivity they do so with a violence that would have delighted Stendhal. B. told me the story of a friend of his, Julian S., who had been in love with a certain lady for ten years, and was jealous of her. One summer evening they were both invited to dine somewhere up the river, and three boats were waiting alongside the bank for the guests. The hostess allotted the places, but in ignorance or forgetfulness of this quite open liaison, she placed S. and his mistress in different boats. S. turned pale, and took his place between two ladies; he struggled to hide his distress, but could only keep gazing at the other boat. When the little flotilla reached the middle of the Thames he could bear it no longer, dived into the water in his evening dress, and swam over to join the one whom he loved.

*　　*　　*

Another English story was told me by M. L. B. It may be called:

THE CORINTHIAN PORCH

Lord and Lady Barchester had spent the forty years of their married life in the same house in Park Lane. But after the War they found themselves in difficulties. Investments had gone wrong; one of their sons had been killed; his widow and children were left on the hands of his parents, and the income tax was five shillings on the pound. Lord Barchester was forced to face the fact that he could not keep up both his family seat in Sussex and the Park Lane house. After long hesitation he at last resolved to discuss his difficulties with his wife. He had long been afraid of distressing her. Thirty years before, there had been stormy times in their married life, but old age had brought peace, indulgence, and fondness.

"My dear," he said, "I am dreadfully sorry, but I can see only one way of ending our days honourably, and I know it will be painful to you. I leave you free to accede to it or to set it aside. Listen: land adjoining the Park has reached a very high price. A certain speculator is anxious to build a block of flats, and he needs our corner as it forms an enclave in his property. He offers to buy it at a price which would not only enable us to find another house in the same district, though a little further back from the Park, but would also let us keep a substantial margin to pass our few remaining years in comfort. Still, I know that you are more attached to Barchester House than I am, and I don't want to do anything you would not like."

Lady Barchester agreed to the exchange, and a few months later the old couple were settled in a new house, a few hundred yards away from the one they had been obliged to leave. It was already in the hands of the housebreakers. When they went out, Lord and Lady Barchester passed daily in front of their old home, and it was strange for them to see the slow undoing of a shape which had been the most essential and stable feature in their universe. When they saw their home roofless they felt as if they themselves were exposed to the wind and rain. Lady Barchester felt the sharpest twinge when the front wall was ripped open and she saw, as if on a stage scene set for all to see, the room that had belonged to Patrick, her dead son, and the room in which she herself had spent nearly forty years.

From the street she looked up at the glazed chintz with its dark background which had lined the walls of her room. Through so many hours of mourning and illness, and of happiness too, had she gazed on it, that the stuff's pattern seemed the very background on which her own life had been woven. A few days later came a great surprise. The workmen had ripped off the chintz and there came into view a black and white wallpaper which she had completely forgotten; but immediately, and with puzzling vividness, that paper evoked her long liaison with Harry Webb. How often, gazing on those Japanese houses, had she spent her mornings in an endless dreaming after reading the delicious letters that Harry wrote to her from the Far East! She had loved him deeply. And now he was Sir Henry Webb, one of His Majesty's Ambassadors.

Soon the rain washed off that black and white paper, and beneath it another was revealed. It was a rather ugly flowered pattern, but Lady Barchester remembered how she chose it with great deliberation at the time of her marriage in the year 1890. In those days she wore blue serge dresses, and yellow amber necklaces; she tried to look like Mrs. Burne Jones and went to tea on Sundays with old William Morris. And whilst those fragments of pink and green paper could be seen, she would pass several times a day in front of the house, for its pattern recalled her young days, when she was in love with Lord Barchester.

At last the walls themselves came down, and one day when Lord and Lady Barchester went out to stroll in the Park together, they saw that nothing was left of the house but the little Corinthian porch over the front door. It was an odd, sad spectacle, for there, at the top of the steps, that porch opened on to a desolation of rubble heaped up beneath a wintry sky. For a long time Lady Barchester watched the clouds passing between the white pillars, and then she said to her husband:

"That porch is linked in my memory with the saddest day of my life. I have never dared to mention it, but we are so old now that it doesn't matter. It was at the time when I loved Harry and you were in love with Sybil. One night I had been to a ball to meet Harry when he came back from Tokio. I had been looking forward to the meeting for weeks, but Harry had really only returned home to become engaged, and he danced the whole evening with a young girl, pretending not to notice me. I cried in the carriage on the way home. I reached the house. I felt so disfigured with my tears that I hadn't the courage to let you see me. I pretended to ring the bell and let the coachman go, and then I stood leaning against one of those pillars, and stayed there for a long time. I was sobbing. It was raining very hard. I knew that you yourself were thinking about another woman and I thought my life was finished. That little porch is going to vanish, and that is what it reminds me of."

Lord Barchester had listened to the story with sympathy and interest. He took his wife's arm affectionately.

"I'll tell you what we shall do," he said. "This porch is the tomb of your memories, and before it is demolished we shall go and buy some flowers together and lay them at the top of the steps."

And the old couple went to a florist's, brought back some roses, and laid them at the foot of one of the Corinthian pillars. Next day the porch had disappeared.

*　　*　　*

AUGUST 28TH.—Rain . . . reading . . . trying to form a clear idea of Adler's psychology.

Like Freud, he insists on the part played by childhood in the formation of character. When children cease to be protected from the universe by a mother or nurse, they all experience a sense of inferiority. They are clumsy; they know nothing of the world; childhood is a period of difficult apprenticeship. But the normal child soon recognizes that he is capable of learning the job of being a man and solving the problems set by life. He then forms an optimistic character and thereafter tries to find his place in society as it exists.

On the other hand, the child who feels abnormal, whether on account of bodily or mental shortcomings, or because he is born into bad surroundings, or because he is unfairly treated by his family, feels a *need for superiority* which is greater in proportion as his sense of inferiority is acute. Throughout his life he will require a compensation, a *margin* of security, because of the memory of his spoilt childhood. The normal being will also need security, but for him the compensation is simple —it lies in society itself. An organized society is merely the sum of compensations necessary for the individuals composing it to feel themselves protected. Granted the existence of this society, normal beings can readily enough realize their desires in it. For instance, when sexual desire comes to life in them, they look simply for the woman capable of loving them; they do not doubt the possibility of finding her, or, having found her, of pleasing her.

The abnormal adolescent, however, feels powerless to satisfy his desires in the social world. His tendency therefore is to isolate himself; he regards himself as in an enemy country; he holds an exaggerated view of the hostility and malevolence of human beings. How can he alter? In the tales he listens to, in works of art, the abnormal man seeks only himself; he takes far more interest in whatever recalls the sadness and seamy side of existence than in things that might possibly make him optimistic. The melancholy man likes melancholy books, the mischievous man likes cruel books. This explains the success of men of genius who have at the same time been invalids (Dostoievsky or Nietzsche), and the comparative unpopularity of Goethe. The born pessimist's attitude towards life is one of escaping, and because of that he will not recognize tenderness or friendship if he encounters either. He will become an anti-social individual, feeling tranquillity only in solitude, or, if he lives amongst other men, requiring a very wide margin of security. ("I feel equal to them only if I am leading them.") Consequently he will be proud, often rebuffed, sometimes wearing a mask of hypocrisy. Incredible pride of small apocalyptic shopkeepers, desiring a revolution or the end of the world for the satisfaction of their vainglorious anxiety. . . .

Let this proud-souled pessmist seek refuge, not in some external catastrophe, but in subjective and inward satisfactions, and he will become a neurotic. The madman lives in a dream world where all his inferiorities find compensation. The neurotic makes his escape without crossing the bounds of madness; he evades the battle under various pretexts, explaining his renunciation of love by saying that he is not interested in women, of honours by disowning ambition or alleging ill-health. These excuses enable him to mask the real social or physiological inferiority which is the root cause of his renunciation.

A favourite method of the neurotic is to prolong in adult life the method he has found successful in childhood, that is to say, the admission of weakness. Many children play a comedy of weakness, and many grown-up women do likewise. In the most favourable circumstances the abnormal man will manage to impose himself on the world by his very neurosis. The man of genius forces the acceptance of his subjective world by other men, because that universe corresponds to a widespread contemporary need for compensation (witness Proust).

To Adler, therefore, every man's will is controlled by a central need—to compensate a childhood inferiority. There is thus formed what he terms an *aim of life*. This aim is so chosen that, if we attain it, our personality will be raised to a point of superiority that will make life supportable. It can be attained by roundabout paths. A man who needs to excuse his failure to himself will say: "I don't succeed because I drink, or because I smoke opium." His drunkenness will keep him from thinking: "I don't succeed because I am an inferior creature," and he will find a comprehending fraternity, even a freemasonry, among drinkers or drug-takers. A woman physiologically incapable of loving will build up for herself a whole system of pride, or hatred of the male, in order to avoid the thought of her physiological infirmity. Others will blame their parents, and a still greater number, society. The pamphleteer is really far less concerned with striking at his victim than with convincing himself of his own worth by damaging the worth of others. The malevolent man is nearly always a weak man, just as the cynic in love is a man who has once been sentimentally unhappy. Every man who feels ill-adjusted to the life of his time will become, if he has talent, a scorner of his age. From adolescence, when men reach what Adler calls the fighting line, there are some who enter the battle on the terms offered, and others who become shirkers. They do not consciously tell themselves: "I realize that it is not easy to come out in the front rank, so I'll do all I can to live as little as possible," but they behave just as if they thought on those lines. They escape from society, declaring that they do not like it, or that they despise it.

A man's actions do not enable one to gauge his character. They are merely signs to be interpreted. Generosity may be serving vanity. The proud man makes a sacrifice for a friend, but in so doing he is putting himself on top of his friend. A woman may with the utmost kindness allow her husband to see other women, or even to be unfaithful to her, but she may do this through pride, and because, knowing the outcome to be inevitable, she prefers to have the illusion of having provoked it. A man will take a modest seat in the back row of a meeting, so as to be invited up to the front. People who always arrive late for dinner, who wait for ten invitations before accepting, who accept only on certain strict conditions, all show their own vanity by these habits; others, again, do likewise by their desire to be present at all fashionable functions. The craving for superiority knows a thousand by-paths. It creates solitaries and men of ambition, nearly all artists, and most saints. We all know persons who, in the first phase of a friendship, give the impression of being passionately interested in others, and are always talking of humanity and of their love for their fellow-men, and then, in a second phase, lift the veil and appear as humanitarians only for vanity.

It should not be supposed that such an inferiority complex is necessarily a flaw in an individual. On the contrary, the absence of some such complex is rare in even the most remarkable men. The entirely normal being is a herd creature; he will accept society because he will there be perfectly at ease. Living will be easy, and average success will be within his reach. He will rarely succeed on a grand scale, because the "will to power" is far stronger in the outlaw. The men who make great revolutions, great empires, great works of art, are nearly always men who have suffered from a sense of inferiority. Byron was strong through his infirmity, Dostoievsky and Flaubert through epilepsy, Napoleon through his unhappy adolescence, Disraeli through his Jewish birth.

But if the inferiority complex thus appears to be almost something desirable, what is the aim of the Adlerian psychology? It is to define in certain cases the individual's goal in life, so that he may understand himself clearly. Not every neurotic succeeds in discovering his compensation. Very often a physiological ill is grafted on to the psychological one. Adler has shown, for instance, that many cases of migraine are mere acts of evasion. They provide an excuse for avoiding struggle. Proust's asthma was doubtless originally an attempt at escape. Adler has had under his care a young woman whose neurosis took the form of an extraordinary activity in small matters. She spent all her time in arranging things, in keeping her accounts with incredible exactness of detail, and her husband and relatives said: "She is killing herself with work!" As a matter of fact she was of lazy temperament, and her anxiety to shun the greater tasks which life offered gave rise to this method of escape.

Why is it often necessary to make the neurotic explain his aim in life? Because nearly always the great evil is the sense of isolation. You harbour in yourself a secret grievance that cuts you off from other people. That isolation is broken by the avowal. It does not give power but it gives peace, because the true aim, the true compensation, is to find self-expression, and to feel that one has been understood. Through expression the patient becomes a match for his inferiority. He has dominated it, and, above all, has fitted it into the social scheme, because other men can now understand it. (And this is why the artist-neurotic is cured by his art. The serenity of the aged Goethe arises from the fact that the adolescent Goethe, in "Werther," killed Werther.)

I should be quite ready to accept Adler's system as a whole. He seems to me mistaken in regarding the aim of life as something completely formed in childhood; for my own part, I can see the aim of life being transformed in the course of life itself. Whenever we experience a new sense of inferiority, a new need for compensation comes into being, and the aim of life alters. For instance, a politician beaten at an election will show hostility to the parliamentary régime, and his aim of life will be to become a writer, perhaps an anti-political writer. A man deceived by women will become a conqueror, in order to fortify his pride. A woman who realizes at twenty that she is ill-adapted for love will construct a philosophy hostile to love.

It might be said, of course, that these ideas exist in a different form in La Rochefoucauld. Using different terms, he showed that the "aim of life" is at the root of most of the virtues. In another sense the essence of the Adlerian remedy was also the "Know thyself" of Thales, and in Spinoza's remark: "An emotion ceases to be a pas-

sion as soon as we form a clear and distinct idea of it."
But ideas have to be refashioned in every epoch in a form
that suits the intellectual habits of that epoch. To Moses
the laws of hygiene had to be divine ordinances; to the
modern man, moral laws have to be medical ordinances.
Yet the laws themselves change but little and slowly.

What should we retain of Adler's case? It is desirable
to avoid the creation of any excessively painful sense of
inferiority, and we should therefore (*a*) give the child an
exact impression of its own strength, not giving it a sense
of being either stronger or weaker than it actually is, and
avoiding alterations in its place in the scale of family
values; (*b*) give young people at the time of the formation of their sexual life opportunities for frank conversation to prevent them from regarding themselves as abnormal beings; (*c*) lessen rivalries, ambition, and inequality. In certain forms ambition may be valuable, but
we have allowed too much scope in life to anti-social
feelings.

The ant suffers. Whence Rotary Clubs, friendly societies, Young Communists' associations—tentative ant-heaps.

* * *

One Day: Personal column of *The Times:* "LADY,
owning new luxury car, will drive anybody anywhere.
Write Box No. . . ."

And in the next column, another personal advertisement: "WHAT does the LORD thy GOD demand of
thee except that thou fear the LORD thy GOD?"

Oxford: A philosophical congress. Prof. Northrop of

Yale reads a paper on the relation between Time and Eternity in the light of contemporary physics. He thinks that hitherto we have attached too much importance to Time, and hopes that Eternity will now resume its fitting place.

Prof. Schlick of Vienna expresses his conviction that we are on the threshold of a new era in philosophy. He opines that books will no longer be written about philosophy, but that *all* books will be written by philosophers. (See *Pickwick Papers, passim.*)

. . *Bristol:* Meeting of the British Association. Professor Appleton describes the echoes of wireless waves, certain of which arrive thirty seconds after the original signal. From what can these waves be reflected? Thirty seconds is too long for the moon, and too short for the sun. A difficult and fascinating subject.

Letters to the Editor: A reader of *The Times* suggests that in future, as the meteorologists seem quite incapable of forecasting conditions, the daily weather report should be compiled by a committee of old Scottish shepherds.

Then, a clergyman writes to record his observation of the games of a squirrel and two magpies. The squirrel climbed the trunk of a tree whilst the two magpies followed it by hopping up from branch to branch. The game was repeated several times over. It was clearly a race. The correspondent is glad to be able to say that the magpies behaved like really sporting birds, and took no unfair advantage of the fact that they could easily have flown.

SEPTEMBER 1ST.—Long talk with Harold B. on individualism. This is a subject on which I am not in agreement with several people whom I hold in the highest respect (Alain, André Siegfried). Both of these eulogize radical individualism. But I believe that real individualism is possible only in a stable society. B. brings me some articles in the *New Republic* by John Dewey, setting forth the problem in a way that I find both fresh and interesting.

Dewey's central idea is that our modern societies, as moulded by centralized industry, are corporative organisms which ought to be controlled by collective decisions and have passed beyond the comprehension and strength of an individual. In industry as in agriculture, a pioneering age did exist. But that age has passed. The bold and picturesque type of economic corsair will disappear. Notwithstanding hostile laws (such as the Sherman Law in the United States), agreements between the producers in a country, and even international agreements, are found to offer the only chance of mastering a machinery which is made fragile by the very fact of its vastness. The machine has killed the independent captain of industry, just as firearms placed in the hands of the masses killed the great feudal barons.

This "collective" character of our age is not peculiar to industry; it holds true in nearly every sphere of human activity. Thus, the United States Government is trying to organize agriculture on collective lines. Sports are team sports, and even the team demands for its support the loyalty of the group from which it emerges. Crime itself, formerly the unruly action of an isolated individual, is becoming the organized activity of a corporate body.

The first feature, therefore, is an epoch of collective action; the second, an epoch of unstable equilibrium. Collective action ensures men's happiness when they wholeheartedly believe in the utility of this activity and feel that it expresses their own will (the ant-hill). It becomes irksome when those who ought to participate in it lose faith in its efficacy. Now the misfortune of an age lies in the fact that many individuals have lost their trust in the code that has hitherto controlled their actions. Incapable of suggesting another code, they are powerless to transform society. But they are stricken, and, finding no remedy, they seek refuge in drink, in sensuality, in mystical sects, or in a swift series of violent spectacles. (Revolt of the ant-hill, analogous to that in the early centuries of the Christian era.)

What can be done to cure this malady of the individual? Put back the clock? Forswear science and the machine? That is very much as if a feudal baron of the sixteenth century had said: "In order to save the noble spirit of feudalism, let us vow to go back to the good old sword of our sires, and never again to use the arquebus and cannon." It is ingenuous to suppose the machine is the cause of our woes. The machine, like nature, is neither the friend nor the foe of mankind. It is itself a part of nature. It can be used for man's happiness if man knows how to master it. It ensures, and ought increasingly to ensure, leisure and an abundance of material benefits. If the workers have been filled with a sense of insecurity in our mechanical civilization, by over-production or by the rapidity of technical advances, that is not the fault of the machine, but the fault of a humanity unable to take the necessary steps in a transitional age to safeguard the general security. Man is not merely subject to history; to a certain extent he makes history. It is certain that our political and economic organization has fallen far behind the progress of our mechanical and scientific organization, that we are suffering from this disparity, and that it is at least partially incumbent on us to supply the remedy.

Men require food, clothes, warmth and light, and our civilization has supplied these boons more abundantly than any other. It has, I think, lessened the suffering caused by disease, poverty and harsh laws. On the other hand, man's need for security, leisure and spiritual balance has not diminished. Leisure will perhaps come through the shortening of working-hours, which is inevitable as being the sole remedy against over-production and unemployment. Security is lacking in the modern world. The workers are not sure of having work; the middle-classes are not sure of the future of their children; states are not sure of living in peace. The most important task of the twentieth century is not so much the progressive conquest of matter as to halt and organize the territory already conquered; and that, as the Greek philosophers said long ago, means the refashioning of man himself.

In Dewey's opinion the cure for the sickness of the individual is to be found in a better political and economic organization of the State. To his opponents he would answer: "You complain of the fact that thought is too collective, but I tell you the real trouble is that it is not collective enough." The mental "standardization" of our day is deplorable, not because it is profound but because it remains superficial. Millions of men accept the same absurdity at the same moment, but in a week have already ceased to believe it. The periods when mankind has known happiness are those during which united and homogeneous groups have freely accepted common and relatively stable beliefs, and those are the very periods which have produced the freest and most original individuals. For there is no freedom in anarchy, intellectual or political. An individual outside any social organization would be an inconceivable monster, and in any case has never existed.

The romantic rebel is not a free individual. In his own way he conforms just as much as the diehard conservative. Passion deprives rebel and reactionary alike of judgment. In order to restore a true spiritual freedom in the modern world, according to Dewey, the peoples of our time must be brought to handle the relations of men with the same objective methods as have enabled humanity to master external things. Science has not accepted matter but transformed it. It must not accept economic anarchy, industrial crises, and wars. No problems are incapable of being treated intelligently and systematically. The real individual is not the man who turns away from the spectacle of the 1932 world and gloomily exclaims: "How I wish I had lived in 1232!" It is the man who realizes that an individual life is possible only within a well-organized society, and offers the best that is in him towards the organization of his contemporary society.

This attitude seems to me desirable; and it is comparable to that of Heard's super-individuals. Is it possible for any large number of men?

"I don't think so," said B.

"Nor do I. But is that any reason for not adopting it?"

"Take care," he said. "You're on the path to socialism if you follow Dewey."

"That doesn't matter to me: I'm not afraid of labels . . . I believe that capitalist society will be led to adopt certain forms of collective activity simply because the complexity of modern societies cannot be squared with a régime of feudal warfares. But these forms of collective action will not necessarily be *state* action; they may well be on a corporation basis."

"And suppose society proves incapable of altering itself and giving up its folly?"

"Then society will perish—but of its own free will."

SEPTEMBER 7TH.—Homeward journey. . . . Sad at leaving our bracken and common, but I promised to visit Geneva for the League of Nations Assembly. Reading on the boat some lectures by a German professor, Wilhelm Haas, on the subject—"What is European civilization?" They are interesting, and supplement very well the thesis of Gerald Heard, especially at a point where Heard seems to me to be incomplete—I mean, the part played in the intellectual drama of humanity by the development of positive science.

In essence Haas' theme is this: the scientific conquest of nature is a new idea and would have seemed very strange to the men of other epochs. To a Greek like Socrates the essential thing was not the mastering of nature by obeying her, but the knowledge of man. True, a Greek science did exist, but it was disinterested. Aristotle held that as soon as a science became technical, the man learned in that science ran the risk of becoming a merchant or a slave. To men of the Middle Ages the conquest of the spiritual world was the only thing of importance; the natural world was something accessory.

In the seventeenth century it came about that disinterested science (mathematics and astronomy) led to the observation of natural phenomena. The stars, their movements simplified by the enormous distances separating them from ourselves, were observed to be subject to fixed and simple laws, and from this came the notion that all natural phenomena could be made the objects of calculation, provided that the scientist observed in them only the measurable quantities. The method was wonderfully successful. Mankind discovered that obedience to the laws of nature enabled him to transform nature. And the result, within three centuries, was practical science, industry, and the immense power of man over matter.

For its essential validity this science required the hypothesis of an inert and mechanical nature. Nature as known to the Greeks, the dwelling-place of the Gods, or the Christian conception of nature, upset on occasion by miracles, or even the purely æsthetic view of nature held by the Chinese, did not concern science. A sacrifice had to be made, and if nature were to be mastered, the soul of nature must be taken from it.

To this the modern man is tempted to reply: "And quite rightly so, because in actual fact nature has no soul." Possibly: but the result has been that, for men of the scientific era, the idea of understanding has become identified with the idea of matter as something abstract and mechanical. When they have sought to examine the human spirit, or history, they have quite naturally fallen back on a method which had proved its efficacy. For three centuries now humane science has followed the lead of the natural sciences. Descartes and Spinoza made a geometry of the study of the passions; Tane, a contemporary of Claude Bernard the physiologist, made a physiology of the same study. In the nineteenth century spiritual values were discounted by many scientists and philosophers; this was done without valid proof, and even contrary to proof, for observation can show more proofs of the importance of the spirit in man than of physicochemical connections. Man's attitude towards himself changes. He no longer believes in his own power. The individual man of the scientific era loses the faculty of feeling himself to be a focus of energy. The Hindu ascetic and the Catholic saint believe in a mysterious power in man, and the primitive man believes in that power because he feels it within him, but Hippolyte Taine and Adrien Sixte assume *a priori* that everything within us happens according to mechanical laws. "Vice and virtue are products, like sugar and sulphuric acid." A disheartening self-abasement, for it robs mankind of his faith in mankind.

The time comes (and it has done so in our own day) when man feels the lack of that power and regrets this sacrifice. He discovers that science does not prove the reality of a universal mechanism. The phenomena of life and spirit have never been capable of explanation by scientific methods. The "profane" success of modern scientists like Eddington, Whitehead, or Louis de Broglie, lies in their support of the compatibility of science with the idea of human freedom. The European mind accepted the sacrifice with enthusiasm; it is now beginning to regret it. Having failed to find happiness in the triumph of a scientific civilization, humanity is revolting against it. And it is curious to note that the present rebellion of the conservative bourgeoisie against the machine has a close analogy to the Rousseauesque sympathies of the nobility about 1760. Just as in Rousseau's time, sentiment is opposed to intelligence: a false opposition, as I think, because man cannot be cut up into distinct faculties except by an artificial operation. But I see clearly (in spite of my sympathies being in the intellectual camp) how much that is genuine and deep-seated lies beneath this rebellion.

The problem, I think, ought to be presented in quite different terms. Why attack scientific civilization? Can it be abolished? Is that desired? Are not the Russians, who did not possess it, now engaged in setting it up for themselves? In any case, is it really true that men were happier long ago, in a pastoral or agricultural civilization?

The yearning for a return to nature is a chronic form of human nostalgia. But the peasant who worked twelve or fourteen hours a day in summer, or his wife and daughter who drudged year in, year out on heavy handicrafts, would tell a very different tale. In any case, the advance of machinery has certainly lessened the evils caused by the first industrial revolution. Read Disraeli's "Sybil," and see whether the English working-classes of his day were freer and less "standardized" individuals than the workers of our own time. Besides, what do these comparisons matter? Dewey is certainly right in saying that the problem is not to escape from our own day, but to understand our own day and to create the age that will follow it.

*　　*　　*

Paris to Geneva by train. Crossing Paris I met Jean Prévost, who gave me a volume of Saint-Evremond for my journey.

"One of the great joys to be found in loving God," he says somewhere, "is to be able to lose those who love Him." My own lack of religion has often made me regret that fond unity existing between friends who hold common, unargued beliefs.

Through the carriage window, the Cathedral of Sens: as lovely as Saint-Wulfran at Abbeville (I don't know why one should call up the other—perhaps those watchtowers). Burgundian villages where the roofs of orange-red tiles blend with the other roofs of bluish slate. The colours of France. . . . To refashion man himself. But wherein? Perhaps by giving him a better understanding of the nature of human societies. We live on a decayed vocabulary. When I came through Paris I was pleased to find at my flat these lines in a pamphlet which three young men had sent me: "There is no opposition between 'individual' and 'social,' for they derive from one another. The liberating truth which we put forward as the fundamental principle of a civilization to be built, is the condition of the liberation of personality. . . . It is treason, therefore, to accept collective society as a makeshift and submit to the machine. It is likewise treason to make collective society an end in itself and deify the machine." Neither submit, nor deify. Dominate. But shall we be willing to do so?

SEPTEMBER 12TH.—*Geneva.*

The Assembly hall looks more like a school than a parliament. . . . Surprising to see greybeards on those benches. . . . The kindergarten of peace. . . . During a speech by Sir Robert Borden which I cannot hear properly, I note on the margin of my agenda paper some

APHORISMS WRITTEN DURING A SESSION
OF THE LEAGUE OF NATIONS

Here is a parliament of all the nations on this globe, met to provide laws for themselves. Which does it look like? A class-room, a town council's room, a Protestant conventicle. This simplicity is reassuring in itself. Anything that reminds men of so many familiar spectacles could only be human. A healthy society, after the pangs of childbirth, must bring forth desks, a speaker's platform, conventions; from this atmosphere of boredom I recognize that the League, a society of nations, has not brought forth a monster.

*   *   *

The annual Assembly is more of a religious ceremony than a political discussion; quite unwittingly the speakers there assume the tone of the preacher; the word "Peace" recurs here in every sentence like the word "God" in other temples, and it is uttered in just the same manner.

*   *   *

Every year, in the first week of September, a great sacred orator (Father Briand, or the Rev. Arthur Henderson) preaches a solemn sermon in the League Assembly on a text of the Covenant. Then the congregation sing their favourite hymns: Hymn No. 159, "Disarmament—Security"; or Hymn No. 163, "Security—Disarmament"; or Hymn No. 137, "Must we, gentlemen, let politics come before economic facts?"

It is an excellent thing for the miscreant to yield to the discipline of the Churches; ceremonial soothes and quells the passions.

*   *   *

In the notes above, and in these that follow, I mean no irony; I am only trying to give an exact description of an institution which I believe to be useful. Its real machinery is more secret. Like the mechanisms of any modern society, it consists of a permanent bureaucracy, sittings of committees, lobby conversations. The Assembly is necessary for the prestige of the League, as reviews and parades are for regimental discipline.

* * *

At Geneva, verbal boldness must be in inverse proportion to the war budget of the Power represented by the orator.

* * *

Taboos can only be raised in a society which is gathering strength. The League is not yet twelve years old; in a decade or two it will be possible to allow irony and enthusiasm. Meanwhile, let everyone get accustomed, without disgust or alarm, to seeing those monstrous creatures—foreigners.

* * *

The institution of Geneva would really be indispensable if it only served to bring hostile statesmen face to face with each other. At a distance the mental picture of an unknown enemy takes on the most detestable features. Face to face, a Rumanian and a Hungarian are astounded to see men, and pleasant men too.

* * *

Whatever surprises is impolite. Commonplaces are comforting. At Geneva the art of saying nothing has been brought to its highest point of perfection. The more empty a speech, the more do the experts in the lobbies exclaim on its subtlety. The few positive elements floating in this transparent void assume, in contrast, a singular brightness, ill-understood by the layman. He tries to judge them on their face value, which is small, and not in relation to the context, which heightens them. But the real expert can discern allusions there, as well hidden as those of the old maids at Combray when they thanked Swann for his roses.

* * *

In the lobbies you will hear certain persons regretting that a speaker was not more precise. Make no mistake: those are his enemies, looking for an imprudence with which to lay him low.

* * *

The happiest result of Geneva is not that it has "given the death-blow to the old diplomacy," but that it has given the tone and subtleties of that diplomacy to the statesmen who despised it. Under various names, Monsieur de Norpois never leaves the Geneva platform.

* * *

Decision at Geneva must be made unanimously. It is therefore necessary to find formulas that seem to be hollow (and enable everyone to vote for them) and yet contain, well tucked away, the necessary undertaking. They manage to do it.

* * *

"Dull yourselves," said Pascal. Devotional practices are a path to faith. The hostile statesmen coming to Geneva and living amongst believers soon feels his contempt being watered down. Every politician has a desire to please. Despite himself, his tone is not that of Berlin, or London, or Rome, or Paris. He still maintains his heresies, but

with the Genevan unction. Before long he will be singing in the choir.

* * *

The lobbies of Geneva are the first sketch of a world
public opinion.

* * *

"These speeches and committees and resolutions soothe
anxiety but do not cure it. . . . A narcotic is not a remedy,
only an expedient." All quite true, but in an acute crisis
the patient must be soothed in order to make his sickness
curable.

* * *

The loves and hatreds of the peoples are based not on
sober thoughts, but on memories, fears and phantasms.
There are such things as collective psychoses. A people,
like an individual, can be the victim of an inferiority complex that makes it shy, timid, and irritable. Thus the
Germans believe they cannot inspire affection, the French
that they cannot be organized, the English that they cannot be logical. These obscure and fallacious ideas should
be studied and stripped bare.

* * *

The mental maladies of nations, like those of individuals, have often a physical cause. An economic crisis
is toxic to the mind and sets up an inexplicable uneasiness.
Research into the stability of prices and monetary reform
will perhaps prove the surest cure for aggressive chau-
vinism.

* * *

The League of Nations is often blamed for the slowness of its methods, but I should be tempted to praise them for that. Every civilization ought to deaden the reflexes of the brute in man by a set of reducing gearratios. In questions affecting territorial claims, a question adjourned is often more than half-solved. "It is urgent that we should wait," a model old diplomat used to say.

* * *

The League of Nations can no more guarantee peace than a doctor can guarantee a cure. Is that any reason for giving up the doctor?

* * *

Whether the peoples like it or not, their destinies are now so interwoven that the League of Nations cannot now disappear. If some catastrophe swept it away to-morrow, it would rise again under another name. As Gilbert Murray has well said, the League may not be efficacious, but it is certainly indispensable.

* * *

Readers of these aphorisms will think me sceptical, and praise or blame me according to their own feelings with regard to the League of Nations. But those who have read this journal will realize, on the contrary, how serious I am in attaching great importance to ceremonial in the collective life of the peoples. Wasn't it on the journey I took on the first day of these holidays that I noted, in connection with Malinowski's book, the importance of the conventions amongst primitive people? In any matter of relations between different peoples we are primitives. It is full circle.

SEPTEMBER 13TH.—I was wrong last month when I criticized Alain's phrase about the pilot in the storm. Here, at Geneva, one realizes better how the man of action ought to steer as the waves come, and beware of far-flung projects. In Time and Reality problems are never as Intellect imagined them. Questions that looked the most dangerous are suddenly resolved one day by circumstances, or by natural changes. Perhaps the Polish Corridor will quite soon cease to be a difficulty. How? Why? We cannot foresee. But it is possible that just when the European perils of 1931 vanish into a thin smoke, other events, inconceivable to-day, will become urgent and formidable. More than once the world believed in a war on account of Morocco; it came on account of a murder in Bosnia. It was with an inaccurate comparison that I answered Alain when I said that "the pilot knows that he is sailing to Havre and is certain of reaching there." For the Ocean of Time has only one coast, that of our birth. We do not know the ever-receding, inaccessible shores towards which the blind winds, the everlasting tides, are driving us. We can only steer towards some great light, such as peace, and try to keep the vessel afloat.

SEPTEMBER 14TH.—I have not been well during the whole of my stay in Geneva. However, I have not been at all unhappy, for I am surrounded by friends. But the nights are hard. Unable to sleep, I re-read this journal.

What are the thoughts to which all this reading and brooding has brought me this summer? To-day, September the fourteenth, nineteen hundred and thirty, looking over a sleeping Geneva, what do I believe?

I believe that the world of appearances is the only one that will ever be known to us, that our spirit cannot attain to an essential reality distinct from these appearances, that in any case the very nature of such a reality is inconceivable to us, and that the sole reality for man is the shadows of the cavern as perceived by him or by other men.

I believe that human wisdom has discovered certain connections between these shadows, and that many of them are obedient to certain laws, possibly statistical but still consistent, which allow men to divine and to shape the future in an always increasing, yet eternally small, measure. Other shadows there are which elude the mind and can be apprehended only by the heart. Others again move remotely in a flux that offers no foothold at all. Disease and war produce evils so terrible that it should be possible to bring men to combine against the fates.

I believe that a man of courage should recognize not only the hypothetical nature of all human knowledge, but also the ability of the intelligence, backed by experience, to make continual adjustment of the hypothesis in order to make it conform as closely as possible to the ever-invisible model whose movements it helps us to foretell.

I believe that the human will, free within those narrow bounds in which more powerful forces enclose it, is, in the actual state of our knowledge, a necessary and possible hypothesis. I believe that man can give pledges and live up to them: I believe that, under the clockwork vault of the stars, he should do his best to create relatively stable societies, subject to conventions recognized as such, but respected because they alone can give a sense of peace and security to savage and unhappy animals. . . .

Three o'clock in the morning. A touch of fever. I must try to sleep.

THE HIDDEN TREASURE

W HAT is the meaning of life?" I brooded.
It was a Sunday in June. The walls were warm
under the glare of sun, and at open windows sat men in
their shirtsleeves dozing over the newspapers. In my post
was a thick, heavy letter from America. I had opened
it first.

"What is the meaning of life?" wrote the American
symposiarch. "The astronomers have taught us that the
whole of human history is but a moment in the trajectory
of a star. The historians have shown us that all progress
is chimerical, that all greatness ends in decadence; the
psychologists, that love is merely a phenomenon of local-
ized congestion. The life of our societies is but a pullulation of human insects, a planetary mildew which will
some day disappear. Nothing is certain, except defeat
and death, a sleep from which no one has yet awoken.
. . . Do you not think that modern Science, by disclosing
these truths and expelling from the heavens the divinities
who formerly dwelt there, has robbed us of the illusions
which alone enabled men to live? If you do not think
so, can you tell us what is the meaning of life to you, what
is the mainspring of your energy? Where do you find
your consolations and hopes? In fact—on what hidden
treasure do you live?"

A whiff of hot tar rose from the street, and the snorting

of a motor-car. A bareheaded woman limped past, carrying cherries in her basket. A butcher's boy made his tricycle zig-zag across the empty burning street. "What is the meaning of life?" I thought. "What is the mainspring of my energy?" I thought. "Upon what hidden treasure are they living, that butcher, that lame woman, and that chauffeur?" I thought. A maidservant leaned out; a policeman looked up. My fancy turned to the fictitious. . . .

I

First of all (I said to myself), a rocket-shell capable of carrying men to the moon has been constructed. Esnault-Pelterie has succeeded not only in going beyond the zone of terrestrial gravity, but also, by means of rockets discharged backward, in checking the downward fall so as to make the shock of landing easy and harmless. A first shell, manned by Frenchmen, has made the circuit round the moon, lateral rockets enabling it to take the necessary turns, and it has come back to its starting-point without serious accident. Some Englishmen have thereupon volunteered to form an expedition to land on the moon itself. They have set off in four shells, taking with them the materials necessary for making oxygen, for reversing the shell and propelling it back to the Earth.

Here it would be necessary to describe the arrival on the Moon, the desolation of the place, the setting-up of the oxygen factory, the solemn establishment of a General Government of the Moon. On a heavenly body having neither atmosphere nor steam, the production of oxygen and of some synthetic foodstuff would be difficult. But there is nothing to prevent the story being set in a future when such a synthesis is practicable.

The next chapter, ten years later, shows the colony prospering. Young people have married, children have been born, the oxygen market is well supplied, the housewives going there every morning with their balloons on their arms; in fact, it is possible to live, to love, to make a career, to think, and to suffer on the Moon. But the colony, with limited mechanical resources, has been unable to build the shell for returning, or even to communicate with the Earth. Meanwhile, all these Englishmen continue to behave just as if they were in England. The Governor, Sir Charles Solomon, and Lady Solomon, dress for dinner every evening. On the King's Birthday, Sir Charles gives the toast of His Majesty, and all the colonists, men and women, murmur "The King!" through their oxygen masks. An affecting picture.

Part two: Two hundred years have elapsed. The Moon is now inhabited by the seventh generation of Terrestrials. The greatly increased population are happy enough, and all these beings who have been born on the Moon can scarcely imagine another type of life. They have been taught in the schools that they are the subjects of an invisible King whose palace is very far away, on the gleaming globe of the Earth, but the best minds don't believe it. British conventions, however, still control the activities of life, and the public laws are promulgated in the name of the King of Great Britain and Ireland, Emperor of India, Protector of the Moon.

The reader then views the birth of an iconoclastic doctrine amongst the Anglo-Lunaries. A group of students and politicians organize a campaign against the persistence of the Terrestrial legend. Who has ever seen this King in whose name they are ruled? Has not the time come to forget these out-of-date Anglo-Terrestrial conventions and to live a free life? Amongst the younger generation these theories meet with great success, but they are a vexation to the Conservative Party. "Beware!" say the Conservatives. "If you strip the Earth planet of our King and of the legendary Englishmen who bequeathed us our traditions, you will be making Lunary life extremely difficult. What meaning will your life have for you then? What will be the mainsprings of your energy? On what hidden treasure will you live?"

And indeed events seem to justify those who argue thus, for this is a period of melancholy and romantic despair amongst the Lunar youth. Attempts at sexual freedom produce deep disorder of the mind. Boredom, as often happens, goes hand in hand with liberty, and riot follows in the wake of boredom. The people are restless, men are disquieted, and literature is excellent. For the first time a great writer appears on the Moon, a lyrical philosopher who rapidly acquires astonishing influence over the young. His most famous book is entitled "The Pastures of the Moon"; and to give a few notions of his teaching, my story would include certain extracts from this work.

"The Pastures of the Moon" is supposed to be addressed to an imaginary disciple, Selenos. "Why, Selenos, do you seek the meaning of life elsewhere than in life itself?

241

Does the King of whom our legends tell really exist? I do not know. What matter to me, Selenos? I know that the mountains of the moon are beautiful when they are lit by the terrestrial crescent. If some day the King should appear in a shell like that of which our poets tell, guided by regal rockets, I shall recognize him. If he remains, as from the day of my birth he has remained, silent and invisible, I shall doubt his reality; but I shall have no doubts, Selenos, of life, of the beauty of the moment, of the happiness of action. The sophists are teaching you to-day that life is but a short movement of the trajectory of a star. What are you, Selenos, to the stars, or the stars to you? They are saying that nothing exists but defeat and death. But I say to you that nothing exists but victory and life. What do we know of our death, Selenos? Either the spirit is immortal and we shall not die, or the spirit dies with the body and we cannot live our death. And so, Selenos, live as if you were eternal, and do not believe that your life is changed because they have proved to you that the Earth is empty. You are not living on the Earth, Selenos, but in yourself, yourself alone." It is in allusion to this famous passage that a Lunary who seems to be out of touch with reality is currently said to be "earthstruck."

2

And this fiction, I thought, would be a possible answer to the American editor.

Opposite me, on the torrid balcony, a woman in a mauve dressing-gown was carefully arranging pots of boxwood, a geranium, a table. On the edge of the gutter a bird had perched, and with quick neat movements of its head was seeking scraps of food. Other fictions could be imagined, I thought. You could imagine an avenue in a park, crossed by two unbroken files of brown ants. One lot are coming from the ant-hill, the others are returning to it. They are all employed on a task of public utility, for they consult together, and each one of them, on meeting the another ant going in the opposite direction, stops it and feels it. At this moment the left-hand line is halted by one ant, doubtless an eloquent one, who is waving his antennæ in the middle of the path.

The antennæ of the Wise Ant say this: "You have been able to believe, and I have believed with you, my brethren, that the world of ants is the only important one, that it is watched over by the Great Ant, and that so lofty and noble a sentiment is devotion to the common ant-hill that it justifies our toils and torments. In very sooth, I told myself, it is hard to carry across these vast and perilous deserts, hemmed in by high mountain ridges of turf, our scraps of straw and our dead insects, with never a moment's rest. It is heroic thus to brave water, landslides, voracious birds, and those enormous twin masses which appear in the sky and crush hundreds of ants in one rhythmic movement. But this heroism, I used to believe, is easy when one is vowed to the most glorious of all ant-hills.

"Alas, my brethren, I have been studying and pondering and comparing, and this is what I have come to understand. This ant-hill of ours, which we have thought to be the centre of the world and the peculiar care of the Great Ant, is just like thousands of other ant-hills, each one of which is inhabited by thousands of ants who believe, every ant-jack of them, that their city is the very navel of the world. Are you astounded? But that is nothing! Ants may form a race beyond numbering, but yet they are only one race amongst thousands of races, one form amid the infinitely multiple forms of life. Do you protest, O ants? There is more to come. Not only is the ant merely one form amongst forms, but—I am afraid to utter the words, so grievously do they wound my pride —but it is one of the weakest and most scorned of forms. Do you wave your antennæ? Learn then as I have done, to divine the thoughts of those twin masses which so rhythmically crush into the dust the heroic legions of the ants. They belong to monstrous beings, so vast that we cannot see them, so powerful that we cannot imagine them, creatures to whom it is humiliating to think: 'We are ourselves but ants in the eyes of God.' You threaten? You turn angry? O, brother ants! You can pardon them, for they too are led astray by pride, even in their humility. The Earth on which they reign is but a splash of mud, and the duration of their race an instant in eternity.

"And there, my brethren, is what I, the Wise Ant, have come to understand by observing men, and the movements of the sands and the stars. So, having seen for myself that all is vanity, I say this to you: 'Why toil? Why carry bits of straw and corpses of butterflies? Why cross the perilous deserts of the avenues in long drudging files?'

"For what will be the fruit of your labour on this earth? You will rear one more generation of ants which in its turn will labour and suffer and be crushed under the huge feet of men. And these ants in their turn will rear other ants, and so on into time infinitely distant and infinitely near when the Earth will be no more than a dead world. That is why I, the Wise Ant, having pondered these matters, now say to you: 'Halt! Cease your vain toils! Be dupes no longer! Know that there is no Great Ant, that progress is illusion, that your desire to work is only a result of heredity, that nothing is certain on the Earth but the defeat and death of ants—a sleep from which there is no awakening. . . .'"

Such is the message transmitted by the antennæ of the Wise Ant whilst he bars the road to the procession of toilers. But a young ant thrusts him quietly aside. "That's all very well, comrade," he says, "but we've got our tunnel to dig."

3

Yes, I thought, that story too would be a possible answer to the American philosopher. Science, he says, shows that the life of our societies is a mere pullulation of human insects, a planetary mildew. But does not even an insect desire to live? Does not a mildew seek to persevere in its existence? In any case, is it true that Science destroys man's faith in himself? What has Science done if it has not offered mankind efficacious prescriptions for the transformation of the world in which he has to live? Before Science, as after it, human societies were mildews. What has changed, except that these growths have altered the planet a little for the better?

"The change," the American philosopher would say, "lies in the fact that before Science these growths did not recognize themselves as such. These insects did not admit that they were insects, but believed in the pre-eminent dignity of man. Demons, genii, gods, leaned always over their activities, dictating them. The hope of a future life made them forget the miseries of earthly life. Rites and Laws, sustained by a supernatural authority, preserved them from doubt and anguish. But what gods to-day lend to Laws the power of their name? Osiris had succeeded to the tribal God, Jupiter to Osiris, Jehovah to Jupiter. Is it in Einstein's or in Eddington's name that you are going to impose limits to desire?"

A puff of wind rippled the shadows of the sun-blinds on the white wall. It is true, I reflected, that man cannot live without rules. But an instinct warns him of them. As soon as some catastrophe shatters the pattern, he weaves it round himself anew. Now he makes it into the commandments of God, now into the teachings of Science, now into the decrees of an earthly King. But what matter? If we obliterate the reality of the symbol, as happened with my Lunaries, are the laws any less wise for that? Shall we not one day end by accepting them for what they are—necessary and shifting conventions? Shall we not one day admit that any proposition beyond the reach of human experience is a thing of no certainty?

We know that we do not know. Is that such a dreadful confession? Is it a new reflection, and did Socrates ever say otherwise?

Evening was falling. Already the concierge in his braces was dragging out his chair on to the pavement. Lights were appearing in the windows of respectable homes, showing the laid tables. What is my hidden treasure, I asked myself? This revulsion from a doctrine? This love of action? The roofs turned suddenly darker, and behind them a milky gleam poured into the sky. O Selenos, I thought. . . . The Moon was rising.

"HOW much?" I asked, indicating to M. Cherkaouen the curved dagger with its almost plain sheath.

He stopped and murmured a few words in Arabic. Bowing, the merchant kissed the plump hand which emerged from the white *gandoura*.

". . ." said the merchant.

M. Cherkaouen smiled in his collar of white beard.

"He said fifty francs. Offer him thirty. . . . That will be all right."

We were in the *souks* of Marrakesh. Tall negroes astride minute donkeys were calling *"Balek!"* as they parted the crowd. As if by miracle the tightly-pressed people on foot opened a passage-way. Between two plains of white cloth a narrow horizontal slit showed the eyes of the women; they seemed beautiful. As M. Cherkaouen passed, the old men sitting in the booths saluted, raising a hand to brow or breast.

"These merchants," he said, "are not like yours. They keep no accounts, and know nothing of inventories or net costs. . . . No. . . . they buy, they sell, they live. . . . If the end of the year leaves them with any money, then some put it into stock, others into land or houses. . . . The wisest buy women, or carpets. . . ."

"Have they no banking accounts?"

We were entering the *souk* of the dyers. The copper

bowls gleamed in the shadows; the air smelt of washed wool and indigo; on to the pegs of one stall an Arab boy was hooking skeins of ruddy violet, of bluish green.

"A Moslem cannot have a banking account," said M. Cherkaouen decisively. "Our religion forbids us to lend with interest. To make money fructify by commerce is lawful, but money by money is against the will of God."

"But, M. Cherkaouen, you are a well-paid official and you have no commerce of your own; don't you bank your money? Do you not buy shares?"

"I?" he said. (We were crossing the *souk* of the smiths; hammers sang; two crystal notes, one high, one low, beat time as we walked.) "I? And how should I own shares without ceasing to be a good Moslem? Yes, it has sometimes happened that I have been obliged to deposit sums of money in a bank, but in such cases I have always warned the banker that I could not accept interest."

"But surely, M. Cherkaouen, a Moslem must think of the future, like a Christian or a Jew. . . . When you are old, or when these merchants can no longer go on working . . ."

"In old age," he said, "a man has few needs, and to satisfy them he can easily sell off part of the property he has gained during the summer of his life. An old man needs women but little, not much food, and a smaller garden for shorter walks."

"But we must anticipate everything, M. Cherkaouen. . . . Suppose the old man lives to be even older than he expected, and has already sold off all his goods, would it not be desirable for him to have a life income, a few pence, a certainty that he would not die of starvation?"

"His children ought to prevent that," he answered.

"And if he has no children, or if they are dead?"

"Then," said he, "God will provide."

*   *   *

We were walking through a cloud of perfume. Rose petals and orange blossom were tumbling from the flat straw baskets. *"Balek!"* cried the donkeymen. The women were buying flowers. *"Salaam!"* said the old men to M. Cherkaouen. The sun was stabbing through the reeds. M. Cherkaouen moved on with his long nomad's stride that pushed the sandal forward.

"God will provide," I reflected. . . . (In front of a tailor's booth two little boys were stretching the black thread and the white thread to be twisted to make a chainstitch broidery under the needle.) "Do you really believe," I said aloud, "that God is for ever leaning over this speck of mud, observing the destiny of each one of us, ready to intervene if the old man dies of hunger or if the innocent man is dispossessed of his wealth?"

"Do you not believe so?" he said, looking at me with surprise.

"I should like to believe it," I said, "but I confess that if I look round me I cannot see the results of this benevolent wisdom. I see the wicked triumphant, the ambitious rewarded, the assassin firm in the saddle, the just man stricken with hideous maladies. I see the coquette surrounded by subjected men and the virtuous woman spurned."

"You think that you see these things," he said, "because you attach too much importance to the present. . . . I too, when young, was indignant when my enemy got the better of me by intrigue. . . . In those days I was eager to defend myself, to give battle in my turn, to denounce falsehood. . . . Afterward I understood better the spectacle of life. . . . I saw that the wheel revolves, that by waiting long enough and without raising my finger, my enemy is entangled in his own falsehoods, totters and falls. . . ."

"What! Will you maintain that you have never beheld the guilty dying unpunished? Then this Morocco of yours is very different from the lands which I have observed! In Europe, in America . . ."

"Excuse me," said M. Cherkaouen. (An old merchant stopped him to sprinkle liquid from a flask on him, and again we were surrounded with the scent of orange flowers.) "Excuse me. . . . Certainly, I too have seen the wicked die before their chastisement. But I know that God will punish their children, or the children of their children, or the tenth generation. . . . And above all I know that it is vain for me to concern myself therewith, for man does not alter that which is written."

"*Balek!*" cried the donkeymen. At the entrance to the *souks,* in the square of Djem-el-Fna, five blind negroes were asking alms. One of them stood alone in front of the group, singing a plaintive phrase over and over again. "Amen" answered the four others, and then the chant began again. The passers-by gave. M. Cherkaouen bade us farewell. Crouching motionless along the walls, all thought banished from their minds, men were sleeping away their lives, with open eyes.

*   *   *

"God will provide," I thought. (The Arab story-teller was talking in the centre of a ring of white cloth.) "Man does not alter that which is written. . . . Ah, how sure of that teaching he seems! What quiet certainty he infuses into his life! But we, the children of Europe and America, are incapable of this passivity; we do alter the things that are written; we do not accept God's universe and God's justice; we look ahead, we calculate, we arrange, we prophesy. . . . Yes," my thoughts ran on, "yes, we prophesy, we make mistakes, we act, we undo our own actions, we produce, and our products overwhelm us with poverty. . . . Are we any wiser than these merchants who buy women and carpets and enjoy the strength of the body whilst it is still young?"

With their large eyes wide open in their heads of antique bronzes, some *chleuh* dancers moved this way and that, tense, working towards some invisible spasm. "Man does not alter that which is written. . . ." I pondered. Who was it who had made almost the same remark to me in a totally different setting? "Man does not alter that which is written. . . ." Yes, at the door of a house in Normandy, looking down a sheltered valley; a hill closed it in; horses were galloping under the gnarled apple-trees; the silence could be felt against the distant hum of a motor. "There is nothing to be done," the banker said to me. . . . "Rash men must be left to

perish," the banker said to me. . . . "Whatever one attempts," he said, "prolongs the crisis by hindering the
action of economic laws." And he stooped to pluck a
sprig of honeysuckle.

"Nature must take her own course," said the financier.
"Man does not alter that which is written," said M. Cherkaouen. A hectic drumming stirred the dancers on. The
cows were slowly turning beside the white barriers. In
misfortune the wisdom of the sedentary and the wisdom
of the nomad joined hands. The Occidental, tamer of
natural forces, accepted for a time the universe of God.
On the dusty square a crouching people unconcernedly
awaited their destiny.

ECONOMIC RELATIVITY

IF, in the year 1240, the peasants of Normandy or Brittany could have had described to them the institutions which seem to us so natural to-day—the independent farmer, the château with no armed men, the administration of justice in the name of the people by regular and official judges—the picture would have surprised them to the point of incredulity.

If, before the War, and apart from socialist or communist circles, an essayist had discussed the chances of the survival of capitalism, he would not have been taken seriously. The régime of private property had every appearance of being one of the necessary outcomes of human nature. A captain of industry had no more doubts about his rights over his own factory than a feudal lord of the twelfth century had about his rights over his fief.

Will capitalism and private property go to join feudalism and seignorial rights in the unfamiliar museums of archaic institutions? A whole political party believes so, and one nation, Russia, is already exploring a new economic system. Has she succeeded? Is it not possible that capitalism, before giving place, like every human creation, to other self-engendered forms, still has years or centuries of vigour within itself? Is it a young institution overcome by growing-pains, or a crumbling system already doomed? What should the capitalist states do to remedy

those infirmities, which could so easily become mortal?—
Such are a few of the questions which, in my opinion,
every enquiring mind should face in the year 1932.

I

One certainty is, that none of these questions would be
so pressing were it not for the Russian experiment. Not
that it is easy at the present moment to give an honest
judgment regarding that experiment. It is one of the
most curious phenomena of our time that impartial men
(or men believing themselves to be so) find it impossible
to obtain trustworthy information regarding conditions in
the new Russia. The existence of a censorship casts suspicion on the testimony of Russians and even on that of
foreign correspondents resident in Russia. The shortness
of their visits, their ignorance of the language, the super-
vision of their guides, deprive the accounts of travellers of
much of their value, and leave them almost completely at
the mercy of the preconceived ideas, favourable or otherwise, which they were anxious to verify when they set out.

In spite of, or possibly because of, this ignorance, Soviet
Russia stimulates the imagination. We do not know
whether it is successful, but we cannot be blind to the
fact that it endures. Its adroit leaders are ingenious in
building up an impression of success. Their Five Year
Plan was a fine discovery. That formula contains a blend
of exactness and mystery which is at once perturbing and
satisfying to the mind. Moreover, it is not merely a formula. The capitalist engineers and business men who
have visited Russia within the last year have come back,

not converted, but surprised. Builders of factories themselves, they cannot withhold admiration from those gigantic examples which are being constructed over there. True, building is not difficult in itself: the problem is not to create a tool-kit, but to use it under conditions of productivity and wages superior to those of the capitalist régimes, and it is not proved that this problem will be solved. No matter: viewed at a distance, the effect produced is striking.

For over two years the capitalist countries have been passing through a formidable crisis. The machine seems to be out of order. The numbers of unemployed rise, and the necessity of providing for them forces the various countries to live on their reserves. It is only natural that communism appears as a refuge to two groups of human beings. One of these consists of the unfortunate people who have lost their fortune or their work, and lay the blame for their personal misfortune on "the system." The other consists of the intellectuals, who are startled by the inability of the capitalists to secure a reasonable organization of production and distribution, and are attracted by the obvious logical strictness of the Russian organization. To both classes of malcontents the U.S.S.R. provides a nucleus of crystallization. The existence of a communist Russia endows the crises of over-production and unemployment with a new character, at once deep-seated and dangerous. But it is none the less certain that since the War these crises in themselves have apparently assumed a more serious and widespread character than formerly. We must seek the reason why.

2

The property-owner's right to do as he pleases with what belongs to him (saving respect for law), and his right to unlimited aggrandizement of his property, are part of a very old-established system which, all in all, has produced wonderful results. Nearly everywhere, and throughout the whole of recorded history, human civilization has rested on this foundation. The hope of gain, the will to increase one's power, the desire to bequeath it to one's children, have produced an energy of toil and a wisdom of saving resulting in that prodigious accumulation of capital which, under the form of houses, cultivated fields, livestock, furniture, objects of art, and every other form of wealth, constitutes the framework of our spiritual civilization. At the present moment one may be the champion or the adversary of capitalism; it seems to me that an historian can hardly fail to recognize the greatness of its effects in the past.

In the nineteenth century, and then in the twentieth, the system of private property was profoundly altered by the development of machinery and the concentration of great industries. That story has often been told, and here I wish only to pick out two points:

(*a*) A new feudalism was created by the great profits made during this period. Family businesses were handed down like feudal holdings in dynasties of manufacturers or traders. Millions of workers accepted the suzerainty of the masters who provided them with work. Until 1880 (and even, in many countries, until 1900) the working classes in practice left political power in the hands of these Notables. The heroic figures of banking, trade, and industry engaged in Homeric battles in which defeat meant bankruptcy, sometimes suicide. As with all the warfares of the castles, the cottages paid a heavy price. But the public likes the tournament, and there are great masters just as once there were great lords. In the United States, a country where the feudalism of business is still strong and primitive, the populace, until the last great slump and notwithstanding frequent wounds from the splinters, admired the way in which the great jousters of Wall Street handled their lances.

(*b*) The development of certain industries has been so rapid that the isolated capitalist has no longer been able to find in his personal profits the new capital so essential to him. Whence has come the flourishing of the joint-stock company, with a total transformation of the nature of property. In Balzac's day a man like old Grandet owned poplars, fields, houses, gold, and, as one part of his fortune, State bonds. At the present day a Parisian wage-earner will own shares in an oil concern with its head office in Amsterdam, in a copper mine which he thinks is in Spain but is really in the Argentine, in a rubber plantation with its trees being tapped in Java or Sumatra. This participation of small investors in great concerns has induced the superficial observer to talk of a democratization of property. But this democracy actually resembles political democracy only inasmuch as they are both plutocracies. These great businesses are administered by a small number of men who remain all-powerful, who settle contracts and fix dividends, and who are freed from all serious control by the very multiplicity of their shareholders.

The consequences of these transformations of private property have not been happy. The results are: discontent on the part of the small capitalist, who has lost the sense of security and confidence; the anarchy of a feudalistic society in which, as everybody strives only to develop his own undertakings without regard to the general requirements of the market, over-production is fatal; the accumulation of vast revenues in the hands of a few men who cannot spend them to satisfy their own needs, and divert these forces from the normal course of the economic cycle, using them to multiply still further means of production which are already too numerous; periodical crises, perhaps inevitable, but the magnitude of which might have been regulated by a more intelligent control over speculation and production; and lastly, unemployment, a grave and automatic consequence of over-production.

A diagnosis of the evils engendered by leaving such complex machinery to its own devices was possible, and was made, in the nineteenth century. But the symptoms then seemed harmless, and indeed negligible. Widening markets had caused the illusion that a continuous expansion of production was possible. By closing a large number of these markets, by industrializing nations which hitherto had only been purchasers, by multiplying the customs barriers of Europe, the War made the oscillations of trade so extremely wide that it became difficult for bourgeois civilization to withstand them. Two attitudes remain possible. The first is to think that these evils are not a necessary outcome of the régime of private property, and that it would become once more efficacious if certain modifications were made in the formulas of our economics. The second, that of the Russians, is to declare that every capitalist society must necessarily produce these harmful results, and that the sole remedy is communism.

3

What elements of strength does communism contain? In the first place, it is an economic dictatorship. In the capitalist world we have had experience of such methods. It is often forgotten that the first great experiment in international socialist economics was made by the Allied Powers between 1915 and 1918. During that period the world's shipping fleets were controlled by the Interallied Shipping Board, and in America the War Industries Board, under the direction of Bernard Baruch, was an economic dictatorship. The results were amazing. Why? Because when the perpetual conflict of individual interests was effaced by the general interest, anarchy was replaced by something approximating to order.

And how were such a renunciation and self-denial then obtained from rebellious human nature? The powerful sentiment of patriotism had sealed the lips of envy, vanity and covetousness. A set of mystical values had been set up, and the individual, bowing before a force greater than himself, accepted the sacrifice. The second positive factor in communism is that it likewise puts forward a set of mystical values. It is blended with patriotism. Russia is playing a hand against the world, and many Russians who do not believe in communism are nevertheless eager to see the triumph of their country. But to members of the party the active force is a really communistic mysticism—the total abandonment of the individual to a task and to hopes which are far greater than himself. It is this mysticism which enables a harsh and exigent dictatorship to endure. The strength of the régime appears to lie in military or police forces, and in fact it is so; but no forcible régime lasts any length of time if it is not upheld by a belief. In the communist party, and particularly amongst the youth, that essential faith exists.

Would it suffice? I do not think so. The number of individuals capable of real sacrifice and selflessness is certainly not negligible, but it cannot be great enough to keep a whole country toiling. When one reads the novels of present-day Russia (for instance, Pilniak's fine book, "The Volga Flows to the Caspian Sea"), one sees how disinterestedness is strengthened by more human passions. I had always wondered what motive springs there could be in the communist economy, to replace for the common man (and it must be admitted that in Russia as elsewhere the common man exists) that desire for gain which is the great motive power of the capitalist economy. They have been made plain to me in Pilniak's book, as also in that of Calvin B. Hoover, and more recently by Stalin's speech on necessary inequalities.

To start with, the idea of gain is not entirely ruled out: "It is inadmissible," says Stalin, "that a locomotive driver should be paid like a copying clerk." When the notion of profit is set aside, that of ambition takes its place, and produces almost identical results. A man in Russia who is a good technician can become a foreman, a factory manager, or an engineer, and these functions have corresponding standards of living, a type of lodging and a prestige amongst women, which are superior to those of the common workman. Like Pilniak, Calvin B. Hoover lets one see that, in Russia, a part equal to that of keenness for profit in the capitalist world is played by political and economic intrigues, manœuvres for self-advancement, talebearing designed to undermine a superior who bars one's road to promotion. Here are to be seen once again the instincts always set free by fanaticism, disguised under a mask of virtue. Stalin's communists are like Cromwell's Puritans. Now, Puritanism and ambition are perhaps even more opposed to the harmonious existence of a society than the love of money, an impersonal and interchangeable form of power. I am doubtful whether humanity would stand to gain much by substituting the god Power for the god Money, or calumny for competition. I don't believe so.

But another and loftier sentiment is evident in the novels of the new Russia. That is, the happiness born of action. The pioneer, the man who, with unresting activity, shapes virgin nature with his own hands, has at all times been a happy man. For two whole centuries America experienced the optimism of the pioneer. After America, Russia is giving free scope to the Men Who Would be Kings. An article by an American engineer in Russian employment has expressed this feeling extremely well: "I am not a communist," he said; "all these doctrines are meaningless to me. All I know is that here I can build the biggest electric power-station, and the finest. What do I care for the rest of it all? I am happy." Read Ilin's short primer, "Moscow Has a Plan," which the Soviets distribute to their school children, and you will see there the Five Year Plan presented as a great and heroic adventure, in a style reminiscent at once of Rudyard Kipling and Walt Whitman. It is only natural that by means of such texts the enthusiasm of young men should have been successfully kindled.

4

Will this mystic enthusiasm prove lasting? Here, as in all things, one should beware of the dangerous profession of prophet. But it is a fine exercise for the wits to study Possibilities. One of these would be the swift disappearance of communism. The Five Year Plan would collapse, the Russian workers would weary of a self-denial proved to be fruitless, and would drive out their masters. This solution does not strike me as likely. The Five Year Plan will not lead Russia into a state of perfect happiness, and will leave the Russian worker with a status which will still be inferior to that of the French or American worker. But it will better his status, and the change will be great enough, with the aid of faith, to make it easy to obtain the allegiance of the Russian masses to a new Plan, which it will be prudent this time to set up for ten or even fifteen years.

It is possible that in the course of these fifteen or twenty years the Soviets will win a good deal of ground from the capitalist states, unless the latter transform their methods. The Soviets are working in a new country, where needs are on a vast scale and the natural resources immense; technical competence is afforded them by German and American engineers; they exercise absolute power. By imposing privations on their people they are building up a reserve capital more quickly than the capitalist would. There is no visible reason why they should not construct a great industrial civilization. The Pharaohs erected the Pyramids, a much more absurd undertaking, and their peoples did not rebel. Mediocre though the early output of communist production may be, it is possible that, doubly aided by foreign collaboration and a coercive system, the Russians might be able, after a series of partial checks, to correct their mistakes.

Russia's real difficulties will start with success. "Nothing fails like success." Let us assume that in thirty years the Soviet régime provides its subjects with a mode of living equal or superior to that of the workers, or even the lower middle-class, in capitalist countries. It is natural then to suppose that the following phenomena will be observed:

(a) The driving force of communist mysticism will lose strength, because all human emotions become enfeebled when they lose the glamour of novelty, because victory will put an end to the thrill of struggle, and because the desire to build and create will no longer find satisfaction. The pioneer clears the land, and it is his destiny to abolish the very background, the very privation, which gave birth to his happiness. The day comes when he replaces hostile nature by the human hive, and on that day he is at once the victor and the dispossessed. The Russians of 1960 will know the same boredom as the Americans of 1927.

(*b*) Russia will doubtless try, as America tried, to prolong the Pioneer period. And then she in her turn will experience over-production. She will find export difficult, because other nations will be bound to protect their own workers. But how, the objector may ask, can over-production arise under a communist régime? Cannot the Soviets increase rations to an unlimited extent, raise the average standard of living, shorten hours of work? And we must loyally admit that this indeed could constitute the superiority of the communist régime over an unreformed capitalist system. But it is not true at this moment, because Russia is in need, and will long remain so, of creating an implement of capital.

(*c*) A lasting improvement of the standards of life would mean the rebirth of a bourgeoisie. The Soviets will be led to distribute so many various products that they will have to grant their wage-earners the right of choice amongst the objects offered and a free disposal of their earnings. From such a right the path towards savings, and then wealth, seems easy, and the slope will be steep. About the end of the twentieth century Russia will discover private property, which will appear as a great revolutionary novelty. Property will bring the rebirth of capitalism, though different from the old form. The cycle will be complete. This at least is one of the possible progressions of the world's history; it is not perhaps the one which will actually take place. But if it be over-ingenuous to believe that capitalism is untouchable, it is no less so to regard communism as a true religion, a logical and perfect form in which human economy will be crystallized for all time.

It is also surprisingly confused thinking to set up individualism against socialism, capitalism against communism, as if one were dealing with clear concepts with well-defined outlines, whereas the reality is complex and shifting, and historical evolution makes human societies oscillate between one system and the other, without being able to stop at either. If our epoch is capable of contributing an original philosophy, it is one of absolute relativity. It is not immoral to be a capitalist, it is not criminal to be a communist; but it would be intelligent to admit that every doctrine is baneful if it is rigid. There is no such thing as economic truth; or rather, every moment has its own economic truth. Just as the scientist adjusts an hypothesis to take account of his experiment, or as the wise military leader accepts the lesson of hard fact, so the economic rulers should hold a doctrine only for the provisional co-ordination of their actions. Capitalism is capable of fashioning the economy of a revolution, and I should like it to do so. But only a process of self-transformation will save it.

THE EARTH-DWELLERS

ANOTHER FRAGMENT FROM A UNIVERSAL HISTORY PUBLISHED
BY THE UNIVERSITY OF * * * IN 1992

....

....

....

BY the end of 1970 friendly relations had been established between the Earth and most of the major planets, and terrestrial scientists became anxious to compare their own hypotheses and doctrines with those of their colleagues in other worlds. But such comparisons were often difficult, because, as is well known, the eminent physicists of Venus, Jupiter and Mars had no perception of either light or sound, and lived in a world of radiations of which we had hitherto been quite ignorant. But the theory of sensorial equivalents made rapid progress, and at the date of writing (1992) it may be said that we are capable of transposing every language of the planetary system into Earth language—except Saturnian.

One of the most interesting discoveries due to this new philology was that of books written about ourselves, the Earth-dwellers, by the scientists of foreign planets. Mankind had not the slightest idea that for millions of years past he had been under observation, thanks to instruments very much more powerful than his own, by the naturalists of Venus, Mars, and even Uranus. Terrestrial science lagged far behind the science of neighbouring bodies, and as our organs were insensitive to the radiations utilized by these observers, it was impossible for us to know that, in the most secret moments of our lives, we were sometimes within the field of vision of a celestial ultra-microscope.

Nowadays these works can be consulted by any scholar in the library of the League of Planets. They provide most commendable reading for young men eager to devote themselves to the learned sciences not only because of their great intrinsic interest, but also because of the sense of humility which they cannot fail to evoke. To observe the incredible errors made by beings of such high intelligence and so wonderfully equipped for research, one cannot refrain from reverting to a number of our own human affirmations, wondering whether we have not observed plants and animals very much as the Martians observed us.

One case in particular strikes us as worthy of careful study: that of the Uranian scholar A E 17, who published his book, "Man and His Life," in 1959.[1] Until the War that book was the standard work not only in Uranus, but also, in translations, amongst the inhabitants of Venus and Mars. To ourselves it is readily accessible because, alone amongst our fellow-planetaries, the Uranians share with us the sense of sight, which makes their vocabulary approximate closely to ours. Moreover, the experiments carried out by A E 17 were such as completely to upset the Earth throughout a period of six months; and we have

[1] Original Uranian edition, 1959. First terrestrial edition, 1982.

access to the terrestrial account of these events in the news-papers and memoirs of the time.

We propose here:

(*a*) To describe briefly a few of the events noted on our own planet in the year 1954;

(*b*) to show what interpretation the eminent A E 17 put on his own experiments.

The Mysterious Springtime

In the month of March, 1954, numerous observers throughout the northern hemisphere gave surprising re-ports of atmospheric conditions. Notwithstanding fine and cool weather, storms of the utmost violence were bursting suddenly within strictly limited zones. Ships' captains and aeroplane pilots reported to the Central Meteorological Bureau that their compasses had for several seconds behaved quite wildly for no conceivable reason. In several places, under a clear sky, people saw what appeared to be the shadow of a huge cloud passing over the ground, although no such cloud was visible. The newspapers pub-lished interviews with the eminent meteorologists, who explained that they had anticipated this phenomenon, which was due to sun-spots and would come to an end with the equinoctial tides. But the advent of the equinox only brought stranger happenings in its wake.

The "Hyde Park Hill" Incident

On the third Sunday in April, the crowds of men and women listening to the open-air orators on their pitch at Marble Arch, suddenly saw passing overhead the shadow of an invisible obstacle mysteriously interposed between the Earth and the sun. A few seconds later, from the Park railings to a point some three or four hundred yards inside the Park, there occurred an abrupt upheaval of the ground. Trees were uprooted and pedestrians tumbled over and buried, whilst those who were on the edge of the disturbed area were dumbfounded to observe that a great funnel at least three hundred feet deep had been scooped out, the soil from which had been thrown up to form a hill of corresponding height.

A policeman, giving evidence next day at the inquest on victims, said: "It all happened just as if a giant had been wielding a spade in the Park. Yes, it was just like some-one using a spade, because the outer edge of the cavity was trim and smooth, while the edge on the side where the hill came consisted of crumbling loose soil, with half-cut heads and bodies protruding from it."

Over three hundred citizens walking in the Park had been buried alive. Some who had only been covered with a light layer of earth managed to extricate themselves with some difficulty. Some, too, suddenly lost their senses and rushed down the steep slope of the ncw hill uttering dreadful shrieks. On the summit of the mound there appeared the upright figure of a Salvation Army preacher, Colonel R. W. Ward, who, with astonishing presence of mind, still shaking the dirt from his hair and clothing, began to bellow: "I told you so, brothers! You have sac-rificed to false gods, and now the Lord God is angered with his people, and the hand of the Lord God has fallen heavy upon us. . . ."

And indeed this inexplicable event bore such a likeness to certain divine punishments as described in Holy Writ, that sceptics amongst the bystanders were instantly converted, and began lives of practising religion to which they have from that moment been steadfast.

The episode enabled people to appreciate the virtues of the Metropolitan Police. Three members of the Force were amongst the victims, but a dozen others, arriving instantly on the scene, set to work on digging with great courage. Telephone messages were sent out at once to the military authorities and fire stations, and General Clark-well, the Commissioner of Police, took command of the rescue forces, and within four hours Hyde Park had resumed its normal appearance. Unfortunately, the dead numbered two hundred.

Scientists gave the most varied explanations of the disaster. The theory of an earthquake, the only reasonable one if the supernatural were ruled out, did not seem plausible, for no shock had been recorded by any seismograph. The public were fairly well satisfied when the experts informed them that it *had* been an earthquake, but an earthquake of a very special sort which they had labelled a "vertical-montiform seismic variant."

The House in the Avenue Victor Hugo

The Hyde Park incident was followed by a considerable number of similar occurrences, which attracted much less public attention because they caused no human fatalities. But at different points these strange mounds were seen taking shape with the same swiftness, each of them bordered by a precipice with sheer, clean-cut fall. In certain places these hills are still in existence: as for instance the one in the plain of Ayen in Périgord, that of Roznov in Wallachia, and that of Itapura in Brazil.

But the mysterious spade which was thus apparently wielded on bare land was now, alas, to attack human erections.

About midday on April 24, a strange noise, compared by some who heard it to that of a whizzing blade, by others to that of an extremely fine and powerful water-jet, astonished the passers-by in the region of Paris bounded approximately by the Arc de Triomphe, the Avenue de la Grande Armée, the Avenue Marceau, and the Avenue Henri Martin.

People happening to be opposite the building known as 66 Avenue Victor Hugo saw an enormous oblique cleft appear across it; the house was shaken by two or three tremors, and suddenly the whole of the top storey, occupied by the servants' rooms, seemed to crumble away as if under powerful pressure. The frenzied inhabitants appeared at the windows and on the balconies. Fortunately, although the building was literally cut in two, it did not collapse. Half-way up the staircase the rescuers came upon the fissure produced by the invisible instrument. It looked exactly as if a blade had cut through the wood of the steps, the carpet, the metal balustrade, following a line at right-angles to these. Everything in its path—furniture, carpets, pictures, books—had been cut in two with a clean stroke, very neatly. By a miracle nobody was injured. A girl sleeping on the third floor found her bed sliced obliquely across; but the cut had just missed her. She had felt no pain, but did experience a shock like that of a weak electric battery.

In this case, too, there were numerous explanations. The word "seismic" was again produced. Certain newspapers accused the architect and proprietor of the building of having used faulty materials in its construction. A communist deputy raised the question in the Chamber.

The Transportation Phenomena

Like the Hyde Park occurrence, the accident in the Avenue Victor Hugo was followed by several almost identical in kind, which we shall not recount, but which ought, as we now see, to have convinced observant minds of a hidden will engaged in the furtherance of a definite plan. In numerous countries, houses, great and small, were sundered by an invisible force. Several farmhouses, one in Massachusetts, another in Denmark, another in Spain, were raised into the air, and dropped back on to the ground, smashed to pieces with their inhabitants. The French Building in New York was cut in two. About fifty men and women met their deaths in these occurrences, but as they took place in very different countries, each isolated case being responsible only for a few victims, and also as nobody could provide an explanation, very little was said about them.

It was different with the subsequent series of happenings, which kept the whole planet in a ferment of excitement throughout May and June, 1954. The first victim was a young negress of Hartford, Connecticut, who was leaving her employers' house one morning when a post-man, the sole witness of the accident, saw her suddenly soar into the air uttering terrible cries. She rose to a height of three hundred feet and then crashed to the ground. The postman declared that he had seen no aerial apparatus of any sort overhead.

The second case of "transportation" was that of a customs official at Calais, who was also seen rising vertically and disappearing at high speed towards the English coast. A few minutes later he was found on the Dover cliffs, dead, but with no visible injuries. He looked as if he had been laid gently down on the ground; he was blue, like a man hanged.

Then began the period of the so-called "successful trans-portations." The first victim to arrive living at the end of his journey was an aged beggar, who was seized by an invisible hand when he was begging for alms in front of Notre Dame, and ten minutes later was deposited in the middle of Piccadilly Circus at the feet of a stupefied policeman. He had not suffered at all, and had the impression of having been conveyed in a closed cabin to which neither wind nor light could penetrate. Eye-witnesses of his departure had observed that he became invisible immediately after he was raised from the ground.

For several weeks longer these "transportations" continued. Once they were known to be quite harmless, they were regarded as rather comical. The choice of the invisible hand seemed to be completely whimsical. Once it was a little girl of Denver, Colorado, who found herself set down in a Russian steppe; another time a Saragossa dentist turned up in Stockholm. The "transportation" which caused most talk was that of the venerable President of the French Senate, M. Paul Reynaud, who was picked up in the Luxembourg gardens and deposited on the shore of Lake Ontario. He took the opportunity of making a journey through Canada, was triumphantly welcomed back at the Bois de Boulogne station, and this unsought publicity was probably largely responsible for his election as President of the Republic, in 1956.

It should be noted that, after their journeys, the subjects of "transportation" were smeared with a reddish liquid, that stained their clothing, for no ascertainable reason. This was the only inconvenience of these otherwise harmless adventures. After about two months they ceased, to be followed by a new and still stranger series which began with the famous episode of the "Two Couples."

The "Two Couples" Episode

The first of the two famous couples was a French one, living in a small house close to Paris, in Neuilly. The husband, Jacques Martin, was on the teaching staff of the Lycée Pasteur, a sporting and scholarly young man, and the author of a remarkable biographical study on Paul Morand. He and his wife had four children. On July 3, towards midnight, Mme. Martin had just fallen asleep when she heard that steam-like whistling which we have already mentioned, felt a slight shaking, and had the impression of being very rapidly raised into the air. Opening her eyes, she was stupefied to see that the pale light of the moon was flooding her room, a whole wall of which had vanished, that she was lying on the edge of a bed cut in two, and that on her left hand, where her husband had been lying a few seconds before, there was a bottomless gulf, above which the stars were glittering. She flung herself in terror towards the still solid edge of the bed, and was amazed (and at the same time reassured) to find that it did not wobble, although it was left with only two legs. Mme. Martin felt that she was rising no higher, but was being moved very fast in a straight line; then she was made aware, by a feeling in the heart like that which one has in a lift descending too quickly, that she was dropping. Imagining that her fall would end with a crash, she had already closed her eyes in anticipation of the final shock. But it was gentle and elastic, and when she looked round her, she could see nothing. The room was dark. Her own narrative continues:

"I put out my arm; everything was solid. The abyss had apparently closed up again. I called my husband's name, thinking that I had been passing through a nightmare and feeling anxious to tell him about it. My groping hand felt a man's arm, and I heard a strong unknown voice say in English: "Oh, my dear, what a fright you gave me!" I started back and wanted to turn on the light, but I could not find the electric switch. "What's wrong?" said the unknown. He himself turned on a light. We both uttered simultaneous cries. In front of me was a fair-haired young Englishman, with a small short nose, rather short-sighted, and still half-asleep, in blue pyjamas. Down the middle of the bed ran a crack;

sheets, mattress and bolster were all cut in two. There
was a difference of three or four inches in the level of the
two portions of the bed.

"When my bedfellow had recovered his wits, his de-
meanour in these difficult circumstances gave me a high
opinion of the British race. After a short but very excusable moment of confusion, his correctness was as complete and natural as if we had been in a drawing-room.
I spoke his language and told him my name. He told me
that his was John Graham. The place we were in was
Richmond. Looking round, I saw that the whole of one
half of my own room had accompanied me: I recognized
my window with its cherry-coloured curtains, the large
photograph of my husband, the small table with books
beside my bed, and even my watch on top of my books.
The other half, Mr. Graham's, was unknown to me. On
the bedside table there were a portrait of a very pretty
woman, photographs of children, some magazines, and a
box of cigarettes. John Graham looked at me for a very
long time, examining the background against which I had
appeared to him, and then said with the utmost seriousness: 'What are you doing here?' I explained that I knew
nothing about it, and pointing to the large portrait, I said:
'This is my husband.' Pointing likewise, he answered:
'This is my wife.' She was delightful, and the disturbing
thought came to me that she was perhaps at that very
moment in the arms of Jacques. 'Do you suppose,' I asked
him, 'that half of your house has been transported to
France at the same time as half of ours has come here?'—
'Why?' he said. He annoyed me. Why, indeed? I knew

nothing about it at all. . . . Because this affair had a sort of natural symmetry of its own.

" 'A queer business,' he said, shaking his head. 'How can it be possible?'—'It isn't possible,' I said, 'but it has happened.'

"At this moment cries were heard apparently coming from upstairs, and the same thought struck us: 'The children?' John Graham jumped out of bed and ran barefoot towards a door, the door of *his* half. He opened it, and I could hear cries, the sound of coughing, and then the Englishman's powerful voice mingling oaths with words of comfort. I made haste to rise, and looked in the mirror. My face looked just as usual. I then noticed that my night-dress was *décolletée* and looked round for my kimono; but I remembered having hung it in the half of the room which had stayed behind. Standing there in front of the mirror, I heard a pitiable voice behind me.

"The cries in the nursery were redoubled, weeping and appeals mingling with them.

" 'Come and help me,' he said in a beseeching tone.

" 'Of course I will . . . but have you got your wife's dressing-gown, and slippers?'

" 'Oh, yes, of course. . . .'

"Handing me his own dressing-gown he showed me the way to the nursery. The children were splendid. I managed to soothe them. It was the youngest, a lovely fair baby, who seemed to be suffering most. I comforted him as best I could, and took his hand; he accepted my presence.

"In this way we spent a couple of hours in that room, both in a state of mental anguish, he thinking of his wife, and I of my husband.

"I asked if we could not telephone to the police. He tried, and found that his telephone had been cut off; his wireless aerial had also been cut; the house must have been looking extremely odd. When dawn appeared, Mr. Graham went out. The children had fallen asleep. In a few minutes he returned for me, saying that really the front of the house was well worth looking at. And it was! The unknown contriver of this miracle had evidently wanted to pick two houses of the same height divided in the same way, and he had succeeded; but the styles were so different that the combined effect took one's breath away. Our house at Neuilly was of brick, very plain, its tall windows framed with stone; the English house was a small black and white cottage, with wide bow-windows. The juxtaposition of these two utterly different halves formed a most ludicrous ensemble—like a Harlequin of Picasso's.

"I urged Mr. Graham to put on his clothes and send off a telegram to France, to find out what had happened to his wife. He told me that the telegraph office did not open till eight o'clock. He was a stolid creature, apparently incapable of conceiving that in such peculiar circumstances, one could infringe regulations and knock up the telegraph-clerk. I shook him energetically, but in vain. All I could get out of him was: 'It only opens at eight.' In the end, about seven o'clock, just when he was going out, we saw a policeman arriving. He was gazing at the house in amazement, and had brought a telegram from the head of the Paris police, asking if I was there and announcing that Mrs. John Graham was safe and sound at Neuilly."

It is not worth while continuing the quotation of this narrative *in extenso*. Suffice it to say that Mrs. Graham tended Mme. Martin's children as devotedly as the latter did the little English ones, that both couples declared themselves charmed by the amiability of their companions in adventure, and that both households remained close friends to their dying days. Mme. Martin was still alive ten years ago, in her family home at Chambourcy (Seine-et-Oise).

The space allotted to this chapter in the general plan of this volume does not allow us to recount the analogous adventures which astonished mankind throughout that month of August, 1954.

The series of "sliced houses" was even longer than that of the "transportations." Over one hundred couples were interchanged in this way, and the changes became a favourite theme with novelists and film-writers. They contained an element of whimsical sensuality which was much to the public's taste. Besides, it was diverting to see (as it really happened) a queen waking up in a policeman's bed, and a ballet-girl in that of the President of the United States. Then the series stopped dead, and gave place to another. It looked as if the mysterious beings who amused themselves by disturbing the lives of humans were capricious, and quick to tire of their games.

The Caging

Early in September, the hand whose power was by now known to all the world fell upon some of the finest minds on its surface. A dozen men, nearly all chemists or physicists, men of the highest achievement, were simultaneously abstracted from different points amongst the civilized countries and transported to a clearing in the Forest of Fontainebleau.

A group of lads who had come there in the early hours of the morning to climb the rocks, noticed some old men wandering forlornly amongst the trees. Seeing that they were in difficulties, the young men tried to approach them to offer help, but were taken aback to find themselves suddenly checked by some transparent but insurmountable resistance. They tried to find a way round the obstacle, but after making a complete circle round the clearing they realized that it was completely ringed by an invisible rampart. One of the scientists was recognized by a few of the youths as their professor, and they called him by name. He did not seem to hear them. Sound could not penetrate the barrier. The celebrated personages were there like caged beasts.

Before very long they seemed to accept the situation. They were observed to be lying down in the sunlight; and then, drawing pieces of paper from their pockets, they began scribbling mathematical formulas and arguing quite cheerfully. One of the young onlookers went off to inform the authorities, and by noon many curious spectators were beginning to come on the scene. By noon the scientists were showing signs of anxiety; they were all of advanced years, and they dragged themselves rather wearily to the edge of the ring, where, seeing that their voices were not reaching anyone, they made signs that they should be supplied with food.

A few officers were present, and one of them had what appeared to be the capital notion of supplying the unfortunate men with supplies by aeroplane. A couple of hours later the drone of a motor was heard, and the pilot, passing skilfully over the circular clearing, dropped some packages of food exactly over the centre. But unfortunately, about sixty feet above the ground the packages were seen to stop in their fall, bounce back and then were left suspended in mid-air. The cage had a roof composed of the same invisible radiations.

Towards nightfall the old men became desperate, signalling that they were dying of hunger and dreaded the night chills. The anguished onlookers could do nothing for them. Were they going to witness the perishing of this remarkable assemblage of great intellects?

In the pale light of the dawn it was at first thought that the situation had not changed, but closer examination showed that quite a new setting had appeared in the centre of the "cage." The invisible hand had staged things so that the packages dropped by the aeroplane were now suspended at the end of a rope about fifteen feet above the ground, whilst alongside this rope hung another which actually reached the ground. To any young man it would have been an easy matter to swing himself up and reach the packages that held the hopes of safety. But unhappily there was little likelihood that any of these venerable men of learning could undertake this difficult gymnastic feat. They were seen walking round the ropes and gauging their strength, but none of them ventured further.

A whole day went by in this way. Night fell. Gradually the curious throng melted away. About midnight one young student took it into his head to ascertain whether the barrier of radiations still held. To his great surprise he found nothing barring his way, walked straight on, and uttered a cry of triumph. The cruel powers which had made men their toys for two whole days were consenting to spare their victims. The scientists were fed and warmed, and none of them succumbed.

*　　*　　*

Such are the chief facts which distinguished this period, at the time inexplicable, but which we now know to have corresponded to a period of experiments on the planet Uranus. We shall now give a few extracts, in our opinion the most interesting, from the book of the famous A E 17.

The reader will understand that we have been obliged to find terrestrial equivalents for the Uranian words, and the translation is only approximate. Uranian time consists of years very much longer than ours, and wherever possible we have made a transposition into terrestrial time. Furthermore, to designate ourselves the Uranians use a word which signifies, roughly, "apterous bipeds"; but this is needlessly complicated and we have in most places substituted the words "men" or "Earth-dwellers." Similarly we have translated the queer word by which they designated our cities by the word "manheaps," which gives in our view a fair suggestion of the associations of analogous ideas. Finally, the reader should not overlook the fact that the Uranian, although endowed like ourselves with the sense of sight, is ignorant of sound. Uranians communicate with each other by means of a special organ consisting of a series of small coloured lamps which flash on and off. Observing that men were without this organ, and being unable to imagine speech, the Uranian naturally supposed that we were incapable of communicating our ideas to each other.

Here we can offer only a few brief excerpts from the book of A E 17 on "Man and His Life." But we strongly advise the student to read the book in its entirety; there is an excellent school edition published with appendix and notes by Professor Fischer of Pekin.

*   *   *

MAN AND HIS LIFE

By

A E 17.

WHEN the surface of the small planets, particularly that of the Earth, is examined through an ordinary telescope, large stains may be noticed, more streaky in texture than those formed by a lake or ocean. If these stains are observed over a long enough period, they are seen to expand throughout several terrestrial centuries, pass through a period of maximum size, and then diminish, or even in some cases disappear. Many observers have thought that they were related to some unhealthy condition of the soil. And indeed nothing could be more like the development and reabsorption of a tumour in an organism. But with the invention of the ultratelemicroscope it has been possible to detect that we are here confronted by an accumulation of living matter. The imperfections of the first apparatus did not allow us to see more than a confused swarming, a sort of throbbing jelly, and excellent observers, such as A 33, then maintained that these terrestrial colonies were composed of animals joined to each other and living a common existence. With our present apparatus it is at once obvious that things are quite otherwise. The individual creatures can be clearly distinguished, and their movements can be followed. The stains observed by A 33 are in point of fact huge nests which can almost be compared to Uranian cities and are known to us as "man-heaps."

The minute animals inhabiting these towns, Men, are apterous biped mammals, with an indifferent electrical system, and generally provided with an artificial epidermis. It was long believed that they secreted this supplementary skin themselves. But my researches enable me to declare that this is not so: they are impelled by a powerful instinct to collect certain animal or vegetable fibres and assemble them in such a way as to form a protection against cold.

I use the word "instinct," and from the outset of this work I must lay stress on a clear indication of my feelings regarding a question which ought never to have been raised and has, especially during recent years, been treated with incredible levity. A curious mode of thought has become habitual amongst our younger naturalists, in attributing to these terrestrial vegetations an intelligence of the same nature as that of the Uranian. Let us leave to others the task of pointing out the distressing nature of such doctrine from the religious point of view. In this book I shall show its absurdity from only the scientific point of view. No doubt the beauty of the spectacle rouses a quite excusable enthusiasm, when one views for the first time under the microscope one of these particles of jelly, and suddenly sees the unfolding of countless lively and interesting scenes—the long streets along which Men pass to and fro, sometimes stopping and apparently exchanging speech; or the small individual nest in which a couple keep watch over a brood of young; or armies on the march; or builders at their work. . . . But for a profitable study of the psychic faculties of these animals it is not enough to profit by the circumstances that chance affords the observer. It is essential to know how to procure the most favourable conditions of observation, and to vary these as much as possible. It is necessary, in a word, to experiment, and thus to build up science on the solid base of fact.

This is what we have sought to do in the course of the long series of experiments reported here. Before embarking on their description I must ask the reader to imagine and to gauge the immense difficulties which such a project was bound to present. Long-distance experiment, no doubt, has become relatively easy since we had at our disposal the W rays, which enable us to grasp, handle, and even transport bodies through interstellar space. But in dealing with creatures so small and fragile as Men, the W rays are very clumsy and brutal instruments. In our first tests it turned out only too often that we killed the animals we desired to observe. Transmitting appliances of extraordinary sensitiveness were required to enable us to reach exactly the point aimed at, and to treat the sensitive matter with the necessary delicacy. In particular, when first carrying out the transference of Men from one point to another on terrestrial territory, we omitted to take full account of these animals' respiratory difficulties. We made them move too rapidly across a thin layer of air which envelops the Earth, and they died of asphyxiation. We had to construct a real box of rays, inside which the swiftness of transportation produced no effect. Similarly, when we first attempted the bisection and transference of nests, we did not make sufficient allowance for the constructional processes used by the Earth-dwellers. Experience taught us to prop up the nests after their division, by the passage of certain massive currents of rays.

The reader will find here a sketch-map of that portion of the terrestrial surface on which our main experiments were carried out. We would ask them particularly to note the two great manheaps on which we made our first tests, and to which we gave the names, later adopted by the astro-sociologists, of "Mad Manheap" and "Rigid Manheap."

These names we chose on account of the singularly different plans of these manheaps, one of which at once impresses the observer by its almost geometrical star-patterns of roadways, whilst the other is a complex maze of rather tortuous streets. Between "Mad Manheap" and "Rigid Manheap" stretches a gleaming line which is believed to be sea. The greatest manheap on the Earth is "Geometrical Manheap," which is even more regular than "Rigid Manheap," but is far distant from the other two, and separated from them by a wider gleaming surface.

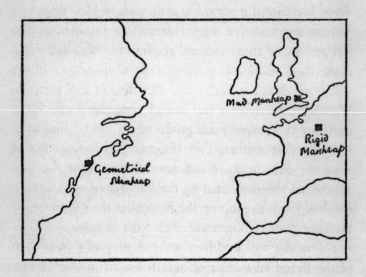

First Attempts

At what point of the Earth was it best to direct our first efforts? How must we interfere with the lives of these animals in such a way as to obtain instructive reactions from them? I must confess to real emotion when I prepared for the first time to operate on the Earth, armed with an apparatus of adequate range.

I had around me four of my young pupils, who were also deeply moved, and in turn we gazed at the charming miniature landscapes in the ultratelemicroscope. Aiming the apparatus at the "Mad Manheap," we sought a fairly open locality so as to see the consequences of our action more clearly. Tiny trees gleamed in the spring sunshine, and multitudes of small motionless insects could be seen forming irregular circles; in the middle of each of these stood an isolated insect. For a moment we speculated on the meaning of this game, but failing to find one, we decided to try an application of the rays. The effect was staggering. A hole was scooped in the ground; some of the insects were buried under the débris; and instantly an astounding activity was loosed. It really looked as if these creatures were intelligently organized. Some went to the rescue of their overwhelmed companions, others went off to get help. We then tried applying the rays on several points of the Earth, but this time we chose uninhabited areas, so as not to endanger our subjects at the very beginning of our researches. We thus learned how to reduce the power of our rays and to operate more skilfully. Being now sure of our means of action, we decided to start the first series of our experiments.

It was my plan to take individuals in a certain manheap, mark them with a touch of a brush, transport them to different points, and then observe whether the transported individual would find his way back to the original manheap. At first, as I have said, we encountered great difficulties, first because the animal died during transference, and then because we had neglected to take into account the artificial epidermis with which these creatures provide themselves. They doff these coverings with the utmost ease, and so once we had set them down again in the midst of a manheap, we lost sight of them. For the subsequent transportations we tried to mark them directly on the body, tearing off the supplementary skin; but in these cases the animal made itself a new skin as soon as it arrived in the manheap.

With a little practice my assistants were at last able to follow one particular animal with the ultratelemicroscope and keep it constantly in sight. They found that in ninety-nine cases out of a hundred, the man returns to his starting-point. I attempted the transference of two males from the same manheap—the "Mad Manheap"—with the extremely remote one which we termed the "Geometrical Manheap." After ten (terrestrial) days my esteemed pupil E X 33, who had followed them night and day with incomparable devotion, showed me them returning to the "Rigid Manheap." They had come back, notwithstanding the fact of their unfamiliarity with the places to which I had transported them; they were individuals of stay-at-home habit (we had kept them under long observation), who were obviously seeing for the first time the country where we had deposited them. How did they find the way back? Their transference had been so rapid that observation was out of the question. What was their guide? Certainly not memory, but a special faculty which we must confine ourselves to noting without claiming to explain it, so remote is it from anything in our own psychology.

These transferences raised another problem. Would the returning individual be recognized by the others? Apparently he is. Generally speaking, great excitement is to be seen in the nest when the absent one reappears. The others place their arms round him and sometimes even place their lips on his. In certain cases, however, the feelings manifested appeared to be those of rage or displeasure.

These first experiments showed that some instinct enables Men to recognize their own manheaps. The second problem to which we turned was to find out whether, amongst these creatures, there existed sentiments akin to those of Uranians, and whether, for instance, conjugal or maternal love could exist on the Earth. Such an hypothesis struck me as absurd; it attributed to the Earth-dweller refinements of feeling which the Uranian has attained only through millions of years of civilization. But the duty of the experimental scientist is to approach his subject with an open mind, and to make all his experiments without any prejudice regarding their outcome.

At night the male Earth-dweller generally rests beside his female. I asked my pupils to bisect some nests in such a way as to separate the male from the female without injuring either, and then to join up one half of Nest A with the half of Nest B, observing whether the little animals took notice of the change. For the experiment to be carried out under normal conditions, it was essential that

the selected nests should closely resemble each other; and
for this reason I instructed my collaborators to select two
nests containing cells of the same size and broods with
the same number of young. E X 33 showed me, not
without pride, two almost identical nests in the "Mad
Manheap" and the "Rigid Manheap," each of them containing a couple with four little ones. The bisection of
the houses, and their transportation, were carried out with
admirable skill by E X 33, and the results were conclusive.
In both cases the couples thus artificially put together by
us showed slight surprise at the moment of waking, ade-
quately accounted for by the movement and shock. Then,
in both cases, they remained together with no attempt at
flight, and in apparently normal attitudes. An almost
incredible fact was that, from the very first moment, each
of the two females tended the other's brood with no sign
of horror or distaste. They were plainly incapable of realizing that they were not dealing with their own offspring.

This experiment was repeated on numerous occasions.
In 93 per cent. cases, the nests and offspring were tended
by both couples. The female retains a stubborn sense of
her proper functions, without having any idea of the individuals towards which she performs this duty. Whether
the children are hers or not, she toils with equal fervour.
It might be thought that this confusion is caused by a close
resemblance between the two nests, but at different stages
we chose nests of quite different appearances, joining up,
for instance, the half of a shabby nest with the half of a
rich nest of a different species. The results were more or

less the same; Man does not distinguish between his own cell and another.

Having thus shown that in the matter of sentiment the Earth-dweller is an animal occupying a very low place in the scale of creation, we sought an appropriate means of gauging his intellectual faculties. The simplest way, it seemed to us, was to isolate a few individuals in a ray-cage and to put at their disposal food which could only be reached by means of more and more complex actions. I took particular pains to choose for this experiment certain Earth-dwellers for whom my colleague X 38 claimed signs of scientific intelligence. In Appendix A will be found the details of this experiment. It showed beyond any possible doubt that the space of time within which Man lives is extremely limited in the past and future, that he immediately forgets, and that he is incapable of imagining the simplest method of self-preservation as soon as he is confronted by problems slightly different from those which he has, by heredity, become used to solving.

After a long period of experimenting on individual Earth-dwellings, my pupils and I became familiar enough with the movements of these animals to be able to observe them in their ordinary life without intervention on our part. It is of the utmost interest to follow, as I have done, the history of a manheap through several terrestrial years.

The origin of these human societies is unknown. Why and how did these animals abandon their freedom to become slaves of the manheap? We cannot tell. It may be that in this grouping process they found a support in warfare against other creatures and against natural forces;

but it is a support for which they pay highly. No animal species is so ignorant as this one of leisure and the joy of living. In the great manheaps, and particularly the "Geometrical Manheap," activity begins at dawn and is prolonged through part of the night. Were this activity necessary, it would be comprehensible; but Man is a creature of such limited nature, so much dominated by his instincts, that he produces hardly anything beyond his requirements. Over and over again have I seen objects accumulating in the reserve stores of a manheap in such numbers that they seemed to be a source of embarrassment; and yet, only a short distance away, another group would continue to manufacture the very same objects.

Little is also known of the division of Mankind into castes. It is established that certain of these animals till the soil and produce nearly all the foodstuffs, whilst others make the supplementary skins or build nests, and others seem to do nothing but move swiftly to and fro over the planet's surface, eating and coupling. Why do the first two classes consent to clothe and feed the third? That remains obscure to me. E X 33 has written a notable thesis seeking to prove that this tolerance has a sexual origin. He has shown that at night, when the individuals of the superior caste foregather, the workers collect round the entrances to these festivities in order to see the half-nude females. According to him, the compensation of the sacrificed classes consists of the æsthetic pleasure provided by the spectacle of these easy existences. The theory strikes me as ingenious, but not so firmly based as to convince me of its truth.

For my own part, I would rather seek an explanation in Man's amazing stupidity. It is a supreme folly to be for ever seeking to explain the actions of Men by Uranian reasonings. That is wrong, profoundly wrong. Man is not guided by a free intelligence. Man obeys a fatal and unconscious incitement; he cannot choose what he shall do; he slides along haphazard, following an irresistible predetermined slope which will bring him to his goal. I amused myself by following the individual existences of certain men in whom the functions of love seemed to be the essentials of their existence. I saw how the conquest of one female to start with brought upon his shoulders all the burdens of nests and young; but not content with that first load, my male would go off in search of a second mate, for whom he set up a new nest. These simultaneous love-affairs led the wretched animal into endless battles of which I was the spectator. It mattered nothing to him; his successive woes seemed to hold no lessons for him, and he went on putting his head into his wretched adventures without seeming to be one whit the wiser after the third than after the first.

One of the strangest proofs of this inability to keep contact with the past and imagine the future, was afforded me by the frightful struggles which I witnessed between individuals of one and the same species. On Uranus it would seem a grotesque idea that one group of Uranians could attack another group, hurling on it projectiles meant to injure it, and trying to asphyxiate it with poisonous gases.

That is what happened on the Earth. Within a few

terrestrial years my observation showed me compact masses of men thus confronting each other, now in one corner of that planet, now in another. Sometimes they fought in the open; sometimes they crouched in earthworks and strove to demolish the adjoining earthworks by showering heavy lumps of metal on them. Note that they themselves were at the same time peppered in the same way. It is a hideous and ridiculous sight. The scenes of horror which one witnesses at these times are such that if these creatures had the slightest faculty for remembering, they would avoid their recurrence for at least several generations. But in the course of even their brief lifetimes, the same men will be seen plunging madly into the same murderous escapades.

Another striking example of this blind subservience of Man to instinct is to be seen in his habit of tirelessly rebuilding manheaps at certain points of the planets where they are fated to destruction. Thus, for instance, I have attentively watched a very populous island where, within eight years, all the nests were destroyed three times by tremors of the outer coating of the Earth. To any sensible observer it is plain that the animals living in these parts ought to migrate. They do nothing of the sort, but pick up once more, with a positively ritual action, the same pieces of wood or iron, and zealously rebuild a manheap which will once more be destroyed in the following year. But, say my critics, however absurd the goal of this activity, it remains true that the activity is regulated, and proves the existence of a directing power, a spirit. Again, a mistaken idea! The swarming of Men disturbed by an earthquake, as I have shown, resembles the movement of gaseous molecules. If the latter be observed individually, they are seen to describe irregular and complicated trajectories, but in combination their great number produces effects of decided simplicity. Similarly, if we demolish a manheap, thousands of insects collide with each other, hamper each other's movements, and show every sign of disorganized excitement; and yet, after a certain time, the manheap is discovered to be built up again.

Such is the strange intellect in which it is now fashionable to see a replica of Uranian reason! But fashion passes, facts remain; and the facts are bringing us back to the good old beliefs regarding the Uranian soul and its privileged destiny. For my own part, I shall be happy if my few experiments, modestly and prudently carried out, have helped towards the downfall of pernicious teachings, and restored these animals to their proper place in the scale of creatures. Curious and worthy of study they certainly are; but the very naïveté and incoherence of Man's behaviour must force us to bear in mind how great is the gulf fixed by the Creator between bestial instinct and the Uranian soul.

Death of A E 17

Happily, A E 17 died before he could witness the first interplanetary war, the establishment of relations between Uranus and the Earth, and the ruin of all his work. His great renown endured to his last days. He was a simple, kindly Uranian, who showed vexation only when contradicted. To ourselves it is an interesting fact that the monument erected to his memory on Uranus bears on its plinth a bas-relief designed from a telephotograpic picture showing a swarming mass of men and women. Its background is strongly reminiscent of Fifth Avenue.

PART III

AMERICA

ADVICE TO A YOUNG FRENCHMAN
LEAVING FOR AMERICA

SINCE you have been making ready for this journey, you have read scores of books about America: forget them. The traveller describing a distant country is tempted to exaggerate its strangeness. My own aim is not to please you but to instruct you. Know, then, that the beings with human faces whom you will find on that other shore, after a week on the ocean, are not so different as you imagine from your friends in Europe, or from yourself. They are men like ourselves, who work and suffer, eat, drink and make love, read the poets, build temples and destroy them, are born and die. When you have observed for yourself that some of them are as fond of Proust and Valéry as you are, when you have seen the paintings of Degas and Renoir in their homes, and heard Debussy and Dukas and Ravel at their concerts, you will doubtless rather shamefacedly drop that extravagant equipment of a spiritual explorer which I see you wearing. You are leaving for America, not for the moon. Keep your mind clear.

Language

Don't imagine you know American because you speak English. You will find yourself mistaken. The ladies of New York, the professors of Harvard, you will understand. But when you come into contact with circles less coloured by European culture you will discover a new language. The existence of racial groupings in America, so important that they have preserved over there a national existence, has enriched the language with Italian, German and Yiddish words; and these have been blended with English rather as Arabic was with Spanish or French in the days of the Moorish invasions. When "Babbitt" was first published in England, it had to have a vocabulary.

American is a much younger language than English. Its words are born from images, as in primitive tongues. Many are short-lived. When I first went there in 1927 everything that was attractive was "cute." In 1931 the word was ludicrous, almost banned. "Awful" in England, *"formidable"* in France, have gone through the same rise and decline. But in America the cycle is more brief, and the vocabulary of each moment is shorter.

You will be surprised at finding over there that the English "yes" is often replaced by a sort of double grunting sound, produced without opening the mouth by first expelling a small quantity of air through the nose and then taking a slight breath. Two quite distinct notes are discernible, the second being the higher, which in unison express a kind of approval at once languid, passive and kindly. The women make even more frequent use of these musical and primitive sounds than the men. I have long wondered about their origin. I think it must be sought in the extreme nervous fatigue of human beings after a day of American city life. This double grunt has an advantage over an articulate sound in that it expresses polite indifference with the very minimum of physical effort.

Conversation

It is a commonplace that conversation does not exist in America. Like all commonplaces this one lacks the finer shades. An after-dinner conversation between professors at Princeton or Yale or Cornell is not unlike a conversation of professors in France or England. I have been at a dinner—a Round Table dinner—in New York where the political conversation was worthy of Léon Berard. A tête-à-tête conversation with an intelligent American woman is one of America's greatest delights. But these joys are few and far between.

And the reason is this: Americans do not allow cooking, "considered as one of the fine arts," an important place in life. Luncheon to them is merely alms to the body; they hurriedly fling it fruit or fish, and return to work. A group of writers, in useful reaction, founded in New York a "Three Hours for Lunch Club," but they are a pleasant exception. Even at dinner general conversation is rare. Each person talks to his neighbour. After dinner the men remain alone, a dreadful custom inherited from England. In New York your host will often suggest taking you on to a theatre, or you will find that he has summoned a pianist, a singer, or a lecturer to the house. The notion of leaving his guests to themselves, and of their finding pleasure in their encounter, amazes and even alarms him. Excessive modesty forbids him to suppose that his friends can possibly be happy just in being under his roof, seeing him and seeing each other. He treats them like children. On Christmas Eve, in some of the most pleasant houses in New York, you will see Christmas trees for grown-ups. What's more, after a dinner-party of remarkable men, with whom really you would like to get into conversation, you will find a conjurer arriving and doing his best to amuse the old gentlemen. You will then understand that the absence of conversation in America comes, not from a void of ideas or wit or information, but from an in-·curable shyness and prodigious self-distrust. In no country will you find such powerlessness in self-expression. It is your part to overcome these resistances and give these "repressed" people the chance of repose and trust.

Drink will help you. In France, I know, you drink little. In America you will have some difficulty in keeping sober. Nearly everywhere you will be offered cocktails, and it will not be easy for you to decline them. In American eyes, Prohibition has set a higher value than ever before on the offer of a drink. The man who pours it out for you is sacrificing a definite part of a supply, a limited wealth. It will hurt him if you seem to undervalue his sacrifice. You have heard a lot about dangerous drinks, and poisonous blends of wine; if you hold back, you will seem to be lacking in trust or in courage. Reflect, to console yourself, that in "dry" homes, the cocktail's place may be taken by a glass of tomato juice.

Realize that in this struggle for drink there is a deeper and nobler element. It is an apprenticeship of liberty, and the American's first revolt against the tyranny of custom. The American needs strong spirits more than the Frenchman or the Italian. Puritanism, and then class respectability, have made him a creature who does not dare to yield to his most natural instincts. Drinking frees him from these secular repressions. "It's only when I've had a drink that I can really be myself," an American said to me. The speak-easy is the only place in New York where men and women meet for the pleasure of being together without requiring a "show" or counting out the minutes. Conversation there is better than in the drawing-rooms, and food is better than in the homes of the wealthy. The father meets his son and daughter there. Family life is reviving there. Do not avoid it, and if you are afraid of clouded wits, do as I do: drink a mouthful, and then absentmindedly leave your full glass on a table.

Intellectual Life

Of all the false notions you may take with you, the most stupid is the legend that America is indifferent to the things of the mind. You will find in that country a literature and an architecture. Painting? We must wait: what I have seen is too much inspired by the modernity of Europe to be truly original. But their books are among the best of our day.

What intellectual life may be in Pittsburgh or Detroit I do not know, but I think you will find New York one of the most mentally stimulating cities of the world. New York is the clearing-house for the ideas of the universe. All the important books of all languages are translated there. A public is found there for Virginia Woolf and

André Gide and Thomas Mann. To-day the most widely-read book in America is by a Swede, to-morrow it will be a Frenchman's, next day a Russian's. Read their young reviews: the *Symposium,* the *Hound and Horn,* the *New Republic.* You will be astonished at the extent of their information and the quality of their judgment.

Of course this universal curiosity is not without its dangers. Mental life suffers in the United States from evils which belong to our epoch but have there assumed a virulent form. The most serious is the rapid wearing-out of ideas. It has been said that the whole American people take up a scientific idea just as they take up a fashion in shoes. That is true. Freud, Behaviourism, the Humanism of Irving Babbitt, the relativity of Einstein, have successively, in elementary form, penetrated the middle-classes much more thoroughly than in Europe. But the American tires of systems as quickly as he becomes infatuated with them. His intellectual fashions are very fleeting. Because the most brilliant minds of Europe go over there to display their range of paradoxes, the blasé American brain craves for spiritual nourishment of a highly flavoured kind. The critical spirit is lacking, not amongst the few, but in the masses. But the masses in Europe, you will say, have little enough of that. Perhaps: but in France they have towards ideas a certain common sense, a traditional mistrust, and in England a splendid indifference and deep contempt, which act as a flywheel and prevent the motors of the mind from jamming. In the United States freshness of mind is greater and curiosity more naïve. That is agreeable, but it entails formidable errors.

So, if you wish to produce a rapid effect upon the crowds in this country, you can. Be brilliant, be cynical. Burn the idols of other men, and idolize what they have burned. Criticize America ferociously. There will be violent reactions; they will help your ephemeral fame. The newspapers will quote your words. You will be famous, and three months later, forgotten. But if you wish, as I hope you do, to bring to these strangers the best of yourself, act in just the contrary way. Be simple; do not force your thought; seek to find precise and subtle shades, as if you were addressing the most cultivated and exacting of your own compatriots. You won't make much of a stir. The reporters will be disappointed at not finding a good headline in what you have said, and will report you in three lines, or not at all. But gradually you will see the sensitive, modest, balanced minds drawing nearer to you. There are many such in the United States. They will fasten on to your person. Not that you are a man of genius, but you can give them something which they lack and which you owe to France—a liking for order in ideas, the art of constructing, a long and inventive tradition in analysis of the feelings. And they, for their part, can bring you freshness of mind and a direct manner of setting moral or metaphysical problems, as if they were completely new. You will teach them maturity. They will reveal youthfulness to you. Is it not from such exchanges that the friendships of peoples and men are formed?

Food

You have been told that the American does not know how to eat? All general statements are misleading. The American cuisine is monotonous (you'll eat chicken every night and ice-cream twice a day), but when that cuisine is simple it is good. Why should one complain in a land where fruits are plentiful and fresh, where the breakfast grape-fruits match the midday persimmons, where botanists, by scientific grafting, have produced a super-fruit in the melon they have named the "Honeydew"? In New England remember the "sea food"; Boston has its fish like Marseilles. In roadside hostelries ask for roast chicken and Lima beans. Beware of salads. American salads are culinary heresies: you will find in them slices of fresh fruit sinfully soaked in oil, scattered pieces of cheese and cabbage, lettuce hearts so dense that your knife cannot deal with them. The bread, often home-made, is varied in shape and flavour. You may regret the French loaf, so nicely salted, but you will like those dinner-rolls with their sprinkling of hard, scented poppy-seeds. Finally, don't be surprised at finding so many dishes decked out with queer, superfluous adornments. This youthful race has more taste for finery than for the pleasures of the palate.

Dress

Wear what you would wear in Paris. Dark, sober clothes in town; tweeds, plus-fours and stockings in the country. In the daytime all the men have taken on that appearance of the well-paid workman which the soft collar gives to a millionaire. The American wage-earner wears a soft cap, sometimes a "derby." He keeps them on his head at work and pulls an overall over his suit. To our European eyes this gives him the appearance of an amateur who has happened to stop accidentally at this job or underneath that car.

But, you ask me, don't all Americans wear the same clothes and the same hat at the same moment? So I have read. Perhaps it was true once. I have never noticed it myself. I have seen "derbies," I have seen cloth caps, and I have seen young men hatless. At Princeton I have heard tell of days when to wear an open shirt-collar *à la* Shelley or Byron was a sign of rebellion to be punished by social ostracism. But these things happened three or four years ago, that is to say, in a distant past. In 1930 a student was free to dress as he chose. There were fashions, of course—a certain beige cashmere pullover, a style in grey flannel trousers—but as fashions they were no stricter than those of Oxford or Cambridge. Only the first-year undergraduate was bound to observe a decent modesty: a black cap was obligatory for him, and coloured neckties forbidden. But after a victory of their team over Yale these young men rebelled, and appeared one morning decked in flaming neckties. The elders capitulated.

Social Usage

Because the United States is a democratic country, you imagine a life free of constraints. That is because you have never studied the morality of primitive peoples. The younger a human group, the more rigid its formalism, because the men therein can be tamed and bent to social life only by strict rules. It is in the oldest aristocracies that the most lax manners and the most free-and-easy grace are to be sought. The pioneer in solitude becomes brutalized. When he starts to live a social life a code and manners have to be imposed upon him. The ceremoniousness of Louis XIV was contrived for the rough nobility of the Fronde. The formality of pioneers is surprising. If you live, as I have done, in an American university town, you will find scores of visiting-cards on your table the day after your arrival. The whole Faculty calls. Even those who find you at home leave a card when they go, and you in your turn, if you have the strength, must return these scores of calls. A telephone invitation is rare, and is held to be contrary to proper usage. If it has been forced by circumstances it is followed by a letter of apology. The smallest events are made the excuse for letters of sympathy or good wishes. An American friend will write and tell you that it was a pleasant dinner the evening before and that he will always remember it. On every occasion gifts are exchanged, small and valueless, but forging links of friendly feeling. When you are tired or overworked you will think these attentions a nuisance. But look closer, and you will see how much they help to build up life in this young society.

Beware of supposing that America, as a country without an hereditary nobility, is a country without hierarchies. I know few nations where the etiquette of scorn has so many forms. The Anglo-Saxons look down on the other races, and they look down on each other. The Southerner looks down on the Northerner, the Easterner looks down on the man from the Middle West. The Americans with two centuries behind them despise those with one, and they despise those with half-a-century, and these refuse to look at newcomers. In the old families, where a son bears his father's name (there is always a Cornelius Vanderbilt or a Percy Pyne, just as there is always a Corisande amongst the Gramonts and a François amongst the La Rochefoucaulds), the name is followed by a numeral. One day they will be talking of John Jacob Astor XVII, as they say Prince Henry XXII of Reuss. In Hollywood the old families are those of the silent film days—such as Douglas Fairbanks and Mary Pickford. They have their English butlers, lace-covered tables, a conservative cuisine, old wines. Charlie Chaplin is the Swann of this old-fashioned society, where people talk in low mournful tones of the good old days when screens were dumb.

American snobbery fastens on to signs of nobility of the most curious kinds; they would have delighted Marcel Proust. It is a social asset to have your telephone number as low as possible. A new-made millionaire will be ready to pay a large sum to the official who allots automobile number-plates in order to secure a figure in the first hundred, when one falls vacant by the extinction of some great name. A box at the Metropolitan Opera House has its own history, like a fauteuil of the French Academy; the names of the successive holders are printed on the programmes. On the occasion of charity performances, when all the boxes are for sale, a *nouveau riche* will find it supremely flattering to his pride to occupy the Astor Box or the Cutting Box.

If you care for happiness, steer clear of professional hostesses; they will devour your time and your strength. Choose a small number of friends. There are certain simple and delightful houses in New York; shun the others. It is different, of course, if for some particular purpose you want to conquer the town. Be more snobbish than the snobs. Your standoffishness will astound them; your silence will perturb them; your capriciousness will hold them spellbound. These people suffer from too rigid a framework in life; shatter the frameworks.

The Sentimental Life

You may arrive convinced by the tales of your fellow-passengers that there is great moral freedom in America. Be cautious. This is the country where women are most closely protected. Adultery is rare; multiple divorce takes its place. The young girls, beautiful and often intelligent, are determined on marriage. What they call their "technique" is an art of love very different from Ovid's. It is true that your status as a foreigner will afford you some security, for the European is desirable as a lover or a friend, but not as a husband. He could not be, like the American, at once generous and free from jealousy. The marriage of a Frenchman and an American woman is one of two spoilt children—an unstable compound. Minds work more simply here. Passion does not play so large a part. You will be surprised how easily a young man, arriving with a girl who seems to you to be "his," puts up with the sight of her giving her attention to another man. Men do not cling as we do to what runs away from them: withdrawal is better than suffering.—"How can you depict men in your novels as being so much taken up with women?" they asked me. "Have your heroes nothing to do?"—Ingenuous, but sincere. Yet if you do touch the heart of one of these splendid creatures, her attachment to you will be all the greater because this perturbed kind of European love will be new to her. The American woman finds slaves; she looks for a master. If you are free, play that hand. It is a fine stake.

*　　*　　*

ENVOI

I should like to tell you more about young men and sports and colleges and girls—they are all a paradise; and about political parties—which are all a hell. But you are going, and I can say only a word. You are going into a land of shyness: don't mislay your sympathy. You are entering the land of kindliness: don't forget your warmheartedness. You are going to the land of youth: don't forget your enthusiasm. A people is a mirror in which every traveller views his own image. In America as everywhere, remember, you will find only what you bring. Fashion within yourself an America of which you will be worthy: that is the only America you will discover.

AMERICA THE UNEXPECTED

I HAVE an aged friend somewhere in Europe who professes violent and very definite ideas regarding the United States. As a matter of fact, they are the more definite because my friend has never crossed the Atlantic. For this very reason no hateful confusion of actual facts has ever troubled the wondrous simplicity of his judgments, and he can wholeheartedly and impenitently call down maledictions on a country which he has never seen and where he knows nobody.

Some time ago I had to confess to him that the University of Princeton had offered me the tenure for a few months of a chair of French literature, and that I was thinking of accepting it. He flung up his hands.

"My poor young friend!" he exclaimed. "Don't do that! You'll never come back alive. You don't know what America is like. It is a country where there is such commotion that you will never have a moment to yourself, where the din is so continuous that you will get neither rest nor sleep, where men die at forty from excessive work and the women leave their homes first thing in the morning to join in the universal hubbub. Mind and intelligence have no value over there. Freedom of thought is non-existent. Human beings have no souls. The only talk you will hear is about money. From childhood you have known the graciousness of a spiritual civilization;

there you will find a civilization of bathrooms and central heating and frigidaires. . . . My dear friend, have you read about the Chicago stockyards? Monstrous, I assure you! Apocalyptic! And those stories in every newspaper about gangs of thugs murdering in broad daylight, and the police hand-in-glove with them . . . ? Really, I am alarmed for your safety. You have a wife and family. . . . Give up this idea, I beg you."

Next day I sailed.

I have now lived for four months in Princeton, New Jersey, and this is the letter I have been writing to my aged friend:

I hardly dare to describe to you the America I have been discovering. You will not believe me; yet what I am going to tell you is simply the exact description of what I have seen. Picture it to yourself: I am living in a pretty provincial town, in a small wooden house surrounded by trees and covered with ivy, the garden of which is separated from the neighbouring gardens only by well-trimmed hedges. Friendly little grey squirrels are playing under my windows. In the street I see a few motor-cars passing, far fewer than in a street in Tours or Avranches, and every hour or two someone strolls past, usually one of my neighbours, a professor like myself. At night the silence is so profound that I sometimes feel restless, and if I wake up suddenly I listen for the distant noise of the Paris tramways.

If I go out I find in one direction a lake, bordered

with maples and willows, in the other, the town, which consists of the University buildings, small houses like my own, and one shopping street, Nassau Street. There, in the mornings, you can see the professors' wives doing their shopping, as used to happen in the provincial towns of France in times gone by. I believe you would find quite a true picture of the life in that main street by reading certain novels of Balzac, which are set in Touraine or Poitou about 1835.

· So much for the hubbub and excitement. As for the social and intellectual life, it cuts me to the quick to tell you, my dear ——, that the picture I contemplate every day is likewise totally different from the one you sketched for me. I talk a great deal with my pupils, with my colleagues, with their wives. Shall I dare to admit that they *have* minds, and some of them very sensitive ones . . . ? And what sort of conversations do we have? Well, it is very odd, but really they are remarkably like those I might have in Paris with intelligent friends. The talk is about the same things and the same books. Marcel Proust, Balzac, Flaubert, Sinclair Lewis and André Siegfried play a great part in our intercourse. The European situation is discussed, sometimes ignorantly, often sympathetically; we even discuss America with as much freedom as you do yourself.

Not a spiritual civilization, you assured me, but one of baths and frigidaires. . . . I'm sorry, my dear ——, but you have a poor hand, and these cards are almost comical. For if I have one grievance against this house, where I have been so happy, it would be its lack of comfort. My American central heating is an aged hot-air apparatus, of a type that no longer exists anywhere in Europe and seems to be blessed with a queer perversity of spirit, for it provides an intolerable warmth on the blazing days when this country's autumn seems like spring, but enters into competition with the frigidaire when the outside temperature drops.

As for my bathroom, it is quite nice to look at, but it is quite chimerical to look for hot water in it, although this circumstance has enabled me to resume a habit of my younger days, taking a cold shower instead of a warm bath. I must apologize for contradicting you on every point, but after all, I can only give you the fruits of my personal experience, can't I? In another house, somewhere else, everything might possibly have been different, but here I have found comforts of the mind rather than of the body.

Finally, you threatened me with terrifying brigands, organized gangs, a life unpoliced and unsafe. But just fancy, my house is not so much as surrounded by a wall; its windows are covered with blinds which a burglar could flick aside with his finger, and when I have to leave it for a few days I don't lock the door, so that the postman can leave my letters and parcels in the entrance hall. Like you, I read in the newspapers of tragic happenings, but we must avoid taking drama as the rule and tragedy as an average representation of life. I assure you that America is not entirely enrolled amongst the gangsters and that few men spend their leisure hours in the Chicago stockvards.

Of course you will tell me that the contrary is true also, and that Princeton is not America. I agree. If I had to paint Pittsburgh or Chicago the picture would be very different. Morand's picture of New York is brilliant and perfectly accurate. But the truth, you will agree, is that the real world is not made up of these crude and simple opposites as our passions would so often like. When Burke was addressing the English in 1793 about France, he said: "I do not know of a method of drawing up an indictment against a whole people. When that people is youthful, alive, and only asking to understand us better, does it not seem more humane, and more wise, to seek to understand it rather than condemn it?"

AMERICAN STUDENTS AND FRENCH NOVELS

I SHOULD like to give an authentic picture of the conversations which a French professor can have with some American pupils. These conversations are frequent, even obligatory, at Princeton. The Professor, of course, gives a course of lectures, during which the pupils take notes, but in the intervals of these the pupils come to his house in groups of six or seven, for more intimate talks. Here the aim is not so much an extension of the lectures as to make the young men talk themselves, to assure oneself that they have read the books of the syllabus, and to accustom them to the expression of their own ideas.

Imagine, then, a glorious autumn day (outside, the maples and sycamores offer a marvellous gamut of red, brick, copper and saffron), and imagine the novice professor awaiting his first tutorial in the tiny drawing-room of his small wooden house. He is not free from anxiety. Will they talk? Will they know French well enough to follow the conversation and take part in it? He has asked them to read the "Princesse de Clèves": will they appreciate these chivalrous lovers, so jealous of their honour, so sensitive to the fine shades of sentiment? He re-reads the opening pages of the novel. . . . The bell rings.

They have arrived in a body, hatless (only first-year men wear a black cap); they look like a pack of young dogs, vigorous and cheerful, enlivened by this sunshine.

They give me their names, which I try my best to remember. There is Plug, a boy from the Middle West, with a formidable American accent; Alexander, lively, charming, rebellious, reminds me of a thoroughbred always pulling on the reins; McCarter, a New Yorker in a black pullover; Meyrovitz has the head of an intellectual, very delicate; Robinson is English; the blond, very frail Arlington, marvellously tailored in light flannel, has lived for a long time in Paris.

I can see at once that I shall have no difficulty in starting conversation; friendly and respectful, they are quite at their ease.

"I should like you to talk first," I said. "Mr. McCarter, how did you like the 'Princesse de Clèves'?"

"So-so," he replied. . . . "I found it well written, but the characters are childish. . . . To begin with, people don't die of love. . . ."

"Are you sure of that?"

"I've never known a case, sir. Nor heard of one . . . I may be wrong, but life seems to me so much simpler than these people want to make it."

"Sure," says Plug. "They were a queer lot, these people long ago; they worked up tragedy everywhere. . . . This morning we were reading 'Phèdre' with M. Coindreau, and I said to him: 'But why does Phèdre make such a bother? I have a friend in Chicago myself who fell in love with his stepmother. He told his father, and his father asked her if *she* loved my friend. And she said she did. So his dad got a divorce and my friend married his stepmother. . . . Now don't you think that's a better way? If Phèdre was a reasonable woman she would not go on moaning about being 'seated in the gloom of the forests,' but she'd have a serious talk with Theseus and marry Hippolytus. Don't you think so, sir?"

"But you forget that Racine knew nothing about divorce, and that possibly Theseus loved Hippolytus. . . . No, I don't agree with you, Mr. Plug. For my own part I find that life is very difficult and that the conflicts of passion are sometimes irremediable."

"Exactly, sir," says Alexander fiercely. "What surprises *me* in the 'Princesse de Clèves' is the ease with which all these men who say they love Mme de Clèves yield their ground to M. de Nemours. . . . Why? Real men wouldn't do that."

I explain something about the chivalrous ideal.

"What you call the chivalrous man," says Robinson, "is really the gentleman. . . . M. de Clèves behaves like a gentleman."

"Possibly," says the charming Alexander, "but all the same, if he had felt a real passion, he would have done something; he'd have taken his wife somewhere far away, or killed Nemours . . . And Mme de Clèves isn't really a passionate woman either. She is always talking about 'safeguarding her glory.' She is like the American women of the eighteen-sixties, always concerned first and foremost with safeguarding their 'respectability.' It's prudent, but not very estimable."

"Is it really true, sir," says Plug, "that these people in the seventeenth century lived like that, and spent their time telling love-stories? Hadn't they anything to do?"

321

"Yes, as a matter of fact they had very little to do. You must bear in mind that the seventeenth century was a time when the French nobility, hitherto warlike and powerful, was moulded to the form of court life by a royal power stronger than itself. These great characters were thus thrust into retirement and needed some way of filling up their leisure. They simply had to be tamed. Whence the Précieuses, the Hôtel de Rambouillet, and later those dissections of sentiment which astonish you. You Americans will soon be coming to the same thing, when your own Louis XIV (who is called Over-production) forces idleness on you against your own will."

They laugh. The talk continues with great animation, and shows me that all of them, except Alexander, who is a romantic, and Meyrovitz, a Spinozaist, are hostile to love viewed as a passion. For next time, I give them "Candide" to read. I think they will enjoy it.

"Sir," Arlington asks me as he goes out, "wasn't the 'Princesse de Clèves' the inspiration for Radiguet's 'Bal du Comte d'Orgel'?"

"Yes. Have you read it?"

"Of course," he said. "Radiguet was a friend of Cocteau, and I read everything Cocteau writes."

* * *

SECOND WEEK.

"Well," I said, "has 'Candide' been a success?"

"A great success," says Alexander, lighting a cigarette. "It's very amusing, but Candide is really too stupid. . . . He never learns a thing from all his calamities."

322

"What! You've not forgotten the end, have you?"

"Yes, at the end he realizes that he must cultivate his garden, but he realizes it too late."

"What exactly does that mean, sir: *'If faut cultiver nôtre jardin'?*" asks Robinson.

"What do you think?"

"It's quite simple," says Alexander. "It means: 'Let's concern ourselves as little as possible with men, who are wicked, or with greatness, which is dangerous, and let us live quietly and go on working'—like Voltaire himself at Ferney."

"Yes," says Robinson the Englishman; "but it can also mean: 'Let us cultivate our inward garden, our spirit.'"

"And it can have an even wider meaning," says Meyrovitz. 'Let us cultivate this planet which is our garden; let us advance the humane sciences and not bother about the universe, which is an absurdity.'"

"Good," I said. "Let's take the first meaning. Do you think that it would be a wise philosophy of life to concern yourself no further with other men, to extirpate all your ambition, and to shut yourself up in your secret garden?"

"An old man's wisdom, perhaps," says Alexander scornfully. "But if I were Candide, I should get bored in my garden and go back to see the world again, with its earthquakes and commercial crises and inquisitors, and—and its excitement!"

"Then do you think, like Martin, that man is doomed to pass from the spasms of anxiety to the lethargy of boredom?"

"I do, sir. . . . I prefer anxiety. . . ."

"For my own part," says McCarter, "I like Martin. He is very intelligent. He says you should work, without too much reasoning. That's the truth."

"Not at all!" says Robinson. "I believe that you have to think in order to cultivate your garden properly. You must have a certain idea of the world and cultivate it in the light of its harmony with a whole. . . . A garden cut off from the rest of the world does not exist."

"I agree," I said. "Martin and Pangloss are both wrong. . . . This world is neither the best nor the worst of all possible worlds; it is the only one, and we have to study it as best we can, in order to lessen by a little the miseries of the human societies that dwell in it."

"But, sir," asks Alexander, "do you believe that they *can* be made less miserable? Is the world any better now than in Voltaire's day?"

"I ask you the same question. . . ."

"No, I don't think it is," he answers. "There is less visible cruelty, but more hidden cruelty. The last war was more hideous than that of the Bulgars and the Abares in 'Candide.' . . . The electric chair is more horrible than the guillotine. . . . Our police are extremely barbarous."

"And what of our material advances—motor-cars, telephones, medicine? Don't they strike you as immense since Voltaire's time?"

I am curious to know the reaction of my young Americans to this subject. To my great surprise the whole class, except McCarter, sides against these comforts.

"Cars and telephones don't add anything to happiness," they declare.

"What!" says McCarter. "In Voltaire's time you had to climb the stairs on foot: now we have elevators. Man is a lazy animal; and therefore elevators add to his happiness."

"When there were no elevators," says Alexander, "there were hardly any storeys."

"Anyhow, sir," breaks in the nasal voice of Plug, who has so far been listening in silence, "if Candide had kept a single one of his Eldorado sheep, which were laden with gold and precious stones, he'd have dodged all his troubles."

*　　*　　*

THIRD WEEK.

Reading: the "Chartreuse de Parme." This time they arrive in high dudgeon.

"Oh! It is far too long!" says McCarter.

"And too boring," says Plug.

"Boring! The 'Chartreuse'! You surprise me, really! I always find it the least boring book in the world."

"Don't exaggerate," says Meyrovitz to his friends. "I certainly was interested in the main story—Clélia, the Duchesse. But as for the rest . . . the comedian, the stories of the archbishop and Rossi—I agree, it's far too long."

"Besides," says Plug, "he's anti-American, this Stendhal. There is a vicious attack on the 'King Dollar.' . . . Was it fashionable, even in 1839, to speak ill of America?"

"He speaks far more ill of France," says Meyrovitz. "Italy seems to be his only object of admiration."

325

"How does Fabrice love Clélia?" asks Alexander. "He barely seems to know her."

"Exactly," I say. "It is one of Stendhal's favourite theories that love increases in the course of absence, through the process which he calls 'crystallization.' . . ." And I explain the story of the bough of Salzburg, which is merely a dead twig if it be not covered with the glittering crystals of the salt. Thus the charm of a woman we love is made up far more from the qualities which our love lends her, than from her actual brilliance. They like that theory.

"It isn't new," says Arlington. "Beauty lies in the eye of the beholder."

"It is always new," I remark. "You will find it again in Proust under the name of subjectivity of the sentiments."

"But I don't understand, sir," says Alexander. "In your lecture this morning you showed us Stendhal as a man of high passions, especially where love was concerned. How can he regard love as a crystallization, that is to say a subjective sentiment, and at the same time be so exalted himself by what is mere illusion?"

"I see no difficulty," says Meyrovitz. "Man can produce his own double. When I go to the theatre I know quite well that the play I am seeing is a mere illusion, that the hero is not a king, that the victim does not die. That doesn't prevent me, after five minutes, from forgetting that I know these things. I am moved, I weep, I laugh. So in love, why shouldn't one believe in the drama?"

"It isn't at all the same thing," answers Alexander. "In

the theatre we accept the play as a play. When we love a girl we want her to be really worthy of being loved."

"Of course!" cries the indignant Plug. "And she is. . . . Not always, but very often. . . . It isn't we who give women their qualities. 'Beauty lies in the eye of the beholder,' I dare say; but sometimes the beauty is likewise in the face of the girl you are looking at. . . . There are some girls, you know, who have real beauty."

"Possibly," says Arlington, rather loftily. "But they're never the ones you love."

"Do you know, sir," says Meyrovitz, "that there is a story very like that of Fabrice, refusing to leave his prison because he may possibly catch a glimpse of his love there? It is in Chaucer, a tale of two brothers shut up in the same prison and both in love with the gaoler's daughter. One gains his liberty, the other remains, and the one who is pardoned can never find consolation."

"Quite true, I remember," says Alexander. "It's a fine story—I'm very fond of it."

"So you see that you are more Stendhalian than you imagine!" I remark.

* * *

FOURTH WEEK.

They arrive much excited by a riot which troubled the campus last night. Coming out from a meeting the young men tore down a statue from its plinth, a figure representing the Christian Student, and bore it off, notwithstanding the Dean, to Nassau Street, where it blocked the traffic for several hours.

"What a crazy notion!" I told them. "Are you ten-

327

year-olds? What harm has this wretched statue done you? Can't you recognize that your Dean is a delightful and cultured man whose word should be respected?"

"The Dean's all right," says Alexander. "We didn't want to annoy him. . . . But believe me, it isn't so absurd as it looks, all this. . . . You must realize that this statue is the symbol of everything we hate. It represents the 'Good Young Man,' with a Bible under one arm and a football under the other. . . . It was presented to the University to honour the type of pious and respectable athlete which our generation holds in horror. . . . It is a state of mind we're attacking, not a statue."

"Every year," says the nasal Plug, "every year the Christian Student gets a lesson. . . . Last year the boys gilded him."

"And they ran a lipstick over the lips of the Medici Venus," adds Meyrovitz.

"Was that symbolic too? But we're a long way from our subject. . . . I should like you to tell me about 'Eugénie Grandet.'"

"I've noticed," says Plug, "that you're very keen on our sticking to the subject in conversation. Is that a French peculiarity?"

"It may be. A taste for unity. Well then . . . who wants to talk about 'Eugénie Grandet'?"

After a moment more of stories pell-mell they settle down to pay homage to Balzac.

"It's far better than the 'Chartreuse de Parme,'" they say.

They like the description of Saumur. Two or three

328

have read other Balzac novels and like them. That active pessimism, that scorn of humanity, that zest for life, the blend seems to be made for them. (For American optimism has greatly altered amongst the present generation; they desire to be thought cynics.) Nevertheless, they proffer a few objections.

"Eugénie is rather a fool," says Alexander. . . . (It was he who said likewise of Candide.) "All she had to do was to join Charles Grandet in the Indies."

"No," says Plug, "she couldn't have done that. It must have been very difficult to get out there in those days; there was no regular service. But what I should have liked is a stronger ending. Why does Balzac marry Eugénie off? That's very flat. She ought to remain an old maid, gradually becoming as miserly as her father, and the book should end with a scene of her refusing two lumps of sugar to old Nanon."

"That would not be at all bad, Mr. Plug. Not that Balzac did not observe that side of the subject. Do you remember? There is a scene where Eugénie answers: 'We shall see,' exactly in the father's tone of voice. . . . But perhaps he has shown himself a greater artist than yourself just by not abusing that possibility. Your end is very good—it is a little too good . . . too much of the 'novel standing like a pyramid' as Flaubert said. You must beware of strength when it is obtained by artificial means."

"Exactly!" says Arlington, "my complaint is that Balzac doesn't beware enough. . . . What annoys me when I read him is that his characters lack the fine shades. Grandet is a miser and nothing else. A human being, after all, is more complex."

"Do you think so? There are some passions which have graduations, and others, on the contrary, which take hold of a man utterly. Avarice is one, fleshly indulgence another . . . Baron Hulot in 'Cousine Bette' is a very true character."

"Tell us, sir," says Plug, "why the brother's creditors are filled with admiration when Grandet pays them the interest on the debt? Wasn't that quite a matter of course?"

Whereupon they engage in a lively argument on business morality. The better I know them, the more I am struck by this habit of always fastening on to questions of practical morality. Pure æsthetics are a matter of indifference to them. They are interested for a time in studying whether a novel is well or badly constructed, but never deeply interested. How should one act?—that is the real problem for them.

After the tutorial McCarter asks me if he can wait for a moment.

"Why, certainly."

And when the others had gone, he asked me abruptly:

"I should like to ask you something, sir. . . . Is incest very common in France?"

"Incest?" I repeat in astonishment. "No, not at all. . . . At any rate, not more than elsewhere. But why?"

"Why, because all the plays and novels we read are full of incest. 'Phèdre' is a story of incest; and 'René,' which I'm reading with the Dean—incest. . . . Your 'Chartreuse de Parme' is an aunt in love with her nephew. And then, yesterday again, 'Eugénie Grandet.' . . ."

"'Eugénie Grandet'?" I exclaim in surprise. "But that is not a story of incest, is it?"

"Oh, yes, it is. . . . It is a cousin in love with her cousin. That makes me just as wild. The other day we had a friend staying at home with us for the week-end who is engaged to his cousin. My sister and I felt quite ill to see him kissing the girl. . . ."

"That is strange," I said. "It's a feeling I don't know at all."

"And then another thing, sir: how emotional all these novels are. . . . I mean, how lacking in calm and indifference all these characters are, Stendhal's as much as Balzac's! How seriously they take their passions!"

"But don't you yourselves have passions that you take seriously?"

"Far less so, sir. Over here you'll see a boy who seems to be in love with a girl. He will see one of his friends take possession of her. But he won't show any displeasure, and perhaps afterwards he will marry the girl just the same. . . . I've often seen that. I don't say it is better."

I question him about his family and upbringing.

"My father was very strict," he says. "I never went out at night until I was sixteen. I have great admiration for my father's and mother's way of life. They were terribly old-fashioned; they loved each other. But certainly they were happy, and they made me happy."

"Then do you think that it would be better for American youth to turn back to these sterner morals?"

331

"I don't think they ought to turn back to the old-style hypocrisy. . . . What we need would be to have freedom but to refrain from using it, through reason. . . . Now, I myself don't care for your nineteenth century, but I do admire the French seventeenth century. The characters in Molière are human beings that I can feel close beside me. . . . They're sad, they're comic, they're reasonable— like the people I see around me. La Rochefoucauld too, that's a man I can understand—or Saint-Simon. The Romantics bore me. Henriette in 'Les Femmes Savantes' would be just the sort of woman I should marry. But not Clélia, nor Eugénie."

He stayed quite a long time. I liked his lively seriousness.

*　　*　　*

FIFTH WEEK.

I gave them a choice between "Madame Bovary" and "L'Education Sentimentale," and I noticed that they were alarmed at the length of both books. Pardonable alarm: they have only a week, and to read a novel of five hundred pages in a foreign language, and with other lectures to attend, is heavy work. The leaves have fallen in the avenue now, and the winter constellations are rising in the clear sky.

"You must be cold. Sit down in front of the fire."

Several of them squat down in front of the fireplace and light cigarettes.

"Well, then, 'L'Education Sentimentale'?"

They exchange glances and laugh.

332

"Terrible!" says Plug, with comical conviction in his huge voice.

"Terrible? In what sense?"

"Terrible. . . . Terribly long! Terribly boring!"

"But Flaubert meant it to be boring. . . . Do you remember the passage of Proust I was reading to you this morning, about that everlasting imperfect tense of Flaubert's which gives his sentences the monotony of a great river?"

"Well, all I can say," answers Plug, "is that if the man wanted to write a boring novel, he sure did so."

Alexander protests:

"Well, *I* read 'Madame Bovary.' . . . It's wonderful, but disheartening. . . . Charles Bovary is too much of a fool; Emma is too stupid in her choice of lovers. . . . Everything becomes petty, shabby, horrible. . . . Life isn't so wretched as all that. . . . Whenever I got through thirty pages I had to stop to look at the sun, or get a breath of air, or a game of tennis. . . . Then I could come back to the sorrowful M. Flaubert with a store of contentment."

I try to expound Flaubert's doctrine: that romanticism is something unavoidable, but always fails because it seeks the unattainable; that every destiny fails because external forces are hostile to the dream (I read them several passages to show how Frédéric Moreau is perpetually escaping instead of living); whence, a scorn for worldly temptations and an escape into art. Man cannot imagine the things he actually has. " 'You depict wine, love and fame, on one condition, my friend—that you are neither drunkard, lover nor soldier.' "

333

"Well, sir," says Plug, "I'd far rather be a drunkard or a lover or a soldier, and not depict anything at all!"

"Yes, Mr. Plug. But that just shows us that you are cut out for a man of action, not for an artist."

"Yes, but why talk of Flaubert's 'admirable' life? If he made a religion of his art, isn't that simply because he was incapable of becoming a drunkard or a lover or a soldier?"

"Partly for that reason. We always lend some support of reason to our most unavoidable actions. . . ."

"It all cuts both ways," says Meyrovitz. "You could also maintain that he could not become a soldier *because* he was an artist."

"No," says Plug. "It is the men who are impotent in action who take refuge in art. . . . You never find the man incapable of art taking refuge in action. . . . A bad writer never becomes a great politician."

"How do I know?" I answer. "In any case, we know of writers who have passed their great creative period and then turn to a life of action. We have our Lamartine, and the English have their Byron."

"What I don't see," says Meyrovitz, "is why art is exempt from Flaubert's nihilism. If everything is illusory, a description of life is also an illusion."

"No, Mr. Meyrovitz, that is precisely what I shall try to show you in connection with Proust and what he called 'Time Recovered.' The special property of a work of art is that it catches a dream and gives stability of outline to an ever-shifting world. . . . Only, in my opinion, there is another method of escaping the dream; and that is,

334

action. Where Flaubert's characters go wrong is in dreaming their loves and their labours. That is why they are unhappy. If Bouvard and Pécuchet had done more farming and read fewer books about agriculture, they would have gathered their crops of vegetables; and they would have found a kind of happiness in that."

"Yes," says Alexander, "if Frédéric were Mme Arnoux's lover instead of imagining her clad as an odalisque before the pictures in the Louvre, he would be less boring, and less melancholy. . . . Dreaming about playing tennis is no good; so is reading books about tennis; but playing tennis is great fun."

" 'The soul's joy lies in doing,' said Shelley," I remind him.

"Do you remember what I said the other day?" asks McCarter. "I can see now why I prefer the people of the seventeenth century to those of the nineteenth. They did less dreaming and they took more action. . . ."

* * *

So the winter passed . . . Zola—Bourget—France—Proust—André Gide. . . . The last day. I looked sadly at the house, already stacked with trunks; I should never see it again. The bell rang, and rang again. One after another, every quarter of an hour, I saw them arriving—Plug, Meyrovitz, Arlington, Robinson, McCarter. Some only came to say good-bye, others to consult me about their theses. Arlington wanted to write about Proust and Freudian psychology, Plug on Balzac and business, Meyrovitz on Stendhal's youth, Alexander on Flaubert, Proust

335

and the objectivity of sentiments. Talking with them, I inwardly summarized my own impressions. Intelligent? Yes, these young men were very intelligent. Literary culture? Very much the same as that of a European of the same age; possibly even better-read. But they are almost totally lacking in historical culture and, except for Meyrovitz, they simply have no idea of what the construction and plan of a work can mean. This indifference to logical order in thought is an Anglo-Saxon trait, but I find it deeper amongst these Americans than in England. They are saved by their youth, by freshness of eye, by newness of words and imagery. A land of nascent poetry, of renascence. Their classical age will come in time.

Next day, in New York, I found a huge basket of white roses in my cabin—with a card. It was Alexander's.

THREE PHANTOMS

I HAVE been spending three months in the Eastern States. Wherever I went, in autumnal woods, in the snow-covered plains, in the streets of New York or Boston, I met three phantoms. So real were they that I sometimes took them for living men.

I often found it hard, when walking the American country-side, to realize that I was separated from the European landscape by an ocean. Against an Ile-de-France blue the fluffy clouds sketched a sky of Corot's or Monet's. But as soon as the eye fell on a house the illusion faded. The American house is redolent of exotic, colonial savours. It is of wood, painted in a grey that is almost white, and it conjures up the films of Chaplin and the stories of the pioneers. To our eyes, accustomed to gauge the solidity of brick or stone, this wood looks flimsy and provisional. A foreigner's mistake: woods here are durable, and many of these houses are old.

In the village graveyards the most worn of the tombstones bear venerable dates. *"Descended from an old English family—He abjured the glories of this World—To shield himself from Sin . . . Anno Domini 1669."* In a Quaker burial-ground near Princeton the stones are unmarked; not so much as a name; no desire to cherish an earthly memory when salvation is all that matters. At

337

the entrance to the ground is a wooden meeting-house, and behind it the pious farmers would tether their horses for shelter during meeting. An ascetic background, which must be evoked if one wishes to understand America.

The men who first landed on these shores of New England were Puritans who had left Europe because Puritanism was persecuted there. They made their perilous voyage in order to found the City of God. Their poetry came from the Bible, their morality from Calvin. For a long time their ministers of religion were also their political heads. And thus there took shape a breed of stern workers, virtuous and intolerant, capable of assuming the strict discipline which was to turn these waste lands and virgin forests into a great country.

That breed still lives. It no longer rules. Puritanism has been sapped by sundry influences, by comfort, by Latin immigration. Middle-class respectability, sentimentalism and prudery have blunted the fine rude vigour of its speech. Modern science has made a breach in its walls as a universal system. Biblical theology has been succeeded by a modernist religion, and amongst some by an absence of any religion. A recent enquiry in a Protestant seminary showed that only twenty out of a hundred future ministers believed in the damnation of unbelievers, and only eight in the literal inspiration of the Bible. The word "sin" has almost vanished from the vocabulary of a 1931 American student. A New York preacher would hardly dare to use it, and it has been said by the Rev. Dr. Shelton, president of the National Bible Institute, that this omission of the word "sin" from sermons is stupefying, considering that sin is a dominating word in the vocabulary of the Bible. Prohibition, a scion of Puritanism, has dealt its sire a mortal blow by making a vice into a rebellion. Habit and fondness have kept a great part of America loyal to the decencies of a family life; but here, there and everywhere, young rebel groups have tried to shake off the old law. Post-War cynicism has confronted nineteenth-century hypocrisy. The medical psychologists, disciples of Freud, aided this movement by providing desire with a vocabulary which enabled people to say anything and to vanquish the old inhibitions. Easy divorce has made marriage a legalized adventure. The descendants of the Puritans have been dabbling in the difficult profession of the libertine.

They have not enjoyed it. The frankest and best of them admit that they are ill at ease. The restless ghosts of the Pilgrim Fathers stalk abroad, and not only round the stones on the graveyard turf. These great Puritan souls are haunting minds which fancied themselves emancipated. The clear-eyed, scientific intelligence of many young Americans attaches no importance to the activities of love. It is a natural instinct which must be satisfied. But as soon as they allow a radicalism of the senses to rule their actions, then, to their surprise, a vexed and unfamiliar voice makes itself heard within them. The Puritan is pushing up his tombstone. The Statue is an ever-present guest at the orgies of a New Jersey Don Juan. As in the "Tannhäuser," so in the American mind, the Pilgrims' Chorus mingles with the music of the Venusberg and distorts it with harsh discordances.

Americans are at once shocked and fascinated by what they call French "realism," the cynicism of a Maupassant hero. The reason why many of them drink is that only intoxication gives the desires strength to drown the Puritan voice. Many of them surrender after a few attempts. "I have tried," a young professor told me, "but I'm not made for a life of freedom. Liberty is movement, and if I am sincere with myself my desire is for immobility. My need is to be quiet, to be in harmony with myself. I am irreligious in my brain, not in my heart." It is this clash which made the American of 1931 so interesting. It is he who has been the creator of a remarkable young literature within a few years. America is looking for a morality. Babbitt himself, in his naïve way, is a character in search of a doctrine. When I was reading French novels with my pupils, it was a rule of life they sought rather than a subject of erudition. Bourget's "Le Disciple" interested them because it sets a problem of free will. They prefer the French sixteenth century to the nineteenth, because it can show them frameworks and moralists.

For the generation reaching the age of twenty to-day is quite different from the one that reached that age just after the War. At that time, as Thomas Beer has remarked, there was mass production of rebels. A Bastille had to be razed every morning. But destroying a Bastille is not building a new city, and the best young minds are wondering what city of the mind they are going to build.

"My father and mother," said one young student to me, "lived in a very strict fashion. . . . I have had a great admiration for their life. There certainly was something bad in the 1880 hypocrisy, but there is plenty of hypocrisy in the aggressive liberty of to-day. . . ."

"Do many of your friends think like you?" I asked.

"Nearly all of them do," he answered. "Few dare to say so. . . . They talk about wine and women, but these things don't amuse them. . . ."

And for an instant I could see the austere features of the Puritan showing on his boyish face.

The seventeenth-century Puritan was in his way heroic. But the ghosts of heroes have not the virtues of heroes, and can only alarm the living. The Puritan ghost has inspired the United States electorate with stern and futile laws, outwardly contrived to tear out "sin" from the human heart. The Puritan ghost has given the New York and Chicago police the task of converting millions of sinners into saints on the Last Day. Now, it is impossible to make the laws of a great country from the conventions of a Methodist community. Walter Lippmann has said that, sooner or later, America will have to bring back its legislative ideal to the point where it coincides with human nature. America will never find her moral equilibrium until she has at last exorcised the Puritan phantom.

The traveller crossing the plains of France, or the English country-side, recognizes a country in which the whole of the land's surface is occupied, and for centuries has been occupied, by man. Every village is a completed thing; one feels that it will hardly now grow any more, that it has found its form, linked to the road or the railway, to the fields and meadows that hem it round. In America the Frenchman emerging from a large town feels himself in the wilds. In Princeton, a small town for all its age, certain streets stop dead on the edge of a wilderness. The asphalt of a well-kept roadway is succeeded without any transition by the yellow grass stretching away to the horizon. The farther one goes from the coast, the more striking this impression becomes. Plains without one human being, vast lakes with small wooden houses on their edge, mere frameworks of towns, sketched rather than constructed, and where placards summon the inhabitants to a town-meeting, rocky valleys, snowy wastes—a land where nature still holds sway, and which has just received its pioneers.

America is a precocious child, whose boldness and dexterity have made one forget its age. She is like one of those adolescent heirs to a great fortune, to whom the elders grudgingly grant a place in the family councils. She holds a majority of the Human Race company stock, but her youthfulness is terrifying. It was about 1810 that the New England farmers, suffering from the economic results of the Napoleonic Wars, came westward in their wide felt hats, with guns slung on their backs and cartridges in their belt, to fell the forests of Indiana and Illinois, and built their first wooden shacks out there. It was in 1869 that two outlandish locomotives with cowcatchers met north of Salt Lake, and the Pacific Railroad made possible the development of the Far West. It was only yesterday that in any period of slump an American could still say, "I'm off!"—and after a few days on horse-back could find new territory, rich and unexploited, where land was given him openhandedly and where any vigorous man was welcome.

During the whole of the nineteenth century such a pioneer was the typical American. He then acquired the traits of character which are proper to founders. The pioneer is kindly, because to him a man is not a competitor but a partner in the war with nature. He is a lover of equality, because birth does not count in the wilderness. He esteems the man of action and looks askance on the dreamer, because in these still frail communities ceaseless activity is essential. He is chivalrous, because women are few and precious, and because in this poorly guarded land a religious respect for women is their sole protection. He hardly troubles about the central government and settles his affairs for himself; in the last resort his sheriff metes out rough and summary justice; sentences are carried out by his militia. He is a nomad, because he has found that the best remedy in case of misfortune is to move off. On political honesty he has not very strict notions, because the nomad, always ready to move away, has not the settled inhabitant's fear of the judgments of the local tribe. Finally, he is an optimist, because he lives in a country which has never failed him, and because he knows that a strong, bold man can always find success a little farther on.

Such was the "pioneer in space," the man of the ever-shifting frontier, whose wide-brimmed hat and galloping horse and long rifle lent life to the films of 1912. But by then, in the real America, he was no more than a cinema hero. After the West he had managed to conquer the Far West. Then he had reached the other coast. Flight into the virgin forest, that romanticism in action, was becoming difficult. For a long time there had been born a new type of American in the East and the Middle West: the "pioneer in time," I shall call him, for it was in the Future that he sought his free lands and virgin forests. Immigration and the birth-rate were quickly multiplying the population of the United States. All speculation (and speculation is always a forecasting of the future) seemed to be guaranteed by the accumulating value of the human capital. For new inventions new industries had to be created. The great game of action could go ahead. A few years ago the Spanish critic, Madariaga, compared America to a vast nursery stocked with marvellous toys. What giant Father Christmas invented the skyscraper? And who was the boy in Detroit who had the splendid notion of giving all the other boys a real car? To the creator of industry, as to the speculator and the banker, woman remained the distant, hardly visible being, to be worshipped and protected. The pioneer in time, until 1924 at any rate, was no less optimistic, individualist, chivalrous, boyish and generous as the pioneer in space had been.

And for a couple of years now it has looked as if the American, in this second dimension, had once again reached the last, unretreating frontier, the coast of the Over-production Ocean. He feels readier than ever to act, to create, to produce. But he can find no more partners

344

to play the other part in the great game—that of consumer. None of the boys is willing to play the horse in the game any more. For the first time since the Pilgrim Fathers watched from their decks the first tokens of land —floating logs, wild birds, the distant scent of woods— the astonished pioneers are wondering whether leisure will not become a duty. It is hard to say whether the present crisis really shows that saturation-point has been reached, and whether American prosperity will henceforth have to be static rather than dynamic. But that time will come, whether in 1932 or in 1950. The pioneer, in space as in time, is a genus doomed by his own success.

We may regret him: he had at once the charm and the awkwardness of happiness. But it is impossible to preserve the traits of childhood in a country which has come of age. Here and there, in a new industry, or in some difficult territory, pioneers will be left; but the men of the nation will have to acquire the habits of the sedentary. The primitive optimism is already visibly waning in the Eastern States. Culture is spreading, and bringing with it, as usual, the painful but healthy sense of doubt. Feminine domination is not ended, but its approaching end can be foreseen in an easier code of morals, the greater zest of young men for thought, and the economic competition of the sexes. The American woman, like the European, will have to learn other methods in order to retain her superiority. Already she is feeling her way towards that. "But men don't live their lives like that," my pupils would say when we read "La Princesse de Clèves." "Men don't waste time in discussing shades of sentiment with women.

. . . Love doesn't hold such an important place in life."—
"Just wait," I told them. "*Your* seventeenth century is
still to come. Only yesterday you were living in the days
of Chrestien de Troyes and chivalrous love. . . . With
age and leisure you will see the appearance of your own
Princesse de Clèves, your own Nouvelle Héloïse, your
own Bovary."

The period of adjustment will be difficult. The pioneer,
superannuated by success, will for some decades be like
those old officers of the Napoleonic armies, put on half-
pay by 1815 and dreaming all their lives of their past
glories. An apprenticeship in leisure is hard for the man
of action. But the Pioneer, like the Puritan, will slowly
be exorcised. "America comes of age"—the title of Siegfried's book is exact in its image. That noisy childhood
is at an end.

In most human groups one can see the emergence above
the generality of men of various chiefs or nobles, to whom
certain privileges are allowed by the people in exchange
for certain services. At first the nobleman's rôle is princi-
pally that of the warlike leader. Whether by strength and
courage, or by skill and duplicity, he protects his vassals
and leads them to victory. At a later stage the feudal lord
maintains internal order. He safeguards the people of his
domains against the onslaughts of other lords; he gives
support to judges and forbids acts of violence amongst his
subjects.

As soon as order becomes the accepted condition in a
country, the people, ungratefully but reasonably, come to

see that the lord presents as many drawbacks as he does advantages. Admittedly, he is a shield against the other seigneurs. But he takes rather too keen a delight in these virtuous combats; all too often he provokes his neighbours and kindles conflict. Besides, he is expensive: his descendants and successors have generally neither the strength nor the caution of their ancestor; the wars of castle against castle endanger humble folk; and so, with the centuries, there is born a desire to get rid of him. No sooner do improved weapons make his castle and his armour vulnerable, than the masses begin to rally to a central government, and that is the end of the great feudal rulers. Useful they have been; they are useful no longer; and they stand condemned. Such was the history of France; such will be the history of America, which, in very many respects, is still in the feudal stage.

One respect which particularly strikes the European in America is the lack of a central government. The Federal Government in Washington has nothing in common, for instance, with a single focus of power like the Government in Paris, as bequeathed to the French Republic by those two great centralizers, Louis XIV and Napoleon. Some of the most important organs of a European government simply do not exist in America. There is, for example, no national Minister of Education. "What about it?" asks the American. "There's one in each State." True, but that multiplicity makes any unity in programme or teaching an impossibility. Moreover, even in the several States, that Minister is not in control of the better universities, which are private institutions. The Presi-

dent, the great parties, State Governors, Senators—all
these powers in the various States are dependent in the
final analysis on what were termed, in the France of
Louis XI, the great vassals.

These great feudal barons of America are money barons.
They belong to nobilities of varying origins. Some have
reached greatness legally, outwardly at least: lords of
banking, industry and commerce. Together with the
Pioneer and the Puritan they have been the makers of this
great country, and many of their families form an aris-
tocracy very like the families of European monarchies.
Mutatis mutandis, their code of morality is closely akin
to that of the medieval lords. They enjoy a fight—bank
against bank, trust against trust, price-cut against price-
thrust. In an industrial age a tourney can only be economic. They are courteous and friendly, and after splin-
tering lances in the lists of Wall Street they will meet face
to face at the dinner-table, amongst the ladies, in the Park
Avenue keeps. Their medieval counterparts endowed
monasteries; these barons endow colleges and stipulate
the saying of prayers for the founder, just like an English
Henry or a French Dagobert.

This pattern of financial feudalism exists also in Europe,
although there it meets with more resistance than in the
United States from less submissive political parties and
from organized bureaucracies. But alongside the nobility
of wealth there is growing up in America a nobility of
adventurers which in Europe has almost completely vanished. Like the Italians in French sixteenth-century politics, the Irish of Tammany Hall, the great Democratic or

Republican bosses, have carved out a place for themselves amongst the national forces. In the formation of this class, bootlegging has played the part of the pirates and nomadic raiders who founded the Norman nobility. The Chicago racketeer is a feudal figure. He threatens the merchant and obtains yearly tribute from him, giving in exchange his protection against other bandits. "He sells you peace," an American writer has said; that is exactly what our Europan lords sold too.

Al Capone is a more powerful and less cruel Gilles de Rais, surrounded like the French Bluebeard by his armed retinue, although Al Capone's bodyguard wear dinner-jackets and have machine guns mounted in their cars. On December 14, 1930, Al Capone, Prince of Chicago, married his sister Mafalda to the brother of Frank Diamond, another powerful lord of Illinois. Like most royal matches, this marriage had been suggested by political advisers and imposed on bride and bridegroom by the heads of the families, and of the armed forces, who with admirable prudence were anxious to tighten the bonds between their fiefs and avoid dangerous rivalries between their vassals. The ceremony took place in church at Cicero, Illinois, a town in the Capone domains. The young heiress wore an ivory satin gown with a train twenty-five feet long. The church was packed with four thousand guests, for whom the two rival gangs had combined to provide yellow and white chrysanthemums. Behind the pillars stood gunmen, their hands in their revolver pockets, anxiously scrutinizing the movements of everyone coming near their masters. The majestic tones of the organ brought tears to the eyes of many of these worthies. Outside the church waited the loyal and fearful throng, greedy for a glimpse of so many heroes.

Why does this warrior feudality retain a power and prestige in America which it has long since lost amongst ourselves? How does the American public amusedly put up with tournaments so dangerous to the onlookers? These are questions which the surprised European asks. He is amazed, for instance, to read in his newspaper of how hold-up men, after armed robbery in broad daylight in one of New York's busiest streets, have been able to escape in a car before the eyes of an indifferent crowd. If a committee of citizens is convoked in some great city to check the "crime wave," the European is dumbfounded to observe that no enthusiasm is roused by so needful a crusade. Later, when he is more familiar with the country, he realizes that as the conception of a central power, the State is infinitely weaker in America than in Europe, there duels of gang-leaders are viewed by the man-in-the-street very much as those of a Montmorency were by an ordinary Frenchman before the time of Richelieu. As for merchants submitted to racketeering, they are in this respect like medieval serfs, preferring the prospect of comparative peace under the thraldom of Al Capone to the protection of a rather powerless police.

But the citizen will tire of these noisy and dangerous games. The natural evolution of the United States is at present hampered by the absurd Prohibition laws, which make half of the population accomplices in fraud. That situation cannot be lasting. If the East alone were con-

350

sulted, Prohibition would to-day be abrogated. The Methodists of the Middle West would be harder to convince; but sooner or later they will have to learn that a régime which makes the richest and most powerful into evaders of the law is compromising the very existence of the State. When that happens, public opinion will abandon its support of the robber barons, and they will disappear.

As for the economic feudalism, I believe that that also is bound in the end to recognize a central power stronger than itself. Economic machinery has become too complex to be left at the mercy of private bickerings. In days when one scientific discovery can within a few months rob thousands of workers of their livelihood, it is essential that a strong authority should be able to supervise its application. In days when the money of humble people is invested in large enterprises, a strict control must necessarily be exercised by representatives of the investors. Willy-nilly, the United States will be led, like Europe, though more slowly, to a strengthening of the central power. But as the Americans have a liking for new formulas, and have the courage to apply them, it would not surprise me to see them inventing a new form of the State, wherein great organizations of workers, producers and consumers, will regulate the country's economic life, and do so quite distinctly from the political parliamentary body. Such, I believe, was also the view of Keyserling. But whatever the form of this central power of the future, the feudal lord, like the Puritan and the pioneer, is bound to alter or to disappear.

They are phantoms, these three, because their kind cannot adapt itself to the world as it is now being shaped. Like all ghosts, they have, and will long have, a real existence in the minds of the living.

It is after the death of certain persons that we realize how large a part they have played in our lives. I do not bemoan the occult presence of the three phantoms. It infuses the American atmosphere with the inconvenience and mystery which enhance the present with the weight and substance of the past. But their image fades and fades. "What city of the future are we going to raise?" asks the young American. None can foretell. But in that city where the men of 1931 will in their turn be the ghosts, there will certainly be no room for the three phantoms, already paling so fast, of pre-War America.

AMERICANS IN CRISIS

IT has happened that two journeys have given me the opportunity of observing the behaviour of the American people in times of prosperity and in times of crisis. The differences were interesting and noteworthy, and possibly enable one to deduce a few general laws regarding the economic behaviour of crowds.

I

The first characteristic which struck the visitor to America before the slump of 1929 was an extraordinary confidence in the future. Nearly every American one met had, during the years 1922-8, succeeded in what he had undertaken. If they were engaged in industry or commerce they told you how the figures of their production or turnover had, in many cases, been doubled or tripled. If they were wage-earners, their wages or rates had risen. Even if they were novelists, the sales of their books reached figures which to a European seemed astronomical. All, or very nearly all, were speculating, and had a friend who had "put them on to a good thing." That stock had risen, all stocks had risen, and next summer they were going to take a trip to Europe.

When a whole human herd is strongly imbued with optimism of this kind, the isolated member of the herd who tries to oppose that optimism is regarded as a traitor.

Which is quite natural. Optimism is a pleasant sensation, and was all the more so in America's case because it extended to the common classes of society, so that the wealthy were able to give themselves up to it with neither remorse nor anxiety. If a few wise men endeavoured to remind people of all-too obvious economic laws, and to show that prices had reached a point where the whole of world credit could not support them, or to evoke memories of previous slumps, the public waxed indignant. "Things were quite different nowadays; we were entering on a new era. Big wages allied with mass production would enable mankind to scale the topmost peaks of prosperity." Prudence and reflection were words of treason. If thinking led to doubts, thought was criminal. In the colleges during those days the man who reflected was regarded by the average student as dangerous. Sport held absolute sway, because sport is a deterrent to thought. The will to optimism brooked no contradiction.

The happy result of this optimism was a great and universal generosity. I had occasion at that time to observe certain charity subscriptions in small towns. People gave not only gladly, but almost luxuriating in their bounty. There was a kind of heady pleasure in flinging away some part of this money which was rising in waves round every American faster than he could spend it. Universities, hospitals, the rebuilding of European towns —everything shared in this largesse. Spending was the great national game. People sought out new objects just for the sake of an opportunity of buying. It was the time when Big Business was exerting itself to make the public "radio-conscious," or "car-conscious." Nor was it hard to create such demands: people then only wanted the chance of desiring something. The publicity "stimulus" automatically produced the "buying" reaction. Like pessimism, economy would have been held criminal.

Naturally, then, the statesmen and business magnates lucky enough to be in power at that moment reaped the benefit of the popularity always attached to success. A victorious general is a general who is present on the day of a great victory. "Love," says Spinoza, "is joy accompanied by the idea of an external cause." When a people feels happy, it loves its leaders. In this battle of non-existent adversaries, Calvin Coolidge was the strategist favoured by the gods. The Wall Street prophets then commanded an almost religious awe. They foretold a rise, and a rise occurred; therefore they were true prophets. It was a time when any man was acclaimed who told the American people: "We have more locomotives, more automobiles, and more frigidaires per head of the population than any nation in the world." I remember at that time hearing a preacher reading statistics of production from the pulpit to prove the loving-kindness of Heaven.

A prosperous people never desire state intervention in private affairs. At the time of my first visit America was the least socialistic country in the world. There was no unemployment legislation as in England or Germany, no civil servants' statute or workers' pensions as in France. The individual was too successful to need any protection. If he had any fears for the future, there were countless stable insurance corporations ready to do business with

355

him. When Keyserling then wrote about the United States he had to coin a word, "privatism," to express the extreme economic individualism of the 1928 American.

This prosperity engendered feelings of indifference, and often of contempt, towards Europe. Indifference, because American prosperity seemed to be independent of European prosperity. The United States was large enough to buy up the fruits of its own productivity. Besides, the U.S.A. was essential for the rebuilding of that unhappy continent always at war with itself. Contempt, because Europe seemed incapable of grasping the elementary truths which had brought happiness to America. Why did not Europe abolish its absurd little frontiers? Why didn't it adopt the policy of high wages? In a few industries (the motor-car in France, shoes in Czechoslovakia, electricity in Germany) Europe tried to adopt American methods of production, but the absence of high wages meant a lack of consumers. In those days an American of the Babbitt type (and it was the period of the widest diffusion of Babbittry) could scarcely speak to a European without preaching to him, like a mature man to a lad. And the result was that the European, rubbed up the wrong way, called down curses on American vainglory, and did not detect the charming qualities of confidence and generosity which went hand-in-hand with that pride.

Finally the traveller at that time would discover in America a small group of rebels, striving rather unhappily and vainly to react against the herd optimism. The herd treated them badly, and, as always happens, their violence was increased by repression. They could be seen in the colleges flaunting their open shirts, *à la* Shelley, in opposition to the stricter costume of the orthodox. All thought took the form of challenge. The opposition was more harsh and satiric than constructive. Morality became free, but without depth of freedom, I mean that natural spontaneous freedom to be seen, for example, in the heroes of Maupassant. Deeds were bold, but hearts remained puritan. In sexual as intellectual life, the reaction was one of defiance rather than sincere conviction.

Another psychological link, more hidden, joined up sexual freedom with economic prosperity. This was the need for excitement which is necessarily engendered by wealth. The link is easy to account for. The man who satisfies every desire as soon as he feels it, is no longer capable of accumulating in his life those long periods of waiting which make true passions: that waiting for money which makes a Père Grandet in Balzac, that waiting for love which makes a Madame Bovary. He craves for a constant series of strong sensations. Speedy change replaces intensity of desire. This is one of the greatest dangers that prosperity brings to happiness. This was more or less the conduct of *Homo Americanus,* so far as a foreign naturalist could observe him during a journey through the Eastern States of the continent in 1927.

2

If the same naturalist returned to New York in 1931, watched the actions of the same "subjects" he studied four years before, and listened to their conversations, he would be surprised to observe how greatly the crisis had altered them.

I shall begin with an observation simply of the outward scene. About Christmas, 1927, I made a round of the New York stores, and I returned to them in December, 1931. The difference was almost incredible. In a certain large bookstore in 1927 it was impossible to find a salesman; in 1931, the shop was almost empty. The husband whom I had seen giving his wife a Christmas present of an exquisite piece of jewellery, now bought her a small object of no value which he would never have dared to show her four years since. The family who, as I knew, came to Paris every winter were now cancelling the trip for economy's sake.

I allow myself these quite commonplace observations in order to reach a very important point touching "behaviour" in times of crisis: namely, that most of the people whose altered courses of action I was examining had no real need to make these economies. Many of them had lost nothing. All, or nearly all of them, in spite of losses, were still extremely rich people, much more so than the majority of Europeans. Why then were they hesitating to spend, here ten dollars or here a hundred, sums which meant nothing to them?

For two reasons. The first was that their confidence in the future had been affected. The slump has, for a time at least, shattered American optimism. Before the crisis it was easy, by applying the appropriate stimulus, to rouse the American's desire to buy. The stimulus has now to be far stronger to obtain the same response. On the other hand, a new desire, totally unknown in America, has been brought into being—the desire for security. There is a French proverb which says that "a scalded cat dreads cold water." A man who has lost his fortune in bad investments is afraid of *any* investment. In 1927 my American taxi-drivers were always telling me about the money they were going to spend. One of them told me he wanted to go to Paris, but that he was waiting until he had $3,000 because he wanted to travel first-class. In 1931 he spoke with horror of the failure of the Bank of the United States, and talked earnestly about savings banks under adequate State control. If there is still one thing which it is easy to sell to the people of the United States at the present time, it is security. In that market the slightest stimulus provokes an instant response.

But why this instinct of amassing on the part of the rich, who have no real anxiety regarding the security of their future? Because when the whole of a human herd has a strong sensation of pessimism or uneasiness, the isolated member of the herd who flaunts his good fortune is regarded as a traitor. Just as in Europe during the War, those families who had lost one of their members, or feared the loss of one, watched with a very natural sense of annoyance the tranquillity of those who were then said to have "cushy jobs," so, under the influence of the slump, the American mass cannot be sympathetic towards the individual who has not felt its effects. The human animal is extremely sensitive to these herd feelings, and reacts very quickly to them. The quality called tact is simply a swift and silent awareness of the hidden feelings of others. It is tact, a sense of shame, and an instinctive prudence, that make the wealthiest men at the present time make a pretence of being hurt. There is a pleasure in sharing the herd's suffering, and a contrasting sense of shame in enjoying things apart from it.

This psychological explanation is so true that it was clearly perceived by the publicity experts, who strive to fight it by demonstrating that patriotism, the general interest, and the welfare of the working classes, must be served by spending. I saw in New York numerous propaganda films designed to prove to the public that the man who invests his money instead of spending it deserves the contempt of the crowd. But these films had little effect. Not until the wealthy classes begin to feel that purchasing power is again normal amongst the poorer classes, will they themselves again feel able to spend without a sense of remorse.

During the recent crisis, that desire to delude oneself into a feeling of having done something to help the herd, took rather perilously sentimental forms. I must say I was shocked by the sight of the ten thousand men selling apples on the New York streets. That was not a remedy for unemployment; it was the illusion of a remedy. The unemployed men were becoming beggars disguised as traders. For five cents the purchasers had the pleasant illusion of being openhanded and helping to cure the national sickness. But they had done nothing, and for the most part were far from having contributed to the unemployment fund a sum proportional to their means. Consequently, it was very bad psychology to let them acquire an easy conscience at so cheap a rate. The notion of salvation through apples was a deplorable survival of the sentimental optimism which ruled America before the slump.

Fortunately for the United States that optimism has yielded place to a spirit at once more critical, more objective, and more healthy. Through the crisis, intelligence has recovered its value. It has been made clear that to be "a regular guy" is not qualification enough for the conduct of big business. Men have begun to pass under stern scrutiny reputations and declarations which in the days of prosperity were accepted as self-evident. When the Wall Street prophets announced for the first time that the end of the slump was at hand, people were tempted to believe them—an old habit acquired under prosperity. When the first prophecy did not come to pass, the American public were astonished; when the second proved false the same public smiled. The third made it indignant; and now whenever the false prophets open their lips, the average American shrugs his shoulders, and the humorist Will Rogers begs the economists to do no more foretelling of "happy days" being here again, because, he says, that would bring bad luck. An intelligent scepticism is spreading. When an orator tells the American people to-day that they are the happiest in the world because they have so many locomotives and trucks and radios, they turn away bored.

Statesmen unlucky enough to be in power during a crisis are held responsible for the public woes. A defeated general is a general who was present on the day of a great defeat. Mr. Robert Marshall has shown that the Presidential elections in the United States depend on rainfall. This is quite natural. Drought means bad harvests. Bad harvests and poor business beget general discontent and political changes.

In times of crisis the individual, being menaced, seeks the protection of the herd. The power of the State is augmented because everyone desires protection. The United States is an individualist country, but in 1930 was falling back on a form of agricultural socialism for their farmers. On every hand the most intelligent business men are asking for agreed understandings in questions of production, and some even desire such understandings to be international. Scorn and indifference regarding European affairs have been replaced by a very keen interest. The Texas planter observes that he cannot sell his cotton to English factories whose hands are idle. The processions of unemployed men teach the American capitalist that Bolshevism in Europe would have grave consequences for himself. The Senate in Washington is still a long way from the realization that America's true interest lies in her becoming part of the League of Nations and helping to safeguard the peace of the world; but the slump has set America on the road towards an understanding with Europe. Add to this the fact that Europe has felt more sympathetic towards America since the crisis; for nations, like individuals, crave to feel that they are not alone in their sufferings.

What was the result of the crisis on the small group of rebels whom we observed in 1927? It would appear that it has drawn this group closer to the herd; or more exactly, that the mass has drawn closer to this group. Men in general are beginning to see that the rebels were right in declaring that there were other things in human life beyond prosperity. Having less money for the pleasures of excitement, they turn towards the pleasures of culture. This, of course, is true as yet only of a select minority; but, for example, in the universities of the Eastern States one no longer finds the young intellectuals spurned by the athletes. The result is that the intellectual ceases to be a rebel and becomes more constructive.

It is too soon to judge what the effects of the crisis have been on sexual behaviour. But I should not be surprised to find it tending to bring back the most emancipated Americans towards a more traditional mode of life, were it only for economic reasons. Frequent divorce and alimony payments are hobbies for people with a superfluity of ready cash.

3

It is clear, then, that the crisis has altered the reactions of *Homo Americanus* at many points. In my opinion the transformation has been operating in a favourable direction; the slump has made the American more mature and more sensible. It remains to ask whether its effects will be lasting.

We must not, I think, here pitch our hopes too high. The experiences which produce deep changes in us are those which are sufficiently recurrent to become habits. The child learns to walk or to eat because he carries out the movements every day. A unique experience teaches little. Now, the great economic crises of the past have always been bridged by periods of prosperity, lasting for seven, eight, or ten years. This is an interval of time long enough for man to become forgetful. The much more terrible and much more important experience of war itself seems always to have been forgotten by humanity after one generation. Who remembers to-day all the wise reflections aroused in our fathers by the crises of 1876, or 1893, or 1907, or 1929?

The present crisis will probably be succeeded by a wave of rising prices and wealth, and perhaps it will sweep away all the new-found wisdom of America. Nevertheless, in the course of the centuries, men have learned a few lessons. It would astonish me if everything of the last three years' teaching were lost. America is young, but she has grown older and riper since 1929. She is reaching that fine but difficult age when, for peoples as for individuals, grown-up responsibilities succeed the optimistic illusions of childhood and the rebellious pessimism of adolescence. She will pass through other crises, like the one which is now working itself out; and we shall pass through them with her. Her friends hope that she will face up to each of them always a little wiser and better prepared. When a rat is brought back, after a long interval, beside the box of foodstuffs which it has formerly learned how to open, it appears at first to have forgotten its past experience, but the observer soon finds that, notwithstanding appearances, the animal remembers, the proof being the fact that it now discovers much more quickly than the first time how to get access to the box. And humanity is like an undying animal brought back every ten or twelve years, by some powerful and invisible investigator, to be confronted by the complex mechanism of economic crisis. In spite of its apparent madness, it does not totally forget past experience.

(1)